Key to the East

Here is a vivid and comprehensive selection of the songs, stories, dramas and scriptures of the great Asian cultures, a collection harvested from the classics of more than 2500 years.

Included in scholarly, readable translations, are stories from *The Thousand and One Nights*, the Indian epic the *Mahabharata*, and *The Tale of Genji*; poems from the Chinese and Japanese and from the *Rubaiyat* of Omar Khayyam; selections from the *Analects* of Confucius, the Buddhist *Dhammapada*, the *Koran*, the *Bhagavad Gita* and *Tao Teh Ching* and many other classics in all literary forms.

Encompassing the literature of five countries— China, India, Arabia, Iran and Japan—and five of the world's major religions, this volume deals with widely divergent cultures, civilizations and attitudes and, in addition to its sheer entertainment, offers a valuable key for understanding the peoples of the East.

"Well timed . . . one of the very few comprehensive and conscientious anthologies of classical Asian literature ever to appear in America."
—Santha Rama Rau, *N. Y. Times Book Review*

The Study of Man from MENTOR and SIGNET Books

(0451)

☐ **THE ORIGIN OF SPECIES by Charles Darwin.** With a special Introduction by Julian Huxley. The famous classic on evolution that exploded into public controversy and revolutionized the course of science. "Next to the *Bible* no work has been quite as influential, in virtually every aspect of human thought, as *The Origin of Species*."
—Ashley Montagu   (621026—$3.50)

☐ **THE ORIGIN by Irving Stone.** A master writer's magnificent saga of Charles Darwin. Spanning half a century and the entire globe, it tells a story of epic proportions, dealing with the life, times, and destiny of the man whose ideas changed forever human-kind's view of itself.   (117611—$4.50)*

☐ **THE NECK OF THE GIRAFFE: Darwin, Evolution and the New Biology by Francis Hitching.** This book brings today's controversy over the theory of evolution—sparked by scientists who accept evolution, but not Darwin's explanation of it—giving all sides a fair and lucid hearing, and giving us an exciting preview of the new theories that may well replace Darwin in the textbooks and in our minds.
(622324—$3.95)

☐ **THE NEW GOLDEN BOUGH, by Sir James Frazer. Abridged. Revised and edited by Theodore Gaster.** Frazer's classic work on ancient and primitive myth, magic, religion, ritual and taboo traces the evolution of human behavior from savage to civilized man. "Dr. Gaster has done for Frazer what it took two men to do for Gibbon."—Arnold Toynbee.   (622081—$5.95)

☐ **KING SOLOMON'S RING by Konrad Z. Lorenz. Foreword by Julian Huxley.** The classic account of animal behavior that sheds new light on man. Scientists swear by it; laymen laugh over it. "Irresistible charm."—*New York Times Book Review*   (113721—$2.25)

*Price $4.95 in Canada

A TREASURY OF
Asian Literature

Edited with an Introduction and Commentaries

by JOHN D. YOHANNAN

A MENTOR BOOK

NEW AMERICAN LIBRARY

NEW YORK AND SCARBOROUGH, ONTARIO

To Caye
*whose instinct guided
when reason failed,
this book is dedicated*

MENTOR TRADEMARK REG. U.S. PAT. OFF. AND FOREIGN COUNTRIES
REGISTERED TRADEMARK—MARCA REGISTRADA
HECHO EN WINNIPEG, CANADA

SIGNET, SIGNET CLASSIC, MENTOR, PLUME, MERIDIAN AND NAL
BOOKS are published *in the United States* by
New American Library,
1633 Broadway, New York, New York 10019,
in Canada by The New American Library of Canada Limited,
81 Mack Avenue, Scarborough, Ontario M1L 1M8

15 16 17 18 19 20 21 22 23

Printed in Canada

Acknowledgments

In compiling a book that draws upon such vast and varied fields of specialization, I have of course incurred a large debt of gratitude that cannot be measured or expressed. I should like, however, to thank the Orientalists who have personally advised me. Though I have not always taken their advice, I trust that I have benefited from much of the help given me by the following scholars:

Of the University of California at Berkeley: Professors Peter A. Boodberg, Donald H. Shively, Walter J. Fischel, Shih-Hsiang Chen, Murray B. Emeneau, and Edward H. Schafer. Of Harvard University: Professors Daniel H. H. Ingalls and James R. Hightower. Of the University of Michigan: Professors Joseph K. Yamagiwa and A. H. Hourani. Of Columbia University: Professor Richard Lane. Of Stanford University: Professors Robert H. Brower, Frederic Spiegelberg, and Shau Wing Chan. Of the Pacific School of Religion in Berkeley: Professor Jack Finegan.

A very special debt of thanks is owed to my friend and teacher Professor Bernhard Geiger of Columbia University for the many pleasant and profitable hours spent with him in translating Persian poetry.

Acknowledgments and thanks are also due to Professor Arthur J. Arberry of Cambridge University and to the other trustees of the E. J. W. Gibb Memorial Trust for permission to print selections from their edition of the *Mathnawi* of Rumi as translated by Reynold A. Nicholson; to Lady Elsa Richmond, who graciously allowed me to use the translations made by her sister, Gertrude Lowthian Bell, in *Poems from the Divan of Hafiz*, and published by William Heinemann; to Professor Chi-Chen Wang and the Columbia University Press for the use of "The Judicial Murder of Tsui Ning" from his *Traditional Chinese Tales;* to Mr. Arthur Waley and the firm of George Allen and Unwin for the chapter from *The Tale of Genji*, and for "Atsumori" from *The Nō Plays of Japan;* to the same firm for selections from M. M. Pickthall's *Meaning of the Glorious Koran;* to Mr. Waley again and to the firm of Lund Humphries Ltd. for the selections from *Japanese Poetry;* to Mr. Harold G. Henderson for his *haiku*, both as published by Houghton Mifflin in his *Bamboo Broom* and from his own manuscript; to Mr. George Keyt and Kutub Publishers of Bombay for the excerpts from *Gita Govinda;* to Mrs. Mary

v

L. Pritchett and the John Day Company for permission to use translations from *The White Pony* by Robert Payne and others; to Lady Judith Blunt-Lytton for use of her parents' version of the Ode by Imr-ul-Kais; to the Cambridge University Press for the selections from Ma'arri and from the *Divan* of Rumi, both in Reynold A. Nicholson's translations.

The other selections in this book are taken from the following sources no longer in copyright: the fables from the *Pancha-tantra* by Charles R. Lanman are from the Warner *Library of the World's Best Literature* (New York, International Society, 1897); the *Tales from the Gulistân or Rose-Garden of the Sheikh Sa'di of Shirâz* are from the book of that name by Sir Richard Burton (London, Philip Allan and Company, 1928); the same translator's "The Lady and Her Five Suitors" is from the *Tales from the Arabian Nights* (New York, Cardinal Pocket Book, 1951); "Sâvitrí; or Love and Death" by Sir Edwin Arnold is from his *Indian Idylls from the Sanskrit of the Mahabharata* (Boston, Roberts Brothers, 1883); the episodes from the *Shahnamah* of Firdausi are from James Atkinson's translation in *Oriental Literature, 1* of *World's Great Classics* (New York, Colonial Press, 1899); Kalidasa's *Sakoontalá* by M. Monier-Williams is from *Hindu Literature* (New York, P. F. Collier and Son, 1900); *The Rubaiyat of Omar Khayyam* in Edward Fitzgerald's First Edition comes from the variorum text published by The Page Company, Boston, 1898; the excerpts from the *Analects* of Confucius are from *The Chinese Classics, a Translation* by James Legge (New York, Alden, 1883); those from the *Tao Teh Ching* are from *The Canon of Reason and Virtue* by Paul Carus (Chicago, Open Court Publishing Company, 1913); those from the *Bhagavad Gita or Song Celestial* are by Edwin Arnold in *Sacred Writings*, Vol. 2, *The Harvard Classics* (New York, P. F. Collier and Son, 1910); those from the *Dhammapada*, translated by F. Max Müller, are from *Sacred Books of the East* (New York, P. F. Collier and Son, 1900).

Finally, I wish to express my thanks to the Fund for the Advancement of Education for making possible a sabbatical year during which much of the work on this book was done; to the librarians of The City College, the University of California, Columbia University, and the New York Public Library for their courteous help while the book was in process of compilation; to my editor, Mr. Richard Walsh, Jr., for encouragement and advice; and to my colleague, Dr. Brooks Wright, for reading a portion of the manuscript.

                                                        J. D. Y.

Contents

4 SCRIPTURE

Contents

Introduction

❧❀☙

I

The Persians used to say of their old capital: *Isfahan nisfi Jehan*—Isfahan is half the world. Our counterpart to this national shibboleth is the concept of a world divided into "East" and "West"—spheres of mutual ignorance, as it were. The vast continent of Asia, with its millennia of history, shrinks astonishingly in our view of things. Jawaharlal Nehru's sharp retaliation is to confine his account of Western civilization to but a small portion of his *Glimpses of World History*.

To be sure, these old clichés and prejudices are slowly being laid away on both sides. Asia and Africa are deigning to learn at least political and natural science from Europe and America. In the West, self-interest is dictating greater awareness of the other half of the world. Two global wars have finally impressed upon Americans the geography of the remoter continents. And we are now conscious that Asia *has* a history that is not merely a part of the "dark backward and abysm of time," even though we are ignorant of it.

In the remedies we are applying to our old myopia, there is a new danger. Our nascent interest in Asia may become limited to economics and geopolitics. Even the study of Oriental languages in our schools appears to subserve those purposes. As for literature, it is perhaps the most neglected of all Oriental studies. We would not think of stating the case for Western civilization without reference to the accumulated writings of more than two thousand years of history; yet we presume to sound out the mystery of various Asian civilizations—the roots of some of which go back even further into the past—without a knowledge of their books.

This neglect cannot be ascribed to English and American Orientalists, who have translated large portions of the classical literature of Asia. Some of their work, to be sure, is in the crabbed language of philological science, but much of it is in extremely graceful English. And some of it has been passed on to the general public. The scholarly translations of Reynold A. Nicholson, A. J. Arberry, Arthur Ryder, and Arthur Waley have had a direct appeal to the unspecialized general reader. Then, too, we have had popular compilations of the scriptures of the world, anthologies of world poetry, and even an anthology of the lyric poetry of Asia (unfortunately now out of print)—all based upon previous scholarship. The need, expressed by Arthur Waley, for "informed summarizers of specialist knowledge ready to act as middlemen between the scholar and the public" has thus been partly met. Yet since the first year of this century there has not been published in America a general collection of the sacred and secular literature of all Asia. (The Garden City Publishing Company in 1938 issued a reprint of a British anthology, *The Coronation Book of Oriental Literature*, now out of print.) This fact, plus the fact that specialized volumes are inaccessible or expensive, has made it fairly impossible for the general reader to form any impression but the most distorted of the classical literatures of very large segments of the human race. The present anthology hopes to supply the deficiency.

I I

Some of the translations here are new, some old. Most of them meet the highest tests of Oriental scholarship, although they were selected on a somewhat different principle. A translation of literary worth at the cost of some faults of scholarship seemed preferable to a simon-pure translation that does not give pleasure in the reading. Or, as a master translator, Edward Fitzgerald, put it: "Better a live sparrow than a stuffed eagle." On the other hand, no rendition has been employed, however graceful, whose author had no acquaintance with the original language. There are here no English translations from German or French versions of Asian works, and no adaptations of English translations by other hands. This principle eliminated Emerson's intuitively inspired "translations" of Persian poetry from German sources and Richard LeGallienne's popular adaptations of the lyrics of Hafiz. The sacrifice seemed warranted. Within these limits, the premium has been placed upon literacy rather than literalness, and upon esthetic rather than historical considerations. Perhaps the single exceptions to this rule are the stories from the *Mathnawi* of Rumi, given in Reynold A. Nicholson's literal rather than his more polished version, which renders somewhat freely.

The editor takes special pride in offering his abridgement of the Indian love poem *Gita Govinda* in the version by Mr. George Keyt of Ceylon, a distinguished artist and author. Hitherto, this admirable translation has not been published in Europe and America. He is equally happy to have Mr. Harold G. Henderson's permission to print for the first time some of that author's translations of Japanese *haiku;* these appear alongside others already familiar to readers of his book *The Bamboo Broom*.

The arrangement of *A Treasury of Asian Literature* is not by geography or chronology, but rather by literary types. It offers some of the best samples of the peculiar literary genius of five national groups with a view to displaying the infinite variety of Asian literature, not its development within national bounds. The absence of prose works from the Persian does not mean that no such works exist, but only that they are not a distinctive achievement of Iranian literature. On the other hand, the absence of Arabian and Persian drama reflects the nearly total neglect of that literary form in Islamic letters. Similarly, the omission of Arabian, Chinese, and Japanese epic writings is a fact of the literary history of those countries. If the reader asks, however, why Indian fiction, Chinese drama, and Vedic and Zoroastrian scriptures have not been included, the only reply is that arbitrary limits had to be placed upon the size of this book.

For the same reason, the entire "modern" era for all five countries is excluded. Asian literatures since the impact of Western civilization might well compose a separate book. So indeed might the very ancient writings of the Near East, including the Egyptian and Babylonian, whose interest is perhaps less literary than archeological. The reader of this anthology has the assurance that the main *living* cultures of Asia—Islam, Hinduism, Buddhism, Confucianism, and Taoism —have made their contribution to it.

III

Those who are interested in the historical development of the literatures of Arabia, Iran, India, China and Japan will find various aids. In a second table of contents, the selections are arranged by countries and in the order of composition. The chronologies at the end of the book provide a historical framework for the readings. The bibliographies extend the limits of this book for the reader who finds its contents insufficient. The headnotes are intended to facilitate reading of the selections and not to yield all vital information about author or work. The footnotes are the translator's except when marked as the editor's, thus: [Ed.].

The spelling of foreign words is unavoidably inconsistent. The editor, in his commentaries, has employed what he believes to be the commonest forms, generally avoiding diacritical marks, but the translators' orthography has been retained in the selections quoted. Hence spellings such as *Shakuntala—Sakoontalá*.

The primary aim of this book is to make available to the lover of literature, in the English language, a body of pleasurable readings which, up to now, he has not been able easily to come by. Many of these Asian writings rightly belong to the world, for literature is reckless of the points of the compass. As Thoreau said, the waters of the Ganges can flow in Walden Pond. Perhaps the reader of the *Gita Govinda*, or the *Genji*, or the *Gulistan* will find that he is not after all learning about Asians, but rather discovering hitherto hidden portions of his own psyche.

JOHN D. YOHANNAN

The City College
New York City

1 STORY

I Parable

FROM The *Panchatantra*

[COMPOSED ABOUT 2ND CENTURY A.D.]

TRANSLATED BY CHARLES R. LANMAN [1850-1941]

The following fables of India are taken from one of the most ancient and most widely traveled cycles of tales. Indeed, a genealogical table showing the various progeny of the hypothetical parent book reads like a roll call of the nations and languages of the world.

The Adam of this family tree is missing—presumably a Sanskrit version which begat all the others, including the later Sanskrit texts. The second generation text is also missing, this one a Pehlevi or middle Persian translation made in A.D. 550. We know of it from its own immediate descendants, an Old Syriac and an Arabic version belonging to the 8th century. From the latter Arabic text —the grandchild of the original—there have come down a dozen or so off-shoots, including a Greek, a modern Persian and a Hebrew translation, all made in the 11th to 13th centuries. The Greek and Persian versions ultimately supplied the sources for La Fontaine's fables. The Hebrew version, having been translated into Latin in the 13th century, fathered two very popular German and Italian texts, the latter in turn begetting the first English account in the racy Elizabethan language of Sir Thomas North. The English versions most widely read today, however, are not North's, but rather translations—such as those below—made from the Sanskrit descendant of the Adam book. Whether the popular Aesop's fables belong to the same family tree or are only distant cousins it is not possible to say.

The *Panchatantra* is ostensibly a group of five discourses in the form of precepts and examples on the art of wise ruling. A somewhat Machiavellian notion of conduct is conveyed, not too different from the advice offered by the Persian poet Sadi in the *Guli-*

15

stan. What the parables often lack in idealism, however, they make up in practical shrewdness and charm of narration. As in all beast fables, apt characterization of both man and beast is the mark of excellence. One wonders whether anything more apropos has ever been said on the conflict between the uncompromisingly scientific and the humanistic mentalities than the story of "The Lion-Makers." Many of the fables in the *Panchatantra* turn up elsewhere—in the *Arabian Nights,* in Aesop, in the *Gulistan,* as well as in European tale cycles of the medieval and renaissance periods. The arrangement of the stories within a framework is of course an ancient device, but only in the *Jatakas* or Buddhist birth fables do we have an example of greater antiquity than is provided by the *Panchatantra.*

THE LION-MAKERS

Even men of learning and noble birth are sometimes devoid of common-sense. For, true is the saying:—

> Book-learning people rightly cherish;
> But gumption's best of all to me.
> Bereft of gumption you shall perish,
> Like to the Lion-makers three.

"How was that?" said the Man-with-the-wheel. And the Gold-magician narrated:

In a certain place there dwelt four brahman youths in the greatest friendship. Three of them had got to the further shore of the ocean of science, but were devoid of common-sense; while the fourth had common-sense only, and no mind for science. Now once upon a time these friends took counsel together, and said, "Of what profit is science, if we cannot go with it to some foreign country and win the favor of princes and make our fortune? Therefore to the Eastern Country let us go." And so it came to pass.

Now after they had gone a little way, the eldest spoke: "There is one among us, the fourth, who has no learning, but only common-sense; and a man can't get presents from kings by common-sense without learning. Not a whit will I give him of all that I gain; so let him go home." And the second said, "Ho there, Gumption! get you homeward, for you have no learning!" But the third made answer, "Alas, it is not fitting so to do: for we have played together since we were boys. So let him come along too. He's a noble fellow, and shall have a share in the riches that we win."

On then they went together, till in a jungle they saw the

bones of a dead lion. Then spoke the first: "Ha! now we can put our book-learning to the test. Here lies some sort of a dead creature: by the power of our learning we'll bring it to life. I'll put the bones together." And that then he did with zeal. The second added flesh, blood, and hide. But just as the third was breathing the breath of life into it, Gumption stopped him and said, "Hold: this is a lion that you are turning out. If you make him alive, he will kill every one of us." Thereupon made answer the other, "Fie, stupid! is learning to be fruitless in my hands?" "Well, then," said Gumption, "just wait a bit till I climb a tree."

Thereupon the lion was brought to life. But the instant this was done, he sprang up and killed the three. Afterwards Gumption climbed down and went home.

Therefore, concluded the Gold-magician, therefore I say:—

> Book-learning people rightly cherish;
> But gumption's best of all to me.
> Bereft of gumption you shall perish,
> Like to the Lion-makers three.

COUNT NOT YOUR CHICKENS BEFORE THEY BE HATCHED

Once upon a time there lived in a certain town a brahman named Luckless. He begged a lot of barley grits; and with what he had left over from his dinner, he filled a jar. This he hung on a low peg in the wall, put his cot beneath it, and looking at it with unaverted gaze, he bethought him:—"This pot is full of barley grits, and, if there comes a famine, will fetch me a hundred pieces of silver. With them I shall buy me a couple of she-goats; and as they will drop kids every six months, I shall soon have a herd from them. For the goats I shall get many cows; for the cows, buffalo-cows; and for them, mares; and when they have foaled, I shall have many horses; and from the sale of them, much gold. With the gold I'll get a house with four rooms, about a court. And then some brahman will come to my house, and give me his lovely daughter, with a rich dowry in marriage.

"She will bear me a son, and I'll name him Soma-çarman. When he's old enough for me to trot him on my knee, I'll take a book, and sitting out behind the stable, I'll study it. Then Soma-çarman, seeing me, and eager to be trotted on my knee, will leave his mother's lap, and in coming to me will get right near the horses' hoofs. And I, full of anger, shall say to my wife. 'Take the child, quick!' She, busy with housework, won't hear me, and I shall get up and give her a kick."

Deep sunk in thought, he gave such a kick that he broke the jar, and the grits ran down over him till he was well whitened.

THE TRANSFORMED MOUSE

On the bank of the Ganges, whose billows are flecked with white foam made by the fish that dart in terror at the roar of the waters breaking on its craggy shores, there is a hermitage filled with ascetics. They are given over to prayer, restraint of the senses, asceticism, study of holy writ, fasting, and meditation. They take very pure and very little water. They mortify the flesh by a diet of bulbs, roots, fruits, and waterplants. They wear only an apron of bast.

There was one among them named Yajnavalkya. He had performed his sacred ablutions in the Ganges, and was about to rinse his mouth, when into his hand there fell from the beak of a hawk a little mouse. On seeing it, he put it on a banyanleaf, bathed again and rinsed his mouth, performed rites of expiation and so forth; and then by the power of his asceticism he changed the mouse into a girl, took her with him to his hermitage, and said to his wife, who was childless, "My dear, take this girl as your daughter, and bring her up carefully."

So the wife reared her, and loved her, and cared for her, till she was twelve years old; and then, seeing the girl was fit to be married, she said to her husband, "Seest thou not, O husband, that the time for our daughter's marriage is slipping by?" "Quite right," said he: "so if she is agreed, I will summon the exalted sun-god, and give her to him to wife." "What's the harm?" said his wife: "do so."

So the sage called the sun. And such was the power of his summons, which was made up of words of the Scripture, that the sun came instantly, saying, "Reverend sir, didst thou call me?" He answered, "Here is my daughter. If she will but choose thee, then take her to wife." And to his daughter he spake, "My child, does the exalted sun, the illumer of the three worlds, please thee?" The girl said, "Father, he is too scorching. I like him not. Call me some one more eminent than he." Then said the hermit to the sun, "Exalted one, is there any one mightier than thou?" And the sun said, "There is one mightier than I,—the cloud; for he covers me, and then none can see me."

So the sage called the cloud, and said, "Daughter, to him do I give thee." "He is too dark and cold," answered she; "so give me to some other, mightier being." Then the sage asked the cloud, "O cloud, is there any mightier even than thou?" "The wind is mightier than I," said the cloud: "when the wind strikes me I am torn to a thousand shreds."

So the sage called the wind and said, "Daughter, does the wind please thee best for a husband?"—"Father, he is too fickle. Bring hither some one mightier even than he." And the sage said, "O wind, is any mightier than thou?" And the wind made answer, "The mountain is mightier than I; for strong as I am, it braces itself and withstands me."

So the sage called the mountain and said, "Daughter, to him do I give thee." She answered and spake, "Father, he is too hard and unyielding. Give me to some other than him." So the sage asked the mountain, "O king of mountains, is there any mightier even than thou?" And the mountain said, "The mice are mightier than I; for they tear and rend my body asunder."

So the sage called a mouse, and showed him to her, and said, "Daughter, to him do I give thee. Does the king of the mice please thee?"

And she, showing her joy at the thought that this one at last was of her own kind, said, "Father, make me a mouse again, and give me to him, in order that I may fulfill my household duties after the manner ordained for my kind." So by the power of his asceticism he made her a mouse again, and gave her to him.

THE GREEDY JACKAL

The brahman said:—

> Excessive greed should ne'er be cherished.
> Have greed—but keep it moderate.
> The all too greedy jackal perished,
> A wooden top-knot on his pate.

"How was that?" asked the brahman woman. And the brahman narrated:

In a certain forest lived a savage tribesman, who, on a day, set out a-hunting. And as he went he met a mighty boar, as big as the peak of Mount Anjana. Straightway drawing his bow till the string touched his ear, he let fly a keen arrow and hit the boar. Full of rage, the boar, with his sharp tusk that gleamed like the young moon's crescent, ripped up the belly of the hunter, that he fell lifeless to earth. But the boar too yielded his life, from the smarting wound of the arrow.

Meantime, a jackal, for whom Fate had ordained a speedy death, roaming for hunger hither and yon, came to the spot. Delighted at the sight of the boar and the hunter, he bethought him: "Ah! Fate is kind to me in giving me this unexpected food. How true is the saying:—

> No finger need'st thou raise! may'st work or sleep!
> But of thy deeds wrought in a former birth,
> The fruit—or good or ill—thou needs must reap!
> Inexorable Karma rules the earth.

And again—

> In whatso time of life, or when, or where,
> In former birth thou didst or good or ill,
> In just that time of life, and then, and there,
> In future birth, of fruit shall have thy fill!

Now I'll manage it so with these carcasses that I shall get a living off them for many days. And to begin withal, I'll eat the sinew which forms the bowstring. For they say:—

> A wise man doth sip the elixir of life,
> Circumspectly and slowly, and heedful.
> Thus enjoy thou the riches thou'st won by thy strife:
> Never take at one time more than needful."

Making up his mind in this way, he took the end of the bow in his mouth, and began to gnaw the sinew. But as soon as his teeth cut through the string, the bow tore through his palate, and came out of his head like a top-knot, and he gave up the ghost. Therefore, continued the brahman, therefore I say:—

> Excessive greed should ne'er be cherished.
> Have greed—but keep it moderate.
> The all too greedy jackal perished,
> A wooden top-knot on his pate.

FROM The *Gulistan* of Sadi

{A.D. 1184-1292?}

TRANSLATED BY SIR RICHARD BURTON {1821-1890}

᚛᚛᚜

Of Sadi, Ralph Waldo Emerson said that he "speaks to all nations, and like Homer, Shakespeare, Cervantes, and Montaigne, is perpetually modern." Emerson thought of the *Gulistan* as one of the bibles of the world, for he found in it "the universality of moral law." One of its English translators, defending some of its morally questionable passages, urged his readers to skip over them "as some of our queasy clergy do in reading the morning and evening lessons" from the Bible. For the most part, however, the obscenities in Sadi are to be found in works other than the *Gulistan;* the latter is an eminently ethical book. If some of its wisdom is more Machiavellian than idealistic, one must credit the harsh realities of the mode of life for which the much-traveled author was prescribing. The book has for centuries been a common reader in Mohammedan schools, and when the British took over the rule of India, there was no better *vade mecum* for their civil servants to use in unriddling the psychology of Moslem India.

The vogue of Sadi antedated that of the other Persian poets in Europe by nearly a century. The *Gulistan* appeared in a Latin translation in 1651 and had soon won the admiration of Voltaire and other savants of the Enlightenment. Its sister book, the *Bostan,* provided an occasion for one of Benjamin Franklin's more charming hoaxes. Having read a parable from it in the works of the English divine, Jeremy Taylor (who had received it from a Latin version), Franklin passed it off as a missing chapter from *Genesis.* The message of the parable on toleration was so pleasing to the rational-minded eighteenth-century readers that it was some time before the fraudulent chapter was discovered to be an English translation of a Latin version of a Persian original.

Like the *Panchatantra,* with which it has some tales in common, the *Gulistan* is a compendium of proverbial wisdom embodied in charming prose tales studded with pithy verses. Edwin Arnold has aptly described it in culinary terms as "an intellectual pillaw; a literary curry; a kebab of versatile genius." It reads human motives shrewdly and shows their wide range, from the meanest personal greed to the sublimest selflessness. Tradition attributes to Sadi a life of over 100 years, during which he is said to have traveled from India in the East to Tripoli in the West. His contacts with men of all faiths, and of none, imparted to his outlook a cosmopolitanism that contrasts starkly with the illiberal views of some of his Western contemporaries—for example, the Crusaders against whom he fought.

The following translation of portions of the *Gulistan* is attributed to Sir Richard Burton though it was probably the product of his collaboration with an Austrian resident of India, E. H. Rehatsek.

᚛᚛᚜

From the *GULISTAN*

II

One of the Kings of Khorâsân had a vision in a dream of Sultân Mahmûd, one hundred years after his death. His whole person appeared to have been dissolved and turned to dust, except his eyes, which were revolving in their orbits and looking about. All the sages were unable to give an interpretation, except a Dervish, who made his salutation and said: "He is still looking amazed how his kingdom belongs to others."

VII

A Pâdshâh was in the same boat with a Persian slave, who had never before been at sea, and experienced the inconvenience of a vessel; he began to cry and to tremble to such a degree that he could not be pacified by kindness, so that at last the King became displeased as the matter could not be remedied.

In that boat there happened to be a philosopher, who said: "With thy permission I shall quiet him."

The Pâdshâh replied: "It will be a great favour."

The philosopher ordered the slave to be thrown into the water, so that he swallowed some of it, whereon he was caught and pulled by his hair to the boat, to the stern of which he clung with both his hands. Then he sat down in a corner, and became quiet. This appeared strange to the King, who knew not what wisdom there was in the proceeding [and asked for it]; he [the philosopher] replied:

"Before he had tasted the calamity of being drowned, he knew not the safety of the boat; thus also a man does not appreciate the value of immunity from a misfortune until it has befallen him."

> O thou full man! Barley-bread pleases thee not;
> She is my sweetheart who appears ugly to thee!
> To the houris of paradise purgatory seems hell;
> Ask the denizens of hell: [to them] purgatory is paradise!

IX

An Arab king was sick in his state of decrepitude, so that all hopes of life were cut off. A trooper entered the gate with the good news that a certain fort had been conquered by the good luck of the King, that the enemies had been captured, and that the whole population of the district had been reduced to obedience. The King heaved a deep sigh and replied:

"This message is not for me, but for my enemies, namely the heirs of the kingdom. I spent my precious life in hopes,

alas! that every desire of my heart will be fulfilled. My wishes
were realised, but to what profit? since there is no hope that
my past life will return. The hand of fate has struck the
drum of departure. O my two eyes, bid farewell to the head;
O palm, forearm, and arm of my hand, all take leave from
each other. Death, the foe of my desires, has fallen on me.
For the last time, O friends! pass near me. My life has
elapsed in ignorance, I have done nothing; be on your guard."

X

I was constantly engaged in prayer, at the head of the prophet
Yahia's tomb in the cathedral mosque of Damascus, when one
of the Arab kings, notorious for his injustice, happened to arrive on a pilgrimage to it, who offered his supplications, and
asked for compliance with his needs.

The Dervish and the plutocrat are slaves on the floor of
this threshold, and those who are the wealthiest are the
most needy.

Then he said to me: "Dervishes being zealous and veracious
in their dealings, unite thy mind to mine,[1] for I am apprehensive of a powerful enemy."

I replied: "Have mercy upon thy feeble subjects, that thou
mayest not be injured by a strong foe. With a powerful arm
and the strength of the wrist to break the five fingers of a poor
man is sin. Let him be afraid who spares not the fallen, because if he falls no one will take hold of his hand. Whoever
sows bad seed and expects good fruit has cudgelled his brains
for nought, and begotten vain imaginations. Extract the cotton
from thy ears, and administer justice to thy people; and if
thou failest to do so, there is a day of retribution."

The sons of Adam are limbs of each other, having been
created of one essence. When the calamity of time afflicts
one limb the other limbs cannot remain at rest. If thou hast
no sympathy for the troubles of others, thou art unworthy to
be called by the name of a man.

XIX

It is related that while some game was being roasted for
Nushirvân the Just [2] during a hunting party, no salt could
be found. Accordingly a boy was sent to an adjoining village
to bring some. Nushirvân said: "Pay for the salt, lest it should
become a custom and the village be ruined." Having been
asked what harm could arise from such a trifling demand,
Nushirvân replied: "The foundation of oppression was small

[1] Meaning, "Unite thy supplications to mine."
[2] Nushirvân—one of the most distinguished of the monarchs of pre-
Islamic Persia, famed for his benevolence and justice. [Ed.]

in the world; but whoever came augmented it, so that it reached its present magnitude. If the king eats one apple from the garden of a subject his slaves will pull him up the tree from the roots. For five eggs, which the Sultân allows to be taken by force, the people belonging to his army will put a thousand fowls on the spit!"

> A tyrant does not remain in the world;
> But the curse on him abides for ever!

XXI

It is narrated that an oppressor of the people [a soldier] hit the head of a pious man with a stone, and that the Dervish, having no means of taking vengeance, preserved the stone till the time arrived when the King became angry with that soldier, and imprisoned him in a well. Then the Dervish made his appearance, and dropped the stone upon his head.

He asked: "Who art thou, and why hast thou hit my head with this stone?"

The man replied: "I am the same person whom thou hast struck on the head with this stone on such and such a day."

The soldier continued: "Where hast thou been all this time?"

The Dervish replied: "I was afraid of thy dignity, but now, when I beheld thee in the well, I made use of the opportunity."

When thou seest an unworthy man in good luck intelligent men have chosen submission. If thou hast not a tearing, sharp nail it will be better not to contend with the wicked. Who grasps with his fist one who has an arm of steel, injures only his own powerless wrist. Wait till inconstant fortune ties his hand, then, to please thy friends, pick out his brains.

XXII

A King was subject to a terrible disease, the mention of which is not sanctioned by custom. The tribe of Yunani [3] physicians agreed that this pain cannot be allayed, except by means of the bile of a person endued with certain qualities. Orders having been issued to search for an individual of this kind, the son of a landholder was discovered to possess the qualities mentioned by the doctors. The King summoned the father and mother of the boy, whose consent he obtained by giving them immense wealth, the Qâzi [4] issued a judicial decree that it is permissible to shed the blood of one subject for the safety of the King, and the executioner was ready to slay the boy, who then looked heavenwards and smiled.

---

[3] Yunani—Greek. [Ed.]
[4] Qâzi—ecclesiastical judge. [Ed.]

The King asked: "What occasion for laughter is there in such a position?"

The youth replied: "A son looks to the affection of his father and mother to bring his case before the Qâzi, and to ask justice from the Pâdshâh; in the present instance, however, the father and mother have for the trash of this world surrendered my blood, the Qâzi has issued a decree to kill me, the Sultân thinks he will recover his health only through my destruction, and I see no other refuge besides God the Most High. To whom shall I complain against thy hand, if I am to seek justice also from thy hand?"

The Sultân became troubled at these words, tears rushed to his eyes, and he said: "It is better for me to perish than to shed innocent blood." He kissed the head and eyes of the youth, presented him with boundless wealth; and it is said that the King also recovered his health during that week.

I also remember the distich recited by the elephant-driver on the bank of the Nile:

"If thou knewest the state of the ant under thy foot,
It is like thy own condition under the foot of an elephant."

XXXI

The viziers of Nushirvân happened to discuss an important affair of State, each giving his opinion according to his knowledge. The King likewise gave his opinion, and Barzachumihr concurred with it. Afterwards the viziers secretly asked him: "What superiority hast thou discovered in the opinion of the King above so many other reflections of wise men?"

The philosopher replied: "Since the termination of the affair is unknown, and it depends upon the will of God whether the opinion of the others will turn out right or wrong, it was better to agree with the opinion of the King; so that, if it should turn out to have been wrong, we may, on account of having followed it, remain free from blame. To proffer an opinion contrary to the King's means to wash the hands in one's own blood; should he in plain day say it is night, it is meet to shout: 'Lo! The moon and the Pleiades!'"

XXXVII

Someone had brought information to Nushirvân the Just that an enemy of his had been removed from this world by God the Most High. He asked: "Hast thou heard anything about His intending to spare me? There is no occasion for our rejoicing at a foe's death, because our own life will also not last for ever."

XLVII

I remember, being pious in my childhood, rising in the night, addicted to devotion and abstinence. One night I was sitting with my father, remaining awake and holding the beloved Qurân in my lap, whilst the people around us were asleep. I said: "Not one of these persons lifts up his head, or makes a genuflection. They are as fast asleep as if they were dead."

He replied: "Darling of thy father! Would that thou wert also asleep, rather than disparaging people."

> The pretender sees no one but himself,
> Because he has the veil of conceit in front;
> If he were endowed with a God-discerning eye,
> He would see that no one is weaker than himself.

LVI

A pious man saw in a dream a Pâdshâh in paradise and a devotee in hell, whereon he asked for the reason of the former's exaltation and the latter's degradation, saying that he had imagined the contrary ought to be the case. He received the following answer: "The Pâdshâh had, for the love he bore to Dervishes, been rewarded with paradise; and the devotee had, for associating with Pâdshâhs, been punished in hell."

LXXI

Having become tired of my friends in Damascus, I went into the desert of Jerusalem and associated with animals, till the time when I became a prisoner of the Franks,[5] who put me to work with infidels in digging the earth of a moat in Tarapolis, when one of the chiefs of Aleppo, with whom I had formerly been acquainted, recognized me, and said: "What state is this?" I recited:

> "I fled from men to mountain and desert,
> Wishing to attend upon no one but God;
> Imagine what my state at present is,
> When I must be satisfied in a stable of wretches."

The feet in chains with friends is better than to be with strangers in a garden.

He took pity on my state and ransomed me for ten *dinârs* from the captivity of the Franks, taking me to Aleppo, where he had a daughter, and married me to her, with a dowry of one hundred *dinârs*. After some time had elapsed, she turned out to be ill-humoured, quarrelsome, disobedient, abusive in her tongue, and embittering my life. A bad wife in a good man's house is his hell in this world already. Alas for a bad

5 Franks—general term for Europeans. [Ed.]

consort, alas! Preserve us, O Lord, from the punishment of fire.

Once she lengthened her tongue of reproach, and said: "Art thou not the man whom my father purchased from the Franks for ten *dinârs?*"

I replied: "Yes, he bought me for ten *dinârs,* and sold me into thy hands for one hundred *dinârs.*"

I heard that a sheep had by a great man been rescued from the jaws and the power of a wolf; in the evening he stroked her throat with a knife, whereon the soul of the sheep complained thus: "Thou hast snatched me away from the claws of a wolf, but at last I see thou art thyself a wolf."

CVII

I never lamented about the vicissitudes of time or complained of the turns of fortune, except on the occasion when I was barefooted and unable to procure slippers. But when I entered the great mosque of Kufah with a sore heart, and beheld a man without feet, I offered thanks to the bounty of God, consoled myself for my want of shoes, and recited: "A roast fowl is to the sight of a satiated man less valuable than a blade of grass on the table; and to him who has no means nor power a burnt turnip is [as good as] a roasted fowl."

CXXVIII

An astrologer, having entered his own house, saw a stranger, and, getting angry, began to insult him, whereon both fell upon each other and fought, so that turmoil and confusion ensued. A pious man who had witnessed the scene exclaimed: "How knowest thou what is in the zenith of the sky if thou art not aware who is in thy house?"

CXXXI

A fellow with a disagreeable voice happened to be reading the Qurân, when a pious man passed near, and asked him what his monthly salary was. He replied: "Nothing."

He further inquired: "Then why takest thou this trouble?"

He replied: "I am reading for God's sake."

He replied: "For God's sake do not read. If thou readest the Qurân thus thou wilt deprive the religion of splendour."

CXXXIX

One of the Ullemma [6] had been asked that, supposing one sits with a moon-faced [beauty] in a private apartment, the doors being closed, companions asleep, passion inflamed, and lust raging, as the Arab says, the date is ripe, and its guardian not forbidding—whether he thought the power of abstinence

6 Ullemma—ecclesiastics. [Ed.]

would cause the man to remain in safety. He replied: "If he remains in safety from the moon-faced one, he will not remain safe from evil speakers."

If a man escapes from his own bad lust he will not escape from the bad suspicions of accusers. It is proper to sit down to one's own work, but it is impossible to bind the tongues of men.

C X L V I

A King of the Arabs, having been informed of the relations subsisting between Laila and Mejnûn,[7] with an account of the latter's insanity, to the effect that he had, in spite of his great accomplishments and eloquence, chosen to roam about in the desert and to let go the reins of self-control from his hands; he ordered him to be brought to his presence, and, this having been done, he began to reprove him, and to ask him what defect he had discovered in the nobility of the human soul, that he adopted the habits of beasts and abandoned the society of mankind?

Mejnûn replied: "Many friends have blamed me for loving her, will they not see her one day and understand my excuse? Would that those who are reproving me could see thy face, O ravisher of hearts! That instead of a lemon, in thy presence they might needlessly cut their hands,[8] that the truth may bear witness to the assertion: 'This is he for whose sake ye blamed me.' "

The King expressed a wish to see the beauty of Laila, in order to ascertain the cause of so much distress; accordingly he ordered her to be searched for. The encampments of various Arab families having been visited, she was found, conveyed to the King, and led into the courtyard of the palace. The King looked at her outward form for some time, and she appeared despicable in his sight, because the meanest handmaids of his harem excelled her in beauty and attractions.

Mejnûn, who shrewdly understood [the thoughts of the King], said: "It would have been necessary to look from the window of Mejnûn's eye at the beauty of Laila, when the mystery of her aspect would have been revealed to thee."

> Who are healthy have no pain from wounds;
> I shall tell my grief to no one but a sympathiser.
> It is useless to speak of bees to one

[7] The story of the crazed love of Mejnûn for the Arab girl Laila is the *Romeo and Juliet* of the Moslem world. [Ed.]

[8] An allusion to a famous scene in the story of Yusuf and Zuleíkha, in which the women friends of Zuleikha, distracted by the beauty of Yusuf, cut their hands instead of the lemons or oranges that they were peeling. [Ed.]

Who never in his life felt their sting.
As long as thy state is not like mine,
My state will be but an idle tale to thee.

CLIV

A Vizier who had a stupid son gave him in charge of a scholar to instruct him, and if possible to make him intelligent. Having been some time under instruction, but ineffectually, the learned man sent one to his father with the words: "The boy is not becoming intelligent, and has made a fool of me."

When a nature is originally receptive, instruction will take effect thereon. No kind of polishing will improve iron whose essence is originally bad. Wash a dog in the seven oceans, he will be only dirtier when he gets wet. If the ass of Jesus be taken to Mekkah he will on his return still be an ass.

MAXIM XXXII

Everyone thinks himself perfect in intellect, and his child in beauty.

A Jew was debating with a Mussalmân till I shook with laughter at their dispute; the Moslem said in anger: "If this deed of mine is not correct, may God cause me to die a Jew."

The Jew said: "I swear by the Pentateuch that if my oath is false, I shall die a Moslem like thee."

Should wisdom disappear from the surface of the earth, still no one will acknowledge his own ignorance.

FROM The *Mathnawi* of Rumi

{A.D. 1207-73}

TRANSLATED BY REYNOLD A. NICHOLSON {1868-1945}

The *Mathnawi*, Rumi's greatest work, has been called by Moslems the Koran of the Persians (the highest compliment that could be paid a book not in the language of *the* Book); by Westerners it has been called *The Divine Comedy* of Islam. It is of course an orthodox book, well grounded in Moslem theology. But it is also the Bible of the Sufis, a mystic order claiming many of the Persian poets. Sufism employs the language of the senses to express the spiritual longing of the devotee for reunion with God, from Whom it is believed that man is separated only by his unawareness of his divine nature. Although originally possibly a protest against the forbidding impersonality of Mohammed's God, Sufism came to be regarded as a sort of hidden or esoteric Islam whose pantheistic God might be equated with Allah. The mystical experience to which it exhorts is intended not to supplant but to supplement the submission denoted by the word Islam.

It is interesting to note that the Rev. Edward B. Cowell, who taught Edward Fitzgerald to read Persian, had only disgust for the doubting quatrains of Omar Khayyam, but he revered the pious *Mathnawi* of Rumi. Another Victorian clergyman, the Rev. William Hastie, fervently hoped to combat the godless quatrains with the devout couplets.

Mathnawi means simply couplets. So great has been the authority of this book that it has pre-empted the name of a verse form as its title, very much as if one should designate *Paradise Lost* "The Blank Verse Poem" or *War and Peace* "The Novel." The *Mathnawi* is a vast poem in six books which by exhortation, example and exposition seeks to lead the would-be Sufi along the path to sainthood. It embodies much ancient folklore, Koranic legends, saints' lives, practical wisdom, lofty homilies and even vulgar tales, but also some of the intensest experiences of the spirit recorded by man.

The following selections are from the illustrative material only —tales told in explanation of points under philosophical discussion. They characteristically reveal a liberal Moslem attitude toward not only the prophet of Islam but also the prophets of Judaism and Christianity. Small portions of the literal translation have been left out here in order to retain the story continuity, the omitted lines being expository rather than narrative.

ᛁᚾᚩᛁᚳᚱᚾᛁ

From the *MATHNAWI*

I

One forenoon a freeborn nobleman arrived and ran into Solomon's hall of justice, his countenance pale with anguish and both lips blue. Then Solomon said, "Good sir, what is the matter?"

He replied, "Azrael [9] cast on me such a look, so full of wrath and hate."

"Come," said the king, "what boon do you desire now? Ask!" "O protector of my life," said he, "command the wind to bear me from here to India. Maybe, when thy slave is come thither he will save his life."

Solomon commanded the wind to bear him quickly over the water to the uttermost part of India. Next day, at the time of conference and meeting, Solomon said to Azrael: "Didst thou look with anger on that Moslem in order that he might wander as an exile far from his home?"

9 Azrael—the angel of death. [Ed.]

Azrael said, "When did I look on him angrily? I saw him as I passed by, and looked at him in astonishment, for God had commanded me, saying, 'Hark, today do thou take his spirit in India.' From wonder I said to myself, 'Even if he has a hundred wings, 'tis a far journey for him to be in India to-day.' "

I I

A certain grammarian embarked in a boat. That self-conceited person turned to the boatman and said, "Have you ever studied grammar?" "No," he replied. The other said, "Half your life is gone to naught."

The boatman became heart-broken with grief, but at the time he refrained from answering.

The wind cast the boat into a whirlpool: the boatman shouted to the grammarian, "Tell me, do you know how to swim?" "No," said he, "O fair-spoken, good-looking man!"

"O grammarian," said he, "your whole life is naught, because the boat is sinking in these whirlpools."

I I I

A certain man came and knocked at a friend's door: his friend asked him, "Who art thou, O trusty one?"

He answered, "I." The friend said, "Begone, 'tis not the time for thee to come in: at a table like this there is no place for the raw."

The wretched man went away, and for a year in travel and in separation from his friend he was burned with sparks of fire. Then he returned and again paced to and fro beside the house of his comrade. He knocked at the door with a hundred fears and respects, lest any disrespectful word might escape from his lips.

His friend called to him, "Who is at the door?" He answered, " 'Tis thou art at the door, O charmer of hearts."

"Now," said the friend, "since thou art I, come in, O myself: there is not room in the house for two I's."

I V

Moses saw a shepherd on the way, who was saying, "O God who choosest whom Thou wilt, where art Thou, that I may become Thy servant and sew Thy shoes and comb Thy head? That I may wash Thy clothes and kill Thy lice and bring milk to Thee, O worshipful One; that I may kiss Thy little hand and rub Thy little foot, and when bedtime comes I may sweep Thy little room. O Thou to whom all my goats be a sacrifice, O Thou in remembrance of whom are my cries of ay and ah!"

The shepherd was speaking foolish words in this wise. Moses said, "Man, to whom is this addressed?"

He answered, "To that One who created us; by whom this earth and sky were brought to sight."

"Hark!" said Moses, "you have become very backsliding; indeed you have not become a Moslem, you have become an infidel. What babble is this? What blasphemy and raving? Stuff some cotton into your mouth! The stench of your blasphemy has made the whole world stinking: your blasphemy has turned the silk robe of religion into rags. Shoes and socks are fitting for you, but how are such things right for One who is a Sun?"

The shepherd said, "O Moses, thou hast closed my mouth and thou hast burned my soul with repentance." He rent his garment and heaved a sigh, and hastily turned his head towards the desert and went his way.

A revelation came to Moses from God—"Thou hast parted My servant from Me. Didst thou come as a prophet to unite, or didst thou come to sever? So far as thou canst, do not set foot in separation: of all things the most hateful to Me is divorce. I have bestowed on every one a special way of acting: I have given to every one a peculiar form of expression. In regard to him it is worthy of praise, and in regard to thee it is worthy of blame: in regard to him honey, and in regard to thee poison. I am independent of all purity and impurity, of all slothfulness and alacrity in worshipping Me. I did not ordain Divine worship that I might make any profit; nay, but that I might do a kindness to My servants. In the Hindoos the idiom of India is praiseworthy; in the Sindians the idiom of Sind is praiseworthy. I am not sanctified by their glorification of Me; 'tis they that become sanctified and pure and radiant. I look not at the tongue and the speech; I look at the inward spirit and the state of feeling. I gaze into the heart to see whether it be lowly, though the words uttered be not lowly, because the heart is the substance, speech; I look at the inward spirit and the state of feeling. I substance is the real object. How much more of these phrases and conceptions and metaphors? I want burning, burning: become friendly with that burning! Light up a fire of love in thy soul, burn thought and expression entirely away! O Moses, they that know the conventions are of one sort, they whose souls and spirits burn are of another sort."

V

The elephant was in a dark house: some Hindus had brought it for exhibition.

In order to see it, many people were going, every one, into that darkness.

As seeing it with the eye was impossible, each one was feeling it in the dark with the palm of his hand.

The hand of one fell on its trunk: he said, "This creature is like a waterpipe."

The hand of another touched its ear: to him it appeared to be like a fan.

Since another handled its leg, he said, "I found the elephant's shape to be like a pillar."

Another laid his hand on its back: he said, "Truly, this elephant was like a throne."

Similarly, when any one heard a description of the elephant, he understood it only in respect of the part that he had touched. If there had been a candle in each one's hand, the difference would have gone out of their words.

VI

Jesus, son of Mary, was fleeing to a mountain: you would say that a lion wished to shed his blood.

A certain man ran after him and said, "Is it well with thee? There is no one in pursuit of thee: why dost thou flee, like a bird?"

But Jesus still kept running with haste so quickly that on account of his haste he did not answer him.

He pushed on in pursuit of Jesus for the distance of one or two fields, and then invoked Jesus with the utmost earnestness, saying, "For the sake of pleasing God, stop one moment, for I have a difficulty concerning thy flight. From whom art thou fleeing in this direction, O noble one? There is no lion pursuing thee, no enemy, and there is no fear or danger."

He said, "I am fleeing from the fool. Begone! I am saving myself. Do not debar me!"

"Why," said he, "art not thou the Messiah by whom the blind and the deaf are restored to sight and hearing?"

He said, "Yea." Said the other, "Art not thou the King in whom the spells of the Unseen World have their abode? —So that when thou chantest those spells over a dead man, he springs up rejoicing like a lion that has caught his prey."

He said, "Yea, I am he." Said the other, "Dost not thou make living birds out of clay, O beauteous one?"

He said, "Yea." Said the other, "Then, O pure Spirit, thou doest whatsoever thou wilt: of whom hast thou fear? With such miraculous evidence, who is there in the world that would not be one of the slaves devoted to thee?"

Jesus said, "By the holy Essence of God, the Maker of the body and the Creator of the soul in eternity; by the sanctity of the pure Essence and Attributes of Him, for whose sake the collar of Heaven is rent,[10] I swear that the

---

[10] I.e. "on whose account Heaven is enraptured."

spells and the Most Great Name which I pronounced over the deaf and the blind were good in their effects. I pronounced them over the stony mountain; it was cloven and tore upon itself its mantle down to the navel. I pronounced them over the corpse; it came to life. I pronounced them over nonentity: it became entity. I pronounced them lovingly over the heart of the fool hundreds of thousands of times, and 'twas no cure for his folly. He became hard rock and changed not from that disposition; he became sand from which no produce grows."

VII

I will tell you the story of Halíma's [11] mystic experience, that her tale may clear away your trouble.

When she parted Mustafá [12] from her milk, she took him up on the palm of her hand as tenderly as though he were sweet basil and roses, causing him to avoid every good or evil hap, that she might commit that spiritual emperor to the care of his grandsire.

Since she was bringing the precious trust in fear for its safety, she went to the Ka'ba and came into the Hatím. [13]

From the air she heard a cry—"O *Hatím*, an exceedingly mighty Sun hath shone upon thee. O *Hatím*, to-day there will suddenly come upon thee a hundred thousand beams from the Sun of munificence. O *Hatím*, to-day there will march into thee with pomp a glorious King, whose harbinger is Fortune. O *Hatím*, to-day without doubt thou wilt become anew the abode of exalted spirits. The spirits of the holy will come to thee from every quarter in troops and multitudes, drunken with desire."

Halíma was bewildered by that voice: neither in front nor behind was any one to be seen. All the six directions were empty of any visible form, and this cry was continuous —may the soul be a ransom for that cry! She laid Mustafá on the earth, that she might search after the sweet sound. Then she cast her eye to and fro, saying, "Where is that king that tells of mysteries? For such a loud sound is arriving from left and right. O Lord, where is he that causes it to arrive?"

When she did not see any one, she became distraught and despairing: her body began to tremble like the willow-bough. She came back towards that righteous child: she did not see Mustafá in his former place. Bewilderment on be-

---

11 Halíma—Mohammed's nurse and foster mother. [Ed.]
12 Mustafá—Mohammed. [Ed.]
13 The name *Hatím* is properly given to a semicircular wall adjoining the north and west corners of the Ka'ba. Here it denotes the space between the wall and the Ka'ba. [The Ka'ba, the object of the Meccan pilgrimage, houses the anciently worshiped Black Stone.—Ed.]

wilderment fell upon her heart: from grief her abode became very dark. She ran to the dwellings hard by and raised an outcry, saying, "Who has carried off my single pearl?"

The Meccans said, "We have no knowledge: we knew not that a child was there."

She shed so many tears and made so much lamentation that those others began to weep because of her grief. Beating her breast, she wept so mightily that the stars were made to weep by her weeping.

An old man with a staff approached her, saying, "Why, what hath befallen thee, O Halíma, that thou didst let such a fire of grief blaze forth from thy heart and consume these bowels of the bystanders with mourning?"

She replied, "I am Mohammed's trusted fostermother, so I brought him back to hand over to his grandsire. When I arrived in the *Hatím* voices were coming down and I was hearing them from the air. When I heard from the air those melodious strains, because of that sound I laid down the infant there, to see whose voice is the origin of this cry, for it is a very beautiful cry and delightful. I saw no sign of any one around me: the cry was not ceasing for one moment. When I returned to my senses from the bewilderments of my heart, I did not see the child there where I had left him: alas for my heart!"

The old man said, "O daughter, do not grieve, for I will show unto thee a queen, who, if she wish, will tell what has happened to the child: she knows the dwelling-place of the child and his setting-out on the way."

Then Halíma said, "Oh, my soul be a ransom for thee, O goodly and fair-spoken Shaykh! Come, show me that queen of clairvoyance who hath knowledge of what has happened to my child."

He brought her to 'Uzzá,[14] saying, "This idol is greatly prized for information concerning the Unseen. Through her we have found thousands that were lost, when we hastened towards her in devotion."

The old man prostrated himself before 'Uzzá and said at once, "O Sovereign of the Arabs, O sea of munificence!" Then he said, "O 'Uzzá, thou hast done many favours to us so that we have been delivered from snares. On account of thy favour the duty of worshipping thee has become obligatory to the Arabs, so that the Arabs have submitted to thee. In hope of thee this Halíma of the tribe Sa'd has come into the shadow of thy willow-bough, for an infant of hers is lost: the name of that child is Mohammed."

When he said "Mohammed," all those idols immediately fell headlong and prostrate, saying, "Begone, O old man! What

14 'Uzzá—the goddess Venus, worshiped by the pagan Arabs. [Ed.]

is this search after that Mohammed by whom we are deposed?
By him we are overthrown and reduced to a collection of
broken stone; by him we are made unsalable and valueless.
Those phantoms which the followers of vain opinion used
to see from us at times [15] during the *Fatra* [16] will disappear
now that his royal court has arrived: the water is come and
has annulled the ablution with sand.[17] Get thee far off, O
old man! Do not kindle mischief! Hark, do not burn us with
the fire of Mohammed's jealousy! Get thee far off, for God's
sake, O old man, lest thou too be burnt by the fire of Fore-
ordainment. What squeezing of the dragon's tail is this? Dost
thou know at all what the announcement of Mohammed's
advent is in its effects? At this news the heart of sea and
mine will surge; at this news the seven heavens will tremble."

When the old man heard these words from the idols, the
ancient old man let his staff drop from his hand; then, from
tremor and fear and dread caused by that proclamation of
the idols, the old man was striking his teeth together. Even as
a naked man in winter, he was shuddering and saying, "O
destruction!"

When Halíma saw the old man in such a state of terror, in
consequence of that marvel the woman lost the power of
deliberation. She said, "O old man, though I am in affliction
on account of the loss of Mohammed, I am in manifold
bewilderment not knowing whether I should grieve or rejoice.
At one moment the wind is making a speech to me, at another moment the stones are schooling me. The wind addresses
me with articulate words, the stones and mountains give me
intelligence of the real nature of things. Once before they
of the Invisible carried off my child—they of the Invisible,
the green-winged ones of Heaven. Of whom shall I complain? To whom shall I tell this plaint? I am become crazy
and in a hundred minds. God's jealousy has closed my lips
so that I am unable to unfold the tale of the mystery: I say
only this much, that my child is lost. If I should say anything else now, the people would bind me in chains as
though I were mad."

The old man said to her, "O Halíma, rejoice; bow down
in thanksgiving and do not rend thy face. Do not grieve: he
will not become lost to thee; nay, but the whole world will
become lost in him. Before and behind him there are always
hundreds of thousands of keepers and guardians watching
over him in jealous emulation. Didst not thou see how those

---

[15] I.e. the divine powers which, as the idolaters falsely imagined, were
sometimes displayed by the idols.
[16] The interval of time between Jesus and Mohammed.
[17] In the absence of water the ritual ablution may be performed with
sand.

idols with all their arts fell headlong at the name of thy child? This is a marvellous epoch on the face of the earth: I have grown old, and I have not seen aught of this kind."

VIII

There was a man, a householder, who had a very sneering, dirty, and rapacious wife. Whatever food he brought home, his wife would consume it, and the man was forced to keep silence.

One day that family man brought home, for a guest, some meat which he had procured with infinite pains. His wife ate it up with *kabáb* and wine: when the man came in, she put him off with useless words.

The man said to her, "Where is the meat? The guest has arrived: one must set nice food before a guest."

"This cat has eaten the meat," she replied: "hey, go and buy some more meat if you can!"

He said to the servant, "O Aybak, fetch the balance: I will weigh the cat."

He weighed her. The cat was half a *mann*. Then the man said, "O deceitful wife, the meat was half a *mann* and one *sitír* over; the cat is just half a *mann*, my lady. If this is the cat, then where is the meat? Or, if this is the meat, where is the cat? Search for her!"

II Prose Fiction

FROM *The Thousand and One Nights*

[COMPILED 13TH-16TH CENTURY A.D.]

TRANSLATED BY SIR RICHARD BURTON [1821-1890]

For a great many European and American readers, Oriental literature means chiefly *The Arabian Nights,* as *The Thousand and One Nights* has been known since its introduction into Europe early in the 18th century. Certainly, no other body of Asian writings, except the Bible, has had so many and so different readers. Men and women, young and old, the literarily naïve and sophisticated, have found an inexhaustible fund of pleasure in these marvelous tales.

The Oriental tinge in 19th century European civilization owes more to them than to any other single factor. One cannot imagine the paintings of Delacroix, the music of Rimski-Korsakov, or the "Turkish" tales of Byron without *The Arabian Nights* as background. Early magazines of the 18th century, both in England and in the American colonies, were filled with imitations of these tales, and the present preoccupation of Hollywood with the theme bids fair to become permanent.

The Arabian Nights obviously makes its appeal to fundamental human drives: sex, the will to power, the hunger of the belly and the thirst of the palate. Critics have attempted to explain the numerous fantasies of food and drink, of delectable maidens in languorous postures, of bottomless hordes of wealth, in terms of the impoverished life of a people confined to the barren desert. But this will hardly answer the question of why they appeal so strongly to 20th century Americans enjoying the highest standard of living ever known. Nor will that explanation jibe with the belief of most scholars that these are not (most of them) Arabian tales, but are rather of Indian, Persian, or Egyptian origin. They took their present shape, to be sure, in the Arabic language, probably in Egypt under the Mameluke Dynasty. But only a few of the stories are of that time and place. The more typical belong to the time of the Caliph Harun-al-Rashid and are probably of Persian invention. Others are traceable to India. Such a one is the tale of "The Lady and Her Five Suitors," here reproduced. Analogues of it are of course to be found in many other literatures; readers of the *Decameron* will remember the first story of the eighth day.

Like Boccaccio's famous cycle of stories, or the *Canterbury Tales* of Chaucer, or the much older *Panchatantra, The Thousand and One Nights* constitutes really only one large tale enclosing a great number of smaller tales. The unifying situation is well known: how the Wazir's daughter Shahrazad undertook to save her gradually diminishing sex from the misogynist King Shahryar, who had been putting his numerous consorts to death at an alarming rate; how she delayed the date of her own execution by protracting the tales until she had presented him with several children; how she won his love by demonstrating the faithfulness of the female; and how finally she proved the cunning of her species by arranging a double wedding in which her sister Dinazad and *his* brother Zaman—whose experiences with women had been equally disillusioning—were also married.

ᛁᚾᛞᛁᚲᛣᛁ

THE LADY AND HER FIVE SUITORS

A woman of the daughters of the merchants was married to a man who was a great traveller. It chanced once that he set out for a far country and was absent so long that his wife, from pure ennui, fell in love with a handsome young man of the sons of the merchants, and they loved each other with exceeding love. One day the youth quarrelled with another man, who lodged a complaint against him with the Chief of Police, and he cast him into prison. When the news came to the merchant's wife, his mistress, she wellnigh lost her wits; then she arose and donning her richest clothes repaired to the house of the Chief of Police. She saluted him and presented a written petition to this purport: "He thou hast clapped in jail is my brother such and such, who fell out with such an one; and those who testified against him bore false witness. He hath been wrongfully imprisoned, and I have none other to come in to me nor to provide for my support; therefore I beseech thee of thy grace to release him."

When the magistrate had read the paper, he cast his eyes on her and fell in love with her forthright; so he said to her, "Go into the house, till I bring him before me; then I will send for thee and thou shalt take him." "O my lord," replied she, "I have none to protect me save Almighty Allah! I am a stranger and may not enter any man's abode." Quoth the Wali, "I will not let him go, except thou come to my home and I take my will of thee." Rejoined she, "If it must be so, thou must needs come to my lodging and sit and sleep the siesta and rest the whole day there." "And where is thy abode?" asked he; and she answered, "In such a place," and appointed him for such a time. Then she went out from him, leaving his heart taken with love of her, and she repaired to the Kazi of the city to whom she said, "O our lord the Kazi!" He exclaimed, "Yes!" and she continued, "Look into my case, and thy reward be with Allah the Most High!" Quoth he, "Who hath wronged thee?" and quoth she, "O my lord, I have a brother and I have none but that one, and it is on his account that I come to thee; because the Wali hath imprisoned him for a criminal and men have borne false witness against him that he is a wrong-doer; and I beseech thee to intercede for him with the Chief of Police."

When the Kazi looked on her, he fell in love with her forthright and said to her, "Enter the house and rest awhile with my handmaids whilst I send to the Wali to release thy brother. If I knew the money-fine which is upon him, I would pay it out of my own purse, so I may have my desire of thee, for thou pleasest me with thy sweet speech." Quoth she, "If thou, O my lord, do thus, we must not blame others." Quoth he, "An thou wilt not come in, wend thy ways." Then said she, "An thou wilt have it so, O our lord, it will be privier and better in my place than in thine, for here are slave-girls and eunuchs and goers-in and comers-out, and indeed I am a woman who wotteth naught of this fashion; but need compelleth." Asked the Kazi, "And where is thy house?"; and she answered, "In such a place," and appointed him for the same day and time as the Chief of Police. Then she went out from him to the Wazir, to whom she proffered her petition for the release from prison of her brother who was absolutely necessary to her; but he also required her of herself, saying, "Suffer me to have my will of thee and I will set thy brother free." Quoth she, "An thou wilt have it so, be it in my house, for there it will be privier both for me and for thee. It is not far distant and thou knowest that which behoveth us women of cleanliness and adornment." Asked he, "Where is thy house?" "In such a place," answered she and appointed him for the same time as the two others.

Then she went out from him to the King of the city and told him her story and sought of him her brother's release. "Who imprisoned him?" inquired he; and she replied, " 'Twas thy Chief of Police." When the King heard her speech, it transpierced his heart with the arrows of love and he bade her enter the palace with him, that he might send to the Kazi and release her brother. Quoth she, "O King, this thing is easy to thee, whether I will or nill; and if the King will indeed have this of me, it is of my good fortune; but, if he come to my house, he will do me the more honour by setting step therein." Quoth the King, "We will not cross thee in this." So she appointed him for the same time as the three others, and told him where her house was.

Then she left him and, betaking herself to a man which was a carpenter, said to him, "I would have thee make me a cabinet with four compartments one above other, each with its door for locking up. Let me know thy hire and I will give it thee." Replied he, "My price will be four dinars; but, O noble lady and well-protected, if thou wilt vouchsafe me thy favours, I will ask nothing of thee." Rejoined she, "An there be no help but that thou have it so, then make thou five compartments with their padlocks"; and she appointed him to bring it exactly on the day required. Said he, "It is well; sit down, O my lady, and I will make it for thee forthright, and after I will come to thee at my leisure." So she sat down by him, whilst he fell to work on the cabinet, and when he had made an end of it she chose to see it at once carried home and set up in the sitting-chamber. Then she took four gowns and carried them to the dyer, who dyed them each of a different color; after which she applied herself to making ready meat and drink, fruits, flowers and perfumes.

Now, when the appointed trysting-day came, she donned her costliest dress and adorned herself and scented herself, then spread the sitting-room with various kinds of rich carpets and sat down to await who should come. And behold, the

Kazi was the first to appear, devancing the rest; and when she saw him, she rose to her feet and kissed the ground before him; then, taking him by the hand, made him sit down by her on the couch and lay with him and fell to jesting and toying with him. By and by, he would have her do his desire, but she said, "O my lord, doff thy clothes and turband and assume this yellow cassock and this headkerchief, whilst I bring thee meat and drink; and after thou shalt win thy will." So saying, she took his clothes and turband and clad him in the cassock and the kerchief; but hardly had she done this, when lo! there came a knocking at the door. Asked he, "Who is that rapping on the door?" and she answered, "My husband." Quoth the Kazi, "What is to be done, and where shall I go?" Quoth she, "Fear nothing, I will hide thee in this cabinet"; and he, "Do as seemeth good to thee." So she took him by the hand and, pushing him into the lowest compartment, locked the door upon him.

Then she went to the house-door, where she found the Wali; so she kissed the ground before him and, taking his hand, brought him into the saloon, where she made him sit down and said to him, "O my lord, this house is thy house; this place is thy place, and I am thy handmaid; thou shalt pass all this day with me; wherefore do thou doff thy clothes and don this red gown, for it is a sleeping-gown." So she took away his clothes and made him assume the red gown and set on his head an old patched rag she had by her; after which she sat by him on the divan and she sported with him while he toyed with her awhile, till he put out his hand to her. Whereupon she said to him, "O our lord, this day is thy day and none shall share in it with thee; but first, of thy favour and benevolence, write me an order for my brother's release from jail that my heart may be at ease." Quoth he, "Hearkening and obedience; on my head and eyes be it!" and wrote a letter to his treasurer, saying: "As soon as this communication shall reach thee, do thou set such an one free, without stay or delay; neither answer the bearer a word." Then he sealed it and she took it from him, after which she began to toy again with him on the divan when, behold, someone knocked at the door. He asked, "Who is that?" and she answered, "My husband." "What shall I do?" said he, and she, "Enter this cabinet, till I send him away and return to thee." So she clapped him into the second compartment from the bottom and padlocked the door on him; and meanwhile the Kazi heard all they said.

Then she went to the house-door and opened it, whereupon, lo! the Wazir entered. She kissed the ground before him and received him with all honor and worship, saying, "O my lord, thou exaltest us by thy coming to our house; Allah never de-

prive us of the light of thy countenance!" Then she seated him
on the divan and said to him, "O my lord, doff thy heavy
dress and turband and don these lighter vestments." So he put
off his clothes and turband and she clad him in a blue cassock
and a tall red bonnet, and said to him, "Erst thy garb was that
of the Wazirate; so leave it to its own time and don this light
gown, which is better fitted for carousing and making merry
and sleep." Thereupon she began to play with him and he
with her, and he would have done his desire of her; but she
put him off, saying, "O my lord, this shall not fail us." As
they were talking there came a knocking at the door, and the
Wazir asked her, "Who is that?"; to which she answered, "My
husband." Quoth he, "What is to be done?" Quoth she, "Enter
this cabinet, till I get rid of him and come back to thee and
fear thou nothing." So she put him in the third compartment
and locked the door on him, after which she went out and
opened the house-door when, lo and behold! in came the King.

As soon as she saw him she kissed the ground before him
and, taking him by the hand, led him into the saloon and
seated him on the divan at the upper end. Then said she to
him, "Verily, O King, thou dost us high honour, and if we
brought thee to gift the world and all that therein is, it would
not be worth a single one of thy steps us-wards." And when
he had taken his seat upon the divan she said, "Give me leave
to speak one word." "Say what thou wilt," answered he, and
she said, "O my lord, take thine ease and doff thy dress and turband." Now his clothes were worth a thousand dinars; and
when he put them off she clad him in a patched gown, worth
at the very most ten dirhams, and fell to talking and jesting
with him; all this while the folk in the cabinet hearing everything that passed, but not daring to say a word. Presently,
the King put his hand to her neck and sought to do his desire
of her; when she said, "This thing shall not fail us, but I had
first promised myself to entertain thee in this sitting-chamber,
and I have that which shall content thee." Now, as they were
speaking, someone knocked at the door and he asked her,
"Who is that?" "My husband," answered she; and he, "Make
him go away of his own good will, or I will fare forth to him
and send him away perforce." Replied she, "Nay, O my lord,
have patience till I send him away by my skilful contrivance."
"And I, how shall I do?" inquired the King; whereupon she
took him by the hand and, making him enter the fourth compartment of the cabinet, locked it upon him. Then she went
out and opened the house-door, when behold, the carpenter
entered and saluted her.

Quoth she, "What manner of thing is this cabinet thou hast
made me?" "What aileth it, O my lady?" asked he, and she

answered, "The top compartment is too strait." Rejoined he, "Not so"; and she, "Go in thyself and see; it is not wide enough for thee." Quoth he, "It is wide enough for four," and entered the fifth compartment, whereupon she locked the door on him. Then she took the letter of the Chief of Police and carried it to the treasurer who, having read and understood it, kissed it and delivered her lover to her. She told him all she had done and he said, "And how shall we act now?" She answered, "We will remove hence to another city, for after this work there is no tarrying for us here." So the twain packed up what goods they had and, loading them on camels, set out forthright for another city.

Meanwhile, the five abode each in his compartment of the cabinet without eating or drinking three whole days, during which time they held their water, until at last the carpenter could retain his no longer; so he staled on the King's head, and the King urined on the Wazir's head, and the Wazir piddled on the Wali and the Wali pissed on the head of the Kazi; whereupon the Judge cried out and said, "What nastiness is this? Doth not what strait we are in suffice us, but you must make water upon us?" The Chief of Police recognized the Kazi's voice and answered, saying aloud, "Allah increase thy reward, O Kazi!" And when the Kazi heard him, he knew him for the Wali. Then the Chief of Police lifted up his voice and said, "What means this nastiness?" and the Wazir answered, saying, "Allah increase thy reward, O Wali!" whereupon he knew him to be the Minister. Then the Wazir lifted up his voice and said, "What means this nastiness?" But when the King heard and recognized his Minister's voice, he held his peace and concealed his affair. Then said the Wazir, "May God damn this woman for her dealing with us! She hath brought hither all the Chief Officers of the State, except the King." Quoth the King, "Hold your peace, for I was the first to fall into the toils of this lewd strumpet." Whereat cried the carpenter, "And I, what have I done? I made her a cabinet for four gold pieces, and when I came to seek my hire, she tricked me into entering this compartment and locked the door on me." And they fell to talking with one another, diverting the King and doing away his chagrin.

Presently the neighbors came up to the house and, seeing it deserted, said one to other, "But yesterday our neighbor, the wife of such an one, was in it; but now no sound is to be heard therein nor is soul to be seen. Let us break open the doors and see how the case stands, lest it come to the ears of the Wali or the King and we be cast into prison and regret not doing this thing before." So they broke open the doors and entered the saloon, where they saw a large wooden cabinet and heard men within groaning for hunger and thirst. Then said one of them, "Is there a Jinni in this cabinet?" and his fellow, "Let us heap fuel about it and burn it with fire." When the Kazi heard this, he bawled out to them, "Do it not!" And they said to one another, "Verily the Jinn make believe to be mortals and speak with men's voices." Thereupon the Kazi repeated somewhat of the Sublime Koran and said to the neighbors, "Draw near to the cabinet wherein we are." So they drew near, and he said, "I am so and so the Kazi, and ye are such an one and such an one, and we are here a company." Quoth the neighbors, "Who brought you here?" And he told them the whole case from beginning to end. Then they fetched a carpenter, who opened the five doors and let out Kazi, Wazir, Wali, King and carpenter in their queer disguises; and each, when he saw how the others were accoutred, fell a-laughing at them.

An Anonymous Chinese Tale

{A.D. 12TH-13TH CENTURIES}

TRANSLATED BY CHI-CHEN WANG {1889-   }

ᴵᴺᵛᵠᵢᶜᵟᴬᴵ

Until recent years fiction was held in as low repute by the Chinese literati as were *The Arabian Nights* in the Islamic Near East. Both belonged, in their origin, on the wrong side of the literary tracks, and their rejection by men of taste did not reflect merely a puritanical code of judgment. *The Arabian Nights* was a coffee-house amusement; most Chinese stories and novels grew up in the colloquial language outside the bounds of respectability. They were narrated by what Arthur Waley has called proletarian open-air storytellers. By a process of accretion they developed into story cycles or full-length novels. Thus their authors, when they can be established at all, are only the narrators of particular—usually later—versions.

To be sure, there are some Chinese stories in the literary tongue. These date back to T'ang times and are generally concerned with supernatural happenings. For contemporary English readers of fiction they hardly have the interest which the more realistic stories of the Sung and later dynasties have. The latter give us charming glimpses of the everyday life of the Chinese people, in whom we recognize our brothers under the skin as we rarely do in the characters of the more refined prose of China. The tales of the supernatural, deriving from a mythology strange to us, tend to stress differences between the reader and the characters about whom he reads.

"The Judicial Murder of Tsui Ning," although it finds a place for the supernatural episode of the King Pacifier, depends for its appeal almost entirely upon the commonplace and the matter of fact. The main story is engagingly unfolded as the second of two instances in proof of a moral maxim to the effect that a joke can have serious consequences. The story develops seriousness in a manner reminiscent of Hawthorne's *Wakefield*, in which too the husband yields to a whimsical impulse that affects his marital life. The anonymous Chinese author is, if anything, more disposed to moralizing than was the Puritan Hawthorne, but it is doubtful whether the English reader can accept as poetic justice the fate which he metes out to his several characters. Liu's wife is absolved of her guilt in the deaths of Tsui Ning and Erh Chieh because she contrives the death of her second husband. Tsui Ning himself is supposedly the victim of judicial murder at the hands of an irate citizenry, but he is more likely to appear to be "framed" by the author, who permits him to be in possession of exactly the amount of money that has been stolen from Liu. While the author's fulminations against lynch law are admirable, we are more likely to give our assent to his conclusion that "good and evil both end up in the grave."

In spite of the obvious defects of the story, however, it has an irresistible manner of intimate narration and a wealth of local color which make it an excellent example of Chinese detective fiction.

ﮩﻨﻤﺠﺌﺤﻤﺌﻰ

THE JUDICIAL MURDER OF TSUI NING

Cleverness and cunning are gifts of Heaven,
Ignorance and stupidity may be feigned.
Jealousy arises often from a narrow heart,
Disputes are set off by thoughtless jokes.
For the heart is more dangerous than the River with its nine bends
And there are evil faces that ten coats of mail cannot conceal.
Wine and women have often caused the downfall of states
But who has ever seen good men spoiled by books?

This poem tells about the difficulties that beset men. The road of life is a tortuous one and the heart of man is hard to fathom. The great Way has receded farther and farther from the world and the ways of men have become more and more multifarious. Every one bustles about for the sake of gain but in their ignorance they often reap nothing but calamities. One should ponder on these thoughts well if one wants to maintain one's life and protect one's family. It is because of this that the ancients used to say:

> There is a season for frowning,
> There is a season for laughing.
> One must consider most carefully
> Before frowning or laughing.

This time [18] I shall tell you about a man who brought death upon himself and several others and ruin to his family because of something he said in jest under the influence of wine. But first let me tell you another story as an introduction.

In the Yuan Feng period (1078–1085) of our dynasty there was a young graduate by the name of Wei Peng-chu, with the derived name Chung-hsiao. He was just eighteen years old and had a wife as pretty "as flower and jade." He had been married for barely a month when "the spring tests approached and the examination halls were thrown open," [19] and Wei had to take leave of his wife, pack his baggage, and set off for the capital to attend the examinations. Said the wife to her husband: "Come back home as soon as you can, whether or not you pass your examinations. Do not leave me all alone."

"Have no fear," replied Wei. "I am going only because I have to think of my career."

Then he set off on his journey and soon reached the capital. There indeed he passed the examinations, the ninth place in the first group. He was appointed to a post in the capital which he assumed with a great deal of pomp and ceremony. Of course he wrote a letter to his wife and sent it by a trusted servant. Besides the usual inquiries after her health and the news of his success, he wrote also the following at the end of the letter: "Since I have no one to look after me in the capital, I have taken a concubine. I look forward to your coming soon, so that we can enjoy our good fortune together."

The servant took the letter and went directly to Wei's home. He congratulated his mistress and presented the letter. After tearing open the letter and reading what it had to say about this and that, she said to the servant: "What a faithless man your master is! Here he has just received his appointment, and yet he has already gotten himself a concubine!"

Whereupon the servant said: "It must be one of the master's

---

[18] *Hui*, the word by which the chapter of popular novels is designated, is actually a numerical classifier equivalent to the English word "time." It is a vestige of the oral origin of popular fiction.
[19] A stock phrase which I have encountered more than a score of times in popular fiction.

jokes, for no such thing had happened when I left the capital. Please do not worry about it. Madame can see for herself when she arrives at the capital."

"I'll give the matter no more thought, then, if that is the case," Madame Wei said, and, as she was not able to secure boats for the journey right away, she wrote a letter to her husband and sent it by someone who happened to be going to the capital. In the meantime she packed and got herself ready for the journey.

When the messenger reached the capital he inquired his way to Wei's house and delivered the letter. Needless to say, he was given food and wine for his trouble.

Now when Wei opened the letter and read it, he found only this: "As you have taken yourself a 'little wife,' I have also taken myself a 'little husband.' We shall set out for the capital together at the first opportunity." This did not disturb Wei at all, for he knew that his wife was only joking.

But it happened that before he had a chance to put the letter away, one of his fellow graduates came to call on him, and as he was one of his intimate friends and knew that Wei did not have his family with him, he went straight to his inner chamber. After a few minutes of conversation, Wei had to excuse himself and leave his friend alone in the room. While the latter was looking at the papers on Wei's desk, he came upon the wife's letter and was so amused by it that he began to read it aloud. Just then Wei came back into the room. He blushed and said, "It is a very stupid thing. She is only joking because I have joked with her." His fellow graduate guffawed and said, "It is hardly a matter to joke about." Then he went away.

Now this fellow was also young and "liked to talk and loved to gossip," and as a result what was said in the letter was soon all over the capital. What was worse was that some of the officials, jealous of Wei's youthful success, took the matter up and impeached Wei in a memorial to the throne, charging him with impropriety and branding him as unfit for the important post which he occupied. Wei was as a consequence demoted and banished to a provincial post. Regret was then useless. Wei's future was completely ruined and he never rose high in official position.

This is a case of a man who lost his opportunity for official advancement because of a joke. Now I shall tell you about another man who, because of a jest uttered under the influence of wine, threw away his own life and caused several people to lose theirs.

How did this happen?

The paths of this world are tortuous and sad
And the jeering mouths of men open and shut
   without cause.
The white clouds have no desire to darken the sky
But the wild wind blows them hither without pause.

Now in the time of Kao Tsung, Hangchou, being the capital, was not inferior in wealth and glory to Kaifeng, the old capital. There lived at that time to the left of the Arrow Bridge a man by the name of Liu Kuei, with the derived name of Chun-chien. He came from an old and solid family but its fortunes had declined during his time. He studied for the examinations at first, but later on he found it impossible to continue his scholarly pursuits and had to change his profession and take up business. He was like a man who enters the priesthood after middle life. He knew nothing of business and as a consequence he lost his capital. He had to give up his large house for a small one and ended up by renting only a few rooms. He had a wife by the name of Wang-shih and a concubine whom he took because Wang-shih did not bear him any children. The latter's name was Chen, the daughter of Chen the pastry peddler, and she was called Erh Chieh.[20] He took her before he became quite destitute. The three of them lived together, without any one else in the family.

Liu Chun-chien was a very good-natured man and was beloved by his neighbors, who used to assure him that his poverty was due to his bad luck and not to any fault of his own and that better days would come when his luck turned. This was what his neighbors said, but his fortune did not grow any better and he lived at home depressed and helpless.

One day as he was sitting home doing nothing, his father-in-law's servant Lao Wang, about seventy years old, came to him and said: "It is the master's birthday and I have been commanded to come and escort the young mistress home for the occasion."

"How stupid of me to forget the Great Mountain's birthday," Liu said. He and his wife gathered together a few articles of clothing that they needed, tied them up in a bundle, and gave it to Lao Wang to carry. Liu instructed Erh Chieh to take care of the house, saying that they would not be able to come back that day, as it was getting late, but that they would surely be back the following evening, and then set out for his father-in-law's house, which was about twenty li from the city.

Arriving there, he greeted his father-in-law but did not

[20] "Sister Two," because she was the "second wife."

have a chance to tell the latter about his troubles as there were many guests present. After the guests went away he was put up in the guest room for the night. It was not until the next morning that his father-in-law came to talk to him, saying: "Brother-in-law,[21] you can't go on like this. Remember the saying: 'He who does nothing will eat a mountain clean and the earth bare,' and the one to the effect that a man's gully is as bottomless as the sea and the days pass like the shuttle. You must look ahead. My daughter married you in the hope that you could provide her with food and clothing. Don't tell me that you want to go on like this!"

Liu sighed and said: "You are quite right, Great Mountain. But 'It is easier to go up the mountain and catch a tiger than to open your mouth to ask for help.' At a time like this there is nothing for me to do but sit and wait. To ask people for help is simply to court failure for one's pain. There are not many people who have my welfare at heart as you do, Great Mountain."

"I do not blame you for feeling the way you do," his father-in-law said. "However, I cannot stand by without doing something for you two. How would you like me to advance you some money for opening a provision store?"

"That would be excellent," Liu said. "I shall always be grateful for your kindness."

After lunch, the father-in-law took out fifteen strings of cash and gave them to Liu, saying, "Take this money for outfitting the store. I shall give you another ten *kuan* when you are ready to open up. As to your wife, I should like to keep her here for the present. On the day of the opening I shall take her to you myself and at the same time wish you luck. What do you think of it?"

Liu thanked his father-in-law again and again and went away carrying the money on his shoulder. It was getting late when he entered the city. As he passed by the house of an acquaintance who was also a tradesman he decided to call on him and seek his advice. So he knocked at the man's gate. The man came out and greeted him, and asked him what had brought him. When Liu told him about his plans, the man said: "I have nothing to do at present and shall be glad to come and help you whenever you need me." "That would be fine," Liu said.

And so they talked about business conditions over a few cups of wine. Liu's capacity for wine was not very large and he soon began to feel the effects of the liquor. He got up

21 That is, "my son's brother-in-law." This is considered more polite because it elevates, so to speak, the person addressed one generation higher than he actually is in relation to the speaker.

and took leave of his host, saying, "Thank you for your hospitality. Please come over to my house tomorrow and talk things over." The man escorted Liu to the head of the street and then went home.

Now if I, the storyteller, and Liu "had been born in the same year and brought up side by side," and if I "could have put my arms around his waist and dragged him back by the hand." [22] Liu would not have suffered the calamity that he did. But because I wasn't there to prevent him, Liu died a more grievous death than Li Ts'un-hsiao of the *Story of the Five Dynasties* [23] and P'eng Yueh of the *Book of Han*.

Now when Liu reached his house and knocked at the gate it was already lamplight time. As Erh Chieh was dozing under the lamp, after waiting for him all day, it was some time before she woke up and said, "I am coming," and then went and opened the gate. Liu went into the room and his concubine relieved him of the load of money and put it on the table, saying: "Where have you got this money from? What is it for?" Now Liu was still under the influence of wine and then too he was annoyed because his concubine had been so slow in answering the gate. He thought he would try to scare her. So he said: "I am afraid you won't like it when I tell you, but you'll have to know sooner or later. I have mortgaged you to a merchant because I am in great need of money. I shall redeem you when things are better with me. That's why I have not mortgaged you for more. But if things should not get any better, I am afraid that I shall have to give you up entirely."

The concubine did not know whether to believe him or not, for she found it difficult not to believe it because of the money right in front of her and she found it difficult to believe that her husband would have the heart to dispose of her thus because both he and his wife had always been so kind to her. The only remark she could make was, "You should have told my parents about it."

Liu said, "Your parents would never have consented if I had told them. After you have gone to that man's house, I shall send some one to break the news to your parents. Perhaps they won't blame me under the circumstances."

The concubine again asked: "Where did you get your wine?" "I drank with the man to bind the contract," Liu answered. "Why hasn't Ta Chieh [24] come back with you?" the concubine asked. "Because she cannot bear to say

---

[22] A formula often introduced by storytellers when their heroes are about to walk into disaster.
[23] Historical romance which rivaled the *Three Kingdoms* in popularity at this early period.
[24] Elder sister; that is, the first wife.

goodby to you," Liu answered. "She will come back after you have left tomorrow. Please understand that I can't help it and that there is no backing out of it."

After saying this, Liu went to bed without undressing, hardly able to hide his amusement. He was soon sound asleep.

But the concubine could not fall asleep. "What sort of man has he sold me to?" she wondered to herself. "I must go to my parents' house and tell them about it. If he did sell me and the man comes for me tomorrow he can look for me at my parents'."

After thus turning the matter in her mind, she piled the money at his feet and taking advantage of his drunken sleep she gathered a few things together and slipped out of the house, pulling the door shut behind her. She went to the house of a neighbor by the name of Chu San and asked Chu's wife to let her stay with them for the night, saying, "My husband has sold me for no good reason at all. I want to let my parents know about it. Please tell him to come to my parents' house if he wants me."

"That's the right thing to do," her neighbors said. "You can go on tomorrow and we shall let your husband know." The next day the concubine took leave of her host and went away.

> A fish that once frees itself from the hook
> Will swim away never to return.

Now to return to Liu Kuei. When he woke up at the third watch the lamp was still burning but there was no sight of his concubine. Thinking that she might be in the kitchen he called to her and asked her to bring him some tea. There was no answer and he fell asleep again after a half-hearted attempt to get up.

Now it happened that a bad man was out that night to steal, having lost at gambling that same day, and he came to Liu's house. He tried the door and it yielded readily as the concubine had only pulled it to after her. He tiptoed into Liu's room and soon discovered the pile of money by Liu's feet. He began to help himself to it but in doing so he woke up Liu, who got up and shouted: "You can't do that! I have borrowed the money in order to go into business to feed myself. What am I to do if you steal it from me?"

The robber did not answer but struck at Liu's face with his fist. The latter dodged and struck back. After battling thus for a while the robber, seeing that he could not get the better of Liu, retreated to the kitchen and there picked up an axe that happened to be handy and struck Liu in the face just as he was about to raise the alarm. As Liu fell, the robber struck him again and alas! Liu became as dead as can be and quite ready to receive the sacrificial offerings of his heirs.

"I had to make a thorough job of it once I began," the robber said, half to himself and half to the corpse before him. "I did not mean to kill you, really; it was you that forced me to it." So saying he turned back to Liu's room and took the rest of the money, wrapped it up securely and went off, pulling the door to after him.

The following morning when the neighbors found that Liu's door was still shut at a late hour, they shouted to him and receiving no answer, they went inside and there they found his body and his concubine gone. They raised the alarm.

Then Chu San, the neighbor at whose house Erh Chieh had stopped for the night, came forward and told the neighbors assembled that the concubine had stopped at his house and had gone early that morning to her parents' house. "We must send some one to find her and at the same time notify Liu's wife," he said, and his suggestion was carried out accordingly.

Now to return to the concubine. She had hardly gone a li or two after she left Chu San's house that morning when her feet began to hurt so that she could not go on but had to sit down by the road and rest herself. Presently a young man carrying a shoulder bag full of money appeared on the scene and stopped to look at her. She was not beautiful but her eyebrows were nicely arched and her teeth bright, and she was undeniably attractive.

> Wild flowers are especially pleasing to the eye
> And country wine goes more to the head.

The young man bowed to her and asked her where she was traveling alone by herself. She returned the bow and told him that she was going to her parents and had stopped to rest. "And where have you come from and where are you going?" she asked. The man, keeping a proper distance, answered: "I have just come from the city where I had gone to sell some silk and I am bound for Chuchiatang." "My parents do not live far from there," the concubine said. "May I go with you?" "Certainly," the man answered. "I shall be honored to escort you there."

The two went on together thus for about two or three li when they noticed two men running after them, running so fast that their feet hardly touched the ground, and they were sweating and panting and their coats were open at the front.

They shouted, "Will the young lady please stop for a moment for we want to have a word with you?"

The concubine and the young man stopped and when the two pursuers caught up with them, each laid his hand on one, saying, "Come along with us, you two!"

The concubine was astonished. The men were her neighbors, one of them being Chu San who had given her shelter for the night. She said, "I told you last night where I was going. Why are you pursuing me?" Chu San said, "There has been a murder in your house; you have to come back with us." "I don't believe you," the concubine said. "I left my husband home last night safe and sound. I must go on to my parents. I cannot come with you." "It is not for you to say whether you'll come or not," Chu San said, and thereupon began to shout for help.

When the young man saw the gravity of the situation he said to Erh Chieh, "You had better go with them since things are as they say. I'll go on myself." "But you can't go," the two neighbors cried, "for since you are found in company with her you will have to explain yourself." "Why can't I?" the young man said. "I have only chanced to meet her on the road; it is not as if we had met by design. The road is a free thoroughfare."

But it was useless for Erh Chieh and the young man to explain themselves. By this time they were surrounded by spectators and they all said that the young man could not go away, especially since:

> He that has done nothing unlawful during the day
> Need have no fear of knocks at his door at night.

"If you don't come with us willingly," the two pursuers said, "it means that you have a guilty conscience and we shall have to force you."

There was nothing for the young man and Erh Chieh to do but go with the two neighbors. When the four of them arrived at Liu Kuei's house there was a curious crowd at the door. Erh Chieh went inside and there found Liu Kuei lying dead on the ground and the fifteen strings of money gone from the bed where she had left them. Her mouth dropped open and her tongue stuck out and thus she remained for a long time. The young man too was frightened, saying, "Oh luckless me! That I should be involved in such a calamity just because I walked a distance with the young lady!" The crowd talked excitedly among themselves.

Then Liu Kuei's wife and her father, old Mr. Wang, came running and stumbling on the scene and burst out crying at the sight of the body.

"Why have you killed your husband," Mr. Wang said to Erh Chieh, "and run away with the money? What have you to say for yourself now that by the justice of Heaven you have been caught?"

The concubine told them what had happened and that she knew nothing of her husband's death, but Liu Kuei's wife said, "It couldn't be! Why should he say that he got the fifteen *kuan* from selling you when my father had given it to him to start a business? It is evident that you have been unfaithful and have plotted the murder with your lover and run away with the money. Your stay at the neighbors' was only a ruse. There is no use denying it, for how can you explain that man found in your company?" Then turning to the young man she made a similar accusation.

"My name is Tsui Ning," the young man explained. "I had never seen the young lady before until I chanced to meet her on the road this morning. I asked her where she was going and we have traveled together only because we were going in the same direction. This is the truth; I know nothing of what happened before that."

But the crowd did not believe what he said. They searched his shoulder bag and found in it exactly fifteen *kuan* of cash. " 'The net of Heaven catches everything though its mesh is wide,' " they cried. "You must have had a part in the murder. If you had made good your escape we would have had to answer for your crime."

Thereupon Liu Kuei's wife caught hold of Erh Chieh and Mr. Wang caught hold of Tsui Ning and they dragged the suspects to the prefect's yamen, with the neighbors following them for witnesses. When the prefect heard that a murder case had come up, he immediately entered the trial hall and summoned all the parties concerned and commanded them each to tell his story.

First old Mr. Wang told the circumstances of the case as he knew them and ended by appealing for justice against the culprits. The prefect then summoned the concubine and commanded her to confess. But Erh Chieh said, "Though I am only Liu Kuei's concubine, he has always been good to me and the mistress too has always been kind and considerate. So why should I want to do this terrible thing?" Then she went on and told exactly what happened after Liu Kuei's return the evening before.

The prefect was inclined to see things as the neighbors did and was eager to have the case closed, so he brushed aside the prisoners' protestations of innocence and had them mercilessly tortured until they confessed to the crime that they did not commit. The confession was duly signed, witnessed by the neighbors, and Erh Chieh and Tsui Ning were put into heavy cangues and shut up in the death prison. The documents of the case were presented to the throne through the usual channels, and in due course the concubine and Tsui Ning were both sentenced to death, the first by quartering and the second by decapitation. The sentences were duly carried out. Even if the two had had mouths all over their bodies they could not have explained away the evidence against them.

> He who is dumb cannot tell of his distress
> Though the gentian root tastes bitter in his mouth.

Now reflect on the circumstance of the case, reader. If Erh Chieh and the young man Tsui Ning had been really guilty of the murder, would they not have fled the scene during the night? Why should the concubine have gone to the neighbors to stay for the night and thus allow herself to be caught the next morning? If the trial official had thought about the matter carefully he would have seen the falsity of the accusation. But, in his eagerness to close the case, he did not think at all. What confession can you not force if you rely on torture alone? But one's deeds are marked in the book of another judge and one is bound to be punished in due time, punished oneself if the judgment is swift or punished through one's descendants if it is slow. The ghosts of these two who have been unjustly put to death will not rest until they have been revenged, of that you may be sure. For this reason alone—to say nothing of the fact that the dead cannot be called back to life and that which has been broken cannot be mended—those in official positions should not try cases carelessly and resort to torture but should try to establish justice by every means possible.

But to return to our story. After the trial, Liu Kuei's wife returned home, and set up a spirit tablet to her husband to observe the period of mourning. When her father suggested that she remarry, she said, "I must at least observe one year of mourning if not the required three." At the end of the year her father sent his old servant Lao Wang to fetch her, saying, "Tell the young mistress to get her things together and come back here. She can remarry now after her year of mourning." As there wasn't much else for her to do, Liu Kuei's wife decided to follow her father's suggestion. She tied her things up in a bundle and gave it to Lao Wang to carry. Then saying goodby to the neighbors, she set out for her father's house. On the way she was caught in the rain and went into the wood to seek shelter, and thereby she

> Drew nearer to death step by step,
> Like sheep and hogs that wander into a butcher's house.

In the wood they suddenly heard a voice shouting: "I am the King Pacifier of the Mountains. Halt, wayfarers, and pay me toll for the use of the road!" Then a man wielding a huge sword jumped out from behind the trees.

Well, Lao Wang's time must have been up, for instead of handing over what he was carrying to the robber, he rushed at him shouting defiance. The robber dodged and Lao Wang fell to the ground by the force of his own headlong rush. "How dare you defy me, little calf," the robber cried with anger, and brought down his sword on the prostrate figure. Blood squirted out and Lao Wang lived no more.

Realizing that it would be useless to try to run away from the robber, Liu Kuei's wife decided to resort to a ruse. She clapped her hands and said, "Well done, well done!" The man stared at her and said, "Who are you?" She answered, "I am an unfortunate woman who has recently lost her husband and was mated to this old man by a deceitful matchmaker. He was no good at all except to eat and eat. You have relieved me of a burden with your sword."

Pleased with her words and seeing that she was not bad looking, the robber said, "Would you be the mistress of my mountain domain?" Since there wasn't much else she could do, she said, "I shall most willingly serve you, great king."

On hearing this the man's anger changed to joy; he threw Lao Wang's body into a swamp, picked up his sword and led Liu Kuei's wife to an isolated house. He picked up a clump of earth and threw it on the roof, whereupon a man opened the door. Inside the robber ordered a sheep killed and wine brought and performed the wedding ceremony with Liu Kuei's wife.

> One knows well that it is not a proper match,
> But it is better than to lose one's life.

After the robber took Liu Kuei's wife, he made several good hauls in succession and became quite rich after about half a year's time. Being a sensible woman, she tried to persuade him to mend his ways. Thus she used to exhort him day and night: "It is said that the water jug will, sooner or later, break over the well platform and that a soldier will die on the battle ground. Just so you will come to a bad end if you keep on doing things against the laws of Heaven. Since we have now accumulated more than enough for the rest of our lives, why don't you give up your present profession and take up some kind of lawful business?"

Finally the robber gave way to her exhortations. He rented a house in the city and opened up a general store. When he could spare the time he would go to the temples to make offerings to atone for his crimes.

One day he said to Liu Kuei's wife: "Though I was a highwayman once, I know well the maxim that each act of injustice must be atoned for, just as a debt must be paid. In my career of evil in the past I have done nothing worse than thieving and robbing except in two cases. In each case I was responsible for killing a man and in one of them I was indirectly responsible for two other lives. These lives have weighed on my mind and I shall not be able to rest in peace until I have hired some priests to pray for their souls."

"How were you responsible for destroying two lives?" Liu Kuei's wife asked.

"One is, as you know, your husband, whom I killed in the forest when he rushed at me. He was an old man and had done nothing against me. His soul must be crying for revenge, especially since I have taken his wife."

"What is done cannot be undone," Liu Kuei's wife said. "Moreover, if you had not killed him we would not have become man and wife. Let us say no more about that. But who was the other man that you killed?"

"It was even a greater crime," the robber said, "for it caused two innocent persons to be put to death." Then he went on and told her about the murder of Liu Kuei, for he was in fact the man who stole into Liu Kuei's house on that fatal night and murdered him in order to make his escape. "These are the worst crimes in my life as a highwayman," he concluded. "I must do something for their souls."

"So this is the man who killed my husband and caused the unjust deaths of Erh Chieh and that young man," Liu Kuei's wife wailed to herself. "Since I was partly responsible for their deaths by my false testimony, their spirits must also hold me responsible." However, she said nothing of her thoughts to the robber but watched her opportunity. When it came she went to the prefect's yamen and shouted for justice.

There was then a new prefect for Linanfu, who had been in his post only half a month. Liu Kuei's wife was brought to him in the trial hall and there weeping and wailing she told her story. The robber was seized and under the prodding of instruments of torture, confessed everything. He was sentenced to death and the case was sent up to the throne for review. An edict was issued after the usual period of sixty days ordering the immediate execution of the robber. The original trial official was demoted for miscarriage of justice, and the authorities were charged to seek out the nearest kin of the concubine and Tsui Ning and to compensate them for the injustice done. Since Liu Kuei's wife had married the robber under duress and since she was instrumental in avenging her husband's death, she was given half of the robber's property, the other half being confiscated.

After watching the execution, Liu Kuei's wife took the robber's head and made offerings at the tomb of her husband and those of the concubine and Tsui Ning. She gave her share of the robber's estate to the temples and devoted the rest of her long life to praying for the dead.

> Good and evil both end up in the grave
> But a jest may bring about untimely death.
> So pray remember always to tell the truth
> For the tongue is ever at the bottom of calamity.

FROM *The Tale of Genji*

by Lady Murasaki Shikibu

{?978-?1031 A.D.}

TRANSLATED BY ARTHUR WALEY {1889-   }

ᛁᚱᚾᚩᚳᛞᛁ

The conscientious reader of Lady Murasaki's *Tale of Genji* in Arthur Waley's English translation can hardly deny that here is one of the world's greatest achievements in the art of the novel. Whether owing to its intrinsic merits in the original Japanese or by virtue of its translator's creative genius, the *Genji* has earned a place with the great European novels of the 19th and 20th centuries. It has a vertical density of texture which one associates with the work of Henry James, a horizontal spaciousness which belongs to Tolstoy, and Marcel Proust's exquisite sense of the dimension of time. If to these analogies one should add Jane Austen's gift for reporting significant social detail and Emily Brontë's feeling for the Gothically romantic, some of the ranging qualities of *The Tale of Genji* might be intimated.

It differs from these European masterworks of the art of fiction most notably in the manner of the unfolding of the plot. In this it has been likened to a Japanese scroll. At any time the scroll presents to our view a vast panorama of persons and events which require that the eye devote several chapters, as it were, to taking in simultaneous actions. As the scroll is rolled in at one end and out at the other, formerly prominent persons and events become peripheral and new data assume the focus of attention. Even the novel's hero, who is central through about four-fifths of the thousand pages of the translation, in the last ten chapters yields the stage to his son. This feature of the architecture of *The Tale of Genji* serves to make Time and Place rather than Action the important elements of the novel.

The society depicted in the *Genji* is that of the court at Kyoto, the capital of Japan during the great Heian age (795–1185 A.D.), for which the model was the T'ang civilization of China. It was an extremely refined society, aptly described by G. B. Sanson as "preoccupied with art and letters, quick to criticise a weak stroke of the brush, a faulty line of verse, a discordant colour or an ungraceful movement; great connoisseurs in emotion and judges of ceremonies and etiquette; sentimentally aware of the sadness of this dew-like fleeting world, but intellectually unconcerned with all its problems; prone to a gentle melancholy but apt to enjoy each transitory moment; and quite without interest in any outlook but their own." If the reader of these words finds a resemblance to the *fin de siècle* decadence of 19th century Europe, he will not be far from the truth. Shortly after the period in question, Japanese society was propelled, by a series of civil wars, into a long age of feudalism.

That the life pictured in this novel was fundamentally the life lived and observed by the authoress can be confirmed by the diaries kept by noble ladies of the court, including one by Lady Murasaki herself. Here are all the evidences of a highly ritualized mode of existence: the elaborate ceremony of dress and discourse, the utter finesse of the combined arts of penmanship and verse-making as applied in courtship, the delicacy of courtship itself from behind the screen, the clandestine rendezvous under dark of night, the native Japanese amorality passing into immorality, and the attendant neuroses requiring not only incantation and exorcism, but also penance.

As a member of the noted Fujiwara family and as a court attendant of the Empress, Lady Murasaki was in an advantageous position to note all this. To render it in a purely distilled form in the *Genji* was the contribution of her gifted pen. The imaginative treatment of the facts of experience she conceived as the novelist's function. Her hero, discussing the origin of the art of fiction, says:

> . . . It happens because the storyteller's own experience of men and things, whether for good or ill—not only what he has passed through himself, but even events which he has only witnessed or been told of—has moved him to an emotion so passionate that he can no longer keep it shut up in his heart.

With appropriate artistic detachment, Lady Murasaki relates the amours, sorrows, introspections, and self-recriminations of her somewhat Byronic hero without any attempt to pass judgment upon his moral vagaries, as though the only ethic she knew was the morality of esthetics.

Efforts have of course been made to equate the characters of the novel with historic personages. The most interesting of these equations is between the authoress herself and the girl Murasaki, who figures prominently in the present chapter. It is more likely that the writer received her name from the character than that the character is a projection of herself.

As revealed in the accompanying genealogical tables (adapted from Arthur Waley's), Prince Genji has already lived fully for his young years before the events of this chapter. His relations with women have ranged from casual flirtations to distracted love, and he is unhappily married at the time. On a visit to a Buddhist retreat he catches sight of the little girl Murasaki and acquires for her an ambiguous feeling which, if it is not yet sexual love, soon becomes that. His comparatively happy life with Murasaki after she becomes his second wife is the subject of a good portion of the novel. But as even the present excerpt shows, the love of any one woman was of Genji's life a thing apart; it was to become Murasaki's whole existence.

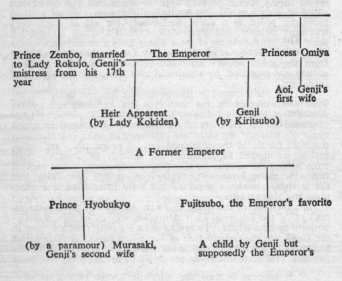

Prince Zembo, married to Lady Rokujo, Genji's mistress from his 17th year — The Emperor — Princess Omiya

Aoi, Genji's first wife

Heir Apparent (by Lady Kokiden) — Genji (by Kiritsubo)

A Former Emperor

Prince Hyobukyo — Fujitsubo, the Emperor's favorite

(by a paramour) Murasaki, Genji's second wife — A child by Genji but supposedly the Emperor's

MURASAKI

He fell sick of an ague, and when numerous charms and spells had been tried in vain, the illness many times returning, someone said that in a certain temple on the Northern Hills there lived a wise and holy man who in the summer of the year before (the ague was then rife and the usual spells were giving no relief) was able to work many signal cures: "Lose no time in consulting him, for while you try one useless means after another the disease gains greater hold upon you." At once he sent a messenger to fetch the holy man, who however replied that the infirmities of old age no longer permitted him to go abroad. "What is to be done?" said Genji; "I must go secretly to visit him"; and taking only four or five trusted servants he set out long before dawn. The place lay somewhat deep into the hills. It was the last day of the third month and in the Capital the blossoms had all fallen. The hill-cherry was not yet out; but as he approached the open country, the mists began to assume strange and lovely forms, which pleased him the more because, being one whose movements were tethered by many proprieties, he had seldom seen such sights before. The temples too delighted him. The holy man lived in a deep cave hollowed out of a high wall of rock. Genji did not send in his name and was in close disguise, but his face was well known and the priest at once recognized him. "Forgive me," he said; "it was you, was it not, who sent for me the other day? Alas, I think no longer of the things of this world and I am afraid I have forgotten how to work my cures. I am very sorry indeed that you have come so far," and pretending to be very much upset, he looked at Genji, laughing. But it was soon apparent that he was a man of very great piety and learning. He wrote out certain talismans and administered them, and read certain spells. By the time this was over, the sun had risen, and Genji went a little way outside the cave and looked around him. From the high ground where he was standing he looked down on a number of scattered hermitages. A winding track led down to a hut which, though it was hedged with the same small brushwood as the rest, was more spaciously planned, having a pleasant roofed alley running out from it, and there were trim copses set around. He asked whose house it was and was told by one of his men that a certain abbot had been living there in retirement for two years. "I know him well," said Genji on hearing the abbot's name; "I should not like to meet him dressed and attended as I am. I hope he will not hear . . ." Just then a party of nicely dressed children came out of the house and began to pluck such flowers as are used for the decoration of altars and holy images. "There are some girls with them," said one of Genji's men. "We cannot suppose that His Reverence keeps them. Who then can they be?" and to satisfy his curiosity he went a little way down the hill and watched them. "Yes, there are some very pretty girls, some of them grown up and others quite children," he came back and reported.

During a great part of the morning Genji was busy with his cure. When at last the ceremony was completed, his attendants, dreading the hour at which the fever usually returned, strove to distract his attention by taking him a little way across the mountain to a point from which the Capital could be seen. "How lovely," cried Genji, "are those distances half-lost in haze, and that blur of shimmering woods

that stretches out on every side. How could anyone be unhappy for a single instant who lived in such a place?" "This
is nothing," said one of his men. "If I could but show you
the lakes and mountains of other provinces, you would soon
see how far they excell all that you here admire"; and he
began to tell him first of Mount Fuji and many another
famous peak, and then of the West Country with all its
pleasant bays and shores, till he quite forgot that it was the
hour of his fever. "Yonder, nearest to us," the man continued, pointing to the sea, "is the bay of Akashi in Harima.
Note it well; for though it is not a very out-of-the-way place,
yet the feeling one has there of being shut off from everything
save one huge waste of sea makes it the strangest and most
desolate spot I know. And there it is that the daughter of a
lay priest who was once governor of the province presides
over a mansion of quite disproportionate and unexpected
magnificence. He is the descendant of a Prime Minister and
was expected to cut a great figure in the world. But he is a
man of very singular disposition and is averse to all society.
For a time he was an officer in the Palace Guard, but he gave
this up and accepted the province of Harima. However, he
soon quarrelled with the local people and, announcing that
he had been badly treated and was going back to the Capital,
he did nothing of the sort, but shaved his head and became a
lay priest. Then instead of settling, as is usually done, on
some secluded hillside, he built himself a house on the seashore, which may seem to you a very strange thing to do; but
as a matter of fact, whereas in that province in one place
or another a good many recluses have taken up their abode,
the mountain-country is far more dull and lonely and would
sorely have tried the patience of his young wife and child; and
so as a compromise he chose the seashore. Once when I was
travelling in the province of Harima I took occasion to visit
his house and noted that, though at the Capital he had lived
in a very modest style, here he had built on the most magnificent and lavish scale, as though determined in spite of what
had happened (now that he was free from the bother of
governing the province) to spend the rest of his days in the
greatest comfort imaginable. But all the while he was making
great preparations for the life to come and no ordained
priest could have led a more austere and pious life."

"But you spoke of his daughter?" said Genji. "She is
passably good-looking," he answered, "and not by any means
stupid. Several governors and officers of the province have
set their hearts upon her and pressed their suit most urgently;
but her father has sent them all away. It seems that though
in his own person so indifferent to worldly glory, he is
determined that this one child, his only object of care, should

make amends for his obscurity, and has sworn that if ever she chooses against his will, and when he is gone flouts his set purpose and injunction to satisfy some idle fancy of her own, his ghost will rise and call upon the sea to cover her."

Genji listened with great attention. "Why, she is like the vestal virgin who may know no husband but the King-Dragon of the Sea," and they laughed at the old ex-Governor's absurd ambitions. The teller of the story was a son of the present Governor of Harima, who from being a clerk in the Treasury had last year been capped an officer of the Fifth Rank. He was famous for his love-adventures and the others whispered to one another that it was with every intention of persuading the lady to disobey her father's injunctions that he had gone out of his way to visit the shore of Akashi.

"I fear her breeding must be somewhat countrified," said one; "it cannot well be otherwise, seeing that she has grown up with no other company than that of her old-fashioned parents—though indeed it appears that her mother was a person of some consequence." "Why, yes," said Yoshikiyo, the Governor's son, "and for this reason she was able to secure little girls and boys from all the best houses in the Capital, persuading them to pay visits to the seaside and be playmates to her own little girl, who thus acquired the most polished breeding." "If an unscrupulous person were to find himself in that quarter," said another, "I fear that despite the dead father's curse he might not find it easy to resist her."

The story made a deep impression upon Genji's imagination. As his gentlemen well knew, whatever was fantastic or grotesque both in people and situations at once strongly attracted him. They were therefore not surprised to see him listen with so much attention. "It is now well past noon," said one of them, "and I think we may reckon that you will get safely through the day without a return of your complaint. So let us soon be starting for home." But the priest persuaded him to stay a little longer: "The sinister influences are not yet wholly banished," he said; "it would be well that a further ritual should continue quietly during the night. By tomorrow morning, I think you will be able to proceed." His gentlemen all urged him to stay; nor was he at all unwilling, for the novelty of such a lodging amused him. "Very well then, at dawn," he said, and having nothing to do till bedtime which was still a long way off, he went out on to the hillside, and under cover of the heavy evening mist loitered near the brushwood hedge. His attendants had gone back to the hermit's cave and only Koremitsu was with him. In the western wing, opposite which he was standing, was a nun at her devotions. The blind was partly raised. He thought she seemed to be dedicating flowers to an image. Sitting near the middle pillar, a sutra-book propped upon a stool by her side, was another nun. She was reading aloud; there was a look of great unhappiness in her face. She seemed to be about forty; not a woman of the common people. Her skin was white and very fine, and though she was much emaciated, there was a certain roundness and fulness in her cheeks, and her hair, clipped short on a level with her eyes, hung in so delicate a fringe across her brow that she looked, thought Genji, more elegant and even fashionable in this convent guise than if her hair had been long. Two very well-conditioned maids waited upon her. Several little girls came running in and out of the room at play. Among them was one who seemed to be about ten years old. She came running into the room dressed in a rather worn white frock lined with stuff of a deep saffron color. Never had he seen a child like this. What an astonishing creature she would grow into! Her hair, thick and wavy, stood out fanwise about her head. She was very flushed and her lips were trembling. "What is it? Have you quarrelled with one of the other little girls?" The nun raised her head as she spoke and Genji fancied that there was some resemblance between her and the child. No doubt she was its mother. "Inu has let out my sparrow—the little one that I kept in the clothes-basket," she said, looking very unhappy. "What a tiresome boy that Inu is!" said one of the two maids. "He deserves a good scolding for playing such a stupid trick. Where can it have got to? And this after we had taken so much trouble to tame it nicely! I only hope the crows have not found it," and so saying she left the room. She was a pleasant-looking woman, with very long, wavy hair. The others called her Nurse Shonagon, and she seemed to be in charge of the child. "Come," said the nun to the little girl, "you must not be such a baby. You are thinking all the time of things that do not matter at all. Just fancy! Even now when I am so ill that any day I may be taken from you, you do not trouble your head about me, but are grieving about a sparrow. It is very unkind, particularly as I have told you I don't know how many times that it is naughty to shut up live things in cages. Come over here!" and the child sat down beside her. Her features were very exquisite; but it was above all the way her hair grew, in cloudy masses over her temples, but thrust back in childish fashion from her forehead, that struck him as marvellously beautiful. As he watched her and wondered what she would be like when she grew up it suddenly occurred to him that she bore no small resemblance to one whom he had loved with all his being,[25] and at the resemblance he secretly wept.

[25] Fujitsubo, who was indeed the child's aunt.

The nun, stroking the child's hair, now said to her: "It's a lovely mop, though you *are* so naughty about having it combed. But it worries me very much that you are still so babyish. Some children of your age are very different. Your dear mother was only twelve when her father died; yet she showed herself quite capable of managing her own affairs. But if I were taken from you now, I do not know what would become of you, I do not indeed," and she began to weep. Even Genji, peeping at the scene from a distance, found himself becoming quite distressed. The girl, who had been watching the nun's face with a strange unchildish intensity, now dropped her head disconsolately, and as she did so her hair fell forward across her cheeks in two great waves of black. Looking at her fondly, the nun recited the poem: "Not knowing if any will come to nurture the tender leaf whereon it lies, how loath is the dewdrop to vanish in the sunny air." To which the waiting-woman replied with a sigh: "O dewdrop, surely you will linger till the young budding leaf has shown in what fair form it means to grow."

At this moment the priest to whom the house belonged entered the room from the other side: "Pray, ladies," he said, "are you not unduly exposing yourselves? You have chosen a bad day to take up your stand so close to the window. I have just heard that Prince Genji has come to the hermit yonder to be cured of an ague. But he has disguised himself in so mean a habit that I did not know him, and have been so near all day without going to pay my respects to him." The nun started back in horror; "How distressing! He may even have passed and seen us . . ." and she hastened to let down the folding blind. "I am really very glad that I am to have an opportunity of visiting this Prince Genji of whom one hears so much. He is said to be so handsome that even austere old priests like myself forget in his presence the sins and sorrows of the life they have discarded and take heart to live a little longer in a world where so much beauty dwells. But you shall hear all about it. . . ."

Before the old priest had time to leave the house Genji was on his way back to the hermit's cave. What an enchanting creature he had discovered! How right too his friends had been on that rainy night when they told him that on strange excursions such as this beauty might well be found lurking in unexpected quarters! How delightful to have strolled out by chance and at once made so astonishing a find! Whose could this exquisite child be? He would dearly love to have her always near him, to be able to turn to her at any moment for comfort and distraction, as once he had turned to the lady in the Palace.

He was already lying down in the hermit's cave when (everything being at very close quarters) he heard the voice of the old priest's disciple calling for Koremitsu. "My master has just learnt," said this disciple, "that you were lodged so near at hand; and though it grieves him that you did not in passing honour him with a visit, he would at once have paid his respects to the Prince, had he not thought that Lord Genji could not be unaware of his presence in the neighbourhood of this hermitage, and might perhaps have refrained from visiting him only because he did not wish to disclose the motive of his present pilgrimage. But my master would remind you," continued the man, "that we too in our poor hut could provide you with straw beds to lie on, and should be sorry if you left without honouring us. . . ."

"For ten days," answered Genji from within, "I have been suffering from an ague which returned so constantly that I was in despair, when someone advised me to consult the hermit of this mountain, whom I accordingly visited. But thinking that it would be very disagreeable for a sage of his repute if in such a case as mine it became known that his treatment had been unsuccessful, I was at greater pains to conceal myself than I should have been if visiting an ordinary wonder-worker. Pray ask your master to accept this excuse and bid him enter the cave." Thus encouraged, the priest presented himself. Genji was rather afraid of him, for though an ecclesiastic he was a man of superior genius, very much respected in the secular world, and Genji felt that it was not at all proper to receive him in the shabby old clothes which he had used for his disguise. After giving some details of his life since he had left the Capital and come to live in retirement on this mountain, the priest begged Genji to come back with him and visit the cold spring which flowed in the garden of his hut. Here was an opportunity to see again the people who had so much interested him. But the thought of all the stories that the old priest might have told them about him made him feel rather uncomfortable. What matter? At all costs he must see that lovely child again and he followed the old priest back to his hut. In the garden the natural vegetation of the hillside had been turned to skilful use. There was no moon, and torches had been lit along the sides of the moat, while fairy lanterns hung on the trees. The front parlour was very nicely arranged. A heavy perfume of costly and exotic scents stole from hidden incense-burners and filled the room with a delicious fragrance. These perfumes were quite unfamiliar to Genji and he supposed that they must have been prepared by the ladies of the inner room, who would seem to have spent considerable ingenuity in the task.

The priest began to tell stories about the uncertainty of this life and the retributions of the life to come. Genji was appalled to think how heavy his own sins had already been. It was bad enough to think that he would have them on his conscience for the rest of his present life. But then there was also the life to come. What terrible punishments he had to look forward to! And all the while the priest was speaking Genji thought of his own wickedness. What a good idea it would be to turn hermit and live in some such place. . . . But immediately his thoughts strayed to the lovely face which he had seen that afternoon and longing to know more of her, "Who lives with you here?" he asked. "It interests me to know, because I once saw this place in a dream and was astonished to recognize it when I came here today." At this the priest laughed: "Your dream seems to have come rather suddenly into the conversation," he said, "but I fear that if you pursue your enquiry, your expectations will be sadly disappointed. You have probably never heard of Azechi no Dainagon, he died so long ago. He married my sister, who after his death turned her back upon the world. Just at that time I myself was in certain difficulties and was unable to visit the Capital; so for company she came to join me here in my retreat."

"I have heard that Azechi no Dainagon had a daughter. Is that so?" said Genji at a venture; "I am sure you will not think I ask the question with any indiscreet intention. . . ." "He had an only daughter who died about ten years ago. Her father had always wanted to present her at Court. But she would not listen, and when he was dead and there was only my sister the nun to look after her, she allowed some wretched go-between to introduce her to Prince Hyobukyo whose mistress she became. His wife, a proud, relentless woman, from the first pursued her with constant vexations and affronts; day in and day out this obstinate persecution continued, till at last she died of heartbreak. They say that unkindness cannot kill; but I shall never say so, for from this cause alone I saw my kinswoman fall sick and perish."

"Then the little girl must be this lady's child," Genji realized at last. And that accounted for her resemblance to the lady in the Palace.[26] He felt more drawn towards her than ever. She was of good lineage, which is never amiss; and her rather rustic simplicity would be an actual advantage when she became his pupil, as he was now determined she should; for it

[26] Fujitsubo, who was Hyobukyo's sister.

would make it the easier for him to mould her unformed tastes to the pattern of his own. "And did the lady whose sad story you have told me leave no remembrance behind her?" asked Genji, still hoping to turn the conversation on to the child herself. "She died only a short while after her child was born, and it too was a girl. The charge of it fell to my sister who is in failing health and feels herself by no means equal to such a responsibility." All was now clear. "You will think it a very strange proposal," said Genji, "but I feel that I should like to adopt this child. Perhaps you would mention this to your sister? Though others early involved me in marriage, their choice proved distasteful to me and having, as it seems, very little relish for society, I now live entirely alone. She is, I quite realize, a mere child, and I am not proposing . . ." Here he paused and the priest answered: "I am very much obliged to you for this offer; but I am afraid it is clear that you do *not* at all realize that the child in question is a mere infant. You would not even find her amusing as a casual distraction. But it is true that a girl as she grows up needs the backing of powerful friends if she is to make her way in the world, and though I cannot promise you that anything will come of it, I ought certainly to mention the matter to her grandmother." His manner had suddenly become somewhat cool and severe. Genji felt that he had been indiscreet and preserved an embarrassed silence. "There is something which I ought to be doing in the Hall of Our Lord Amida," the priest presently continued, "so I must take leave of you for a while. I must also read my vespers; but I will rejoin you afterwards," and he set out to climb the hill. Genji felt very disconsolate. It had begun to rain; a cold wind blew across the hill, carrying with it the sound of a waterfall—audible till then as a gentle intermittent plashing, but now a mighty roar; and with it, somnolently rising and falling, mingled the monotonous chanting of the scriptures. Even the most unimpressionable nature would have been plunged into melancholy by such surroundings. How much the more so Prince Genji, as he lay sleepless on his bed, continually planning and counter-planning! The priest had spoken of "vespers," but the hour was indeed very late. It was clear however that the nun was still awake, for though she was making as little noise as possible, every now and then her rosary would knock with a faint click against the praying-stool. There was something alluring in the sound of this low, delicate tapping. It seemed to come from quite close. He opened a small space between the screens which divided the living-room from the inner chamber and rustled his fan. He had the impression that someone in the inner room after a little hesitation had come towards the screen as though saying to herself, "It cannot be so, yet I could have sworn I heard . . ." and then retreated a little, as though thinking, "Well, it was only my fancy after all!" Now she seemed to be feeling her way in the dark, and Genji said aloud, "Follow the Lord Buddha and though your way lie in darkness yet shall you not go astray." Suddenly hearing his clear young voice in the darkness, the woman had not at first the courage to reply. But at last she managed to answer: "In which direction, please, is He leading me? I am afraid I do not quite understand." "I am sorry to have startled you," said Genji. "I have only this small request to make: that you will carry to your mistress the following poem: 'Since first he saw the green leaf of the tender bush, never for a moment has the dew of longing dried from the traveller's sleeve.' " "Surely you must know that there is no one here who understands messages of that kind," said the woman; "I wonder whom you mean?" "I have a particular reason for wishing your mistress to receive the message," said Genji, "and I should be obliged if you would contrive to deliver it." The nun at once perceived that the poem referred to her grandchild and supposed that Genji, having been wrongly informed about her age, was intending to make love to her. But how had he discovered her grand-daughter's existence? For some while she pondered in great annoyance and perplexity, and at last answered prudently with a poem in which she said that "he who was but spending a night upon a traveller's dewy bed could know little of those whose home was forever upon the cold moss of the hillside." Thus she turned his poem to a harmless meaning. "Tell her," said Genji when the message was brought back, "that I am not accustomed to carry on conversations in this indirect manner. However shy she may be, I must ask her on this occasion to dispense with formalities and discuss this matter with me seriously!" "How can he have been thus misinformed?" said the nun, still thinking that Genji imagined her granddaughter to be a grown-up woman. She was terrified at being suddenly commanded to appear before this illustrious personage and was wondering what excuse she would make. Her maids, however, were convinced that Genji would be grievously offended if she did not appear, and at last, coming out from the women's chamber, she said to him: "Though I am no longer a young woman, I very much doubt whether I ought to come like this. But since you sent word that you have serious business to discuss with me, I could not refuse. . . ." "Perhaps," said Genji, "you will think my proposal both ill-timed and frivolous. I can only assure you that I mean it very seriously. Let Buddha judge . . ." But here he broke off, intimidated by her age and gravity. "You have certainly chosen a very strange manner of communicating this proposal to me. But though you have not yet said what it is, I am sure you are quite in earnest about it." Thus encouraged, Genji continued. "I was deeply touched by the story of your long widowhood and of your daughter's death. I too, like this poor child, was deprived in earliest infancy of the one being who tenderly loved me, and in my childhood suffered long years of loneliness and misery. Thus we are both in like case, and this has given me so deep a sympathy for the child that I long to make amends for what she has lost. It was, then, to ask if you would consent to let me play a mother's part that at this strange and inconvenient hour I trespassed so inconsiderately upon your patience." "I am sure that you are meaning to be very kind," said the nun, "but—forgive me—you have evidently been misinformed. There is indeed a girl living here under my charge; but she is a mere infant and could not be of the slightest interest to you in any way, so that I cannot consent to your proposal." "On the contrary," said Genji, "I am perfectly conversant with every detail concerning this child; but if you think my sympathy for her exaggerated or misplaced, pray pardon me for having mentioned it." It was evident that he did not in the least realize the absurdity of what he had proposed, and she saw no use in explaining herself any further. The priest was now returning and Genji, saying that he had not expected she would at once fall in with his idea and was confident that she would soon see the matter in a different light, closed the screen behind her.

The night was almost over. In a chapel near by, the Four Meditations of the Law Flower were being practised. The voices of the ministrants who were now chanting the Litany of Atonement came floating on the gusty mountain-wind, and with this solemn sound was mingled the roar of hurrying waters. "Startled from my dream by a wandering gust of the mountain gale, I heard the waterfall, and at the beauty of its music wept." So Genji greeted the priest; and he in turn replied with the poem, "At the noise of a torrent wherein I daily fill my bowl I am scarce likely to start back in wonder and delight." "I get so used to it," he added apologetically. A heavy mist covered the morning sky, and even the chirruping of the mountain-birds sounded muffled and dim. Such a variety of flowers and blossoming trees (he did not know their names) grew upon the hillside that the rocks seemed to be spread with a many-coloured embroidery. Above all he marvelled at the exquisite stepping of the deer who moved across the slope, now treading daintily, now suddenly pausing; and as he watched them the last remnants of his sickness were dispelled by sheer delight. Though the hermit had little use of his limbs, he managed by hook or crook to perform the mystic motions of the Guardian Spell,[27] and though his aged voice was husky and faltering, he read the sacred text with great dignity and fervour. Several of Genji's friends now arrived to congratulate him upon his recovery, among them a messenger from the Palace. The priest from the hut below brought a present of strange-looking roots for which he had gone deep into the ravine. He begged to be excused from accompanying Genji on his way. "Till the end of the year," he said, "I am bound by a vow which must deprive me of what would have been a great pleasure," and he handed Genji the stirrup-cup. "Were I but able to follow my own desires," said Genji taking the cup, "I would not leave these hills and streams. But I hear that my father the Emperor is making anxious enquiry after me. I will come back before the blossom is over." And he recited the verse, "I will go back to the men of the City and tell them to come quickly, lest the wild wind outstripping them should toss these blossoms from the cherry bough." The old priest, flattered by Genji's politeness and captivated by the charm of his voice, answered with the poem: "Like one who finds the aloe-tree in bloom, to the flower of the mountain-cherry I no longer turn my gaze." "I am not after all quite so great a rarity as the aloe-flower," said Genji, smiling.

Next the hermit handed him a parting-cup, with the poem: "Though seldom I open the pine-tree door of my mountain-cell, yet have I now seen face to face the flower few live to see," and as he looked up at Genji, his eyes filled with tears. He gave him, to keep him safe in future from all harm, a magical wand; and seeing this the nun's brother in his turn presented a rosary brought back from Korea by Prince Shotoku. It was ornamented with jade and was still in the same Chinese-looking box in which it had been brought from that country. The box was in an open-work bag, and a five-leafed pine-branch was with it. He also gave him some little vases of blue crystal to keep his medicines in, with sprays of cherry-blossom and wistaria along with them, and such other presents as the place could supply. Genji had sent to the

---

[27] The Guardian Spell (*goshin*) is practiced as follows:

The ministrant holds the palms of his hands together with middle fingers touching and extended, first fingers separated and bent, tips of thumbs and little fingers bunched together, and third fingers in line with middle fingers so as to be invisible from in front. With hands in this sacred pose (*mudra*) he touches the worshipper on forehead, left and right shoulder, heart and throat. At each contact he utters the spell

ON · BASARA GONJI HARAJUBATA · SOHAKA

which is corrupt Sanskrit and means "I invoke thee, thou diamond-fiery very majestic Star." The deity here invoked is Vairocana, favourite Buddha of the Mystic Sect.

Capital for gifts with which to repay his reception in the mountain. First he gave a reward to the hermit, then distributed alms to the priests who had chanted liturgies on his behalf, and finally he gave useful presents to the poor villagers of the neighbourhood. While he was reading a short passage from the scriptures in preparation for his departure, the old priest went into his house and asked his sister the nun whether she had any message for the Prince. "It is very hard to say anything at present," she said. "Perhaps if he still felt the same inclination four, or five years hence, we might begin to consider it." "That is just what I think," said the priest.

Genji saw to his regret that he had made no progress whatever. In answer to the nun's message he sent a small boy who belonged to the priest's household with the following poem: "Last night indeed, though in the greyness of twilight only, I saw the lovely flower. But today a hateful mist has hidden it utterly from my sight." The nun replied: "That I may know whether indeed it pains you so deeply to leave this flower, I shall watch intently the motions of this hazy sky." It was written in a noteworthy and very aristocratic hand, but quite without the graces of deliberate artistry. While his carriage was being got ready, a great company of young lords arrived from the Great Hall, saying that they had been hard put to it to discover what had become of him and now desired to give him their escort. Among them were To no Chujo, Sachu Ben, and other lesser lords, who had come out of affection for the Prince. "We like nothing better than waiting upon you," they said, rather aggrieved, "it was not kind of you to leave us behind." "But having come so far," said another, "it would be a pity to go away without resting for a while under the shadow of these flowering trees"; whereupon they all sat down in a row upon the moss under a tall rock and passed a rough earthenware wine-jar from hand to hand. Close by them the stream leaped over the rocks in a magnificent cascade. To no Chujo pulled out a flute from the folds of his dress and played a few trills upon it. Sachu Ben, tapping idly with his fan, began to sing "The Temple of Toyora." The young lords who had come to fetch him were all persons of great distinction; but so striking was Genji's appearance as he sat leaning disconsolately against the rock that no eye was likely to be turned in any other direction. One of his attendants now performed upon the reed-pipe; someone else turned out to be a skilful *sho* [28] player. Presently the old priest came out of his house carrying a zithern, and putting it into Genji's hands begged him to play something, "that the birds of the mountain

[28] A Chinese instrument; often translated "mouth-organ."

may rejoice." He protested that he was not feeling at all in the mood to play; but yielding to the priest's persuasion, he gave what was really not at all a contemptible performance. After that, they all got up and started for home. Everyone on the mountain, down to the humblest priest and youngest neophyte, was bitterly disappointed at the shortness of his stay, and there were many tears shed; while the old nun within doors was sorry to think that she had had but that one brief glimpse of him and might never see him again. The priest declared that for his part he thought the Land of the Rising Sun in her last degenerate days ill-deserved that such a Prince should be born to her, and he wiped his eyes. The little girl too was very much pleased with him and said he was a prettier gentleman than her own father. "If you think so, you had better become his little girl instead," said her nurse. At which the child nodded, thinking that it would be a very good plan indeed; and in future the best-dressed person in the pictures she painted was called "Prince Genji," and so was her handsomest doll.

On his return to the Capital he went straight to the Palace and described to his father the experiences of the last two days. The Emperor thought him looking very haggard and was much concerned. He asked many questions about the hermit's magical powers, to all of which Genji replied in great detail. "He ought certainly to have been made Master Magician long ago," said His Majesty. "His ministrations have repeatedly been attended with great success, but for some reason his services have escaped public acknowledgment," and he issued a proclamation to this effect. The Minister of the Left came to meet him on his way from the Presence and apologized for not having come with his sons to bring him back from the mountain. "I thought," he said, "that as you had gone there secretly, you would dislike being fetched; but I very much hope that you will now come and spend a few days with us quietly; after which I shall esteem it a privilege to escort you to your palace." He did not in the least want to go, but there was no escape. His father-in-law drove him to the Great Hall in his own carriage, and when the bullocks had been unyoked dragged it in at the gate with his own hands. Such treatment was certainly meant to be very friendly; but Genji found the Minister's attentions merely irritating.

Aoi's quarters had, in anticipation of Genji's coming, just been put thoroughly to rights. In the long interval since he last visited her many changes had been made; among other improvements, a handsome terrace had been built. Not a thing was out of its right place in this supremely well-ordered house. Aoi, as usual, was nowhere to be seen. It was only after repeated entreaties by her father that she at last consented to appear in her husband's presence. Posed like a princess in a picture she sat almost motionless. Beautiful she certainly was. "I should like to tell you about my visit to the mountain, if only I thought that it would interest you at all or draw an answer from you. I hate to go on always like this. Why are you so cold and distant and proud? Year after year we fail to reach an understanding and you cut yourself off from me more completely than before. Can we not manage for a little while to be on ordinary terms? It seems rather strange, considering how ill I have been, that you should not attempt to enquire after my health. Or rather, it is exactly what I should expect; but nevertheless I find it extremely painful." "Yes," said Aoi, "it is extremely painful when people do not care what becomes of one." She glanced back over her shoulder as she spoke, her face full of scorn and pride, looking uncommonly handsome as she did so. "You hardly ever speak," said Genji, "and when you do, it is only to say unkind things and twist one's harmless words so that they seem to be insults. And when I try to find some way of helping you for a while at least to be a little less disagreeable, you become more hopelessly unapproachable than ever. Shall I one day succeed in making you understand . . . ?" and so saying he went into their bedroom. She did not follow him. He lay for a while in a state of great annoyance and distress. But, probably because he did not really care about her very much one way or the other, he soon became drowsy and all sorts of quite different matters drifted through his head. He wanted as much as ever to have the little girl in his keeping and watch her grow to womanhood. But the grandmother was right; the child was too absurdly young, and it would be very difficult to broach the matter again. Would it not however be possible to contrive that she should be brought to the Capital? It would be easy then to find excuses for fetching her and she might, even through some such arrangement as that, become a source of constant delight to him. The father, Prince Hyobukyo, was of course a man of very distinguished manners; but he was not at all handsome. How was it that the child resembled one of her aunts and was so unlike all the rest? He had an idea that Fujitsubo and Prince Hyobukyo were children of the same mother, while the others were only half-sisters. The fact that the little girl was closely related to the lady whom he had loved for so long made him all the more set upon securing her, and he began to puzzle his head for some means of bringing this about.

Next day he wrote his letter of thanks to the priest. No doubt it contained some allusion to his project. To the nun he wrote: "Seeing you so resolutely averse to what I had proposed, I refrained from justifying my intentions so fully as I could have wished. But should it prove that, even by the few words I ventured to speak, I was able to convince you that this is no mere whim or common fancy, how happy would such news make me." On a slip of paper folded small and tucked into the letter he wrote the poem: "Though with all my heart I tried to leave it behind me, never for a moment has it left me—the fair face of that mountain-flower!" Though she had long passed the zenith of her years the nun could not but be pleased and flattered by the elegance of the note; for it was not only written in an exquisite hand, but was folded with a careless dexterity which she greatly admired. She felt very sorry for him, and would have been glad, had it been in her conscience, to have sent him a more favorable reply. "We were delighted," she wrote, "that being in the neighborhood you took occasion to pay us a visit. But I fear that when (as I very much hope you will) you come here purposely to visit us, I shall not be able to add anything to what I have said already. As for the poem which you enclose, do not expect her to answer it, for she cannot yet write her 'Naniwa Zu' [29] properly, even letter by letter. Let me then answer it for her: 'For as long as the cherry-blossoms remain unscattered upon the shore of Onoe where wild storms blow —so long have you till now been constant!' For my part, I am very uneasy about the matter."

The priest replied to the same effect. Genji was very much disappointed and after two or three days he sent for Koremitsu and gave him a letter for the nun, telling him at the same time to find out whatever he could from Shonagon, the child's nurse. "What an impressionable character he is," thought Koremitsu. He had only had a glimpse of the child; but that had sufficed to convince him that she was a mere baby, though he remembered thinking her quite pretty. What trick would his master's heart be playing upon him next?

The old priest was deeply impressed by the arrival of a letter in the hands of so special and confidential a messenger. After delivering it, Koremitsu sought out the nurse. He repeated all that Genji had told him to say and added a great deal of general information about his master. Being a man of many words he talked on and on, continually introducing some new topic which had suddenly occurred to him as relevant. But at the end of it all Shonagon was just as puzzled as everyone else had been to account for Genji's interest in

[29] A song the words of which were used as a first writing lesson.

a child so ridiculously young. His letter was very deferential. In it he said that he longed to see a specimen of her childish writing done letter by letter, as the nun had described. As before, he enclosed a poem: "Was it the shadows in the mountain well that told you my purpose was but jest?" [30] To which she answered, "Some perhaps that have drawn in that well now bitterly repent. Can the shadows tell me if again it will be so?" and Koremitsu brought a spoken message to the same effect, together with the assurance that so soon as the nun's health improved, she intended to visit the Capital and would then communicate with him again. The prospect of her visit was very exciting.

About this time Lady Fujitsubo fell ill and retired for a while from the Palace. The sight of the Emperor's grief and anxiety moved Genji's pity. But he could not help thinking that this was an opportunity which must not be missed. He spent the whole of that day in a state of great agitation, unable whether in his own house or at the Palace to think of anything else or call upon anyone. When at last the day was over, he succeeded in persuading her maid Omyobu to take a message. The girl, though she regarded any communication between them as most imprudent, seeing a strange look in his face like that of one who walks in a dream, took pity on him and went. The Princess looked back upon their former relationship as something wicked and horrible and the memory of it was a continual torment to her. She had determined that such a thing must never happen again.

She met him with a stern and sorrowful countenance, but this did not disguise her charm, and as though conscious that he was unduly admiring her she began to treat him with great coldness and disdain. He longed to find some blemish in her, to think that he had been mistaken, and be at peace.

I need not tell all that happened. The night passed only too quickly. He whispered in her ear the poem: "Now that at last we have met, would that we might vanish forever into the dream we dreamed tonight!" But she, still conscience-stricken: "Though I were to hide in the darkness of eternal sleep, yet would my shame run through the world from tongue to tongue." And indeed, as Genji knew, it was not without good cause that she had suddenly fallen into this fit of apprehension and remorse. As he left, Omyobu came running after him with his cloak and other belongings which he had left behind. He lay all day upon his bed in great torment. He sent a letter, but it was returned unopened. This had happened many times in the past, but now it filled him with such consternation that for two or three days he was

[30] There is here a pun, and a reference to poem 3807 in the *Manyoshu*.

completely prostrate and kept his room. All this while he was in constant dread lest his father, full of solicitude, should begin enquiring what new trouble had overtaken him. Fujitsubo, convinced that her ruin was accomplished, fell into a profound melancholy and her health grew daily worse. Messengers arrived constantly from the Court begging her to return without delay; but she could not bring herself to go. Her disorder had now taken a turn which filled her with secret foreboding, and she did nothing all day long but sit distractedly wondering what would become of her. When the hot weather set in she ceased to leave her bed at all. Three months had now passed and there was no mistaking her condition. Soon it would be known and everywhere discussed. She was appalled at the calamity which had overtaken her. Not knowing that there was any cause for secrecy, her people were astonished that she had not long ago informed the Emperor of her condition. Speculations were rife, but the question was one which only the Princess herself was in a position definitely to solve. Omyobu and her old nurse's daughter who waited upon her at her toilet and in the bathhouse had at once noted the change and were somewhat taken aback. But Omyobu was unwilling to discuss the matter. She had an uncomfortable suspicion that it was the meeting which she arranged that had now taken effect with cruel promptness and precision. It was announced in the Palace that other disorders had misled those about her and prevented them from recognizing the true nature of her condition. This explanation was accepted by everyone.

The Emperor himself was full of tender concern, and though messengers kept him constantly informed, the gloomiest doubts and fancies passed continually through his mind. Genji was at this time visited by a most terrifying and extraordinary dream. He sent for interpreters, but they could make little of it. There were indeed certain passages to which they could assign no meaning at all; but this much was clear: the dreamer had made a false step and must be on his guard. "It was not *my* dream," said Genji, feeling somewhat alarmed. "I am consulting you on behalf of someone else," and he was wondering what this "false step" could have been when news reached him of the Princess's condition. This then was the disaster which his dream had portended! At once he wrote her an immense letter full of passionate self-reproaches and exhortations. But Omyobu, thinking that it would only increase her agitation, refused to deliver it, and he could trust no other messenger. Even the few wretched lines which she had been in the habit of sending to him now and again had for some while utterly ceased.

In her seventh month she again appeared at Court. Overjoyed at her return, the Emperor lavished boundless affection upon her. The added fulness of her figure, the unwonted pallor and thinness of her face gave her, he thought, a new and incomparable charm. As before, all his leisure was spent in her company. During this time several Court festivals took place and Genji's presence was constantly required; sometimes he was called upon to play the *koto* or flute, sometimes to serve his father in other ways. On such occasions, strive as he might to show no trace of embarrassment or agitation, he feared more than once that he had betrayed himself; while to her such confrontations were one long torment.

The nun had somewhat improved in health and was now living in the Capital. He had enquired where she was lodging and sent messages from time to time, receiving (which indeed was all he expected) as little encouragement as before. In the last months his longing for the child had increased rather than diminished, but day after day went by without his finding any means to change the situation. As the autumn drew to its close, he fell into a state of great despondency. One fine moonlit night when he had decided, against his own inclination, to pay a certain secret visit,[31] a shower came on. As he had started from the Palace and the place to which he was going was in the suburbs of the Sixth Ward, it occurred to him that it would be disagreeable to go so far in the rain. He was considering what he should do when he noticed a tumbled-down house surrounded by very ancient trees. He asked whose this gloomy and desolate mansion might be, and Koremitsu, who, as usual, was with him, replied: "Why that is the late Azechi no Dainagon's house. A day or two ago I took occasion to call there and was told that my Lady the nun has grown very weak and does not know what goes on about her." "Why did you not tell me this before?" said Genji deeply concerned; "I should have called at once to convey my sympathy to her household. Pray go in at once and ask for news." Koremitsu accordingly sent one of the lesser attendants to the house, instructing him to give the impression that Genji had come on purpose to enquire. When the man announced that Prince Genji had sent him for news and was himself waiting outside, great excitement and consternation prevailed in the house. Their mistress, the servants said, had for several days been lying in a very parlous condition and could not possibly receive a visit. But they dared not simply send so distinguished a visitor away, and hastily tidying the southern parlour, they bustled him into it, saying,

31 To Lady Rokujo.

"You must forgive us for showing you into this untidy room. We have done our best to make it presentable. Perhaps, on a surprise visit, you will forgive us for conducting you to such an out-of-the-way closet. . . ." It was indeed not at all the kind of room that he was used to. "I have been meaning for a long while to visit this house," said Genji; "but time after time the proposals which I made in writing concerning a certain project of mine were summarily rejected and this discouraged me. Had I but known that your mistress's health had taken this turn for the worse. . . ." "Tell him that at this moment my mind is clear, though it may soon be darkened again. I am deeply sensible of the kindness he has shown in thus visiting my death-bed, and regret that I cannot speak with him face to face. Tell him that if by any chance he has not altered his mind with regard to the matter that he has discussed with me before, by all means let him, when the time has come, number her among the ladies of his household. It is with great anxiety that I leave her behind me and I fear that such a bond with earth may hinder me from reaching the life for which I have prayed."

Her room was so near and the partition so thin that as she gave Shonagon her message he could hear now and again the sound of her sad, quavering voice. Presently he heard her saying to someone, "How kind, how very kind of him to come. If only the child were old enough to thank him nicely!" "It is indeed no question of kindness," said Genji to Shonagon. "Surely it is evident that only some very deep feeling would have driven me to display so zealous a persistency! Since first I saw this child, a feeling of strange tenderness towards her possessed me, and it has grown to such a love as cannot be of this world only.[32] Though it is but an idle fancy, I have a longing to hear her voice. Could you not send for her before I go?" "Poor little thing," said Shonagon. "She is fast asleep in her room and knows nothing of all our troubles." But as she spoke there was a sound of someone moving in the women's quarters and a voice suddenly was heard saying: "Grandmother, Grandmother! Prince Genji who came to see us in the mountains is here, paying a visit. Why do you not let him come and talk to you?" "Hush, child, hush!" cried all the gentlewomen, scandalized. "No, no," said the child; "Grandmother said that when she saw this prince it made her feel better at once. I was not being silly at all." This speech delighted Genji; but the gentlewomen of the household thought the child's incursion painful and unseemly, and pretended not to hear her last remark. Genji gave up the idea of paying a real visit and drove back to his house,

[32] Arises out of some connection in a previous existence.

thinking as he went that her behaviour was indeed still that of a mere infant. Yet how easy and delightful it would be to teach her!

Next day he paid a proper visit. On his arrival he sent in a poem written on his usual tiny slip of paper: "Since first I heard the voice of the young crane, my boat shows a strange tendency to stick among the reeds!" It was meant for the little girl and was written in a large, childish hand, but very beautifully, so that the ladies of the house said as soon as they saw it, "This will have to go into the child's copybook."

Shonagon sent him the following note: "My mistress, feeling that she might not live through the day, asked us to have her moved to the temple in the hills, and she is already on her way. I shall see to it that she learns of your enquiry, if I can but send word to her before it is too late." The letter touched him deeply.

During these autumn evenings his heart was in a continual ferment. But though all his thoughts were occupied in a different quarter, yet owing to the curious relationship in which the child stood to the being who thus obsessed his mind, the desire to make the girl his own throughout this stormy time grew daily stronger. He remembered the evening when he had first seen her and the nun's poem, "Not knowing if any will come to nurture the tender leaf. . . ." She would always be delightful; but in some respects she might not fulfil her early promise. One must take risks. And he made the poem: "When shall I see it lying in my hand, the young grass of the moor-side that springs from purple [33] roots?" In the tenth month the Emperor was to visit the Suzaku-in for the Festival of Red Leaves. The dancers were all to be sons of the noblest houses. The most accomplished among the princes, courtiers and other great gentlemen had been chosen for their parts by the Emperor himself, and from the Royal Princes and State Ministers downward everyone was busy with continual practises and rehearsals. Genji suddenly realized that for a long while he had not enquired after his friends on the mountain. He at once sent a special messenger who brought back this letter from the priest: "The end came on the twentieth day of last month. It is the common lot of mankind; yet her loss is very grievous to me!" This and more he wrote, and Genji, reading the letter, was filled with a bitter sense of life's briefness and futility. And what of the child concerning whose future the dead woman had shown such anxiety? He could not remember his own mother's death at all distinctly; but some dim recollection

---

[33] Purple is *murasaki* in Japanese. From this poem the child is known as Murasaki; and hence the authoress derived the nickname by which she too is known.

still floated in his mind and gave to his letter of condolence an added warmth of feeling. It was answered, not without a certain self-importance, by the nurse Shonagon.

After the funeral and mourning were over, the child was brought back to the Capital. Hearing of this he allowed a short while to elapse and then one fine, still night went to the house of his own accord. This gloomy, decaying, half-deserted mansion must, he thought, have a most depressing effect upon the child who lived there. He was shown into the same small room as before. Here Shonagon told him between her sobs the whole tale of their bereavement, at which he too found himself strangely moved. "I would send my little mistress to His Highness her father's," she continued, "did I not remember how cruelly her poor mother was used in that house. And I would do it still if my little lady were a child in arms who would not know where she had been taken to nor what the people there were feeling towards her. But she is now too big a girl to go among a lot of strange children who might not treat her kindly. So her poor dead grandmother was always saying down to her last day. You, Sir, have been very good to us, and it would be a great weight off my mind to know that she was coming to you, even if it were only for a little while; and I would not worry you with asking what was to become of her afterwards. Only for her sake I am sorry indeed that she is not some years older, so that you might make a match of it. But the way she has been brought up has made her young even for her age." "You need not so constantly remind me of her childishness," said Genji. "Though it is indeed her youth and helplessness which move my compassion, yet I realize (and why should I hide it from myself or from you?) that a far closer bond unites our souls. Let me tell her myself what we have just now decided," and he recited a poem in which he asked if "like the waves that lap the shore where young reeds grow he must advance only to recede again." "Will she be too much surprised?" he added. Shonagon, saying that the little girl should by all means be fetched, answered his poem with another in which she warned him that he must not expect her to "drift seaweedlike with the waves," before she understood his intention. "Now, what made you think I should send you away without letting her see you?" she asked, speaking in an offhand, familiar tone which he found it easy to pardon. His appearance, which the gentlewomen of the house studied with great care while he sat waiting for the child and singing to himself a verse of the song "Why so hard to cross the hill?" made a deep impression upon them, and they did not forget that moment for a long while after.

The child was lying on her bed weeping for her grandmother. "A gentleman in a big cloak has come to play with you," said one of the women who were waiting upon her. "I wonder if it is your father." At this she jumped up and cried out: "Nurse, where is the gentleman in a cloak? Is he my father?" and she came running into the room. "No," said Genji, "it is not your father; but it is someone else who wants you to be very fond of him. Come. . . ." She had learnt from the way people talked about him that Prince Genji was someone very important, and feeling that he must really be very angry with her for speaking of him as the "gentleman in a cloak" she went straight to her nurse and whispered, "Please, I am sleepy." "You must not be shy of me any more," said Genji. "If you are sleepy, come here and lie on my knee. Will you not even come and talk to me?" "There," said Shonagon, "you see what a little savage she is," and pushed the child towards him. She stood listlessly by his side, passing her hand under her hair so that it fell in waves over her soft dress or clasping a great bunch of it where it stuck out thick around her shoulders. Presently he took her hand in his; but at once, in terror of this close contact with someone to whom she was not used, she cried out, "I said I wanted to go to bed," and snatching her hand away she ran into the women's quarters. He followed her crying, "Dear one, do not run away from me! Now that your granny is gone, you must love me instead." "Well!" gasped Shonagon, deeply shocked. "No, that is too much! How can you bring yourself to say such a wicked thing to the poor child? And it is not much use *telling* people to be fond of one, is it?" "For the moment, it may not be," said Genji. "But you will see that strange things happen if one's heart is set upon a thing as mine is now."

Hail was falling. It was a wild and terrible night. The thought of leaving her to pass it in this gloomy and half-deserted mansion immeasurably depressed him and snatching at this excuse for remaining near her: "Shut the partition-door!" he cried. "I will stay for a while and play the watchman here on this terrible night. Draw near to me, all of you!" and so saying, as though it were the most natural thing in the world, he picked up the child in his arms and carried her to her bed. The gentlewomen were far too astonished and confounded to budge from their seats; while Shonagon, though his high-handed proceedings greatly agitated and alarmed her, had to confess to herself that there was no real reason to interfere, and could only sit moaning in her corner. The little girl was at first terribly frightened. She did not know what he was going to do with her and shuddered violently. Even the feel of his delicate, cool skin when he drew her to him gave her goose-flesh. He saw this; but none the less he began gently and carefully to remove her outer garments, and laid her down. Then, though he knew quite well that she was still frightened of him, he began talking to her softly and tenderly: "How would you like to come with me one day to a place where there are lots of lovely pictures and dolls and toys?" And he went on to speak so feelingly of all the things she was most interested in that soon she felt almost at home with him. But for a long while she was restless and did not go properly to sleep. The storm still raged. "Whatever should we have done if this gentleman had not been here?" whispered one of the women; "I know that for my part I should have been in a terrible fright. If only our little lady were nearer to his age!" Shonagon, still mistrustful, sat quite close to Genji all the while.

At last the wind began to drop. The night was far spent; but his return at such an hour would cause no surprise! "She has become so dear to me," said Genji, "that, above all at this sad time in her life, I am loath to leave her even for a few short hours. I think I shall put her somewhere where I can see her whenever I wish. I wonder that she is not frightened to live in such a place as this." "I think her father spoke of coming to fetch her," said Shonagon; "but that is not likely to be till the Forty-nine Days are up." "It would of course under ordinary circumstances be natural that her father should look after her," admitted Genji; "but as she has been brought up entirely by someone else she has no more reason to care for him than for me. And though I have known her so short a time, I am certainly far fonder of her than her father can possibly be." So saying he stroked the child's hair and then reluctantly, with many backward glances, left the room. There was now a heavy white fog, and hoar-frost lay thick on the grass. Suddenly he found himself wishing that it were a real love-affair, and he became very depressed. It occurred to him that on his way home he would pass by a certain house which he had once familiarly frequented. He knocked at the door, but no one answered. He then ordered one of his servants who had a strong voice to recite the following lines: "By my Sister's gate though morning fog makes all the world still dark as night, I could not fail to pause." When this had been sung twice, the lady sent an impertinent coxcomb of a valet to the door, who having recited the poem, "If you disliked the hedge of fog that lies about this place, a gate of crazy wicker would not keep you standing in the street," at once went back again into the house. He waited; but no one else came to the door, and though he was in no mood to go dully home since it was now broad daylight, what else could be done? At his palace he lay for a long while smiling to himself with pleasure as he recollected the child's pretty speeches and ways. Towards noon he rose and began to write a letter to her; but he could not find the right words, and after many times laying his brush aside he determined at last to send her some nice pictures instead.

That day Prince Hyobukyo paid his long-promised visit to the late nun's house. The place seemed to him even more ruinous, vast and antiquated than he remembered it years ago. How depressing it must be for a handful of persons to live in these decaying halls, and looking about him he said to the nurse: "No child ought to live in a place like this even for a little while. I must take her away at once; there is plenty of room in my house. You" (turning to Shonagon) "shall be found a place as a Lady-in-Waiting there. The child will be very well off, for there are several other young people for her to play with." He called the little girl to him and noticing the rich perfume that clung to her dress since Genji held her in his arms, the Prince said, "How nicely your dress is scented. But isn't it rather drab?" No sooner had he said this than he remembered that she was in mourning, and felt slightly uncomfortable. "I used sometimes to tell her grandmother," he continued, "that she ought to let her come to see me and get used to our ways, for indeed it was a strange upbringing for her to live alone year in year out with one whose health and spirits steadily declined. But she for some reason was very unfriendly towards me, and there was in another quarter [34] too a reluctance which I fear even at such a time as this may not be wholly overcome. . . ." "If that is so," said Shonagon, "dull as it is for her here, I do not think she should be moved till she is a little better able to shift for herself."

For days on end the child had been in a terrible state of grief, and not having eaten the least bite of anything she was grown very thin, but was none the less lovely for that. He looked at her tenderly and said: "You must not cry any more now. When people die, there is no help for it and we must bear it bravely. But now all is well, for I have come instead. . . ." But it was getting late and he could not stay any longer. As he turned to go he saw that the child, by no means consoled at the prospect of falling under his care, was again crying bitterly. The Prince, himself shedding a few tears, did his best to comfort her: "Do not grieve so," he said, "today or tomorrow I will send for you to come and live with me," and with that he departed. Still the child wept and no way could be found to distract her thoughts. It was not of course that she had any anxiety about her own future, for about such matters she had not yet begun to think at all;

[34] His wife.

but only that she had lost the companion from whom for years on end she had never for a moment been separated. Young as she was, she suffered so cruelly that all her usual games were abandoned, and though sometimes during the day her spirits would a little improve, as night drew on she became so melancholy that Shonagon began to wonder how much longer things would go on like this, and in despair at not being able to comfort her, would herself burst into tears.

Presently Koremitsu arrived with a message saying that Genji had intended to visit them, but owing to a sudden command from the Palace was unable to do so, and being very much perturbed at the little one's grievous condition had sent for further news. Having delivered this message, Koremitsu brought in some of Genji's servants whom he had sent to mount guard over the house that night. "This kindness is indeed ill-placed," said Shonagon. "It may not seem to him of much consequence that his gentlemen should be installed here; but if the child's father hears of it, we servants shall get all the blame for the little lady's being given away to a married gentleman. It was you who let it all begin, we shall be told. Now be careful," she said turning to her fellow-servants, "do not let her even mention these watchmen to her father." But alas, the child was quite incapable of understanding such a prohibition, and Shonagon, after pouring out many lamentations to Koremitsu, continued: "I do not doubt but that in due time she will somehow become his wife, for so their fate seems to decree. But now and for a long while there can be no talk of any such thing, and this, as he has roundly told me, he knows as well as the rest of us. So what he is after I cannot for the life of me imagine. Only today when Prince Hyobukyo was here he bade me keep a sharp eye upon her and not let her be treated with any indiscretion. I confess when he said it I remembered with vexation certain liberties which I have allowed your master to take, thinking little enough of them at the time." No sooner had she said this than she began to fear that Koremitsu would put a worse construction on her words than she intended, and shaking her head very dolefully she relapsed into silence. Nor was she far wrong, for Koremitsu was indeed wondering of what sort Genji's misdemeanors could have been.

On hearing Koremitsu's report Genji's heart was filled with pity for the child's state and he would like to have gone to her at once. But he feared that ignorant people would misunderstand these frequent visits and, thinking the girl older than she was, spread foolish scandals abroad. It would be far simpler to fetch her to his palace and keep her there. All through the day he sent numerous letters, and at dusk Koremitsu again went to the house saying that urgent business had once more prevented Genji from visiting them, for which remissness he tendered his apologies. Shonagon answered curtly that the girl's father had suddenly decided to fetch her away next day and that they were too busy to receive visits: "The servants are all in a fluster at leaving this shabby old house where they have lived so long and going to a strange, grand place. . . ." She answered his further questions so briefly and seemed so intent upon her sewing that Koremitsu went away.

Genji was at the Great Hall, but as usual he had been unable to get a word out of Aoi and in a gloomy mood he was plucking at his zithern and singing, "Why sped you across field and hill so fast upon this rainy night?" [35]

The words of the song were aimed at Aoi and he sang them with much feeling. He was thus employed when Koremitsu arrived at the Great Hall. Genji sent for him at once and bade him tell his story. Koremitsu's news was very disquieting. Once she was in her father's palace it would look very odd that Genji should fetch her away, even if she came willingly. It would inevitably be rumored abroad that he had made off with her like a child-snatcher, a thief. Far better to anticipate his rival and exacting a promise of silence from the people about her, carry her off to his own palace immediately. "I shall go there at daybreak," he said to Koremitsu. "Order the carriage that I came here in, it can be used just as it is, and see to it that one or two attendants are ready to go with me." Koremitsu bowed and retired.

Genji knew that whichever course he chose, there was bound to be a scandal so soon as the thing became known. Inevitably gossips would spread the report that, young though she was, the child by this time knew well enough why she had been invited to live with Prince Genji in his palace. Let them draw their own conclusions. That did not matter. There was a much worse possibility. What if Hyobukyo found out where she was? His conduct in abducting another man's child would appear in the highest degree outrageous and discreditable. He was sorely puzzled, but he knew that if he let this opportunity slip he would afterwards bitterly repent it, and long before daybreak he started on his way. Aoi was cold and sullen as ever. "I have just remembered something very important which I must see about at home," he said; "I shall not be long," and he slipped out so quietly that the servants of the house did not know that he was gone. His cloak was brought to him from his own apartments and he drove off attended only by Koremitsu who followed on horseback. After much knocking they succeeded in getting the gate

[35] The song is addressed by a girl to a suspicious lover; Genji reverses the sense.

opened, but by a servant who was not in the secret. Koremitsu ordered the man to pull in Genji's carriage as quietly as he could and himself went straight to the front door, which he rattled, coughing as he did so that Shonagon might know who was there. "My lord is waiting," he said when she came to the door. "But the young lady is fast asleep," said Shonagon; "His Highness has no business to be up and about at this time of night." She said this thinking that he was returning from some nocturnal escapade and had only called there in passing. "I hear," said Genji now coming forward, "that the child is to be moved to her father's and I have something of importance which I must say to her before she goes." "Whatever business you have to transact with her, I am sure she will give the matter her closest attention," scoffed Shonagon. Matters of importance indeed, with a child of ten! Genji entered the women's quarters. "You cannot go in there," cried Shonagon in horror; "several aged ladies are lying all undressed. . . ." "They are all fast asleep," said Genji. "See, I am only rousing the child," and bending over her: "The morning mist is rising," he cried, "it is time to wake!" And before Shonagon had time to utter a sound he had taken the child in his arms and begun gently to rouse her. Still half-dreaming, she thought it was the prince her father who had come to fetch her. "Come," said Genji while he put her hair to rights, "your father has sent me to bring you back with me to his palace." For a moment she was dazed to find that it was not her father and shrank from him in fright. "Never mind whether it is your father or I," he cried; "it is all the same," and so saying he picked her up in his arms and carried her out of the inner room. "Well!" cried out Koremitsu and Shonagon in astonishment. What would he do next? "It seems," said Genji, "that you were disquieted at my telling you I could not visit her here as often as I wished and would make arrangements for her to go to a more convenient place. I hear that you are sending her where it will be even more difficult for me to see her. Therefore . . . make ready one or the other of you to come with me."

Shonagon, who now realized that he was going to make off with the child, fell into a terrible fluster. "O, Sir," she said, "you could not have chosen a worse time. Today her father is coming to fetch her, and whatever shall I say to him? If only you would wait, I am sure it would all come right in the end. But by acting so hastily you will do yourself no good and leave the poor servants here in a sad pickle." "If that is all," cried Genji, "let them follow as soon as they choose," and to Shonagon's despair he had the carriage brought in. The child stood by weeping and bewildered. There seemed no way of preventing him from carrying out his purpose and gathering together the child's clothes that she had been sewing the night before, the nurse put on her own best dress and stepped into the carriage. Genji's house was not far off and they arrived before daylight. They drew up in front of the western wing and Genji alighted. Taking the child lightly in his arms, he set her on the ground. Shonagon, to whom these strange events seemed like a dream, hesitated as though still uncertain whether she should enter the house or no. "There is no need for you to come in if you do not want to," said Genji. "Now that the child herself is safely here I am quite content. If you had rather go back, you have only to say so and I will escort you."

Reluctantly she left the carriage. The suddenness of the move was in itself enough to have upset her; but she was also worrying about what Prince Hyobukyo would think when he found that his child had vanished. And indeed what *was* going to become of her? One way or another all her mistresses seemed to be taken from her and it was only when she became frightened of having wept for so long on end that she at last dried her eyes and began to pray.

The western wing had long been uninhabited and was not completely furnished; but Koremitsu had soon fitted up screens and curtains where they were required. For Genji makeshift quarters were soon contrived by letting down the side-wings of his screen-of-honor. He sent to the other part of the house for his night things and went to sleep. The child, who had been put to bed not far off, was still very apprehensive and ill at ease in these new surroundings. Her lips were trembling, but she dared not cry out loud. "I want to sleep with Shonagon," she said at last in a tearful, babyish voice. "You are getting too big to sleep with a nurse," said Genji who had heard her. "You must try and go to sleep nicely where you are." She felt very lonely and lay weeping for a long while. The nurse was far too much upset to think of going to bed and sat up for the rest of the night in the servants' quarters crying so bitterly that she was unconscious of all that went on around her.

But when it grew light she began to look about her a little. Not only this great palace with its marvellous pillars and carvings, but the sand in the courtyard outside which seemed to her like a carpet of jewels made so dazzling an impression upon her that at first she felt somewhat overawed. However, the fact that she was now no longer in a household of women gave her an agreeable sense of security.

It was the hour at which business brought various strangers to the house. There were several men walking just outside her window and she heard one of them whisper to another: "They say that someone new has come to live here. Who can it be, I wonder? A lady of note, I'll warrant you."

Bath water was brought from the other wing, and steamed rice for breakfast. Genji did not rise till far on into the morning. "It is not good for the child to be alone," he said to Shonagon, "so last night before I came to you I arranged for some little people to come and stay here," and so saying he sent a servant to "fetch the little girls from the eastern wing." He had given special orders that they were to be as small as possible and now four of the tiniest and prettiest creatures imaginable arrived upon the scene.

Murasaki was still asleep, lying wrapped in Genji's own coat. It was with difficulty that he roused her. "You must not be sad any more," he said. "If I were not very fond of you, should I be looking after you like this? Little girls ought to be very gentle and obedient in their ways." And thus her education was begun.

She seemed to him, now that he could study her at leisure, even more lovely than he had realized and they were soon engaged in an affectionate conversation. He sent for delightful pictures and toys to show her and set to work to amuse her in every way he could. Gradually he persuaded her to get up and look about her. In her shabby dress made of some dark grey material she looked so charming now that she was laughing and playing, with all her woes forgotten, that Genji too laughed with pleasure as he watched her. When at last he retired to the eastern wing, she went out of doors to look at the garden. As she picked her way among the trees and along the side of the lake, and gazed with delight upon the frosty flower-beds that glittered gay as a picture, while a many-coloured throng of unknown people passed constantly in and out of the house, she began to think that this was a very nice place indeed. Then she looked at the wonderful pictures that were painted on all the panels and screens and quite lost her heart to them.

For two or three days Genji did not go to the Palace, but spent all his time amusing the little girl. Finally he drew all sorts of pictures for her to put into her copybook, showing them to her one by one as he did so. She thought them the loveliest set of pictures she had ever seen. Then he wrote part of the *Musashi-no* poem.[36] She was delighted by the way it was written in bold ink-strokes on a background stained with purple. In a smaller hand was the poem: "Though the parent-root [37] I cannot see, yet tenderly I love its offshoot [38]

---

[36] "Though I know not the place, yet when they told me this was the moor of Musashi the thought flashed through my mind: 'What else indeed could it be, since all its grass is purple-dyed?'"
[37] Fujitsubo. The fuji flower is also purple (*murasaki*) in colour.
[38] The child Murasaki, who was Fujitsubo's niece. Musashi was famous for the purple dye extracted from the roots of a grass that grew there.

—the dewy plant that grows upon Musashi Moor." "Come," said Genji while she was admiring it, "you must write something too." "I cannot write properly yet," she answered, looking up at him with a witchery so wholly unconscious that Genji laughed. "Even if you cannot write properly it will never do for us to let you off altogether. Let me give you a lesson." With many timid glances towards him she began to write. Even the childish manner in which she grasped the brush gave him a thrill of delight which he was at a loss to explain. "Oh, I have spoiled it," she suddenly cried out and blushing hid from him what she had written. But he forced her to let him see it and found the poem: "I do not know what put Musashi into your head and am very puzzled. What plant is it that you say is a relative of mine?" It was written in a large childish hand which was indeed very undeveloped, but was nevertheless full of promise. It showed a strong resemblance to the late nun's writing. He felt certain that if she were given up-to-date copybooks she would soon write very nicely.

Next they built houses for the dolls and played so long at this game together that Genji forgot for a while the great anxiety [39] which was at that time preying upon his mind.

The servants who had been left behind at Murasaki's house were extremely embarrassed when Prince Hyobukyo came to fetch her. Genji had made them promise for a time at any rate to tell no one of what had happened and Shonagon had seemed to agree that this was best. Accordingly he could get nothing out of them save that Shonagon had taken the child away with her without saying anything about where she was going. The Prince felt completely baffled. Perhaps the grandmother had instilled into the nurse's mind the idea that things would not go smoothly for the child at his palace. In that case the nurse with an excess of craftiness might, instead of openly saying that she feared the child would not be well treated under his roof, have thought it wiser to make off with her when opportunity offered. He went home very depressed, asking them to let him know instantly if they had any news, a request which again embarrassed them. He also made enquiries of the priest at the temple in the hills, but could learn nothing. She had seemed to him to be a most lovable and delightful child; it was very disappointing to lose sight of her in this manner. The princess his wife had long ago got over her dislike of the child's mother and was indignant at the idea that she was not to be trusted to do her duty by the child properly.

Gradually the servants from Murasaki's house assembled at her new home. The little girls who had been brought to

[39] The pregnancy of Fujitsubo.

play with her were delighted with their new companion and they were soon all playing together very happily.

When her prince was away or busy, on dreary evenings she would still sometimes long for her grandmother the nun and cry a little. But she never thought about her father whom she had never been used to see except at rare intervals. Now indeed she had "a new father" of whom she was growing every day more fond. When he came back from anywhere she was the first to meet him and then wonderful games and conversations began, she sitting all the while on his lap without the least shyness or restraint. A more charming companion could not have been imagined. It might be that when she grew older, she would not always be so trustful. New aspects of her character might come into play. If she suspected, for example, that he cared for someone else, she might resent it, and in such a case all sorts of unexpected things are apt to happen; but for the present she was a delightful plaything. Had she really been his daughter, convention would not have allowed him to go on much longer living with her on terms of such complete intimacy; but in a case like this he felt that such scruples were not applicable.

III Epic

FROM The *Mahabharata*

{5TH TO 1ST CENTURY B.C.}

TRANSLATED BY SIR EDWIN ARNOLD {1832-1904}

The two great epic poems of India have been traditionally compared with the two epics of Greek literature. The *Mahabharata* is the *Iliad* of India, embodying as it does the older materials. The *Ramayana* takes its story from an episode in the *Mahabharata* and gives it a romantic treatment in the form of *kavya* or court poetry, much as the story of the *Odyssey* is derived from the account of the fall of Ilium. Since the hero Rama is one of the avatars of the god Vishnu, the *Ramayana* is probably the more popular of the two works. The *Mahabharata,* however, is the true epic of India because it is a primitive poem or *itihasa* and contains a full store of the mythology and religion of the Hindus.

Actually, the *Mahabharata* is a group of poems in one. The

epic story of the great wars between the two branches of the Bharata family (the Pandavas and the Kuravas) embraces only about a fifth of the whole work, which runs to about 100,000 slokas or double octosyllabic couplets, and is contained in eighteen books and a supplement. Embodied are, besides the famous devotional poem the *Bhagavad Gita,* numerous stories which serve as illustrative or instructional material, particularly in the worship of Vishnu and Shiva.

The tale of Sâvitrî is such a narrative. It is told to the exiled king of the Pandavas by way of consoling him for the plight of his much-tried queen, Draupadi. Sâvitrî takes her place alongside the more famous Sita (heroine of the *Ramayana*) and the admirable Shakuntala (whose story is also told in the *Mahabharata*) as the type of ideal Indian womanhood. Devoted and long-suffering like the Hebraic Ruth whom she resembles, she shows at the same time a winning sort of aggressiveness. Her colloquy with Yama, the god of death, in behalf of her doomed spouse, Satyavan, forms the climax of the tale. The good-humored if gloomy god is understandably charmed from his dread intent by her sweet words, and the piously filial Satyavan is returned to his grieving parents.

A few lines from the introduction and conclusion of Arnold's translation are omitted.

৸৩৻৩৶

SÂVITRÎ; OR, LOVE AND DEATH

There was a Raja, pious-minded, just,—
King of the Mâdras,—valiant, wise, and true;
Victorious over sense, a worshipper;
Liberal in giving, prudent, dear alike
To peasant and to townsman; one whose joy
Lived in the weal of all men—Aswapati—
Patient, and free of any woe, he reigned,
Save that his manhood passing, left him lone,
A childless lord; for this he grieved; for this
Heavy observances he underwent,
Subduing needs of flesh, and oftentimes
Making high sacrifice to Sâvitrî;
While, for all food, at each sixth watch he took
A little measured dole; and thus he did
Through sixteen years, (most excellent of Kings!)
Till at the last, divinest Sâvitrî
Grew well-content, and, taking shining shape,
Rose through the flames of sacrifice and showed
Unto that prince her heavenly countenance.
"Raja," the Goddess said—the Gift-bringer—
"Thy piety, thy purity, thy fasts,
The largesse of thy hands, thy heart's wide love,

Thy strength of faith, have pleased me. Choose some boon.
Thy dearest wish, Monarch of Mâdra, ask;
It is not meet such merit go in vain."

The Raja answered: "Goddess, for the sake
Of children I did bear these heavy vows:
If thou art well-content, grant me, I pray,
Fair babes, continuers of my royal line;
This is the boon I choose, obeying law:
For—say the holy seers—the first great law
Is that a man leave seed."

          The Goddess said:
"I knew thine answer, Raja, ere it came;
And He, the Maker of all, hath heard my word
That this might be, The self-existent One
Consenteth. Born there shall be unto thee
A girl more sweet than any eyes have seen;
There is not found on earth so fair a maid!
I that rejoice in the Great Father's will
Know this and tell thee."

          "Oh, so may it be!"
The Raja cried, once and again; and she,
The Goddess, smiled anew, and vanished so;
While Aswapati to his palace went.
There dwelled he, doing justice to all folk;
Till, when the hour was good, the wise King lay
With her that was his first and fairest wife,
And she conceived a girl (a girl, my liege!
Better than many boys), which wonder grew
In darkness,—as the Moon among the stars
Grows from a ring of silver to a round
In the month's waxing days,—and when time came
The Queen a daughter bore, with lotus-eyes,
Lovely of mould. Joyous that Raja made
The birth-feast; and because the fair gift fell
From Sâvitrî the Goddess, and because
It was her day of sacrifice, they gave
The name of "Sâvitrî" unto the child.
In grace and beauty grew the maid, as if
Lakshmi's [40] own self had taken woman's form.
And when swift years her gracious youth made ripe,
Like to an image of dark gold she seemed
Gleaming, with waist so fine, and breasts so deep,
And limbs so rounded. When she moved, all eyes
Gazed after her, as though an Apsara [41]

---

[40] Lakshmi—the beautiful spouse of the god Vishnu. [Ed.]
[41] Apsara—celestial water nymph. [Ed.]

Had lighted out of Swarga. Not one dared,
Of all the noblest lords, to ask for wife
That miracle, with eyes purple and soft
As lotus-petals, that pure perfect maid,
Whose face shed heavenly light where she did go.

Once she had fasted, laved her head, and bowed
Before the shrine of Agni,[42]—as is meet,—
And sacrificed, and spoken what is set
Unto the Brahmans—taking at their hands
The unconsuméd offerings, and so passed
Into her father's presence—bright as 'Sri,[43]
If 'Sri were woman! Meekly at his feet
She laid the blossoms; meekly bent her head,
Folded her palms, and stood, radiant with grace,
Beside the Raja. He, beholding her
Come to her growth, and thus divinely fair,
Yet sued of none, was grieved at heart and spake:
"Daughter, 'tis time we wed thee, but none comes
Asking thee; therefore, thou thyself some youth
Choose for thy lord, a virtuous prince: whoso
Is dear to thee, he shall be dear to me;
For this the rule is by the sages taught—
Hear the commandment, noble maid—'That sire
Who giveth not his child in marriage
Is blamable; and blamable that king
Who weddeth not; and blamable that son
Who, when his father dieth, guardeth not
His mother.' Heeding this," the Raja said,
"Haste thee to choose, and so choose that I bear
No guilt, dear child, before the all-seeing Gods."

Thus spake he; from the royal presence then
Elders and ministers dismissing. She,—
Sweet Sâvitrî,—low lying at his feet,
With soft shame heard her father, and obeyed.
Then, on a bright car mounting, companied
By ministers and sages, Sâvitrî
Journeyed through groves and pleasant woodland-towns
Where pious princes dwelled, in every spot
Paying meet homage at the Brahmans' feet;
And so from forest unto forest passed,
In all the Tirthas making offerings:
Thus did the Princess visit place by place.

[42] Agni—god of fire, after Indra the most worshipped of Vedic gods.
[Ed.]
[43] 'Sri—title of Krishna, beloved reincarnation of the god Vishnu. [Ed.]

The King of Mâdra sat among his lords
With Narada beside him, counselling:
When—(son of Bhârat!) entered Sâvitrî;
From passing through each haunt and hermitage,
Returning with those sages. At the sight
Of Narad seated by the Raja's side,
Humbly she touched the earth before their feet
With bended forehead.

> Then spake Narada:
"Whence cometh thy fair child? and wherefore, King,
Being so ripe in beauty, giv'st thou not
The Princess to a husband?"

> "Even for that
She journeyed," quoth the Raja; "being come,
Hear for thyself, great Rishi, what high lord
My daughter chooseth." Then, being bid to speak
Of Narad and the Raja, Sâvitrî
Softly said this: "In Chalva reigned a prince,
Lordly and just, Dyumutsena named,
Blind, and his only son not come to age;
And this sad king an enemy betrayed
Abusing his infirmity, whereby
Of throne and kingdom was that king bereft;
And with his queen and son, a banished man,
He fled into the wood; and, 'neath its shades,
A life of holiness doth daily lead.
This Raja's son, born in the court, but bred
'Midst forest peace,—royal of blood, and named
Prince Satyavan,—to him my choice is given."

"Aho!" cried Narad, "evil is this choice
Which Sâvitrî hath made, who, knowing not,
Doth name the noble Satyavan her lord:
For, noble is the Prince, sprung of a pair
So just and faithful found in word and deed
The Brahmans styled him 'Truth-born' at his birth.
Horses he loved, and ofttimes would he mould
Coursers of clay, or paint them on the wall;
Therefore 'Chitraśwa' was he also called."

Then spake the King: "By this he shall have grown—
Being of so fair birth—either a prince
Of valor, or a wise and patient saint."

Quoth Narad: "Like the sun is Satyavan
For grace and glory; like Vrihaspati
For counsel; like Mahendra's self for might;
And hath the patience of th' all-bearing earth."

"Is he a liberal giver?" asked the King;
"Loveth he virtue? Wears he noble airs?
Goeth he like a prince, with sweet proud looks?"

"He is as glad to give, if he hath store,
As Rantideva," Narada replied.
"Pious he is; and true as Shivi was,
The son of Usinara; fair of form
(Yayâti was not fairer); sweet of looks
(The Aświns not more gracious); gallant, kind,
Reverent, self-governed, gentle, equitable,
Modest, and constant. Justice lives in him,
And Honor guides. Those who do love a man
Praise him for manhood; they that seek a saint
Laud him for purity, and passions tamed."

"A prince thou showest us," the Raja said,
"All virtues owning. Tell me of some faults,
If fault he hath."

                    "None lives," quoth Narada,
"But some fault mingles with his qualities;
And Satyavan bears that he cannot mend.
The blot which spoils his brightness, the defect
Forbidding yonder Prince, Raja, is this,—
'Tis fated he shall die after a year:
Count from today one year, he perisheth!"

"My Sâvitrî," the King cried; "go, dear child,
Some other husband choose. This hath one fault;
But huge it is, and mars all nobleness:
At the year's end he dies;—'tis Narad's word,
Whom the gods teach."

                    But Sâvitrî replied:
"Once falls a heritage; once a maid yields
Her maidenhood; once doth a father say,
'Choose, I abide thy choice.' These three things done,
Are done forever. By my Prince to live
A year, or many years; be he so great
As Narada hath said, or less than this;
Once have I chosen him, and choose not twice!
My heart resolved, my mouth hath spoken it,
My hand shall execute;—this is my mind!"

Quoth Narad: "Yea, her mind is fixed, O King,
And none will turn her from the path of truth!
Also the virtues of Prince Satyavan
Shall in no other man be found. Give thou
Thy child to him. I gainsay not."

Therewith
The Raja sighed: "Nay, what must be, must be.
She speaketh sooth: and I will give my child,
For thou our Guru art."

Narada said:
"Free be the gift of thy fair daughter, then;
May happiness yet light!—Raja, I go."
So went that sage, returning to his place;
And the King bade the nuptials be prepared.
He bade that all things be prepared,—the robes,
The golden cups; and summoned priest and sage,
Brahman and Rity-yaj and Purôhit;
And, on a day named fortunate, set forth
With Sâvitrî. In the mid-wood they found
Dyumutsena's sylvan court: the King,
Alighting, paced with slow steps to the spot
Where sat the blind lord underneath a sal,
On mats woven of kusa grass. Then passed
Due salutations; worship, as is meet:—
All courteously the Raja spake his name,
All courteously the blind King gave to him
Earth, and a seat, and water in a jar;
Then asked, "What, Maharaja, bringeth thee?"
And Aswapati, answering, told him all.
With eyes fixed full upon Prince Satyavan
He spake: "This is my daughter, Sâvitrî;
Take her from me to be wife to thy son,
According to the law; thou know'st the law."
Dyumutsena said: "Forced from our throne,
Wood-dwellers, hermits, keeping state no more,
We follow right, and how would right be done
If this most lovely lady we should house
Here, in our woods, unfitting home for her?"
Answered the Raja: "Grief and joy we know,
And what is real and seeming,—she and I;
Nor fits this fear with our unshaken minds.
Deny thou not the prayer of him who bows
In friendliness before thee; put not by
His wish who comes well-minded unto thee;
Thy stateless state shows noble; thou and I
Are of one rank; take then this maid of mine
To be thy daughter, since she chooseth me
Thy Satyavan for son."

The blind lord spake:
"It was of old my wish to grow akin,
Raja, with thee, by marriage of our blood;

But ever have I answered to myself,
'Nay, for thy realm is lost;—forego this hope!'
Yet now, so let it be, since so thou wilt;
My welcome guest thou art. Thy will is mine."

Then gathered in the forest all those priests,
And with due rites the royal houses bound
By nuptial tie. And when the Raja saw
His daughter, as befits a princess, wed,
Home went he, glad. And glad was Satyavan,
Winning that beauteous spouse, with all gifts rich;
And she rejoiced to be the wife of him,
So chosen of her soul. But when her sire
Departed, from her neck and arms she stripped
Jewels and gold, and o'er her radiant form
Folded the robe of bark and yellow cloth
Which hermits use; and all hearts did she gain
By gentle actions, soft self-government,
Patience, and peace. The Queen had joy of her
For tender services and mindful cares;
The blind King took delight to know her days
So holy, and her wise words so restrained;
And with her lord in sweet converse she lived
Gracious and loving, dutiful and dear.

But while in the deep forest softly flowed
This quiet life of love and holiness,
The swift moons sped; and always in the heart
Of Sâvitrî, by day and night, there dwelt
The words of Narada,—those dreadful words!

Now, when the pleasant days were passed, which brought
The day of Doom, and Satyavan must die
(For hour by hour the Princess counted them,
Keeping the words of Narada in heart),
Bethinking on the fourth noon he should die,
She set herself to make the "Threefold Fast,"
Three days and nights foregoing food and sleep;
Which, when the King Dyumutsena heard,
Sorrowful he arose, and spake her thus:
"Daughter, a heavy task thou takest on;
Hardly the saintliest soul might such abide."
But Sâvitrî gave answer: "Have no heed:
What I do set myself I will perform;
The vow is made, and I shall keep the vow."
"If it be made," quoth he, "it must be kept;
We cannot bid thee break thy word, once given."

With that the King forbade not, and she sat
Still, as though carved of wood, three days and nights.
But when the third night passed, and brought the day
Whereon her lord must die, she rose betimes,
Made offering on the altar flames, and sang
Softly the morning prayers; then, with clasped palms
Laid on her bosom, meekly came to greet
The King and Queen, and lowlily salute
The gray-haired Brahmans. Thereupon those saints—
Resident in the woods—made answer mild
Unto the Princess: "Be it well with thee,
And with thy lord, for these good deeds of thine."
"May it be well!" she answered; in her heart
Full mournfully that hour of fate awaiting
Foretold of Narad.

                    Then they said to her:
"Daughter, thy vow is kept. Come, now, and eat."
But Sâvitrî replied: "When the sun sinks
This evening, I will eat,—that is my vow."

So when they could not change her, afterward
Came Satyavan, the Prince, bound for the woods,
An axe upon his shoulder; unto whom
Wistfully spake the Princess: "Dearest Lord,
Go not alone to-day; let me come too;
I cannot be apart from thee to-day."

"Why not 'to-day'?" quoth Satyavan. "The wood
Is strange to thee, Belovèd, and its paths
Rough for thy tender feet; besides, with fast
Thy soft limbs faint; how wilt thou walk with me?"

"I am not weak nor weary," she replied,
"And I can walk. Say me not nay, sweet Lord,
I have so great a heart to go with thee."

"If thou hast such good heart," answered the Prince,
"I shall say yea; but first entreat the leave
Of those we reverence, lest a wrong be done."

So, pure and dutiful, she sought that place
Where sat the King and Queen, and, bending low,
Murmured request: "My husband goeth straight
To the great forest, gathering fruits and flowers;
I pray your leave that I may be with him.
To make the Agnihôtra sacrifice

Fetcheth he those, and will not be gainsaid,
But surely goeth. Let me go. A year
Hath rolled since I did fare from th' hermitage
To see our groves in bloom. I have much will
To see them now."

The old King gently said:
"In sooth it is a year since she was given
To be our son's wife, and I mind me not
Of any boon the loving heart hath asked,
Nor any one untimely word she spake;
Let it be as she prayeth. Go, my child;
Have care of Satyavan, and take thy way."

So, being permitted of them both, she went,—
That beauteous lady,—at her husband's side,
With aching heart, albeit her face was bright.
Flower-laden trees her large eyes lighted on,
Green glades where pea-fowl sported, crystal streams,
And soaring hills whose green sides burned with bloom,
Which oft the Prince would bid her gaze upon;
But she as oft turned those great eyes from them
To look on him, her husband, who must die
(For always in her mind were Narad's words).
And so she walked behind him, guarding him,
Bethinking at what hour her lord must die,
Her true heart torn in twain, one half to him
Close-cleaving, one half watching if Death come.

Then, having reached where woodland fruits did grow,
They gathered those, and filled a basket full;
And afterwards the Prince plied hard his axe,
Cutting the sacred fuel. Presently
There crept a pang upon him; a fierce throe
Burned through his brows, and, all asweat, he came
Feebly to Sâvitrî, and moaned: "O wife,
I am thus suddenly too weak for work;
My veins throb, Sâvitrî; my blood runs fire;
It is as if a threefold fork were plunged
Into my brain. Let me lie down, fair Love!
Indeed, I cannot stand upon my feet."

Thereon that noble lady, hastening near,
Stayed him, that would have fallen, with quick arms;
And, sitting on the earth, laid her lord's head
Tenderly in her lap. So bent she, mute,
Fanning his face, and thinking 'twas the day—
The hour—which Narad named—the sure fixed date
Of dreadful end—when, lo! before her rose

A shade majestic. Red his garments were,
His body vast and dark; like fiery suns
The eyes which burned beneath his forehead-cloth;
Armed was he with a noose, awful of mien.
This Form tremendous stood by Satyavan,
Fixing its gaze upon him. At the sight
The fearful Princess started to her feet.
Heedfully laying on the grass his head,
Up started she, with beating heart, and joined
Her palms for supplication, and spake thus
In accents tremulous: "Thou seem'st some god;
Thy mien is more than mortal; make me know
What god thou art, and what thy purpose here."
And Yama said (the dreadful God of death):
"Thou art a faithful wife, O Sâvitrî,
True to thy vows, pious, and dutiful;
Therefore I answer thee. Yama I am!
This Prince, thy lord, lieth at point to die;
Him will I straightway bind and bear from life;
This is my office, and for this I come."

Then Sâvitrî spake sadly: "It is taught,
Thy messengers are sent to fetch the dying;
Why is it, Mightiest, thou art come thyself?"

In pity of her love, the Pitiless
Answered,—the King of all the Dead replied:
"This was a Prince unparalleled, thy lord;
Virtuous as fair, a sea of goodly gifts,
Not to be summoned by a meaner voice
Than Yama's own: therefore is Yama come."

With that the gloomy God fitted his noose,
And forced forth from the Prince the soul of him—
Subtile, a thumb in length—which being reft,
Breath stayed, blood stopped, his body's grace was gone,
And all life's warmth to stony coldness turned.
Then, binding it, the Silent Presence bore
Satyavan's soul away toward the South.

But Sâvitrî the Princess followed him;
Being so bold in wifely purity,
So holy by her love: and so upheld,
She followed him.

                    Presently Yama turned.
"Go back," quoth he; "pay him the funeral dues.
Enough, O Sâvitrî! is wrought for love;
Go back! too far already hast thou come."

Then Sâvitrî made answer: "I must go
Where my lord goes, or where my lord is borne;
Nought other is my duty. Nay, I think,
By reason of my vows, my services
Done to the Gurus, and my faultless love,
Grant but thy grace, I shall unhindered go.
The sages teach that to walk seven steps,
One with another, maketh good men friends;
Beseech thee, let me say a verse to thee:—

> Be master of thyself, if thou wilt be
> Servant of Duty. Such as thou shalt see
> Not self-subduing, do no deeds of good
> In youth or age, in household or in wood.
> But wise men know that virtue is best bliss,
> And all by some one way may reach to this.
> It needs not men should pass through orders four
> To come to knowledge: doing right is more
> Than any learning; therefore sages say
> Best and most excellent is Virtue's way."

Spake Yama then: "Return! yet I am moved
By those soft words; justly their accents fell,
And sweet and reasonable was their sense.
See, now, thou faultless one. Except this life
I bear away, ask any boon from me;
It shall not be denied."

Sâvitrî said:

"Let, then, the King, my husband's father, have
His eyesight back, and be his strength restored,
And let him live anew, strong as the sun."

"I give this gift," Yama replied: "thy wish,
Blameless, shall be fulfilled. But now go back;
Already art thou wearied, and our road
Is hard and long. Turn back, lest thou, too, die."

The Princess answered: "Weary am I not,
So I walk nigh my lord. Where he is borne,
Thither wend I. Most mighty of the gods,
I follow whereso'er thou takest him.
A verse is writ on this, if thou wouldst hear:—

> There is nought better than to be
> With noble souls in company:
> There is nought dearer than to wend
> With good friends faithful to the end.
> This is the love whose fruit is sweet;
> Therefore to bide therein is meet."

Spake Yama, smiling: "Beautiful! Thy words
Delight me; they are excellent, and teach
Wisdom unto the wise, singing soft truth.
Look, now! except the life of Satyavan,
Ask yet another—any—boon from me."

Sâvitrî said: "Let, then, the pious King,
My husband's father, who hath lost his throne,
Have back the Râj; and let him rule his realm
In happy righteousness. This boon I ask."

"He shall have back the throne," Yama replied,
"And he shall reign in righteousness: these things
Will surely fall. But thou, gaining thy wish,
Return anon; so shalt thou 'scape sore ill."

"Ah, awful God! who hold'st the world in leash,"
The Princess said, "restraining evil men,
And leading good men,—even unconscious,—there
Where they attain, hear yet these famous words:—

"The constant virtues of the good are tenderness and love
To all that lives—in earth, air, sea—great, small—below,
        above,
Compassionate of heart, they keep a gentle thought for each,
Kind in their actions, mild in will, and pitiful of speech;
Who pitieth not he hath not faith; full many an one so lives,
But when an enemy seeks help the good man gladly gives."

"As water to the thirsting," Yama said,
"Princess, thy words melodious are to me.
Except the life of Satyavan thy lord,
Ask one boon yet again, for I will grant."

Answer made Sâvitrî: "The King, my sire,
Hath no male child. Let him see many sons
Begotten of his body, who may keep
The royal line long regnant. This I ask."

"So it shall be!" the Lord of death replied;
"A hundred fair preservers of his race
Thy sire shall boast. But this wish being won,
Return, dear Princess; thou hast come too far."

"It is not far for me," quoth Sâvitrî,
"Since I am near my husband; nay, my heart
Is set to go as far as to the end;
But hear these other verses, if thou wilt:—

        "By that sunlit name thou bearest,
            Thou, Vaivaswata! art dearest;
        Those that as their Lord proclaim thee,

       King of Righteousness do name thee:
       Better than themselves the wise
       Trust the righteous. Each relies
       Most upon the good, and makes
       Friendship with them. Friendship takes
       Fear from hearts; yet friends betray,
       In good men we may trust alway."

"Sweet lady," Yama said, "never were words
Spoke better; never truer heard by ear;
Lo! I am pleased with thee. Except this soul,
Ask one gift yet again, and get thee home."

"I ask thee, then," quickly the Princess cried,
"Sons, many sons, born of my body: boys;
Satyavan's children; lovely, valiant, strong;
Continuers of their line. Grant this, kind God."

"I grant it," Yama answered; "thou shalt bear
Those sons thy heart desireth, valiant, strong.
Therefore go back, that years be given thee.
Too long a path thou treadest, dark and rough."

But, sweeter than before, the Princess sang:—
       "In paths of peace and virtue
       Always the good remain;
       And sorrow shall not stay with them,
       Nor long access of pain;
       At meeting or at parting
       Joys to their bosom strike;
       For good to good is friendly,
       And virtue loves her like.
       The great sun goes his journey
       By their strong truth impelled;
       By their pure lives and penances
       Is earth itself upheld;
       Of all which live or shall live
       Upon its hills and fields,
       Pure hearts are the 'protectors,'
       For virtue saves and shields.

       "Never are noble spirits
       Poor while their like survive;
       True love has gems to render,
       And virtue wealth to give.
       Never is lost or wasted
       The goodness of the good;
       Never against a mercy,
       Against a right, it stood;

And seeing this, that virtue
Is always friend to all,
The virtuous and true-hearted,
Men their 'protectors' call."

"Line for line, Princess! as thou sangest so,"
Quoth Yama, "all that lovely praise of good,
Grateful to hallowed minds, lofty in sound,
And couched in dulcet numbers—word by word—
Dearer thou grew'st to me. O thou great heart,
Perfect and firm! ask any boon from me,—
Ask an incomparable boon!"

                         She cried
Swiftly, no longer stayed: "Not heaven I crave,
Nor heavenly joys, nor bliss incomparable,
Hard to be granted even by thee; but *him*,
My sweet lord's life, without which I am dead;
Give me that gift of gifts! I will not take
Aught less without him,—not one boon,—no praise,
No splendors, no rewards,—not even those sons
Whom thou didst promise. Ah, thou wilt not, now,
Bear hence the father of them, and my hope!
Make thy free word good; give me Satyavan
Alive once more."

                    And thereupon the God—
The Lord of Justice, high Vaivaswata—
Loosened the noose and freed the Prince's soul,
And gave it to the lady, saying this,
With eyes grown tender: "See, thou sweetest queen
Of women, brightest jewel of thy kind!
Here is thy husband. He shall live and reign
Side by side with thee,—saved by thee,—in peace,
And fame, and wealth, and health, many long years;
For pious sacrifices world-renowned.
Boys shalt thou bear to him, as I did grant,—
Kshatriya kings, fathers of kings to be,
Sustainers of thy line. Also, thy sire
Shall see his name upheld by sons of sons,
Like the immortals, valiant, Mâlavas."

These gifts the awful Yama gave, and went
Unto his place; but Sâvitrî—made glad,
Having her husband's soul—sped to the glade
Where his corse lay. She saw it there, and ran,
And, sitting on the earth, lifted its head,
And lulled it on her lap full tenderly.
Thereat warm life returned: the white lips moved;

The fixed eyes brightened, gazed, and gazed again;
As when one starts from sleep and sees a face—
The well-belovèd's—grow clear, and, smiling, wakes,
So Satyavan. "Long have I slumbered, Dear,"
He sighed, "why didst thou not arouse me? Where
Is gone that gloomy man that haled at me?"

Answered the Princess: "Long, indeed, thy sleep,
Dear Lord, and deep; for he that haled at thee
Was Yama, God of Death; but he is gone;
And thou, being rested and awake, rise now,
If thou canst rise; for, look, the night is near!"

Thus, newly living, newly waked, the Prince
Glanced all around upon the blackening groves,
And whispered: "I came forth to pluck the fruits,
O slender-waisted, with thee: then, some pang
Shot through my temples while I hewed the wood,
And I lay down upon thy lap, dear wife,
And slept. This do I well remember. Next—
Was it a dream,—that vast, dark, mighty One
Whom I beheld? Oh, if thou saw'st and know'st,
Was it in fancy, or in truth, he came?"

Softly she answered: "Night is falling fast;
To-morrow I will tell thee all, dear Lord.
Get to thy feet, and let us seek our home.
Guide us, ye Gods! the gloom spreads fast around;
The creatures of the forest are abroad,
Which roam and cry by night. I hear the leaves
Rustle with beasts that creep. I hear this way
The yells of prowling jackals; beasts do haunt
In the southern wood; their noises make me fear."

"The wood is black with shadows," quoth the Prince;
"You would not know the path; you could not see it;
We cannot go."

        She said: "There was to-day
A fire within this forest, and it burned
A withered tree; yonder the branches flame.
I'll fetch a lighted brand and kindle wood:
See! there is fuel here. Art thou so vexed
Because we cannot go? Grieve not. The path
Is hidden, and thy limbs are not yet knit.
To-morrow, when the way grows clear, depart;
But, if thou wilt, let us abide to-night."

And Satyavan replied: "The pains are gone
Which racked my brow; my limbs seem strong again;
Fain would I reach our home, if thou wilt aid.

Ever betimes I have been wont to come
At evening to the place where those we love
Await us. Ah, what trouble they will know,
Father and mother, searching now for us!
They prayed me hasten back. How they will weep,
Not seeing me; for there is none save me
To guard them. 'Quick return,' they said; 'our lives
Live upon thine; thou art our eyes, our breath,
Our hope of lineage; unto thee we look
For funeral cakes, for mourning feasts, for all.'
What will these do alone, not seeing me,
Who am their stay? Shame on the idle sleep
And foolish dreams which cost them all this pain!
I cannot tarry here. My sire belike,
Having no eyes, asks at this very hour
News of me from each one that walks the wood.
Let us depart. Not, Sâvitrî, for us
Think I, but for those reverend ones at home,
Mourning me now. If they fare well, 't is well
With me; if ill, nought's well; what would please them
Is wise and good to do."

                    Thereat he beat
Faint hands, eager to go; and Sâvitrî,
Seeing him weeping, wiped his tears away,
And gently spake: "If I have kept the fast,
Made sacrifices, given gifts, and wrought
Service to holy men, may this black night
Be bright to those and thee; for we will go.
I think I never spoke a false word once
In all my life, not even in jest; I pray
My truth may help to-night them, thee, and me!"

"Let us set forth," he cried; "if any harm
Hath fallen on those so dear, I could not live;
I swear it by my soul! As thou art sweet,
Helpful, and virtuous, aid me to depart."

Then Sâvitrî arose, and tied her hair,
And lifted up her lord upon his feet;
Who, as he swept the dry leaves from his cloth,
Looked on the basket full of fruit. "But thou,"
The Princess said, "to-morrow shalt bring these;
Give me thine axe, the axe is good to take."
So saying, she hung the basket on a branch,
And in her left hand carrying the axe,
Came back, and laid his arm across her neck,
Her right arm winding round him. So they went.

FROM The *Shahnamah* of Firdausi

{A.D. 932-1020}

TRANSLATED BY JAMES ATKINSON {1780-1852}

In the middle years of the 19th century, when Matthew Arnold was looking about for a theme that would lift English poetry out of the querulousness that characterized the Victorian mood, he hit upon the story of the combat between the legendary Persian warrior Rustem and his son Sohráb. Here was a bit of action out of the clear, untainted ages when emotions were elemental and grand, before the disease of modern life, with its Faustian intro-spectiveness, had set in. The famous poem which he wrote on the subject, based less on Firdausi's epic than on secondhand accounts of it, has given Firdausi his largest fame in English-speaking circles. Other popular retellings of episodes from the *Shahnamah* have made the myths of ancient Persia almost as familiar to Eng-lish and American children as the hero tales of Greece and Rome.

But the curiosity of the 20th century about the nature of myth has extended the area of interest in the *Shahnamah*. Jungian psychologists will not easily permit a father-son combat to pass as a mere adventure tale. The Sohráb and Rustem episode has re-ceived serious treatment by folklorists. Whether this tale of a son-killing father represents the protest of a matriarchal society or is the statement of a more immediate Freudian family situation, the reader may judge. At any rate, the myth has recoiled upon Matthew Arnold, who has been charged with projecting his own suppressed desire to do battle with a stronger father, the renowned Thomas Arnold of Rugby.

This episode from the *Shahnamah* is but the best known of many stories about the Persian champion Rustem, and he is but the most famous of the numerous large figures—legendary, semi-legendary, and historical—who move about in the pages of a vast and wandering epic. Firdausi, the father of modern Persian poetry, collected the old Iranian legends that had been submerged by the Mohammedan conquest of his land and retold them in a book of 60,000 couplets that is seven times the length of the *Iliad*. Always regarded by the Persians as their national poem, it has in the recent revival of that land come into a new life. Verses from it are recited on holiday occasions, and Firdausi's leading position in the annals of Persian literature has been unmistakably reaffirmed.

The first selection relates the meeting of Rustem with the maiden Tahmíneh, following the loss of his horse Rakush in Tartar territory. Their marriage, Rustem's departure, and the sub-sequent birth of the powerful boy Sohráb are quickly told, as well as the mother's decision to keep the news from the father. But with fatal inevitability, Sohráb grows up to become the champion of the Túránian hordes (also called Tartars or Turks), led by

Afrásiáb, Rustem's deadly enemy. The scheme to bring father
and son to battle with one another is hatched and the catastrophe
ominously forecast.

The second selection shows the working out of Afrásiáb's plan
by the uncontrollable hand of fate. The captive Persian, Hujír,
treacherously refuses to disclose the identity of Rustem to Sohráb,
who is therefore compelled to fight the Persian champion, by
whom he is at last felled. On the Persian side King Káús refuses
the balm that might have saved the life of Sohráb, and the two an-
tagonists are left isolated from their war-lords, the one to die,
the other to mourn. There remains only to tell the story of the
mother's grief and her consequent death.

ﻟﻤﺰﻗﺤﺴﺎ

THE BIRTH OF SOHRÁB

One watch had passed, and still sweet slumber shed
Its magic power around the hero's head—
When forth Tahmíneh came—a damsel held
An amber taper, which the gloom dispelled,
And near his pillow stood; in beauty bright,
The monarch's daughter struck his wondering sight.
Clear as the moon, in glowing charms arrayed,
Her winning eyes the light of heaven displayed;
Her cypress form entranced the gazer's view,
Her waving curls, the heart, resistless, drew,
Her eye-brows like the Archer's bended bow;
Her ringlets, snares; her cheek, the rose's glow,
Mixed with the lily—from her ear-tips hung
Rings rich and glittering, star-like; and her tongue,
And lips, all sugared sweetness—pearls the while
Sparkled within a mouth formed to beguile.
Her presence dimmed the stars, and breathing round
Fragrance and joy, she scarcely touched the ground,
So light her step, so graceful—every part
Perfect, and suited to her spotless heart.

Rustem, surprised, the gentle maid addressed,
And asked what lovely stranger broke his rest.
"What is thy name," he said—"what dost thou seek
Amidst the gloom of night? Fair vision, speak!"

"O thou," she softly sigh'd, "of matchless fame!
With pity hear, Tahmíneh is my name!
The pangs of love my anxious heart employ,
And flattering promise long-expected joy;
No curious eye has yet these features seen,
My voice unheard, beyond the sacred screen.

How often have I listened with amaze,
To thy great deeds, enamoured of thy praise;
How oft from every tongue I've heard the strain,
And thought of thee—and sighed, and sighed again.
The ravenous eagle, hovering o'er his prey,
Starts at thy gleaming sword and flies away:
Thou art the slayer of the Demon brood,
And the fierce monsters of the echoing wood.
Where'er thy mace is seen, shrink back the bold,
Thy javelin's flash all tremble to behold.
Enchanted with the stories of thy fame,
My fluttering heart responded to thy name;
And whilst their magic influence I felt,
In prayer for thee devotedly I knelt;
And fervent vowed, thus powerful glory charms,
No other spouse should bless my longing arms.
Indulgent heaven propitious to my prayer,
Now brings thee hither to reward my care.
Túrán's dominions thou hast sought, alone,
By night, in darkness—thou, the mighty one!
O claim my hand, and grant my soul's desire;
Ask me in marriage of my royal sire;
Perhaps a boy our wedded love may crown,
Whose strength like thine may gain the world's
  renown.
Nay more—for Samengán will keep my word—
Rakush to thee again shall be restored."

The damsel thus her ardent thought expressed,
And Rustem's heart beat joyous in his breast,
Hearing her passion—not a word was lost,
And Rakush safe, by him still valued most;
He called her near; with graceful step she came,
And marked with throbbing pulse his kindled flame.

And now a Múbid,[44] from the Champion-knight,
Requests the royal sanction to the rite;
O'erjoyed, the King the honoured suit approves,
O'erjoyed to bless the doting child he loves,
And happier still, in showering smiles around,
To be allied to warrior so renowned.
When the delighted father, doubly blest,
Resigned his daughter to his glorious guest,
The people shared the gladness which it gave,
The union of the beauteous and the brave.
To grace their nuptial day—both old and young,
The hymeneal gratulations sung:
"May this young moon bring happiness and joy,

[44] Zoroastrian priest. [Ed.]

And every source of enmity destroy."
The marriage-bower received the happy pair,
And love and transport shower'd their blessings
    there.

Ere from his lofty sphere the morn had thrown
His glittering radiance, and in splendour shone,
The mindful Champion, from his sinewy arm
His bracelet drew, the soul-ennobling charm;
And, as he held the wondrous gift with pride,
He thus address'd his love-devoted bride!
"Take this," he said, "and if, by gracious heaven,
A daughter for thy solace should be given,
Let it among her ringlets be displayed,
And joy and honour will await the maid;
But should kind fate increase the nuptial-joy,
And make thee mother of a blooming boy,
Around his arm this magic bracelet bind,
To fire with virtuous deeds his ripening mind;
The strength of Sám will nerve his manly form,
In temper mild, in valour like the storm;
His not the dastard fate to shrink, or turn
From where the lions of the battle burn;
To him the soaring eagle from the sky
Will stoop, the bravest yield to him, or fly;
Thus shall his bright career imperious claim
The well-won honours of immortal fame!"
Ardent he said, and kissed her eyes and face,
And lingering held her in a fond embrace.
When the bright sun his radiant brow displayed,
And earth in all its loveliest hues arrayed,
The Champion rose to leave his spouse's side,
The warm affections of his weeping bride.
For her, too soon the winged moments flew,
Too soon, alas! the parting hour she knew;
Clasped in his arms, with many a streaming tear,
She tried, in vain, to win his deafen'd ear;
Still tried, ah fruitless struggle! to impart,
The swelling anguish of her bursting heart.
The father now with gratulations due
Rustem approaches, and displays to view
The fiery war-horse—welcome as the light
Of heaven, to one immersed in deepest night;
The Champion, wild with joy, fits on the rein,
And girds the saddle on his back again;
Then mounts, and leaving sire and wife behind,
Onward to Sístán rushes like the wind.

But when returned to Zábul's [45] friendly shade,
None knew what joys the Warrior had delayed;
Still, fond remembrance, with endearing thought,
Oft to his mind the scene of rapture brought.

When nine slow-circling months had roll'd away,
Sweet-smiling pleasure hailed the brightening day—
A wondrous boy Tahmíneh's tears supprest,
And lull'd the sorrows of her heart to rest;
To him, predestined to be great and brave,
The name Sohráb his tender mother gave;
And as he grew, amazed, the gathering throng,
View'd his large limbs, his sinews firm and strong;
His infant years no soft endearment claimed:
Athletic sports his eager soul inflamed;
Broad at the chest and taper round the loins,
Where to the rising hip the body joins;
Hunter and wrestler; and so great his speed,
He could o'ertake, and hold the swiftest steed.
His noble aspect, and majestic grace,
Betrayed the offspring of a glorious race.
How, with a mother's ever anxious love,
Still to retain him near her heart she strove!
For when the father's fond inquiry came,
Cautious, she still concealed his birth and name,
And feign'd a daughter born, the evil fraught
With misery to avert—but vain the thought;
Not many years had passed, with downy flight,
Ere he, Tahmíneh's wonder and delight,
With glistening eye, and youthful ardour warm,
Filled her foreboding bosom with alarm.
"O now relieve my heart!" he said, "declare,
From whom I sprang and breathe the vital air.
Since, from my childhood I have ever been,
Amidst my play-mates of superior mien;
Should friend or foe demand my father's name,
Let not my silence testify my shame!
If still concealed, you falter, still delay,
A mother's blood shall wash the crime away."

"This wrath forego," the mother answering cried,
And joyful hear to whom thou art allied.
A glorious line precedes thy destined birth,
The mightiest heroes of the sons of earth.
The deeds of Sám remotest realms admire,
And Zál, and Rustem thy illustrious sire!" [46]

[45] Zabulistan was Rustem's home province.
[46] Sám and Zál were Rustem's grandfather and father respectively. [Ed.]

In private, then, she Rustem's letter placed
Before his view, and brought with eager haste
Three sparkling rubies, wedges three of gold,
From Persia sent—"Behold," she said, "behold
Thy father's gifts, will these thy doubts remove
The costly pledges of paternal love!
Behold this bracelet charm, of sovereign power
To baffle fate in danger's awful hour;
But thou must still the perilous secret keep,
Nor ask the harvest of renown to reap;
For when, by this peculiar signet known,
Thy glorious father shall demand his son,
Doomed from her only joy in life to part,
O think what pangs will rend thy mother's heart!—
Seek not the fame which only teems with woe;
Afrásiyáb is Rustem's deadliest foe!
And if by him discovered, him I dread,
Revenge will fall upon thy guiltless head."
    The youth replied: "In vain thy sighs and tears,
The secret breathes and mocks thy idle fears.
No human power can fate's decree control,
Or check the kindled ardour of my soul.
Then why from me the bursting truth conceal?
My father's foes even now my vengeance feel;
Even now in wrath my native legions rise,
And sounds of desolation strike the skies;
Káús himself, hurled from his ivory throne,
Shall yield to Rustem the imperial crown,
And thou, my mother, still in triumph seen,
Of lovely Persia hailed the honoured queen!
Then shall Túrán unite beneath my band,
And drive this proud oppressor from the land!
Father and Son, in virtuous league combined,
No savage despot shall enslave mankind;
When Sun and Moon o'er heaven refulgent blaze,
Shall little stars obtrude their feeble rays?"
    He paused, and then: "O mother, I must now
My father seek, and see his lofty brow;
Be mine a horse, such as a prince demands,
Fit for the dusty field, a warrior's hands;
Strong as an elephant his form should be,
And chested like the stag, in motion free,
And swift as bird, or fish; it would disgrace
A warrior bold on foot to show his face."

    The mother, seeing how his heart was bent,
His day-star rising in the firmament,
Commands the stables to be searched to find

Among the steeds one suited to his mind;
Pressing their backs he tries their strength and nerve,
Bent double to the ground their bellies curve;
Not one, from neighbouring plain and mountain
     brought,
Equals the wish with which his soul is fraught;
Fruitless on every side he anxious turns,
Fruitless, his brain with wild impatience burns,
But when at length they bring the destined steed,
From Rakush bred, of lightning's winged speed,
Fleet, as the arrow from the bow-string flies,
Fleet, as the eagle darting through the skies,
Rejoiced he springs, and, with a nimble bound,
Vaults in his seat, and wheels the courser round;
"With such a horse—thus mounted, what remains?
Káús, the Persian King, no longer reigns!"
High flushed he speaks—with youthful pride elate,
Eager to crush the Monarch's glittering state;
He grasps his javelin with a hero's might,
And pants with ardour for the field of fight.

Soon o'er the realm his fame expanding spread,
And gathering thousands hasten'd to his aid.
His Grand-sire, pleased, beheld the warrior-train
Successive throng and darken all the plain;
And bounteously his treasures he supplied,
Camels, and steeds, and gold.—In martial pride,
Sohráb was seen—a Grecian helmet graced
His brow—and costliest mail his limbs embraced.

Afrásiyáb now hears with ardent joy,
The bold ambition of the warrior-boy,
Of him who, perfumed with the milky breath
Of infancy, was threatening war and death,
And bursting sudden from his mother's side,
Had launched his bark upon the perilous tide.

The insidious King sees well the tempting hour,
Favouring his arms against the Persian power,
And thence, in haste, the enterprise to share,
Twelve thousand veterans selects with care;
To Húmán and Bármán the charge consigns,
And thus his force with Samengán combines;
But treacherous first his martial chiefs he prest,
To keep the secret fast within their breast:—
"For this bold youth must not his father know,
Each must confront the other as his foe—
Such is my vengeance! With unhallowed rage,
Father and Son shall dreadful battle wage!
Unknown the youth shall Rustem's force withstand,

And soon o'erwhelm the bulwark of the land.
Rustem removed, the Persian throne is ours,
An easy conquest to confederate powers;
And then, secured by some propitious snare,
Sohráb himself our galling bonds shall wear.
Or should the Son by Rustem's falchion bleed,
The father's horror at that fatal deed,
Will rend his soul, and 'midst his sacred grief,
Káús in vain will supplicate relief."

The tutored chiefs advance with speed, and bring
Imperial presents to the future king;
In stately pomp the embassy proceeds;
Ten loaded camels, ten unrivalled steeds,
A golden crown, and throne, whose jewels bright
Gleam in the sun, and shed a sparkling light.
A letter too the crafty tyrant sends,
And fraudful thus the glorious aim commends.—
"If Persia's spoils invite thee to the field,
Accept the aid my conquering legions yield;
Led by two Chiefs of valour and renown,
Upon thy head to place the kingly crown."

Elate with promised fame, the youth surveys
The regal vest, the throne's irradiant blaze,
The golden crown, the steeds, the sumptuous load
Of ten strong camels, craftily bestowed;
Salutes the Chiefs, and views on every side,
The lengthening ranks with various arms supplied.
The march begins—the brazen drums resound,
His moving thousands hide the trembling ground;
For Persia's verdant land he wields the spear,
And blood and havoc mark his groaning rear.

THE DEATH OF SOHRÁB

Now war and vengeance claim,
Collected thought and deeds of mighty name;
The jointed mail his vigorous body clasps,
His sinewy hand the shining javelin grasps;
Like a mad elephant he meets the foe,
His steed a moving mountain—deeply glow
His cheeks with passionate ardour, as he flies
Resistless onwards, and with sparkling eyes,
Full on the centre drives his daring horse—
The yielding Persians fly his furious course;
As the wild ass impetuous springs away,
When the fierce lion thunders on his prey.

By every sign of strength and martial power,
They think him Rustem in his direst hour;
On Káus now his proud defiance falls,
Scornful to him the stripling warrior calls:
"And why art thou misnamed of royal strain?
What work of thine befits the tented plain?
This thirsty javelin seeks thy coward breast;
Thou and thy thousands doomed to endless rest.
True to my oath, which time can never change,
On thee, proud King! I hurl my just revenge.
The blood of Zind inspires my burning hate,
And dire resentment hurries on thy fate;
Whom canst thou send to try the desperate strife?
What valiant Chief, regardless of his life?
Where now can Fríburz, Tús, Gíw, Gúdarz, be,
And the world-conquering Rustem, where is he?"
     No prompt reply from Persian lip ensued—
Then rushing on, with demon-strength endued,
Sohráb elate his javelin waved around,
And hurled the bright pavilion to the ground;
With horror Káus feels destruction nigh,
And cries: "For Rustem's needful succour fly!
     This frantic Túrk, triumphant on the plain,
     Withers the souls of all my warrior train."
That instant Tús the mighty Champion sought,
And told the deeds the Tartar Chief had wrought.
" 'Tis ever thus, the brainless Monarch's due!
Shame and disaster still his steps pursue!"
This saying, from his tent he soon descried,
The wild confusion spreading far and wide;
And saddled Rakush—whilst, in deep dismay,
Girgín incessant cried—"Speed, speed, away."
Rehám bound on the mace, Tús promptly ran,
And buckled on the broad Burgustuwán.
Rustem, meanwhile, the thickening tumult hears
And in his heart, untouched by human fears,
Says: "What is this, that feeling seems to stun!
This battle must be led by Ahirmun,[47]
The awful day of doom must have begun."
In haste he arms, and mounts his bounding steed,
The growing rage demands redoubled speed;
The leopard's skin he o'er his shoulders throws,
The regal girdle round his middle glows.
High wave his glorious banners; broad revealed,
The pictured dragons glare along the field

---

[47] Ahrimun, the spirit of evil. [Ed.]

Borne by Zúára.[48] When, surprised, he views
Sohráb, endued with ample breast and thews,
Like Sám Suwár, he beckons him apart;
The youth advances with a gallant heart,
Willing to prove his adversary's might,
By single combat to decide the fight;
And eagerly, "Together brought," he cries,
"Remote from us be foemen, and allies,
And though at once by either host surveyed,
Ours be the strife which asks no mortal aid."

Rustem, considerate, view'd him o'er and o'er,
So wondrous graceful was the form he bore,
And frankly said: "Experience flows with age,
And many a foe has felt my conquering rage;
Much have I seen, superior strength and art
Have borne my spear thro' many a demon's heart;
Only behold me on the battle plain,
Wait till thou see'st this hand the war sustain,
And if on thee should changeful fortune smile,
Thou needst not fear the monster of the Nile!
But soft compassion melts my soul to save,
A youth so blooming with a mind so brave!"

The generous speech Sohráb attentive heard,
His heart expanding glowed at every word:
"One question answer, and in answering show,
That truth should ever from a warrior flow;
Art thou not Rustem, whose exploits sublime,
Endear his name thro' every distant clime?"
"I boast no station of exalted birth,
No proud pretensions to distinguished worth;
To him inferior, no such powers are mine,
No offspring I of Nírum's glorious line!"
The prompt denial dampt his filial joy,
All hope at once forsook the Warrior-boy,
His opening day of pleasure, and the bloom
Of cherished life, immersed in shadowy gloom.
Perplexed with what his mother's words implied;—
A narrow space is now prepared, aside,
For single combat. With disdainful glance
Each boldly shakes his death-devoting lance,
And rushes forward to the dubious fight;
Thoughts high and brave their burning souls excite;
Now sword to sword; continuous strokes resound,
Till glittering fragments strew the dusty ground.
Each grasps his massive club with added force,

[48] Zúára, Rustem's brother. [Ed.]

The folding mail is rent from either horse;
It seemed as if the fearful day of doom
Had, clothed in all its withering terrors, come.
Their shattered corslets yield defence no more—
At length they breathe, defiled with dust and gore;
Their gasping throats with parching thirst are dry,
Gloomy and fierce they roll the lowering eye,
And frown defiance. Son and Father driven
To mortal strife! are these the ways of Heaven?
The various swarms which boundless ocean breeds,
The countless tribes which crop the flowery meads,
All know their kind, but hapless man alone
Has no instinctive feeling for his own!
Compell'd to pause, by every eye surveyed,
Rustem, with shame, his wearied strength betrayed;
Foil'd by a youth in battle's mid career,
His groaning spirit almost sunk with fear;
Recovering strength, again they fiercely meet;
Again they struggle with redoubled heat;
With bended bows they furious now contend;
And feather'd shafts in rattling showers descend;
Thick as autumnal leaves they strew the plain,
Harmless their points, and all their fury vain.
And now they seize each other's girdle-band;
Rustem, who, if he moved his iron hand,
Could shake a mountain, and to whom a rock
Seemed soft as wax, tried, with one mighty stroke,
To hurl him thundering from his fiery steed,
But Fate forbids the gallant youth should bleed;
Finding his wonted nerves relaxed, amazed
That hand he drops which never had been raised
Uncrowned with victory, even when demons fought,
And pauses, wildered with despairing thought.
Sohráb again springs with terrific grace,
And lifts, from saddle-bow, his ponderous mace;
With gather'd strength the quick-descending blow
Wounds in its fall, and stuns the unwary foe;
Then thus contemptuous: "All thy power is gone;
Thy charger's strength exhausted as thy own;
Thy bleeding wounds with pity I behold;
O seek no more the combat of the bold!"

Rustem to this reproach made no reply,
But stood confused—meanwhile, tumultuously
The legions closed; with soul-appalling force,
Troop rushed on troop, o'erwhelming man and horse;
Sohráb, incensed, the Persian host engaged,

Furious along the scattered lines he raged;
Fierce as a wolf he rode on every side,
The thirsty earth with streaming gore was dyed.
Midst the Túránians, then, the Champion sped,
And like a tiger heaped the fields with dead.
But when the Monarch's danger struck his thought,
Returning swift, the stripling youth he sought;
Grieved to the soul, the mighty Champion view'd
His hands and mail with Persian blood imbrued;
And thus exclaimed with lion-voice—"O say,
Why with the Persians dost thou war to-day?
Why not with me alone decide the fight,
Thou'rt like a wolf that seek'st the fold by night."

To this Sohráb his proud assent expressed—
And Rustem, answering, thus the youth addressed.
"Night-shadows now are thickening o'er the plain,
The morrow's sun must see our strife again;
In wrestling let us then exert our might!"
He said, and eve's last glimmer sunk in night.

Thus as the skies a deeper gloom displayed,
The stripling's life was hastening into shade!

The gallant heroes to their tents retired,
The sweets of rest their wearied limbs required:
Sohráb, delighted with his brave career,
Describes the fight in Húmán's anxious ear:
Tells how he forced unnumbered Chiefs to yield,
And stood himself the victor of the field!
"But let the morrow's dawn," he cried, "arrive,
And not one Persian shall the day survive;
Meanwhile let wine its strengthening balm impart,
And add new zeal to every drooping heart."
The valiant Gíw with Rustem pondering stood,
And, sad, recalled the scene of death and blood;
Grief and amazement heaved the frequent sigh,
And almost froze the crimson current dry.
Rustem, oppressed by Gíw's desponding thought,
Amidst his Chiefs the mournful Monarch sought;
To him he told Sohráb's tremendous sway,
The dire misfortunes of this luckless day;
Told with what grasping force he tried, in vain,
To hurl the wondrous stripling to the plain:
"The whispering zephyr might as well aspire
To shake a mountain—such his strength and fire.
But night came on—and, by agreement, we
Must meet again to-morrow—who shall be
Victorious, Heaven knows only:—for by Heaven,
Victory or death to man is ever given."

This said, the King, o'erwhelmed in deep despair,
Passed the dread night in agony and prayer.

The Champion, silent, joined his bands at rest,
And spurned at length despondence from his breast;
Removed from all, he cheered Zúára's heart,
And nerved his soul to bear a trying part:—
"Ere early morning gilds the ethereal plain,
In martial order range my warrior-train;
And when I meet in all his glorious pride,
This valiant Túrk whom late my rage defied,
Should fortune's smiles my arduous task requite,
Bring them to share the triumph of my might;
But should success the stripling's arm attend,
And dire defeat and death my glories end,
To their loved homes my brave associates guide;
Let bowery Zábul all their sorrows hide—
Comfort my venerable father's heart;
In gentlest words my heavy fate impart.
The dreadful tidings to my mother bear,
And soothe her anguish with the tenderest care;
Say, that the will of righteous Heaven decreed,
That thus in arms her mighty son should bleed.
Enough of fame my various toils acquired,
When warring demons, bathed in blood, expired.
Were life prolonged a thousand lingering years,
Death comes at last and ends our mortal fears;
Kirshásp, and Sám, and Narímán, the best
And bravest heroes, who have ever blest
This fleeting world, were not endued with power,
To stay the march of fate one single hour;
The world for them possessed no fixed abode,
The path to death's cold regions must be trod;
Then, why lament the doom ordained for all?
Thus Jemshíd fell, and thus must Rustem fall."

When the bright dawn proclaimed the rising day,
The warriors armed, impatient of delay;
But first Sohráb, his proud confederate nigh,
Thus wistful spoke, as swelled the boding sigh—
"Now, mark my great antagonist in arms!
His noble form my filial bosom warms;
My mother's tokens shine conspicuous here,
And all the proofs my heart demands, appear;
Sure this is Rustem, whom my eyes engage!
Shall I, O grief! provoke my Father's rage?
Offended Nature then would curse my name,

And shuddering nations echo with my shame."
He ceased, then Húmán: "Vain, fantastic thought,
Oft have I been where Persia's Champion fought;
And thou hast heard, what wonders he performed,
When, in his prime, Mázinderán was stormed;
That horse resembles Rustem's, it is true,
But not so strong, nor beautiful to view."

   Sohráb now buckles on his war attire,
His heart all softness, and his brain all fire;
Around his lips such smiles benignant played,
He seemed to greet a friend, as thus he said:—
"Here let us sit together on the plain,
Here, social sit, and from the fight refrain;
Ask we from heaven forgiveness of the past,
And bind our souls in friendship that may last;
Ours be the feast—let us be warm and free,
For powerful instinct draws me still to thee;
Fain would my heart in bland affection join,
Then let thy generous ardour equal mine;
And kindly say, with whom I now contend—
What name distinguished boasts my warrior-friend!
Thy name unfit for champion brave to hide,
Thy name so long, long sought, and still denied;
Say, art thou Rustem, whom I burn to know?
Ingenuous say, and cease to be my foe!"

   Sternly the mighty Champion cried, "Away—
Hence with thy wiles—now practised to delay;
The promised struggle, resolute, I claim,
Then cease to move me to an act of shame."
Sohráb rejoined—"Old man! thou wilt not hear
The words of prudence uttered in thine ear;
Then, Heaven! look on."

              Preparing for the shock,
Each binds his charger to a neighbouring rock;
And girds his loins, and rubs his wrists, and tries
Their suppleness and force, with angry eyes;
And now they meet—now rise, and now descend,
And strong and fierce their sinewy arms extend;
Wrestling with all their strength they grasp and
     strain,
And blood and sweat flow copious on the plain;
Like raging elephants they furious close;
Commutual wounds are given, and wrenching blows.
Sohráb now clasps his hands, and forward springs
Impatiently, and round the Champion clings;
Seizes his girdle belt, with power to tear
The very earth asunder; in despair

Rustem, defeated, feels his nerves give way,
And thundering falls. Sohráb bestrides his prey:
Grim as the lion, prowling through the wood,
Upon a wild ass springs, and pants for blood.
His lifted sword had lopt the gory head,
But Rustem, quick, with crafty ardour said:—
"One moment, hold! what, are our laws unknown?
A Chief may fight till he is twice o'erthrown;
The second fall, his recreant blood is spilt,
These are our laws, avoid the menaced guilt."

Proud of his strength, and easily deceived,
The wondering youth the artful tale believed;
Released his prey, and, wild as wind or wave,
Neglecting all the prudence of the brave,
Turned from the place, nor once the strife renewed,
But bounded o'er the plain and other cares pursued,
As if all memory of the war had died,
All thoughts of him with whom his strength was
      tried.

Húmán, confounded at the stripling's stay,
Went forth, and heard the fortune of the day;
Amazed to find the mighty Rustem freed,
With deepest grief he wailed the luckless deed.
"What! loose a raging lion from the snare,
And let him growling hasten to his lair?
Bethink thee well; in war, from this unwise,
This thoughtless act what countless woes may rise;
Never again suspend the final blow,
Nor trust the seeming weakness of a foe!"
"Hence with complaint," the dauntless youth replied,
"To-morrow's contest shall his fate decide."

When Rustem was released, in altered mood
He sought the coolness of the murmuring flood;
There quenched his thirst; and bathed his limbs, and
      prayed,
Beseeching Heaven to yield its strengthening aid.
His pious prayer indulgent Heaven approved,
And growing strength through all his sinews moved;
Such as erewhile his towering structure knew,
When his bold arm unconquered demons slew.
Yet in his mien no confidence appeared,
No ardent hope his wounded spirits cheered.

Again they met. A glow of youthful grace,
Diffused its radiance o'er the stripling's face,
And when he saw in renovated guise,
The foe so lately mastered; with surprise,

He cried—"What! rescued from my power, again
Dost thou confront me on the battle plain?
Or, dost thou, wearied, draw thy vital breath,
And seek, from warrior bold, the shaft of death?
Truth has no charms for thee, old man; even now,
Some further cheat may lurk upon thy brow;
Twice have I shown thee mercy, twice thy age
Hath been thy safety—twice it soothed my rage."
Then mild the Champion: "Youth is proud and vain!
The idle boast a warrior would disdain;
This aged arm perhaps may yet control,
The wanton fury that inflames thy soul!"
　　Again, dismounting, each the other viewed
With sullen glance, and swift the fight renewed;
Clenched front to front, again they tug and bend,
Twist their broad limbs as every nerve would rend;
With rage convulsive Rustem graps him round;
Bends his strong back, and hurls him to the ground;
Him, who had deemed the triumph all his own;
But dubious of his power to keep him down,
Like lightning quick he gives the deadly thrust,
And spurns the Stripling weltering in the dust.
—Thus as his blood that shining steel imbrues,
Thine too shall flow, when Destiny pursues;
For when she marks the victim of her power,
A thousand daggers speed the dying hour.
Writhing with pain Sohráb in murmurs sighed—
And thus to Rustem—"Vaunt not, in thy pride;
Upon myself this sorrow have I brought,
Thou but the instrument of fate—which wrought
My downfall; thou are guiltless—guiltless quite;
O! had I seen my father in the fight,
My glorious father! Life will soon be o'er,
And his great deeds enchant my soul no more!
Of him my mother gave the mark and sign,
For him I sought, and what an end is mine!
My only wish on earth, my constant sigh,
Him to behold, and with that wish I die.
But hope not to elude his piercing sight,
In vain for thee the deepest glooms of night;
Couldst thou through Ocean's depths for refuge fly,
Or midst the star-beams track the upper sky!
Rustem, with vengeance armed, will reach thee there,
His soul the prey of anguish and despair."

　　An icy horror chills the Champion's heart,
His brain whirls round with agonizing smart;
O'er his wan cheek no gushing sorrows flow,

Senseless he sinks beneath the weight of woe;
Relieved at length, with frenzied look, he cries:
"Prove thou art mine, confirm my doubting eyes!
For I am Rustem!" Piercing was the groan,
Which burst from his torn heart—as wild and lone,
He gazed upon him. Dire amazement shook
The dying youth, and mournful thus he spoke:
"If thou art Rustem, cruel is thy part,
No warmth paternal seems to fill thy heart;
Else hadst thou known me when, with strong desire,
I fondly claimed thee for my valiant sire;
Now from my body strip the shining mail,
Untie these bands, ere life and feeling fail;
And on my arm the direful proof behold!
Thy sacred bracelet of refulgent gold!
When the loud brazen drums were heard afar,
And, echoing round, proclaimed the pending war,
Whilst parting tears my mother's eyes o'erflowed,
This mystic gift her bursting heart bestowed:
'Take this,' she said, 'thy father's token wear,
And promised glory will reward thy care.'
The hour is come, but fraught with bitterest woe,
We meet in blood to wail the fatal blow."

The loosened mail unfolds the bracelet bright,
Unhappy gift! to Rustem's wildered sight;
Prostrate he falls—"By my unnatural hand,
My son, my son is slain—and from the land
Uprooted."—Frantic, in the dust his hair
He rends in agony and deep despair;
The western sun had disappeared in gloom,
And still, the Champion wept his cruel doom;
His wondering legions marked the long delay,
And, seeing Rakush riderless astray,
The rumour quick to Persia's Monarch spread,
And there described the mighty Rustem dead.
Káús, alarmed, the fatal tidings hears;
His bosom quivers with increasing fears.
"Speed, speed, and see what has befallen to-day
To cause these groans and tears—what fatal fray!
If he be lost, if breathless on the ground,
And this young warrior, with the conquest crowned—
Then must I, humbled, from my kingdom torn,
Wander like Jemshíd, through the world forlorn."

The army roused, rushed o'er the dusty plain,
Urged by the Monarch to revenge the slain;
Wild consternation saddened every face,
Tús winged with horror sought the fatal place,

And there beheld the agonizing sight—
The murderous end of that unnatural fight.
Sohráb, still breathing, hears the shrill alarms,
His gentle speech suspends the clang of arms:
"My light of life now fluttering sinks in shade,
Let vengeance sleep, and peaceful vows be made.
Beseech the King to spare this Tartar host,
For they are guiltless, all to them is lost;
I led them on, their souls with glory fired,
While mad ambition all my thoughts inspired.
In search of thee, the world before my eyes,
War was my choice, and thou the sacred prize;
With thee, my sire! in virtuous league combined,
No tyrant King should persecute mankind.
That hope is past—the storm has ceased to rave—
My ripening honours wither in the grave;
Then let no vengeance on my comrades fall,
Mine was the guilt, and mine the sorrow, all;
How often have I sought thee—oft my mind
Figured thee to my sight—o'erjoyed to find
My mother's token; disappointment came,
When thou denied thy lineage and thy name;
Oh! still o'er thee my soul impassioned hung,
Still to my father fond affection clung!
But fate, remorseless, all my hopes withstood,
And stained thy reeking hands in kindred blood."
His faltering breath protracted speech denied:
Still from his eye-lids flowed a gushing tide;
Through Rustem's soul redoubled horror ran,
Heart-rending thoughts subdued the mighty man,
And now, at last, with joy-illumined eye,
The Zábul bands their glorious Chief descry;
But when they saw his pale and haggard look,
Knew from what mournful cause he gazed and shook,
With downcast mien they moaned and wept aloud;
While Rustem thus addressed the weeping crowd:
"Here ends the war! let gentle peace succeed,
Enough of death, I—I have done the deed!"
Then to his brother, groaning deep, he said—
"O what a curse upon a parent's head!
But go—and to the Tartar say—no more,
Let war between us steep the earth with gore."
Zúára flew and wildly spoke his grief,
To crafty Húmán, the Túránian Chief,
Who, with dissembled sorrow, heard him tell
The dismal tidings which he knew too well;
"And who," he said, "has caused these tears to flow?

Who, but Hujír? He might have stayed the blow,
But when Sohráb his Father's banners sought;
He still denied that here the Champion fought;
He spread the ruin, he the secret knew,
Hence should his crime receive the vengeance due!"
Zúára, frantic, breathed in Rustem's ear,
The treachery of the captive Chief, Hujír;
Whose headless trunk had weltered on the strand,
But prayers and force withheld the lifted hand.

Then to his dying son the Champion turned,
Remorse more deep within his bosom burned;
A burst of frenzy fired his throbbing brain;
He clenched his sword, but found his fury vain;
The Persian Chiefs the desperate act represt,
And tried to calm the tumult in his breast:
Thus Gúdarz spoke—"Alas! wert thou to give
Thyself a thousand wounds, and cease to live;
What would it be to him thou sorrowest o'er?
It would not save one pang—then weep no more;
For if removed by death, O say, to whom
Has ever been vouchsafed a different doom?
All are the prey of death—the crowned, the low,
And man, through life, the victim still of woe."
Then Rustem: "Fly! and to the King relate,
The pressing horrors which involve my fate;
And if the memory of my deeds e'er swayed
His mind, O supplicate his generous aid;
A sovereign balm he has whose wondrous power,
All wounds can heal, and fleeting life restore;
Swift from his tent the potent medicine bring."
—But mark the malice of the brainless King!
Hard as the flinty rock, he stern denies
The healthful draught, and gloomy thus replies:
"Can I forgive his foul and slanderous tongue?
The sharp disdain on me contemptuous flung?
Scorned 'midst my army by a shameless boy,
Who sought my throne, my sceptre to destroy!
Nothing but mischief from his heart can flow,
Is it, then, wise to cherish such a foe?
The fool who warms his enemy to life,
Only prepares for scenes of future strife."
Gúdarz, returning, told the hopeless tale—
And thinking Rustem's presence might prevail;
The Champion rose, but ere he reached the throne,
Sohráb had breathed the last expiring groan.

Now keener anguish rack'd the father's mind,
Reft of his son, a murderer of his kind;
His guilty sword distained with filial gore,
He beat his burning breast, his hair he tore;
The breathless corse before his shuddering view,
A shower of ashes o'er his head he threw;
"In my old age," he cried, "what have I done?
Why have I slain my son, my innocent son!
Why o'er his splendid dawning did I roll
The clouds of death—and plunge my burthened soul
In agony? My son! from heroes sprung;
Better these hands were from my body wrung;
And solitude and darkness, deep and drear,
Fold me from sight than hated linger here.
But when his mother hears, with horror wild,
That I have shed the life-blood of her child,
So nobly brave, so dearly loved, in vain,
How can her heart that rending shock sustain?"

Now on a bier the Persian warriors place
The breathless Youth, and shade his pallid face;
And turning from that fatal field away,
Move towards the Champion's home in long array.
Then Rustem, sick of martial pomp and show,
Himself the spring of all this scene of woe,
Doomed to the flames the pageantry he loved,
Shield, spear, and mace, so oft in battle proved;
Now lost to all, encompassed by despair;
His bright pavilion crackling blazed in air;
The sparkling throne the ascending column fed;
In smoking fragments fell the golden bed;
The raging fire red glimmering died away,
And all the Warrior's pride in dust and ashes lay.

Káús, the King, now joins the mournful Chief,
And tries to soothe his deep and settled grief;
For soon or late we yield our vital breath,
And all our worldly troubles end in death!
"When first I saw him, graceful in his might,
He looked far other than a Tartar knight;
Wondering I gazed—now Destiny has thrown
Him on thy sword—he fought, and he is gone;
And should even Heaven against the earth be hurled,
Or fire inwrap in crackling flames the world,
That which is past—we never can restore,
His soul has travelled to some happier shore.
Alas! no good from sorrow canst thou reap,
Then wherefore thus in gloom and misery weep?"

But Rustem's mighty woes disdained his aid,
His heart was drowned in grief, and thus he said:
"Yes, he is gone! to me for ever lost!
O then protect his brave unguided host;
From war removed and this detested place,
Let them, unharmed, their mountain-wilds retrace;
Bid them secure my brother's will obey,
The careful guardian of their weary way,
To where the Jihún's distant waters stray."
To this the King: "My soul is sad to see
Thy hopeless grief—but, since approved by thee,
The war shall cease—though the Túránian brand
Has spread dismay and terror through the land."
     The King, appeased, no more with vengeance
          burned,
The Tartar legions to their homes returned;
The Persian warriors, gathering round the dead,
Grovelled in dust, and tears of sorrow shed;
Then back to loved Irán their steps the monarch led.
     But Rustem, midst his native bands, remained,
And further rites of sacrifice maintained;
A thousand horses bled at his command,
And the torn drums were scattered o'er the sand;
And now through Zábul's deep and bowery groves,
In mournful pomp the sad procession moves.
The mighty Chief on foot precedes the bier;
His Warrior-friends, in grief assembled near:
The dismal cadence rose upon the gale,
And Zál astonished heard the piercing wail;
He and his kindred joined the solemn train;
Hung round the bier and wondering viewed the
          slain.
"There gaze, and weep!" the sorrowing Father said,
"For there, behold my glorious offspring dead!"
The hoary Sire shrunk backward with surprise,
And tears of blood o'erflowed his aged eyes;
And now the Champion's rural palace gate
Receives the funeral group in gloomy state;
Rúdábeh loud bemoaned the Stripling's doom;
Sweet flower, all drooping in the hour of bloom,
His tender youth in distant bowers had past,
Sheltered at home he felt no withering blast;
In the soft prison of his mother's arms,
Secure from danger and the world's alarms.
O ruthless Fortune! flushed with generous pride,
He sought his sire, and thus unhappy, died.
     Rustem again the sacred bier unclosed;

Again Sohráb to public view exposed;
Husbands, and wives, and warriors, old and young,
Struck with amaze, around the body hung,
With garments rent and loosely flowing hair;
Their shrieks and clamours filled the echoing air;
Frequent they cried: "Thus Sám the Champion slept!
Thus sleeps Sohráb!" Again thy groaned, and wept.

  Now o'er the corpse a yellow robe is spread,
The aloes bier is closed upon the dead;
And, to preserve the hapless hero's name,
Fragrant and fresh, that his unblemished fame
Might live and bloom through all succeeding days,
A mound sepulchral on the spot they raise,
Formed like a charger's hoof.

                In every ear
The story has been told—and many a tear,
Shed at the sad recital. Through Túrán,
Afrásiyáb's wide realm, and Samengán,
Deep sunk the tidings—nuptial bower, and bed,
And all that promised happiness, had fled!

  But when Tahmíneh heard this tale of woe,
Think how a mother bore the mortal blow!
Distracted, wild, she sprang from place to place;
With frenzied hands deformed her beauteous face;
The musky locks her polished temples crowned.
Furious she tore, and flung upon the ground;
Starting, in agony of grief, she gazed—
Her swimming eyes to Heaven imploring raised;
And groaning cried: "Sole comfort of my life!
Doomed the sad victim of unnatural strife,
Where art thou now with dust and blood defiled?
Thou darling boy, my lost, my murdered child!
When thou wert gone—how, night and lingering
    day,
Did thy fond mother watch the time away;
For hope still pictured all I wished to see,
Thy father found, and thou returned to me,
Yes—thou, exulting in thy father's fame!
And yet, nor sire nor son, nor tidings, came:
How could I dream of this? ye met—but how?
That noble aspect—that ingenuous brow,
Moved not a nerve in him—ye met—to part,
Alas! the life-blood issuing from the heart.
Short was the day which gave to me delight,
Soon, soon, succeeds a long and dismal night;
On whom shall now devolve my tender care?
Who, loved like thee, my bosom-sorrows share?

Whom shall I take to fill thy vacant place,
To whom extend a mother's soft embrace?
Sad fate! for one so young, so fair, so brave,
Seeking thy father thus to find a grave.
These arms no more shall fold thee to my breast,
No more with thee my soul be doubly blest;
No, drowned in blood thy lifeless body lies,
For ever torn from these desiring eyes;
Friendless, alone, beneath a foreign sky,
Thy mail thy death-clothes—and thy father, by;
Why did not I conduct thee on the way,
And point where Rustem's bright pavilion lay?
Thou hadst the tokens—why didst thou withhold
Those dear remembrances—that pledge of gold?
Hadst thou the bracelet to his view restored,
Thy precious blood had never stained his sword."

    The strong emotion choked her panting breath,
Her veins seemed withered by the cold of death:
The trembling matrons hastening round her
    mourned,
With piercing cries, till fluttering life returned;
Then gazing up, distraught, she wept again,
And frantic, seeing 'midst her pitying train,
The favourite steed—now more than ever dear,
The hoofs she kissed, and bathed with many a tear;
Clasping the mail Sohráb in battle wore,
With burning lips she kissed it o'er and o'er;
His martial robes she in her arms comprest,
And like an infant strained them to her breast;
The reins, and trappings, club, and spear, were
    brought,
The sword, and shield, with which the Stripling
    fought,
These she embraced with melancholy joy,
In sad remembrance of her darling boy.
And still she beat her face, and o'er them hung,
As in a trance—or to them wildly clung—
Day after day she thus indulged her grief,
Night after night, disdaining all relief;
At length worn out—from earthly anguish riven,
The mother's spirit joined her child in Heaven.

2 DRAMA

Shakuntala by Kálidása

{FLOURISHED ABOUT 5TH CENTURY A.D.}

TRANSLATED BY M. MONIER-WILLIAMS {1819-1899}

For Western readers at any rate, the high-water mark of not only Indian but perhaps all Asian literature must be represented by *Shakuntala*. Since this drama was introduced to European readers by Sir William Jones in the late 18th century, it has delighted—besides Goethe, who adopted its form of the prologue for his *Faust*—countless readers and probably as many attendants of the professional and amateur stage. *Shakuntala* has that rare ability of a translated work to efface differences of race, culture and language and to speak directly across the page or the footlights.

This fact is the more remarkable since the conventions of the Indian stage are not the same as those of the Western, though attempts have been made to establish the fact of a Greek influence. The key factor in the Indian drama is sentiment. This is not the same thing as emotion, which is personal and might therefore be disagreeable. It is rather a disinterested and hence always pleasant feeling, produced in the reader or viewer by the proper blending of characters, time, place, actor's gestures and voice, poetic and rhetorical devices, etc. The play employs all these to create, not a reasonable facsimile of life, but a pleasurable sense of life without its accidental defects. Thus the Indian drama is frankly romantic and escapist.

To this end, there is excluded from the viewer's sight all unpleasant action capable of marring the delicate sentiment after which the dramatist is striving. Ideally, there must be on the stage no fighting or other violence, no deaths, no marriages or other rituals, not even any kissing. The sense of all these things happening must be suggested, however, and in this lies the art of the Indian drama. One is tempted to see in this principle an analogy to T. S. Eliot's concept of the "objective correlative," that emotion produced in the reader by a right combination of poetic factors and corresponding to, but not identical with, the emotion experienced by the author.

Yet despite obvious differences, *Shakuntala* must appear to readers of poetic drama to belong to the same genre as *The Tempest* or *As You Like It*. Here are the charmingly contrasted jaded court and unspoilt forest; the cynically commenting king's attendant, a sort of Brahman Touchstone; the delightfully coy maidens who serve Shakuntala (these may indeed recall three little maids from another Asian seminary!); and the comic relief of the constabulary. But Kálidása's true kinship with Shakespeare rests upon his status as a poet of nature. He is most characteristic in the lyrical passages descriptive of the fauna and flora of his native land. Even the topmost achievement of this drama, its heroine, is in part creditable to her creator's love of wild life. For Shakuntala is, as it were, half bird (like her counterpart Rima in Hudson's *Green Mansions*), her name being derived from the *shakuntas* or birds with which she held such easy converse. Yet it is as womankind that she ultimately triumphs. The ordeal which she brings upon herself (by an unthinking show of inhospitality to the sage Durvasas while distracted by love) matures her in the knowledge of love and prepares her for the life which, by her hitherto secret noble origin, she was destined to live.

The character of King Dushyanta is somewhat less sympathetic. He has a natural Brahmanical stiffness, but he labors under the greater difficulty—occasioned by the *Mahabharata* legend which provides the story—of having to treat the girl Shakuntala somewhat cavalierly. To be sure Kálidása has considerably psychologized the story. He explains the king's forgetfulness of his unceremonious marriage to Shakuntala by the curse which Durvasas places upon the lovers. Similarly, recollection is effected by the recovery of the lost ring which symbolizes their union. This much supernatural machinery we can accept as easily as we do Shakespeare's ghosts or fairies.

What the reader may miss in Kálidása—and it chiefly has been held against him by those who would refuse him a place beside the great dramatists of the world—is the quality which Matthew Arnold called "high seriousness." There are in Indian drama no probings of the dark recesses of the human heart, as in Greek or Elizabethan tragedy. Tragedy, indeed, there cannot be. Hinduism does not grant sufficient free will to man to permit of his grappling with the moral ambiguities that produce tragedy. Sadness and melancholy there may be; but the ultimate destinies are well controlled, and sunlight at last prevails.

From what little is known of Kálidása, the moderacy of his temperament would further conduce to such happy resolution of human problems. The hallmark of his work has been said to be a Vergilian golden mean. The Olympian—or shall we say Himalayan—calm with which he views the affairs of men may indeed denote the completeness with which he accepted the tenets of Hinduism. From his name it would appear that he was a follower of Kali, the consort of Shiva; but whether Vishnuite or Shivaite, he must have found in the caste system of Brahmanism, and in the several philosophies which expounded its teachings, a proper ordering of the values he would live by. Quite appropriately he marks the zenith in that great flowering of Sanskrit literature which occurred after Buddhism had failed permanently to alter the religion of the Hindus.

DRAMATIS PERSONAE

DUSHYANTA: *King of India.*

MÁTHAVYA: *the Jester, friend and companion of the King.*

KANWA: *chief of the Hermits, foster-father of Sakoontalá.*

ŚÁRNGARAVA, ŚÁRADWATA: *two Bráhmans, belonging to the hermitage of Kanwa.*

MITRÁVASU: *brother-in-law of the King, and Superintendent of the city police.*

JÁNUKA, SÚCHAKA: *two constables.*

VÁTÁYANA: *the Chamberlain or attendant on the women's apartments.*

SOMARÁTA: *the domestic Priest.*

KARABHAKA: *a messenger of the Queen-mother.*

RAIVATAKA: *the warder or door-keeper.*

MÁTALI: *charioteer of Indra.*

SARVA-DAMANA: *afterwards Bharata, a little boy, son of Dushyanta by Sakoontalá.*

KAŚYAPA: *a divine sage, progenitor of men and gods, son of Maríchi and grandson of Brahmá.*

ŚAKOONTALÁ: *daughter of the sage Viśwámitra and the nymph Menaká, foster-child of the hermit Kanwa.*

PRIYAMVADÁ and ANASÚYÁ: *female attendants, companions of Sakoontalá.*

GAUTAMÍ: *a holy matron, Superior of the female inhabitants of the hermitage.*

VASUMATÍ: *the Queen of Dushyanta.*

SÁNUMATÍ: *a nymph, friend of Sakoontalá.*

TARALIKÁ: *personal attendant of the King.*

CHATURIKÁ: *personal attendant of the Queen.*

VETRAVATÍ: *female warder, or door-keeper.*

PARABARITIKÁ and MADHUKARIKÁ: *maidens in charge of the royal gardens.*

SUVRATÁ: *a nurse.*

ADITI: *wife of Kaśyapa; grand-daughter of Brahmá, through her father, Daksha.*

CHARIOTEER, FISHERMAN, OFFICERS, and HERMITS.

PROLOGUE

Benediction

Iśa preserve you! he who is revealed
In these eight forms by man perceptible—
Water, of all creation's works the first;
The fire that bears on high the sacrifice

Presented with solemnity to heaven;
The Priest, the holy offerer of gifts;
The Sun and Moon, those two majestic orbs,
Eternal marshallers of day and night;
The subtle Ether, vehicle of sound,
Diffused throughout the boundless universe;
The Earth, by sages called "The place of birth
Of all material essences and things";
And Air, which giveth life to all that breathe.

STAGE-MANAGER [*after the recitation of the benediction, looking towards the tiring-room*]: Lady, when you have finished attiring yourself, come this way.

ACTRESS [*entering*]: Here I am, Sir; what are your commands?

STAGE-MANAGER: We are here before the eyes of an audience of educated and discerning men; and have to represent in their presence a new drama composed by Kálidása, called "Śakoontalá, or the Lost Ring." Let the whole company exert themselves to do justice to their several parts.

ACTRESS: You, Sir, have so judiciously managed the cast of the characters, that nothing will be defective in the acting.

STAGE-MANAGER: Lady, I will tell you the exact state of the case.

No skill in acting can I deem complete,
Till from the wise the actor gain applause:
Know that the heart e'en of the truly skilful,
Shrinks from too boastful confidence in self.

ACTRESS [*modestly*]: You judge correctly. And now, what are your commands?

STAGE-MANAGER: What can you do better than engage the attention of the audience by some captivating melody?

ACTRESS: Which among the seasons shall I select as the subject of my song?

STAGE-MANAGER: You surely ought to give the preference to the present Summer season that has but recently commenced, a season so rich in enjoyment. For now

Unceasing are the charms of halcyon days,
When the cool bath exhilarates the frame;
When sylvan gales are laden with the scent
Of fragrant Pátalas; when soothing sleep
Creeps softly on beneath the deepening shade;
And when, at last, the dulcet calm of eve
Entrancing steals o'er every yielding sense.

ACTRESS: I will.

Fond maids, the chosen of their hearts to please,
Entwine their ears with sweet Śirísha flowers,

Whose fragrant lips attract the kiss of bees
That softly murmur through the summer hours.

STAGE-MANAGER: Charmingly sung! The audience are motionless as statues, their souls riveted by the enchanting
strain. What subject shall we select for representation,
that we may insure a continuance of their favor?

ACTRESS: Why not the same, Sir, announced by you at first?
Let the drama called "Sakoontalá, or the Lost Ring," be
the subject of our dramatic performance.

STAGE-MANAGER: Rightly reminded! For the moment I had
forgotten it.

Your song's transporting melody decoyed
My thoughts, and rapt with ecstasy my soul;
As now the bounding antelope allures
The King Dushyanta on the chase intent.   [*Exeunt.*

ACT FIRST

Scene—A Forest

*Enter King Dushyanta, armed with a bow and arrow, in a
chariot, chasing an antelope, attended by his Charioteer.*

CHARIOTEER [*looking at the deer, and then at the King*]:
Great Prince,
When on the antelope I bend my gaze,
And on your Majesty, whose mighty bow
Has its string firmly braced; before my eyes
The god that wields the trident seems revealed,
Chasing the deer that flies from him in vain.

KING: Charioteer, this fleet antelope has drawn us far from
my attendants. See! there he runs:—
Aye and anon his graceful neck he bends
To cast a glance at the pursuing car;
And dreading now the swift-descending shaft,
Contracts into itself his slender frame:
About his path, in scattered fragments strewn,
The half-chewed grass falls from his panting mouth;
See! in his airy bounds he seems to fly,
And leaves no trace upon th' elastic turf.   [*With
astonishment.*
How now! swift as is our pursuit, I scarce can see him.

CHARIOTEER: Sire, the ground here is full of hollows; I have
therefore drawn in the reins and checked the speed of
the chariot. Hence the deer has somewhat gained upon
us. Now that we are passing over level ground, we shall
have no difficulty in overtaking him.

KING: Loosen the reins, then.

CHARIOTEER: The King is obeyed. [*Drives the chariot at full speed.*]

> Great Prince, see! see!
> Responsive to the slackened rein, the steeds
> Chafing with eager rivalry, career
> With emulative fleetness o'er the plain;
> Their necks outstretched, their waving plumes, that late
> Fluttered above their brows, are motionless;
> Their sprightly ears, but now erect, bent low;
> Themselves unsullied by the circling dust,
> That vainly follows on their rapid course.

KING [*joyously*]: In good sooth, the horses seem as if they would outstrip the steeds of Indra and the Sun.[1]

> That which but now showed to my view minute
> Quickly assumes dimension; that which seemed
> A moment since disjoined in diverse parts,
> Looks suddenly like one compacted whole;
> That which is really crooked in its shape
> In the far distance left, grows regular;
> Wondrous the chariot's speed, that in a breath,
> Makes the near distant and the distant near.

> Now, Charioteer, see me kill the deer. [*Takes aim.*

A VOICE [*behind the scenes*]: Hold, O King! this deer belongs to our hermitage. Kill it not! kill it not!

CHARIOTEER [*listening and looking*]: Great King, some hermits have stationed themselves so as to screen the antelope at the very moment of its coming within range of your arrow.

KING [*hastily*]: Then stop the horses.

CHARIOTEER: I obey. [*Stops the chariot.*

> *Enter a Hermit, and two others with him.*

HERMIT [*raising his hand*]: This deer, O King, belongs to our hermitage. Kill it not! kill it not!

> Now heaven forbid this barbèd shaft descend
> Upon the fragile body of a fawn,
> Like fire upon a heap of tender flowers!
> Can thy steel bolts no meeter quarry find
> Than the warm life-blood of a harmless deer?
> Restore, great Prince, thy weapon to its quiver;
> More it becomes thy arms to shield the weak,
> Than to bring anguish on the innocent.

KING: 'Tis done. [*Replaces the arrow in its quiver.*

---

[1] The speed of the chariot resembled that of the wind and the sun. Indra was the god of the firmament or atmosphere. The sun, in Hindoo mythology, is represented as seated in a chariot drawn by seven green horses, having before him a lovely youth without legs, who acts as charioteer, and who is Aruna, or the Dawn personified.

HERMIT: Worthy is this action of a Prince, the light of Puru's race.

Well does this act befit a Prince like thee,
Right worthy is it of thine ancestry.
Thy guerdon be a son of peerless worth,
Whose wide dominion shall embrace the earth.

BOTH THE OTHER HERMITS [*raising their hands*] : May heaven indeed grant thee a son, a sovereign of the earth from sea to sea!

KING [*bowing*] : I accept with gratitude a Bráhman's benediction.

HERMIT: We came hither, mighty Prince, to collect sacrificial wood. Here on the banks of the Málíní you may perceive the hermitage of the great sage Kanwa. If other duties require not your presence, deign to enter and accept our hospitality.

When you behold our penitential rites
Performed without impediment by Saints
Rich only in devotion, then with pride
Will you reflect, Such are the holy men
Who call me Guardian; such the men for whom
To wield the bow I bare my nervous arm,
Scarred by the motion of the glancing string.

KING: Is the Chief of your Society now at home?

HERMIT: No; he has gone to Soma-tírtha to propitiate Destiny, which threatens his daughter Sakoontalá with some calamity; but he has commissioned her in his absence to entertain all guests with hospitality.

KING: Good! I will pay her a visit. She will make me acquainted with the mighty sage's acts of penance and devotion.

HERMIT: And we will depart on our errand. [*Exit with his companions.*

KING: Charioteer, urge on the horses. We will at least purify our souls by a sight of this hallowed retreat.

CHARIOTEER: Your Majesty is obeyed.
[*Drives the chariot with great velocity.*

KING [*looking all about him*]: Charioteer, even without being told, I should have known that these were the precincts of a grove consecrated to penitential rites.

CHARIOTEER: How so?

KING: Do not you observe?

Beneath the trees, whose hollow trunks afford
Secure retreat to many a nestling brood
Of parrots, scattered grains of rice lie strewn.
Lo! here and there are seen the polished slabs
That serve to bruise the fruit of Ingudí

The gentle roe-deer, taught to trust in man,
Unstartled hear our voices. On the paths
Appear the traces of bark-woven vests
Borne dripping from the limpid fount of waters.
And mark!
Laved are the roots of trees by deep canals,
Whose glassy waters tremble in the breeze;
The sprouting verdure of the leaves is dimmed
By dusky wreaths of upward curling smoke
From burnt oblations; and on new-mown lawns
Around our car graze leisurely the fawns.

CHARIOTEER: I observe it all.

KING [*advancing a little further*]: The inhabitants of this
sacred retreat must not be disturbed. Stay the chariot,
that I may alight.

CHARIOTEER: The reins are held in. Your Majesty may
descend.

KING [*alighting*]: Charioteer, groves devoted to penance must
be entered in humble attire. Take these ornaments.
[*Delivers his ornaments and bow to the Charioteer.*]
Charioteer, see that the horses are watered, and attend
to them until I return from visiting the inhabitants of
the hermitage.

CHARIOTEER: I will.   [*Exit.*

KING [*walking and looking about*]:Here is the entrance to
the hermitage. I will now go in.
   [*Entering he feels a throbbing sensation in his arm.*
Serenest peace is in this calm retreat,
By passion's breath unruffled; what portends
My throbbing arm? Why should it whisper here
Of happy love? Yet everywhere around us
Stand the closed portals of events unknown.

A VOICE [*behind the scenes*]: This way, my dear companions;
this way.

KING [*listening*]:Hark! I hear voices to the right of yonder
grove of trees. I will walk in that direction. [*Walking
and looking about.*]
Ah! here are the maidens of the hermitage coming this
way to water the shrubs, carrying watering-pots proportioned to their strength. [*Gazing at them.*] How graceful they look!
In palaces such charms are rarely ours;
The woodland plants outshine the garden flowers.
I will conceal myself in this shade and watch them.
                              [*Stands gazing at them.*

*Enter Śakoontalá, with her two female companions, em-
ployed in the manner described.*

ŚAKOONTALÁ: This way, my dear companions; this way.

ANASÚYA: Dear Śakoontalá, one would think that Father Kanwa had more affection for the shrubs of the hermitage even than for you, seeing he assigns to you who are yourself as delicate as the fresh-blown jasmine, the task of filling with water the trenches which encircle their roots.

ŚAKOONTALÁ: Dear Anasúyá, although I am charged by my good father with this duty, yet I cannot regard it as a task. I really feel a sisterly love for these plants. [*Continues watering the shrubs.*

KING: Can this be the daughter of Kanwa? The saintly man, though descended from the great Kaśyapa, must be very deficient in judgment to habituate such a maiden to the life of a recluse.

The sage who would this form of artless grace
Inure to penance—thoughtlessly attempts
To cleave in twain the hard acacia's stem
With the soft edge of a blue lotus leaf.

Well! concealed behind this tree, I will watch her without raising her suspicions. [*Conceals himself.*

ŚAKOONTALÁ: Good. Anasúyá, Priyamvadá has drawn this bark-dress too tightly about my chest. I pray thee, loosen it a little.

ANASÚYÁ: I will [*Loosens it.*

PRIYAMVADÁ [*smiling*]: Why do you lay the blame on me? Blame rather your own blooming youthfulness which imparts fulness to your bosom.

KING: A most just observation!

This youthful form, whose bosom's swelling charms
By the bark's knotted tissue are concealed,
Like some fair bud close folded in its sheath,
Gives not to view the blooming of its beauty.

But what am I saying? In real truth, this bark-dress, though ill-suited to her figure, sets it off like an ornament.

The lotus with the Saivala entwined
Is not a whit less brilliant: dusky spots
Heighten the lustre of the cold-rayed moon:
This lovely maiden in her dress of bark
Seems all the lovelier. E'en the meanest garb
Gives to true beauty fresh attractiveness.

ŚAKOONTALÁ [*looking before her*]: Yon Keśara-tree beckons to me with its young shoots, which, as the breeze waves them to and fro, appear like slender figures. I will go and attend to it. [*Walks towards it.*

PRIYAMVADÁ: Dear Śakoontalá, prithee, rest in that attitude one moment.

ŚAKOONTALÁ: Why so?

PRIYAMVADÁ: The Keśara-tree, whilst your graceful form
bends about its stem, appears as if it were wedded to
some lovely twining creeper.

ŚAKOONTALÁ : Ah! saucy girl, you are most appropriately
named Priyamvadá ("Speaker of flattering things").

KING: What Priyamvadá says, though complimentary, is
nevertheless true. Verily,
Her ruddy lip vies with the opening bud;
Her graceful arms are as the twining stalks;
And her whole form is radiant with the glow
Of youthful beauty, as the tree with bloom.

ANASÚYÁ: See, dear Śakoontalá, here is the young jasmine,
which you named "the Moonlight of the Grove," the
self-elected wife of the mango-tree. Have you forgotten
it?

ŚAKOONTALÁ: Rather will I forget myself. [*Approaching the
plant and looking at it.*] How delightful is the season
when the jasmine-creeper and the mango-tree seem
thus to unite in mutual embraces! The fresh blossoms
of the jasmine resemble the bloom of a young bride,
and the newly-formed shoots of the mango appear to
make it her natural protector. [*Continues gazing at it.*

PRIYAMVADÁ [*smiling*] : Do you know, my Anasúyá, why
Śakoontalá gazes so intently at the jasmine?

ANASÚYÁ: No, indeed, I cannot imagine. I pray thee tell me.

PRIYAMVADÁ: She is wishing that as the jasmine is united
to a suitable tree, so, in like manner, she may obtain
a husband worthy of her.

ŚAKOONTALÁ: Speak for yourself, girl; this is the thought
in your own mind. [*Continues watering the flowers.*

KING: Would that my union with her were permissible! and
yet I hardly dare hope that the maiden is sprung from
a caste different from that of the Head of the her-
mitage. But away with doubt:
That she is free to wed a warrior-king
My heart attests. For, in conflicting doubts,
The secret promptings of the good man's soul
Are an unerring index of the truth.
However, come what may, I will ascertain the fact.

ŚAKOONTALÁ [*in a flurry*]: Ah! a bee, disturbed by the
sprinkling of the water, has left the young jasmine,
and is trying to settle on my face. [*Attempts to
drive it away.*

KING [*gazing at her ardently*]: Beautiful! there is something
charming even in her repulse.
Where'er the bee his eager onset plies,
Now here, now there, she darts her kindling eyes:

What love hath yet to teach, fear teaches now,
The furtive glances and the frowning brow. [*In a tone of
envy.*

Ah happy bee! how boldly dost thou try
To steal the lustre from her sparkling eye;
And in thy circling movements hover near,
To murmur tender secrets in her ear;
Or, as she coyly waves her hand, to sip
Voluptuous nectar from her lower lip!
While rising doubts my heart's fond hopes destroy,
Thou dost the fulness of her charms enjoy.

ŚAKOONTALÁ: This impertinent bee will not rest quiet. I
must move elsewhere. [*Moving a few steps off, and casting a glance around.*] How now! he is following me
here. Help! my dear friends, help! deliver me from the
attacks of this troublesome insect.

PRIYAMVADÁ AND ANASÚYÁ: How can we deliver you? Call
Dushyanta to your aid. The sacred groves are under
the king's special protection.

KING: An excellent opportunity for me to show myself. Fear
not—[*Checks himself when the words are half-uttered.
Aside.*] But stay, if I introduce myself in this manner,
they will know me to be the King. Be it so, I will accost
them, nevertheless.

ŚAKOONTALÁ [*moving a step or two further off*]: What! it
still persists in following me.

KING [*advancing hastily*]: When mighty Puru's offspring
sways the earth,
And o'er the wayward holds his threatening rod,
Who dares molest the gentle maids that keep
Their holy vigils here in Kanwa's grove?

[*All look at the King, and are embarrassed.*

ANASÚYÁ: Kind Sir, no outrage has been committed; only
our dear friend here was teased by the attacks of a
troublesome bee. [*Points to Śakoontalá.*

KING [*turning to Śakoontalá*]: I trust all is well with your
devotional rites? [*Śakoontalá stands confused and silent.*

ANASÚYÁ: All is well, indeed, now that we are honored by
the reception of a distinguished guest. Dear Śakoontalá, go, bring from the hermitage an offering of flowers, rice, and fruit. This water that we have brought
with us will serve to bathe our guest's feet.

KING: The rites of hospitality are already performed; your
truly kind words are the best offering I can receive.

PRIYAMVADÁ: At least be good enough, gentle Sir, to sit
down awhile, and rest yourself on this seat shaded by
the leaves of the Saptaparna tree.

KING: You, too, must all be fatigued by your employment.

ANASÚYÁ: Dear Sakoontalá, there is no impropriety in our sitting by the side of our guest: come, let us sit down here.   [*All sit down together.*

SAKOONTALÁ [*aside*]: How is it that the sight of this man has made me sensible of emotions inconsistent with religious vows?

KING [*gazing at them all by turns*]: How charmingly your friendship is in keeping with the equality of your ages and appearance!

PRIYAMVADÁ [*aside to Anasúyá*]: Who can this person be, whose lively yet dignified manner, and polite conversation, bespeak him a man of high rank?

ANASÚYÁ: I too, my dear, am very curious to know. I will ask him myself. [*Aloud.*] Your kind words, noble Sir, fill me with confidence, and prompt me to inquire of what regal family our noble guest is the ornament? what country is now mourning his absence? and what induced a person so delicately nurtured to expose himself to the fatigue of visiting this grove of penance?

SAKOONTALÁ [*aside*]: Be not troubled, O my heart, Anasúyá is giving utterance to thy thoughts.

KING [*aside*]: How now shall I reply? shall I make myself known, or shall I still disguise my real rank? I have it; I will answer her thus. [*Aloud.*] I am the person charged by his majesty, the descendant of Puru, with the administration of justice and religion; and am come to this sacred grove to satisfy myself that the rites of the hermits are free from obstruction.

ANASÚYÁ: The hermits, then, and all the members of our religious society have now a guardian.

[*Sakoontalá gazes bashfully at the King.*

PRIYAMVADÁ AND ANASÚYÁ [*perceiving the state of her feelings, and of the King's. Aside to Sakoontalá*]: Dear Sakoontalá, if father Kanwa were but at home to-day—

SAKOONTALÁ [*angrily*]: What if he were?

PRIYAMVADÁ AND ANASÚYÁ: He would honor this our distinguished guest with an offering of the most precious of his possessions.

SAKOONTALÁ: Go to! you have some silly idea in your minds. I will not listen to such remarks.

KING: May I be allowed, in my turn, to ask you maidens a few particulars respecting your friend?

PRIYAMVADÁ AND ANASÚYÁ: Your request, Sir, is an honor.

KING: The sage Kanwa lives in the constant practice of austerities. How, then, can this friend of yours be called his daughter?

ANASÚYÁ: I will explain to you, Sir. You have heard of an illustrious sage of regal caste, Viśwámitra, whose family name is Kaúsika.

KING: I have.

ANASÚYÁ: Know that he is the real father of our friend. The venerable Kanwa is only her reputed father. He it was who brought her up, when she was deserted by her mother.

KING: "Deserted by her mother!" My curiosity is excited; pray let me hear the story from the beginning.

ANASÚYÁ: You shall hear it, Sir. Some time since, this sage of regal caste, while performing a most severe penance on the banks of the river Godávarí, excited the jealousy and alarm of the gods; insomuch that they despatched a lovely nymph named Menaká to interrupt his devotions.

KING: The inferior gods, I am aware, are jealous of the power which the practice of excessive devotion confers on mortals.

ANASÚYÁ: Well, then, it happened that Viśwámitra, gazing on the bewitching beauty of that nymph at a season when, spring being in its glory—

　　　　　[Stops short, and appears confused.

KING: The rest may be easily divined. Śakoontalá, then, is the offspring of the nymph.

ANASÚYÁ: Just so.

KING: It is quite intelligible.

How could a mortal to such charms give birth?
The lightning's radiance flashes not from earth.

　　　　[Śakoontalá remains modestly seated with downcast eyes.
Aside. And so my desire has really scope for its indulgence. Yet I am still distracted by doubts, remembering the pleasantry of her female companions respecting her wish for a husband.

PRIYAMVADÁ [*looking with a smile at Śakoontalá, and then turning towards the King*]: You seem desirous, Sir, of asking something further.

　　　　[Śakoontalá makes a chiding gesture with her finger.

KING: You conjecture truly. I am so eager to hear the particulars of your friend's history, that I have still another question to ask.

PRIYAMVADÁ: Scruple not to do so. Persons who lead the life of hermits may be questioned unreservedly.

KING: I wish to ascertain one point respecting your friend—

Will she be bound by solitary vows
Opposed to love, till her espousals only?
Or ever dwell with these her cherished fawns,
Whose eyes, in lustre vieing with her own,
Return her gaze of sisterly affection?

PRIYAMVADÁ: Hitherto, Sir, she has been engaged in the practice of religious duties, and has lived in subjection to her foster-father; but it is now his fixed intention to give her away in marriage to a husband worthy of her.

KING [*aside*]: His intention may be easily carried into effect.
Be hopeful, O my heart, thy harrowing doubts
Are past and gone; that which thou didst believe
To be as unapproachable as fire,
Is found a glittering gem that may be touched.

ŚAKOONTALÁ [*pretending anger*]: Anasúyá, I shall leave you.

ANASÚYÁ: Why so?

ŚAKOONTALÁ: That I may go and report this impertinent Priyamvadá to the venerable matron, Gautamí.[2]

ANASÚYÁ: Surely, dear friend, it would not be right to leave a distinguished guest before he has received the rights of hospitality, and quit his presence in this wilful manner.
     [*Śakoontalá, without answering a word, moves away.*

KING [*making a movement to arrest her departure, but checking himself. Aside*]: Ah! a lover's feelings betray themselves by his gestures.
When I would fain have stayed the maid, a sense
Of due decorum checked my bold design:
Though I have stirred not, yet my mien betrays
My eagerness to follow on her steps.

PRIYAMVADÁ [*holding Śakoontalá back*]: Dear Śakoontalá, it does not become you to go away in this manner.

ŚAKOONTALÁ [*frowning*]: Why not, pray?

PRIYAMVADÁ: You are under a promise to water two more shrubs for me. When you have paid your debt, you shall go, and not before.   [*Forces her to turn back.*

KING: Spare her this trouble, gentle maiden. The exertion of watering the shrubs has already fatigued her.
The water-jar has overtasked the strength
Of her slim arms; her shoulders droop, her hands
Are ruddy with the glow of quickened pulses;
E'en now her agitated breath imparts
Unwonted tremor to her heaving breast;
The pearly drops that mar the recent bloom
Of the Sirísha pendant in her ear,
Gather in clustering circles on her cheek;
Loosed is the fillet of her hair: her hand
Restrains the locks that struggle to be free.
Suffer me, then, thus to discharge the debt for you.

[*Offers a ring to Priyamvadá. Both the maidens, reading the name Dushyanta on the seal, look at each other with surprise.*

[2] The Matron or Superior of the female part of the society of hermits. Her authority resembled that of an abbess in a convent of nuns.

KING: Nay, think not that I am King Dushyanta. I am only the king's officer, and this is the ring which I have received from him as my credentials.

PRIYAMVADÁ: The greater the reason you ought not to part with the ring from your finger. I am content to release her from her obligation at your simple request. [*With a smile.*] Now, Śakoontalá my love, you are at liberty to retire, thanks to the intercession of this noble stranger, or rather of this mighty prince.

ŚAKOONTALÁ [*aside*]: My movements are no longer under my own control. [*Aloud.*] Pray, what authority have you over me, either to send me away or keep me back?

KING [*gazing at Śakoontalá. Aside*]: Would I could ascertain whether she is affected towards me as I am towards her! At any rate, my hopes are free to indulge themselves. Because,

Although she mingles not her words with mine,
Yet doth her listening ear drink in my speech;
Although her eye shrinks from my ardent gaze,
No form but mine attracts its timid glances.

A VOICE [*behind the scenes*]: O hermits, be ready to protect the animals belonging to our hermitage. King Dushyanta, amusing himself with hunting, is near at hand.

Lo! by the feet of prancing horses raised,
Thick clouds of moving dust, like glittering swarms
Of locusts in the glow of eventide,
Fall on the branches of our sacred trees;
Where hang the dripping vests of woven bark,
Bleached by the waters of the cleansing fountain.
    And see!
Scared by the royal chariot in its course,
With headlong haste an elephant invades
The hallowed precincts of our sacred grove;
Himself the terror of the startled deer,
And an embodied hindrance to our rites.
The hedge of creepers clinging to his feet,
Feeble obstruction to his mad career,
Is dragged behind him in a tangled chain;
And with terrific shock one tusk he drives
Into the riven body of a tree,
Sweeping before him all impediments.

KING [*aside*]: Out upon it! my retinue are looking for me, and are disturbing this holy retreat. Well! there is no help for it; I must go and meet them.

PRIYAMVADÁ AND ANASÚYÁ: Noble Sir, we are terrified by the accidental disturbance caused by the wild elephant. Permit us to return into the cottage.

KING [*hastily*]: Go, gentle maidens. It shall be our care that no injury happen to the hermitage.   [*All rise up.*

PRIYAMVADÁ AND ANASÚYÁ: After such poor hospitality we are ashamed to request the honor of a second visit from you.

KING: Say not so. The mere sight of you, sweet maidens, has been to me the best entertainment.

ŚAKOONTALÁ: Anasúyá, a pointed blade of Kuśa-grass [3] has pricked my foot; and my bark-mantle is caught in the branch of a Kuruvaka bush. Be so good as to wait for me until I have disentangled it.

[*Exit with her two companions, after making pretexts for delay, that she may steal glances at the King.*

KING: I have no longer any desire to return to the city. I will therefore rejoin my attendants, and make them encamp somewhere in the vicinity of this sacred grove. In good truth, Śakoontalá has taken such possession of my thoughts, that I cannot turn myself in any other direction.

My limbs drawn onward leave my heart behind,
Like silken pennon borne against the wind.

ACT SECOND

Scene—A Plain on the Skirts of the Forest

Enter the Jester, Máthavya, in a melancholy mood.

MÁTHAVYA [*sighing*]: Heigh-ho! what an unlucky fellow I am! worn to a shadow by my royal friend's sporting propensities. "Here's a deer!" "There goes a boar!" "Yonder's a tiger!" This is the only burden of our talk, while in the heat of the meridian sun we toil on from jungle to jungle, wandering about in the paths of the woods, where the trees afford us no shelter. Are we thirsty? We have nothing to drink but the foul water of some mountain stream, filled with dry leaves which give it a most pungent flavor. Are we hungry? We have nothing to eat but roast game, which we must swallow down at odd times, as best we can. Even at night there is no peace to be had. Sleeping is out of the question, with joints all strained by dancing attendance upon my sporting friend; or if I do happen to doze, I am awakened at the very earliest dawn by the horrible din of a lot of rascally beaters and huntsmen, who must needs

---

[3] A grass held sacred by the Hindoos and freely used at their religious ceremonies. Its leaves are very long and taper to a needle-like point.

surround the wood before sunrise, and deafen me with their clatter. Nor are these my only troubles. Here's a fresh grievance, like a new boil rising upon an old one! Yesterday, while we were lagging behind, my royal friend entered yonder hermitage after a deer; and there, as ill-luck would have it, caught sight of a beautiful girl, called Sakoontalá, the hermit's daughter. From that moment, not another thought about returning to the city! and all last night, not a wink of sleep did he get for thinking of the damsel. What is to be done? At any rate, I will be on the watch for him as soon as he has finished his toilet. [*Walking and looking about.*] Oh! here he comes, attended by the Yavana women with bows in their hands, and wearing garlands of wild flowers. What shall I do? I have it. I will pretend to stand in the easiest attitude for resting my bruised and crippled limbs. [*Stands leaning on a staff.*

Enter King Dushyanta, followed by a retinue in the manner described.

KING: True, by no easy conquest may I win her,
Yet are my hopes encouraged by her mien.
Love is not yet triumphant; but, methinks,
The hearts of both are ripe for his delights.
[*Smiling.*] Ah! thus does the lover delude himself; judging of the state of his loved one's feelings by his own desires. But yet,
The stolen glance with half-averted eye,
The hesitating gait, the quick rebuke
Addressed to her companion, who would fain
Have stayed her counterfeit departure; these
Are signs not unpropitious to my suit.
So eagerly the lover feeds his hopes,
Claiming each trivial gesture for his own.

MÁTHAVYA [*still in the same attitude*]: Ah, friend, my hands cannot move to greet you with the usual salutation. I can only just command my lips to wish your majesty victory.

KING: Why, what has paralyzed your limbs?

MÁTHAVYA: You might as well ask me how my eye comes to water after you have poked your finger into it.

KING: I don't understand you; speak more intelligibly.

MÁTHAVYA: Ah, my dear friend, is yonder upright reed transformed into a crooked plant by its own act, or by the force of the current?

KING: The current of the river causes it, I suppose.

MÁTHAVYA: Aye; just as you are the cause of my crippled limbs.

KING: How so?

MÁTHAVYA: Here are you living the life of a wild man of the woods in a savage, unfrequented region, while your state affairs are left to shift for themselves; and as for poor me, I am no longer master of my own limbs, but have to follow you about day after day in your chases after wild animals, till my bones are all crippled and out of joint. Do, my dear friend, let me have one day's rest.

KING [*aside*]: This fellow little knows, while he talks in this manner, that my mind is wholly engrossed by recollections of the hermit's daughter, and quite as disinclined to the chase as his own.

No longer can I bend my well-braced bow
Against the timid deer; nor e'er again
With well-aimed arrows can I think to harm
These her beloved associates, who enjoy
The privilege of her companionship;
Teaching her tender glances in return.

MÁTHAVYA [*looking in the King's face*]: I may as well speak to the winds, for any attention you pay to my requests. I suppose you have something on your mind, and are talking it over to yourself.

KING [*smiling*]: I was only thinking that I ought not to disregard a friend's request.

MÁTHAVYA: Then may the King live forever!   [*Moves off*.

KING: Stay a moment, my dear friend. I have something else to say to you.

MÁTHAVYA: Say on, then.

KING: When you have rested, you must assist me in another business, which will give you no fatigue.

MÁTHAVYA: In eating something nice, I hope.

KING: You shall know at some future time.

MÁTHAVYA: No time better than the present.

KING: What ho! there.

WARDER [*entering*]: What are your Majesty's commands?

KING: O Raivataka! bid the General of the forces attend.

WARDER: I will, Sire. [*Exit and reënters with the General*.] Come forward, General; his Majesty is looking towards you, and has some order to give you.

GENERAL [*looking at the King*]: Though hunting is known to produce ill effects, my royal master has derived only benefit from it. For

Like the majestic elephant that roams
O'er mountain wilds, so does the King display
A stalwart frame, instinct with vigorous life.
His brawny arms and manly chest are scored

By frequent passage of the sounding string;
Unharmed he bears the mid-day sun; no toil
His mighty spirit daunts; his sturdy limbs,
Stripped of redundant flesh, relinquish nought
Of their robust proportions, but appear
In muscle, nerve, and sinewy fibre cased.
 [*Approaching the King.*] Victory to the King! We have tracked the wild beasts to their lairs in the forest. Why delay, when everything is ready?

KING: My friend Máthavya here has been disparaging the chase, till he has taken away all my relish for it.

GENERAL [*aside to Máthavya*]: Persevere in your opposition, my good fellow; I will sound the King's real feelings, and humor him accordingly. [*Aloud.*] The blockhead talks nonsense, and your Majesty, in your own person, furnishes the best proof of it. Observe, Sire, the advantage and pleasure the hunter derives from the chase.

Freed from all grosser influences, his frame
Loses its sluggish humors, and becomes
Buoyant, compact, and fit for bold encounter.
'Tis his to mark with joy the varied passions,
Fierce heats of anger, terror, blank dismay,
Of forest animals that cross his path.
Then what a thrill transports the hunter's soul,
When, with unerring course, his driven shaft
Pierces the moving mark! Oh! 'tis conceit
In moralists to call the chase a vice;
What recreation can compare with this?

MÁTHAVYA [*angrily*]: Away! tempter, away! The King has recovered his senses, and is himself again. As for you, you may, if you choose, wander about from forest to forest, till some old bear seizes you by the nose, and makes a mouthful of you.

KING: My good General, as we are just now in the neighborhood of a consecrated grove, your panegyric upon hunting is somewhat ill-timed, and I cannot assent to all you have said. For the present,

All undisturbed the buffaloes shall sport
In yonder pool, and with their ponderous horns
Scatter its tranquil waters, while the deer,
Couched here and there in groups beneath the shade
Of spreading branches, ruminate in peace.
And all securely shall the herd of boars
Feed on the marshy sedge; and thou, my bow,
With slackened string enjoy a long repose.

GENERAL: So please your Majesty, it shall be as you desire.

KING: Recall, then, the beaters who were sent in advance to

surround the forest. My troops must not be allowed to disturb this sacred retreat, and irritate its pious inhabitants.

Know that within the calm and cold recluse
Lurks unperceived a germ of smothered flame,
All-potent to destroy; a latent fire
That rashly kindled bursts with fury forth:—
As in the disc of crystal that remains
Cool to the touch, until the solar ray
Falls on its polished surface, and excites
The burning heat that lies within concealed.

GENERAL: Your Majesty's commands shall be obeyed.

MÁTHAVYA: Off with you, you son of a slave! Your nonsense won't go down here, my fine fellow.   [*Exit General.*

KING [*looking at his attendants*]: Here, women, take my hunting-dress; and you, Raivataka, keep guard carefully outside.

ATTENDANTS: We will, sire.   [*Exeunt.*

MÁTHAVYA: Now that you have got rid of these plagues, who have been buzzing about us like so many flies, sit down, do, on that stone slab, with the shade of the tree as your canopy, and I will seat myself by you quite comfortably.

KING: Go you, and sit down first.

MÁTHAVYA: Come along, then.

[*Both walk on a little way, and seat themselves.*

KING: Máthavya, it may be said of you that you have never beheld anything worth seeing: for your eyes have not yet looked upon the loveliest object in creation.

MÁTHAVYA: How can you say so, when I see your Majesty before me at this moment?

KING: It is very natural that everyone should consider his own friend perfect; but I was alluding to Sakoontalá, the brightest ornament of these hallowed groves.

MÁTHAVYA [*aside*]: I understand well enough, but I am not going to humor him. [*Aloud.*] If, as you intimate, she is a hermit's daughter, you cannot lawfully ask her in marriage.[4] You may as well, then, dismiss her from your mind, for any good the mere sight of her can do.

KING: Think you that a descendant of the mighty Puru could fix his affections on an unlawful object?

Though, as men say, the offspring of the sage,
The maiden to a nymph celestial owes
Her being, and by her mother left on earth,
Was found and nurtured by the holy man
As his own daughter, in this hermitage;—

[4] The king must marry within the warrior caste. [Ed.]

So, when dissevered from its parent stalk,
Some falling blossom of the jasmine, wafted
Upon the sturdy sunflower, is preserved
By its support from premature decay.

MÁTHAVYA [*smiling*]: This passion of yours for a rustic maiden,
when you have so many gems of women at home in
your palace, seems to me very like the fancy of a man
who is tired of sweet dates, and longs for sour tamarinds
as a variety.

KING: You have not seen her, or you would not talk in this
fashion.

MÁTHAVYA: I can quite understand it must require something
surpassingly attractive to excite the admiration of such
a great man as you.

KING: I will describe her, my dear friend, in a few words—
Man's all-wise Maker, wishing to create
A faultless form, whose matchless symmetry
Should far transcend Creation's choicest works,
Did call together by his mighty will,
And garner up in his eternal mind,
A bright assemblage of all lovely things:—
And then, as in a picture, fashion them
Into one perfect and ideal form.
Such the divine, the wondrous prototype,
Whence her fair shape was moulded into being.

MÁTHAVYA: If that's the case, she must indeed throw all other
beauties into the shade.

KING: To my mind she really does.
This peerless maid is like a fragrant flower,
Whose perfumed breath has never been diffused;
A tender bud, that no profaning hand
Has dared to sever from its parent stalk;
A gem of priceless water, just released
Pure and unblemished from its glittering bed.
Or may the maiden haply be compared
To sweetest honey, that no mortal lip
Has sipped; or, rather to the mellowed fruit
Of virtuous actions in some former birth,
Now brought to full perfection? Lives the man
Whom bounteous heaven has destined to espouse her?

MÁTHAVYA: Make haste, then, to her aid; you have no time
to lose, if you don't wish this fruit of all the virtues to
drop into the mouth of some greasy-headed rustic of
devout habits.

KING: The lady is not her own mistress, and her foster-father
is not at home.

MÁTHAVYA: Well, but tell me, did she look at all kindly upon you?

KING: Maidens brought up in a hermitage are naturally shy and reserved; but for all that,

She did look towards me, though she quick withdrew
Her stealthy glances when she met my gaze;
She smiled upon me sweetly, but disguised
With maiden grace the secret of her smiles.
Coy love was half unveiled; then, sudden checked
By modesty, left half to be divined.

MÁTHAVYA: Why, of course, my dear friend, you never could seriously expect that at the very first sight she would fall over head and ears in love with you, and without more ado come and sit in your lap.

KING: When we parted from each other, she betrayed her liking for me by clearer indications, but still with the utmost modesty.

Scarce had the fair one from my presence passed,
When, suddenly, without apparent cause,
She stopped, and counterfeiting pain, exclaimed,
"My foot is wounded by this prickly grass."
Then glancing at me tenderly, she feigned
Another charming pretext for delay,
Pretending that a bush had caught her robe,
And turned as if to disentangle it.

MÁTHAVYA: I trust you have laid in a good stock of provisions, for I see you intend making this consecrated grove your game-preserve, and will be roaming here in quest of sport for some time to come.

KING: You must know, my good fellow, that I have been recognized by some of the inmates of the hermitage. Now I want the assistance of your fertile invention, in devising some excuse for going there again.

MÁTHAVYA: There is but one expedient that I can suggest. You are the King, are you not?

KING: What then?

MÁTHAVYA: Say you have come for the sixth part of their grain, which they owe you for tribute.

KING: No, no, foolish man; these hermits pay me a very different kind of tribute, which I value more than heaps of gold or jewels; observe,

The tribute which my other subjects bring
Must moulder into dust, but holy men
Present me with a portion of the fruits
Of penitential services and prayers—
A precious and imperishable gift.

A VOICE [*behind the scenes*]: We are fortunate; here is the
　　object of our search.

KING [*listening*]: Surely those must be the voices of hermits,
　　to judge by their deep tones.

WARDER [*entering*]: Victory to the King! two young hermits
　　are in waiting outside, and solicit an audience of your
　　Majesty.

KING: Introduce them immediately.

WARDER: I will, my liege. [*Goes out, and reënters with two
　　young Hermits.*] This way, Sirs, this way.

　　　　　　　　　　[*Both the Hermits look at the King.*

FIRST HERMIT: How majestic is his mien, and yet what
　　confidence it inspires! But this might be expected in a
　　king whose character and habits have earned for him
　　a title only one degree removed from that of a Saint.

　　In this secluded grove, whose sacred joys
　　All may participate, he deigns to dwell
　　Like one of us; and daily treasures up
　　A store of purest merit for himself,
　　By the protection of our holy rites.
　　In his own person wondrously are joined
　　Both majesty and saintlike holiness:—
　　And often chanted by inspirèd bards,
　　His hallowed title of "Imperial Sage"
　　Ascends in joyous accents to the skies.

SECOND HERMIT: Bear in mind, Gautama, that this is the
　　great Dushyanta, the friend of Indra.

FIRST HERMIT: What of that?

SECOND HERMIT: Where is the wonder if his nervous arm,
　　Puissant and massive as the iron bar
　　That binds a castle-gateway, singly sways
　　The sceptre of the universal earth,
　　E'en to its dark-green boundary of waters?
　　Or if the gods, beholden to his aid
　　In their fierce warfare with the powers of hell,
　　Should blend his name with Indra's in their songs
　　Of victory, and gratefully accord
　　No lower meed of praise to his braced bow,
　　Than to the thunders of the god of heaven?

BOTH THE HERMITS [*approaching*]: Victory to the King!

KING [*rising from his seat*]: Hail to you both!

BOTH THE HERMITS: Heaven bless your Majesty!

　　　　　　　　　　　　　　[*They offer fruits.*

KING [*respectfully receiving the offering*]: Tell me, I pray you,
　　the object of your visit.

BOTH THE HERMITS: The inhabitants of the hermitage, having

heard of your Majesty's sojourn in our neighborhood, make this humble petition.

KING: What are their commands?

BOTH THE HERMITS: In the absence of our Superior, the great Sage Kanwa, evil demons are disturbing our sacrificial rites.[5] Deign, therefore, accompanied by your charioteer, to take up your abode in our hermitage for a few days.

KING: I am honored by your invitation.

MÁTHAVYA [*aside*]: Most opportune and convenient, certainly!

KING [*smiling*]: Ho! there, Raivataka! Tell the charioteer from me to bring round the chariot with my bow.

WARDER: I will, Sire.   [*Exit.*

BOTH THE HERMITS [*joyfully*]: Well it becomes the King by acts of grace
  To emulate the virtues of his race.
  Such acts thy lofty destiny attest;
  Thy mission is to succor the distressed.

KING [*bowing to the Hermits*]: Go first, reverend Sirs, I will follow you immediately.

BOTH THE HERMITS: May victory attend you!   [*Exeunt.*

KING: My dear Máthavya, are you not full of longing to see Sakoontalá?

MÁTHAVYA: To tell you the truth, though I was just now brimful of desire to see her, I have not a drop left since this piece of news about the demons.

KING: Never fear; you shall keep close to me for protection.

MÁTHAVYA: Well, you must be my guardian-angel, and act the part of a very Vishnu [6] to me.

WARDER [*entering*]: Sire, the chariot is ready, and only waits to conduct you to victory. But here is a messenger named Karabhaka, just arrived from your capital, with a message from the Queen, your mother.

KING [*respectfully*]: How say you? a messenger from the venerable Queen?

WARDER: Even so.

KING: Introduce him at once.

WARDER: I will, Sire. [*Goes out, and reënters with Karabhaka.*] Behold the King! Approach.

KARABHAKA: Victory to the King! The Queen-mother bids me say that in four days from the present time she intends celebrating a solemn ceremony for the advancement and preservation of her son. She expects that your Majesty will honor her with your presence on that occasion.

KING: This places me in a dilemma. Here, on the one hand,

---

[5] The religious rites of holy men were often disturbed by certain evil spirits called Rákshasas, who were the determined enemies of piety and devotion.
[6] Vishnu, the Preserver, was one of the three principal gods.

is the commission of these holy men to be executed; and, on the other, the command of my revered parent to be obeyed. Both duties are too sacred to be neglected. What is to be done?

MÁTHAVYA: You will have to take up an intermediate position between the two, like King Triśanku, who was suspended between heaven and earth, because the sage Viśwámitra commanded him to mount up to heaven, and the gods ordered him down again.

KING: I am certainly very much perplexed. For here,

Two different duties are required of me
In widely distant places; how can I
In my own person satisfy them both?
Thus is my mind distracted and impelled
In opposite directions, like a stream
That, driven back by rocks, still rushes on,
Forming two currents in its eddying course.

[*Reflecting.*] Friend Máthavya, as you were my play-fellow in childhood, the Queen has always received you like a second son; go you, then, back to her and tell her of my solemn engagement to assist these holy men. You can supply my place in the ceremony, and act the part of a son to the Queen.

MÁTHAVYA: With the greatest pleasure in the world; but don't suppose that I am really coward enough to have the slightest fear of those trumpery demons.

KING [*smiling*]: Oh! of course not; a great Bráhman like you could not possibly give way to such weakness.

MÁTHAVYA: You must let me travel in a manner suitable to the King's younger brother.

KING: Yes, I shall send my retinue with you, that there may be no further disturbance in this sacred forest.

MÁTHAVYA [*with a strut*]: Already I feel quite like a young prince.

KING [*aside*]: This is a giddy fellow, and in all probability he will let out the truth about my present pursuit to the women of the palace. What is to be done? I must say something to deceive him. [*Aloud to Máthavya, taking him by the hand.*] Dear friend, I am going to the hermitage wholly and solely out of respect for its pious inhabitants, and not because I have really any liking for Sakoontalá, the hermit's daughter. Observe,

What suitable communion could there be
Between a monarch and a rustic girl?
I did but feign an idle passion, friend,
Take not in earnest what was said in jest.

MÁTHAVYA: Don't distress yourself; I quite understand.

[*Exeunt.*

PRELUDE TO ACT THIRD

Scene—The Hermitage

Enter a young Bráhman, carrying bundles of Kuśa-grass for the use of the sacrificing priests.

YOUNG BRÁHMAN: How wonderful is the power of King Dushyanta! No sooner did he enter our hermitage, than we were able to proceed with our sacrificial rites, unmolested by the evil demons.

No need to fix the arrow to the bow;
The mighty monarch sounds the quivering string,
And, by the thunder of his arms dismayed,
Our demon foes are scattered to the wind.

I must now, therefore, make haste and deliver to the sacrificing priests these bundles of Kuśa-grass, to be strewn round the altar. [*Walking and looking about; then addressing someone off the stage.*] Why, Priyamvadá, for whose use are you carrying that ointment of Usíra-root and those lotus leaves with fibres attached to them? [*Listening for her answer.*] What say you?—that Śakoontalá is suffering from fever produced by exposure to the sun, and that this ointment is to cool her burning frame? Nurse her with care, then, Priyamvadá, for she is cherished by our reverend Superior as the very breath of his nostrils. I, for my part, will contrive that soothing waters, hallowed in the sacrifice, be administered to her by the hands of Gautamí. [*Exit.*]

ACT THIRD

Scene—The Sacred Grove

Enter King Dushyanta, with the air of one in love.

KING [*sighing thoughtfully*]: The holy sage possesses magic power
In virtue of his penance; she, his ward,
Under the shadow of his tutelage
Rests in security. I know it well;
Yet sooner shall the rushing cataract
In foaming eddies re-ascend the steep,
Than my fond heart turn back from its pursuit.

God of Love! God of the flowery shafts! [7] we are all of
us cruelly deceived by thee, and by the Moon, however
deserving of confidence you may both appear.

For not to us do these thine arrows seem
Pointed with tender flowerets; not to us
Doth the pale moon irradiate the earth
With beams of silver fraught with cooling dews:—
But on our fevered frames the moon-beams fall
Like darts of fire, and every flower-tipped shaft
Of Káma, as it probes our throbbing hearts,
Seems to be barbed with hardest adamant.

Adorable god of love! hast thou no pity for me? [*In a
tone of anguish.*] How can thy arrows be so sharp when
they are pointed with flowers? Ah! I know the reason:

E'en now in thine unbodied essence lurks
The fire of Śiva's anger, like the flame
That ever hidden in the secret depths
Of ocean, smoulders there unseen. How else
Couldst thou, all immaterial as thou art,
Inflame our hearts thus fiercely?—thou, whose form
Was scorched to ashes by a sudden flash
From the offended god's terrific eye.

Yet, methinks,
Welcome this anguish, welcome to my heart
These rankling wounds inflicted by the god,
Who on his scutcheon bears the monster-fish
Slain by his prowess: welcome death itself,
So that, commissioned by the lord of love,
This fair one be my executioner.

Adorable divinity! Can I by no reproaches excite your
commiseration?

Have I not daily offered at thy shrine
Innumerable vows, the only food
Of thine ethereal essence? Are my prayers
Thus to be slighted? Is it meet that thou
Shouldst aim thy shafts at thy true votary's heart,
Drawing thy bow-string even to thy ear?

[*Pacing up and down in a melancholy manner.*] Now
that the holy men have completed their rites, and have
no more need of my services, how shall I dispel my
melancholy? [*Sighing.*] I have but one resource. Oh for
another sight of the idol of my soul! I will seek her.
[*Glancing at the sun.*] In all probability, as the sun's
heat is now at its height, Śakoontalá is passing her time

---

[7] Káma, the Hindoo Cupid, or god of love. He has five arrows, each
tipped with the blossom of a flower, which pierce the heart through
the five senses.

under the shade of the bowers on the banks of the
Málini, attended by her maidens. I will go and look for
her there. [*Walking and looking about.*] I suspect the
fair one has but just passed by this avenue of young
trees.

Here, as she tripped along, her fingers plucked
The opening buds: these lacerated plants,
Shorn of their fairest blossoms by her hand,
Seem like dismembered trunks, whose recent wounds
Are still unclosed; while from the bleeding socket
Of many a severed stalk, the milky juice
Still slowly trickles, and betrays her path.

[*Feeling a breeze.*] What a delicious breeze meets me in
this spot!

Here may the zephyr, fragrant with the scent
Of lotuses, and laden with the spray
Caught from the waters of the rippling stream,
Fold in its close embrace my fevered limbs.

[*Walking and looking about.*] She must be somewhere
in the neighborhood of this arbor of overhanging creep-
ers, enclosed by plantations of cane.   [*Looking down.*
For at the entrance here I plainly see
A line of footsteps printed in the sand.
Here are the fresh impressions of her feet;
Their well-known outline faintly marked in front,
More deeply towards the heel; betokening
The graceful undulation of her gait.

I will peep through those branches. [*Walking and looking. With transport.*] Ah! now my eyes are gratified by
an entrancing sight. Yonder is the beloved of my heart
reclining on a rock strewn with flowers, and attended
by her two friends. How fortunate! Concealed behind
the leaves, I will listen to their conversation, without
raising their suspicions.

[*Stands concealed, and gazes at them.*

*Sakoontalá and her two attendants, holding fans in their
hands, are discovered as described.*

PRIYAMVADÁ *and* ANASÚYÁ [*fanning her. In a tone of affection*]: Dearest Śakoontalá, is the breeze raised by these
broad lotus leaves refreshing to you?

ŚAKOONTALÁ: Dear friends, why should you trouble yourselves
to fan me?

[*Priyamvadá and Anasúyá look sorrowfully at one another.*

KING: Śakoontalá seems indeed to be seriously ill. [*Thoughtfully.*] Can it be the intensity of the heat that has affected

her? or does my heart suggest the true cause of her
malady? [*Gazing at her passionately.*] Why should I
doubt it?

The maiden's spotless bosom is o'erspread
With cooling balsam; on her slender arm
Her only bracelet, twined with lotus stalks,
Hangs loose and withered; her recumbent form
Expresses languor. Ne'er could noon-day sun
Inflict such fair disorder on a maid—
No, love, and love alone, is here to blame.

PRIYAMVADÁ [*aside to Anasúyá*]: I have observed. Anasúyá, that Śakoontalá has been indisposed ever since her
first interview with King Dushyanta. Depend upon it,
her ailment is to be traced to this source.

ANASÚYÁ: The same suspicion, dear Priyamvadá, has crossed
my mind. But I will at once ask her and ascertain the
truth. [*Aloud.*] Dear Śakoontalá, I am about to put a
question to you. Your indisposition is really very serious.

ŚAKOONTALÁ [*half-rising from her couch*]: What were you
going to ask?

ANASÚYÁ: We know very little about love-matters, dear
Śakoontalá; but for all that, I cannot help suspecting
your present state to be something similar to that of the
lovers we have read about in romances. Tell us frankly
what is the cause of your disorder. It is useless to apply
a remedy, until the disease be understood.

KING: Anasúyá bears me out in my suspicion.

ŚAKOONTALÁ [*aside*]: I am, indeed, deeply in love; but cannot
rashly disclose my passion to these young girls.

PRIYAMVADÁ: What Anasúyá says, dear Śakoontalá, is very
just. Why give so little heed to your ailment? Every day
you are becoming thinner; though I must confess your
complexion is still as beautiful as ever.

KING: Priyamvadá speaks most truly.

Sunk is her velvet cheek; her wasted bosom
Loses its fulness; e'en her slender waist
Grows more attenuate; her face is wan,
Her shoulders droop;—as when the vernal blasts
Sear the young blossoms of the Mádhaví,
Blighting their bloom; so mournful is the change,
Yet in its sadness, fascinating still,
Inflicted by the mighty lord of love
On the fair figure of the hermit's daughter.

ŚAKOONTALÁ: Dear friends, to no one would I rather reveal
the nature of my malady than to you; but I should only
be troubling you.

PRIYAMVADÁ *and* ANASÚYÁ: Nay, this is the very point about

which we are so solicitous. Sorrow shared with affectionate friends is relieved of half its poignancy.

KING: Pressed by the partners of her joys and griefs,
Her much beloved companions, to reveal
The cherished secret locked within her breast,
She needs must utter it; although her looks
Encourage me to hope, my bosom throbs
As anxiously I listen for her answer.

ŚAKOONTALÁ: Know then, dear friends, that from the first moment the illustrious Prince, who is the guardian of our grove, presented himself to my sight—

[*Stops short, and appears confused.*

PRIYAMVADÁ *and* ANASÚYÁ: Say on, dear Śakoontalá, say on.

ŚAKOONTALÁ: Ever since that happy moment, my heart's affections have been fixed upon him, and my energies of mind and body have all deserted me, as you see.

KING [*with rapture*]: Her own lips have uttered the words I most longed to hear.
Love lit the flame, and Love himself allays
My burning fever, as when gathering clouds
Rise o'er the earth in summer's dazzling noon,
And grateful showers dispel the morning heat.

ŚAKOONTALÁ: You must consent, then, dear friends, to contrive some means by which I may find favor with the King, or you will have ere long to assist at my funeral.

KING [*with rapture*]: Enough! These words remove all my doubts.

PRIYAMVADÁ [*aside to Anasúyá*]: She is far gone in love, dear Anasúyá, and no time ought to be lost. Since she has fixed her affections on a monarch who is the ornament of Puru's line, we need not hesitate for a moment to express our approval.

ANASÚYÁ: I quite agree with you.

PRIYAMVADÁ [*aloud*]: We wish you joy, dear Śakoontalá. Your affections are fixed on an object in every respect worthy of you. The noblest river will unite itself to the ocean, and the lovely Mádhaví-creeper clings naturally to the Mango, the only tree capable of supporting it.

KING: Why need we wonder if the beautiful constellation Viśákhá pines to be united with the Moon.

ANASÚYÁ: By what stratagem can we best secure to our friend the accomplishment of her heart's desire, both speedily and secretly?

PRIYAMVADÁ: The latter point is all we have to think about. As to "speedily," I look upon the whole affair as already settled.

ANASÚYÁ: How so?

PRIYAMVADÁ: Did you not observe how the King betrayed his liking by the tender manner in which he gazed upon her, and how thin he has become the last few days, as if he had been lying awake thinking of her?

KING [*looking at himself*]: Quite true! I certainly am becoming thin from want of sleep:—

> As night by night in anxious thought I raise
> This wasted arm to rest my sleepless head,
> My jewelled bracelet, sullied by the tears
> That trickle from my eyes in scalding streams,
> Slips towards my elbow from my shrivelled wrist.
> Oft I replace the bauble, but in vain;
> So easily it spans the fleshless limb
> That e'en the rough and corrugated skin,
> Scarred by the bow-string, will not check its fall.

PRIYAMVADÁ [*thoughtfully*]: An idea strikes me, Anasúyá. Let Śakoontalá write a love-letter; I will conceal it in a flower, and contrive to drop it in the King's path. He will surely mistake it for the remains of some sacred offering, and will, in all probability, pick it up.

ANASÚYÁ: A very ingenious device! It has my entire approval; but what says Śakoontalá?

ŚAKOONTALÁ: I must consider before I can consent to it.

PRIYAMVADÁ: Could you not, dear Śakoontalá, think of some pretty composition in verse, containing a delicate declaration of your love?

ŚAKOONTALÁ: Well, I will do my best; but my heart trembles when I think of the chances of a refusal.

KING [*with rapture*]: Too timid maid, here stands the man from whom

> Thou fearest a repulse; supremely blessed
> To call thee all his own. Well might he doubt
> His title to thy love; but how couldst thou
> Believe thy beauty powerless to subdue him?

PRIYAMVADÁ *and* ANASÚYÁ: You undervalue your own merits, dear Śakoontalá. What man in his senses would intercept with the skirt of his robe the bright rays of the autumnal moon, which alone can allay the fever of his body?

ŚAKOONTALÁ [*smiling*]: Then it seems I must do as I am bid.
[*Sits down and appears to be thinking.*

KING: How charming she looks! My very eyes forget to wink, jealous of losing even for an instant a sight so enchanting.

> How beautiful the movement of her brow,
> As through her mind love's tender fancies flow!
> And, as she weighs her thoughts, how sweet to trace
> The ardent passion mantling in her face!

ŚAKOONTALÁ: Dear girls, I have thought of a verse, but I have no writing-materials at hand.

PRIYAMVADÁ: Write the letters with your nail on this lotus
    leaf, which is smooth as a parrot's breast.

ŚAKOONTALÁ [*after writing the verse*]: Listen, dear friends,
    and tell me whether the ideas are appropriately expressed.

PRIYAMVADÁ *and* ANASÚYÁ: We are all attention.

ŚAKOONTALÁ [*reads*]:
    I know not the secret thy bosom conceals,
      Thy form is not near me to gladden my sight;
    But sad is the tale that my fever reveals,
      Of the love that consumes me by day and by night.

KING [*advancing hastily towards her*]:
    Nay, Love does but warm thee, fair maiden—thy frame
      Only droops like the bud in the glare of the noon;
    But me he consumes with a pitiless flame,
      As the beams of the day-star destroy the pale moon.

PRIYAMVADÁ *and* ANASÚYÁ [*looking at him joyfully, and rising
    to salute him*]: Welcome, the desire of our hearts, that
    so speedily presents itself! [*Śakoontalá makes an effort
                               to rise.*

KING: Nay, trouble not thyself, dear maiden,
    Move not to do me homage; let thy limbs
    Still softly rest upon their flowery couch,
    And gather fragrance from the lotus stalks
    Bruised by the fevered contact of thy frame.

ANASÚYÁ: Deign, gentle Sir, to seat yourself on the rock on
    which our friend is reposing.

           [*The King sits down. Śakoontalá is confused.*

PRIYAMVADÁ: Anyone may see at a glance that you are deeply
    attached to each other. But the affection I have for my
    friend prompts me to say something of which you hardly
    require to be informed.

KING: Do not hesitate to speak out, my good girl. If you omit
    to say what is in your mind, you may be sorry for it
    afterwards.

PRIYAMVADÁ: Is it not your special office as a King to remove
    the suffering of your subjects who are in trouble?

KING: Such is my duty, most assuredly.

PRIYAMVADÁ: Know, then, that our dear friend has been
    brought to her present state of suffering entirely through
    love for you. Her life is in your hands; take pity on her
    and restore her to health.

KING: Excellent maiden, our attachment is mutual. It is I
    who am the most honored by it.

ŚAKOONTALÁ [*looking at Priyamvadá*]: What do you mean by
    detaining the King, who must be anxious to return to
    his royal consorts after so long a separation?

KING: Sweet maiden, banish from thy mind the thought
  That I could love another. Thou dost reign

Supreme, without a rival, in my heart,
And I am thine alone: disown me not,
Else must I die a second deadlier death—
Killed by thy words, as erst by Káma's shafts.

ANASÚYÁ: Kind Sir, we have heard it said that kings have many favorite consorts. You must not, then, by your behavior towards our dear friend, give her relations cause to sorrow for her.

KING: Listen, gentle maiden, while in a few words I quiet your anxiety.

Though many beauteous forms my palace grace,
Henceforth two things alone will I esteem
The glory of my royal dynasty;—
My sea-girt realm, and this most lovely maid.

PRIYAMVADÁ *and* ANASÚYÁ: We are satisfied by your assurances.

PRIYAMVADÁ [*glancing on one side*]: See, Anasúyá, there is our favorite little fawn running about in great distress, and turning its eyes in every direction as if looking for its mother; come, let us help the little thing to find her.
[*Both move away.*

ŚAKOONTALÁ: Dear friends, dear friends, leave me not alone and unprotected. Why need you both go?

PRIYAMVADÁ *and* ANASÚYÁ: Unprotected! when the Protector of the world is at your side. [*Exeunt.*

ŚAKOONTALÁ: What! have they both really left me?

KING: Distress not thyself, sweet maiden. Thy adorer is at hand to wait upon thee.

Oh, let me tend thee, fair one, in the place
Of thy dear friends; and, with broad lotus fans,
Raise cooling breezes to refresh thy frame;
Or shall I rather, with caressing touch,
Allay the fever of thy limbs, and soothe
Thy aching feet, beauteous as blushing lilies?

ŚAKOONTALÁ: Nay, touch me not. I will not incur the censure of those whom I am bound to respect.
[*Rises and attempts to go.*

KING: Fair one, the heat of noon has not yet subsided, and thy body is still feeble.

How canst thou quit thy fragrant couch of flowers,
And from thy throbbing bosom cast aside
Its covering of lotus leaves, to brave
With weak and fainting limbs the noon-day heat?
[*Forces her to turn back.*

ŚAKOONTALÁ: Infringe not the rules of decorum, mighty descendant of Puru. Remember, though I love you, I have no power to dispose of myself.

KING: Why this fear of offending your relations, timid maid?

When your venerable foster-father hears of it, he will
not find fault with you. He knows that the law permits
us to be united without consulting him.

In Indra's heaven, so at least 'tis said,
No nuptial rites prevail,[8] nor is the bride
Led to the altar by her future spouse;
But all in secret does the bridegroom plight
His troth, and each unto the other vow
Mutual allegiance. Such espousals, too,
Are authorized on earth, and many daughters
Of royal saints thus wedded to their lords,
Have still received their father's benison.

ŚAKOONTALÁ: Leave me, leave me; I must take counsel with
my female friends.

KING: I will leave thee when—

ŚAKOONTALÁ: When?

KING: When I have gently stolen from thy lips
Their yet untasted nectar, to allay
The raging of my thirst, e'en as the bee
Sips the fresh honey from the opening bud.

[*Attempts to raise her face. Śakoontalá tries to prevent him.*

A VOICE [*behind the scenes*]: The loving birds, doomed by
fate to nightly separation, must bid farewell to each
other, for evening is at hand.

ŚAKOONTALÁ [*in confusion*]: Great Prince, I hear the voice of
the matron Gautamí. She is coming this way, to inquire
after my health. Hasten and conceal yourself behind the
branches.

KING: I will.　　　　　　　　　　　　　　　　　[*Conceals himself.*

*Enter Gautamí with a vase in her hand, preceded by two
attendants.*

ATTENDANTS: This way, most venerable Gautamí.

GAUTAMÍ [*approaching Śakoontalá*]: My child, is the fever of
thy limbs allayed?

ŚAKOONTALÁ: Venerable mother, there is certainly a change
for the better.

GAUTAMÍ: Let me sprinkle you with this holy water, and all
your ailments will depart. [*Sprinkling Śakoontalá on the
head.*] The day is closing, my child; come, let us go to
the cottage.　　　　　　　　　　　　　　[*They all move away.*

ŚAKOONTALÁ [*aside*]: Oh my heart! thou didst fear to taste of
happiness when it was within thy reach. Now that the
object of thy desires is torn from thee, how bitter will
be thy remorse, how distracting thine anguish! [*Moving

---

8 A marriage without the usual ceremonies is called Gándharva. It was
supposed to be the form of marriage prevalent among the nymphs of
Indra's heaven.

on a few steps and stopping. Aloud.] Farewell! bower of
creepers, sweet soother of my sufferings, farewell! may
I soon again be happy under thy shade.

[*Exit reluctantly with the others.*

KING [*returning to his former seat in the arbor. Sighing*]:
Alas! how many are the obstacles to the accomplishment
of our wishes!

Albeit she did coyly turn away
Her glowing cheek, and with her fingers guard
Her pouting lips, that murmured a denial
In faltering accents, she did yield herself
A sweet reluctant captive to my will,
As eagerly I raised her lovely face:
But ere with gentle force I stole the kiss,
Too envious Fate did mar my daring purpose.

Whither now shall I betake myself? I will tarry for a
brief space in this bower of creepers, so endeared to me
by the presence of my beloved Śakoontalá.

[*Looking round.*

Here printed on the flowery couch I see
The fair impression of her slender limbs;
Here is the sweet confession of her love,
Traced with her nail upon the lotus leaf—
And yonder are the withered lily stalks
That graced her wrist. While all around I view
Things that recall her image, can I quit
This bower, e'en though its living charm be fled?

A VOICE [*in the air*]: Great King,
Scarce is our evening sacrifice begun,
When evil demons, lurid as the clouds
That gather round the dying orb of day,
Cluster in hideous troops, obscene and dread,
About our altars, casting far and near
Terrific shadows, while the sacred fire
Sheds a pale lustre o'er their ghostly shapes.

KING: I come to the rescue, I come. [*Exit.*

PRELUDE TO ACT FOURTH

Scene—The Garden of the Hermitage

Enter Priyamvadá and Anasúyá in the act of gathering flowers.

ANASÚYÁ: Although, dear Priyamvadá, it rejoices my heart
to think that Śakoontalá has been happily united to a
husband in every respect worthy of her, by the form of
marriage prevalent among Indra's celestial musicians,

nevertheless, I cannot help feeling somewhat uneasy in my mind.

PRIYAMVADÁ: How so?

ANASÚYÁ: You know that the pious King was gratefully dismissed by the hermits on the successful termination of their sacrificial rites. He has now returned to his capital, leaving Śakoontalá under our care; and it may be doubted whether, in the society of his royal consorts, he will not forget all that has taken place in this hermitage of ours.

PRIYAMVADÁ: On that score be at ease. Persons of his noble nature are not so destitute of all honorable feeling. I confess, however, that there is one point about which I am rather anxious. What, think you, will father Kanwa say when he hears what has occurred?

ANASÚYÁ: In my opinion, he will approve the marriage.

PRIYAMVADÁ: What makes you think so?

ANASÚYÁ: From the first, it was always his fixed purpose to bestow the maiden on a husband worthy of her; and since heaven has given her such a husband, his wishes have been realized without any trouble to himself.

PRIYAMVADÁ [*looking at the flower-basket*]: We have gathered flowers enough for the sacred offering, dear Anasúyá.

ANASÚYÁ: Well, then, let us now gather more, that we may have wherewith to propitiate the guardian-deity of our dear Śakoontalá.

PRIYAMVADÁ: By all means.   [*They continue gathering.*

A VOICE [*behind the scenes*]: Ho there! See you not that I am here?

ANASÚYÁ [*listening*]: That must be the voice of a guest announcing his arrival.

PRIYAMVADÁ: Surely, Śakoontalá is not absent from the cottage. [*Aside.*] Her heart at least is absent, I fear.

ANASÚYÁ: Come along, come along; we have gathered flowers enough.   [*They move away.*

THE SAME VOICE [*behind the scenes*]: Woe to thee, maiden, for daring to slight a guest like me!

Shall I stand here unwelcomed; even I,
A very mine of penitential merit,
Worthy of all respect? Shalt thou, rash maid,
Thus set at nought the ever sacred ties
Of hospitality? and fix thy thoughts
Upon the cherished object of thy love,
While I am present? Thus I curse thee, then—
He, even he of whom thou thinkest, he
Shall think no more of thee; nor in his heart
Retain thy image. Vainly shalt thou strive
To waken his remembrance of the past;

He shall disown thee, even as the sot,
Roused from his midnight drunkenness, denies
The words he uttered in his revellings.

PRIYAMVADÁ: Alas! alas! I fear a terrible misfortune has
occurred. Sakoontalá, from absence of mind, must have
offended some guest whom she was bound to treat with
respect. [*Looking behind the scenes.*] Ah! yes; I see,
and no less a person than the great sage Durvasas,
who is known to be most irascible. He it is that has
just cursed her, and is now retiring with hasty strides,
trembling with passion, and looking as if nothing could
turn him. His wrath is like a consuming fire.

ANASÚYÁ: Go quickly, dear Priyamvadá, throw yourself at
his feet, and persuade him to come back, while I prepare
a propitiatory offering for him, with water and refresh-
ments.

PRIYAMVADÁ: I will.   [*Exit.*

ANASÚYÁ [*advancing hastily a few steps and stumbling*]: Alas!
alas! this comes of being in a hurry. My foot has slipped
and my basket of flowers has fallen from my hand.
                            [*Stays to gather them up.*

PRIYAMVADÁ [*reëntering*]: Well, dear Anasúyá, I have done
my best; but what living being could succeed in pacifying
such a cross-grained, ill-tempered old fellow? However,
I managed to mollify him a little.

ANASÚYÁ [*smiling*]: Even a little was much for him. Say on.

PRIYAMVADÁ: When he refused to turn back, I implored his
forgiveness in these words: "Most venerable sage, pardon, I beseech you, this first offense of a young and
inexperienced girl, who was ignorant of the respect due
to your saintly character and exalted rank."

ANASÚYÁ: And what did he reply?

PRIYAMVADÁ: "My word must not be falsified; but at the sight
of the ring of recognition the spell shall cease." So saying, he disappeared.

ANASÚYÁ: Oh! then we may breathe again; for now I think
of it, the King himself, at his departure, fastened on
Sakoontalá's finger, as a token of remembrance, a ring
on which his own name was engraved. She has, therefore, a remedy for her misfortune at her own command.

PRIYAMVADÁ: Come, dear Anasúyá, let us proceed with our
religious duties.   [*They walk away.*

PRIYAMVADÁ [*looking off the stage*]: See, Anasúyá, there sits
our dear friend, motionless as a statue, resting her face
on her left hand, her whole mind absorbed in thinking
of her absent husband. She can pay no attention to
herself, much less to a stranger.

ANASÚYÁ: Priyamvadá, let this affair never pass our lips. We must spare our dear friend's feelings. Her constitution is too delicate to bear much emotion.

PRIYAMVADÁ: I agree with you. Who would think of watering a tender jasmine with hot water?

ACT FOURTH

Scene—The Neighborhood of the Hermitage

Enter one of Kanwa's pupils, just arisen from his couch at the dawn of day.

PUPIL: My master, the venerable Kanwa, who is but lately returned from his pilgrimage, has ordered me to ascertain how the time goes. I have therefore come into the open air to see if it be still dark. [*Walking and looking about.*] Oh! the dawn has already broken.

Lo! in one quarter of the sky, the Moon,
Lord of the herbs and night-expanding flowers,
Sinks towards his bed behind the western hills;
While in the east, preceded by the Dawn,
His blushing charioteer, the glorious Sun
Begins his course, and far into the gloom
Casts the first radiance of his orient beams.
Hail! co-eternal orbs, that rise to set,
And set to rise again; symbols divine
Of man's reverses, life's vicissitudes.
    And now,
While the round Moon withdraws his looming disc
Beneath the western sky, the full-blown flower
Of the night-loving lotus sheds her leaves
In sorrow for his loss, bequeathing nought
But the sweet memory of her loveliness
To my bereavèd sight: e'en as the bride
Disconsolately mourns her absent lord,
And yields her heart a prey to anxious grief.

ANASÚYÁ [*entering abruptly*]: Little as I know of the ways of the world, I cannot help thinking that King Dushyanta is treating Śakoontalá very improperly.

PUPIL: Well, I must let my revered preceptor know that it is time to offer the burnt oblation.   [*Exit.*

ANASÚYÁ: I am broad awake, but what shall I do? I have no energy to go about my usual occupations. My hands and feet seem to have lost their power. Well, Love has gained his object; and Love only is to blame for having induced our dear friend, in the innocence of her heart, to confide in such a perfidious man. Possibly, however, the imprecation of Durvasas may be already taking effect. Indeed, I cannot otherwise account for the King's strange conduct, in allowing so long a time to elapse without even a letter; and that, too, after so many promises and protestations. I cannot think what to do, unless we send him the ring which was to be the token of recognition. But which of these austere hermits could we ask to be the bearer of it? Then, again, Father Kanwa has just returned from his pilgrimage: and how am I to inform him of Sakoontalá's marriage to King Dushyanta, and her expectation of being soon a mother? I never could bring myself to tell him, even if I felt that Sakoontalá had been in fault, which she certainly has not. What is to be done?

PRIYAMVADÁ [*entering; joyfully*]: Quick! quick! Anasúyá! come and assist in the joyful preparations for Sakoontalá's departure to her husband's palace.

ANASÚYÁ: My dear girl, what can you mean?

PRIYAMVADÁ: Listen, now, and I will tell you all about it. I went just now to Sakoontalá, to inquire whether she had slept comfortably—

ANASÚYÁ: Well, well; go on.

PRIYAMVADÁ: She was sitting with her face bowed down to the very ground with shame, when Father Kanwa entered and, embracing her, of his own accord offered her his congratulations. "I give thee joy, my child," he said, "we have had an auspicious omen. The priest who offered the oblation dropped it into the very center of the sacred fire, though thick smoke obstructed his vision. Henceforth thou wilt cease to be an object of compassion. This very day I purpose sending thee, under the charge of certain trusty hermits, to the King's palace; and shall deliver thee into the hands of thy husband, as I would commit knowledge to the keeping of a wise and faithful student."

ANASÚYÁ: Who, then, informed the holy Father of what passed in his absence?

PRIYAMVADÁ: As he was entering the sanctuary of the consecrated fire, an invisible being chanted a verse in celestial strains.

ANASÚYÁ [*with astonishment*]: Indeed! pray repeat it.

PRIYAMVADÁ [*repeats the verse*]:

Glows in thy daughter King Dushyanta's glory,
   As in the sacred tree the mystic fire.
Let worlds rejoice to hear the welcome story;
   And may the son immortalize the sire.

ANASÚYÁ [*embracing Priyamvadá*]: Oh, my dear Priyamvadá,

what delightful news! I am pleased beyond measure; yet when I think that we are to lose our dear Śakoontalá this very day, a feeling of melancholy mingles with my joy.

PRIYAMVADÁ: We shall find means of consoling ourselves after her departure. Let the dear creature only be made happy, at any cost.

ANASÚYÁ: Yes, yes, Priyamvadá, it shall be so; and now to prepare our bridal array. I have always looked forward to this occasion, and some time since, I deposited a beautiful garland of Keśara flowers in a cocoa-nut box, and suspended it on a bough of yonder mango-tree. Be good enough to stretch out your hand and take it down, while I compound unguents and perfumes with this consecrated paste and these blades of sacred grass.

PRIYAMVADÁ: Very well.

[*Exit Anasúyá. Priyamvadá takes down the flowers.*

A VOICE [*behind the scenes*]: Gautamí, bid Sárngarava and the others hold themselves in readiness to escort Śakoontalá.

PRIYAMVADÁ [*listening*]: Quick, quick, Anasúyá! They are calling the hermits who are to go with Śakoontalá to Hastinápur.

ANASÚYÁ [*reëntering, with the perfumed unguents in her hand*]: Come along then, Priyamvadá; I am ready to go with you. [*They walk away.*

PRIYAMVADÁ [*looking*]: See! there sits Śakoontalá, her locks arranged even at this early hour of the morning. The holy women of the hermitage are congratulating her, and invoking blessings on her head, while they present her with wedding-gifts and offerings of consecrated wild-rice. Let us join them. [*They approach.*

Śakoontalá is seen seated, with women surrounding her, occupied in the manner described.

FIRST WOMAN [*to Śakoontalá*]: My child, may'st thou receive the title of "Chief-queen," and may thy husband delight to honor thee above all others!

SECOND WOMAN: My child, may'st thou be the mother of a hero!

THIRD WOMAN: My child, may'st thou be highly honored by thy lord!

[*Exeunt all the women, excepting Gautamí, after blessing Śakoontalá.*

PRIYAMVADÁ *and* ANASÚYÁ [*approaching*]: Dear Śakoontalá we are come to assist you at your toilet, and may a blessing attend it!

ŚAKOONTALÁ: Welcome, dear friends, welcome. Sit down here.

PRIYAMVADÁ *and* ANASÚYÁ [*taking the baskets containing the bridal decorations, and sitting down*]: Now, then, dearest, prepare to let us dress you. We must first rub your limbs with these perfumed unguents.

ŚAKOONTALÁ: I ought indeed to be grateful for your kind offices, now that I am so soon to be deprived of them. Dear, dear friends, perhaps I shall never be dressed by you again. [*Bursts into tears.*

PRIYAMVADÁ *and* ANASÚYÁ: Weep not, dearest, tears are out of season on such a happy occasion.

[*They wipe away her tears and begin to dress her.*

PRIYAMVADÁ: Alas! these simple flowers and rude ornaments which our hermitage offers in abundance, do not set off your beauty as it deserves.

Enter two young Hermits, bearing costly presents.

BOTH HERMITS: Here are ornaments suitable for a queen.

[*The women look at them in astonishment.*

GAUTAMÍ: Why, Nárada, my son, whence came these?

FIRST HERMIT: You owe them to the devotion of Father Kanwa.

GAUTAMÍ: Did he create them by the power of his own mind?

SECOND HERMIT: Certainly not; but you shall hear. The venerable sage ordered us to collect flowers for Śakoontalá from the forest-trees; and we went to the wood for that purpose, when

Straightway depending from a neighboring tree
Appeared a robe of linen tissue, pure
And spotless as a moon-beam—mystic pledge
Of bridal happiness; another tree
Distilled a roseate dye wherewith to stain
The lady's feet; and other branches near
Glistened with rare and costly ornaments.
While, 'midst the leaves, the hands of forest-nymphs,
Vying in beauty with the opening buds,
Presented us with sylvan offerings.

PRIYAMVADÁ [*looking at Śakoontalá*]: The wood-nymphs have done you honor, indeed. This favor doubtless signifies that you are soon to be received as a happy wife into your husband's house, and are from this forward to become the partner of his royal fortunes.

[*Sakoontalá appears confused.*

FIRST HERMIT: Come, Gautamí; Father Kanwa has finished his ablutions. Let us go and inform him of the favor we have received from the deities who preside over our trees.

SECOND HERMIT: By all means.   [*Exeunt.*

PRIYAMVADÁ *and* ANASÚYÁ: Alas! what are we to do? We are unused to such splendid decorations, and are at a loss how to arrange them. Our knowledge of painting must be our guide. We will dispose the ornaments as we have seen them in pictures.

ŚAKOONTALÁ: Whatever pleases you, dear girls, will please me. I have perfect confidence in your taste.

[*They commence dressing her.*

Enter Kanwa, having just finished his ablutions.

KANWA: This day my loved one leaves me, and my heart
Is heavy with its grief: the streams of sorrow
Choked at the source, repress my faltering voice.
I have no words to speak; mine eyes are dimmed
By the dark shadows of the thoughts that rise
Within my soul. If such the force of grief
In an old hermit parted from his nursling,
What anguish must the stricken parent feel—
Bereft forever of an only daughter?

[*Advances towards Śakoontalá.*

PRIYAMVADÁ *and* ANASÚYÁ: Now, dearest Śakoontalá, we have finished decorating you. You have only to put on the two linen mantles.   [*Śakoontalá rises and puts them on.*

GAUTAMÍ: Daughter, see, here comes thy foster-father; he is eager to fold thee in his arms; his eyes swim with tears of joy. Hasten to do him reverence.

ŚAKOONTALÁ [*reverently*]: My father, I salute you.

KANWA: My daughter,
May'st thou be highly honored by thy lord,
E'en as Yayáti Śarmishthá adored!
And, as she bore him Puru, so may'st thou
Bring forth a son to whom the world shall bow!

GAUTAMÍ: Most venerable father, she accepts your benediction as if she already possessed the boon it confers.

KANWA: Now come this way, my child, and walk reverently round these sacrificial fires.   [*They all walk round.*

KANWA [*repeats a prayer in the metre of the Rig-veda*]:
Holy flames, that gleam around
Every altar's hallowed ground;
Holy flames, whose frequent food
Is the consecrated wood,
And for whose encircling bed,
Sacred Kuśa-grass is spread;
Holy flames, that waft to heaven
Sweet oblations daily given,

Mortal guilt to purge away;—
Hear, oh hear me, when I pray—
Purify my child this day!
    Now then, my daughter, set out on thy journey. [*Looking on one side.*] Where are thy attendants, Śárngarava and the others?

YOUNG HERMIT [*entering*]: Here we are, most venerable father.

KANWA: Lead the way for thy sister.

ŚÁRNGARAVA: Come, Śakoontalá, let us proceed.

                        [*All move away.*

KANWA: Hear me, ye trees that surround our hermitage!
Śakoontalá ne'er moistened in the stream
Her own parched lips, till she had fondly poured
Its purest water on your thirsty roots;
And oft, when she would fain have decked her hair
With your thick-clustering blossoms, in her love
She robbed you not e'en of a single flower.
Her highest joy was ever to behold
The early glory of your opening buds:
Oh, then, dismiss her with a kind farewell!
This very day she quits her father's home,
To seek the palace of her wedded lord.

                  [*The note of a Köil is heard.*

Hark! heard'st thou not the answer of the trees,
Our sylvan sisters, warbled in the note
Of the melodious Köil? they dismiss
Their dear Śakoontalá with loving wishes.

VOICES [*in the air*]:
Fare thee well, journey pleasantly on amid streams
Where the lotuses bloom, and the sun's glowing beams
Never pierce the deep shade of the wide-spreading trees,
While gently around thee shall sport the cool breeze;
Then light be thy footsteps and easy thy tread,
Beneath thee shall carpets of lilies be spread.
Journey on to thy lord, let thy spirit be gay,
For the smiles of all Nature shall gladden thy way.

            [*All listen with astonishment.*

GAUTAMÍ: Daughter! the nymphs of the wood, who love thee with the affection of a sister, dismiss thee with kind wishes for thy happiness. Take thou leave of them reverentially.

ŚAKOONTALÁ [*bowing respectfully and walking on. Aside to her friend*]: Eager as I am, dear Priyamvadá, to see my husband once more, yet my feet refuse to move, now that I am quitting forever the home of my girlhood.

PRIYAMVADÁ: You are not the only one, dearest, to feel the bitterness of parting. As the time of separation ap-

proaches, the whole grove seems to share your anguish.
In sorrow for thy loss, the herd of deer
Forget to browse; the peacock on the lawn
Ceases its dance; the very trees around us
Shed their pale leaves, like tears, upon the ground.

ŚAKOONTALÁ [*recollecting herself*]: My father, let me, before
I go, bid adieu to my pet jasmine, the Moonlight of
the Grove. I love the plant almost as a sister.

KANWA: Yes, yes, my child, I remember thy sisterly affection
for the creeper. Here it is on the right.

ŚAKOONTALÁ [*approaching the jasmine*]: My beloved jasmine,
most brilliant of climbing plants, how sweet it is to see
thee cling thus fondly to thy husband, the mango-tree;
yet, prithee, turn thy twining arms for a moment in this
direction to embrace thy sister; she is going far away,
and may never see thee again.

KANWA: Daughter, the cherished purpose of my heart
Has ever been to wed thee to a spouse
That should be worthy of thee; such a spouse
Hast thou thyself, by thine own merits, won.
To him thou goest, and about his neck
Soon shalt thou cling confidingly, as now
Thy favorite jasmine twines its loving arms
Around the sturdy mango. Leave thou it
To its protector—e'en as I consign
Thee to thy lord, and henceforth from my mind
Banish all anxious thought on thy behalf.
Proceed on thy journey, my child.

ŚAKOONTALÁ [*to Priyamvadá and Anasúyá*]: To you, my sweet
companions, I leave it as a keepsake. Take charge of it
when I am gone.

PRIYAMVADÁ *and* ANASÚYÁ [*bursting into tears*]: And to whose
charge do you leave us, dearest? Who will care for us
when you are gone?

KANWA: For shame, Anasúyá! dry your tears. Is this the way
to cheer your friend at a time when she needs your
support and consolation?   [*All move on.*

ŚAKOONTALÁ: My father, see you there my pet deer, grazing
close to the hermitage? She expects soon to fawn, and
even now the weight of the little one she carries hinders
her movements. Do not forget to send me word when
she becomes a mother.

KANWA: I will not forget it.

ŚAKOONTALÁ [*feeling herself drawn back*]: What can this be,
fastened to my dress?   [*Turns round.*

KANWA: My daughter,
It is the little fawn, thy foster-child.
Poor helpless orphan! it remembers well

How with a mother's tenderness and love
Thou didst protect it, and with grains of rice
From thine own hand didst daily nourish it;
And, ever and anon, when some sharp thorn
Had pierced its mouth, how gently thou didst tend
The bleeding wound, and pour in healing balm.
The grateful nursling clings to its protectress,
Mutely imploring leave to follow her.

ŚAKOONTALÁ: My poor little fawn, dost thou ask to follow
an unhappy woman who hesitates not to desert her
companions? When thy mother died, soon after thy
birth, I supplied her place, and reared thee with my own
hand; and now that thy second mother is about to
leave thee, who will care for thee? My father, be thou
a mother to her. My child, go back, and be a daughter
to my father.   [*Moves on, weeping.*

KANWA: Weep not, my daughter, check the gathering tear
That lurks beneath thine eyelid, ere it flow
And weaken thy resolve; be firm and true—
True to thyself and me; the path of life
Will lead o'er hill and plain, o'er rough and smooth,
And all must feel the steepness of the way;
Though rugged be thy course, press boldly on.

ŚÁRNGARAVA: Venerable sire! the sacred precept is—"Accompany thy friend as far as the margin of the first stream."
Here then, we are arrived at the border of a lake. It is
time for you to give us your final instructions and
return.

KANWA: Be it so; let us tarry for a moment under the shade
of this fig-tree.   [*They do so.*

KANWA [*aside*]: I must think of some appropriate message
to send to his majesty King Dushyanta.   [*Reflects.*

ŚAKOONTALÁ [*aside to Anasúyá*]: See, see, dear Anasúyá, the
poor female Chakraváka-bird, whom cruel fate dooms
to nightly separation from her mate, calls to him in
mournful notes from the other side of the stream, though
he is only hidden from her view by the spreading leaves
of the water-lily. Her cry is so piteous that I could
almost fancy she was lamenting her hard lot in intelligible words.

ANASÚYÁ: Say not so, dearest.
Fond bird! though sorrow lengthen out her night
Of widowhood, yet with a cry of joy
She hails the morning light that brings her mate
Back to her side. The agony of parting
Would wound us like a sword, but that its edge
Is blunted by the hope of future meeting.

KANWA: Sárngarava, when you have introduced Śakoontalá

into the presence of the King, you must give him this
message from me.

SÁRNGARAVA: Let me hear it, venerable father.

KANWA: This is it—

Most puissant prince! we here present before thee
One thou art bound to cherish and receive'
As thine own wife; yea, even to enthrone
As thine own queen—worthy of equal love
With thine imperial consorts. So much, Sire,
We claim of thee as justice due to us,
In virtue of our holy character—
In virtue of thine honorable rank—
In virtue of the pure spontaneous love
That secretly grew up 'twixt thee and her,
Without consent or privity of us.
We ask no more—the rest we freely leave
To thy just feeling and to destiny.

SÁRNGARAVA: A most suitable message. I will take care to
deliver it correctly.

KANWA: And now, my child, a few words of advice for thee.
We hermits, though we live secluded from the world,
are not ignorant of worldly matters.

SÁRNGARAVA: No, indeed. Wise men are conversant with all
subjects.

KANWA: Listen, then, my daughter. When thou reachest thy
husband's palace, and art admitted into his family,

Honor thy betters; ever be respectful
To those above thee; and, should others share
Thy husband's love, ne'er yield thyself a prey
To jealousy; but ever be a friend,
A loving friend, to those who rival thee
In his affections. Should thy wedded lord
Treat thee with harshness, thou must never be
Harsh in return, but patient and submissive.
Be to thy menials courteous, and to all
Placed under thee, considerate and kind.
Be never self-indulgent, but avoid
Excess in pleasure; and, when fortune smiles,
Be not puffed up. Thus to thy husband's house
Wilt thou a blessing prove, and not a curse.
What thinks Gautamí of this advice?

GAUTAMÍ: An excellent compendium, truly, of every wife's
duties! Lay it well to heart, my daughter.

KANWA: Come, my beloved child, one parting embrace for
me and for thy companions, and then we leave thee.

SAKOONTALÁ: My father, must Priyamvadá and Anasúyá
really return with you? They are very dear to me.

KANWA: Yes, my child; they, too, in good time, will be given in marriage to suitable husbands. It would not be proper for them to accompany thee to such a public place. But Gautamí shall be thy companion.

ŚAKOONTALÁ [*embracing him*]: Removed from thy bosom, my beloved father, like a young tendril of the sandal-tree torn from its home in the western mountains, how shall I be able to support life in a foreign soil?

KANWA: Daughter, thy fears are groundless:—
Soon shall thy lord prefer thee to the rank
Of his own consort; and unnumbered cares
Befitting his imperial dignity
Shall constantly engross thee. Then the bliss
Of bearing him a son—a noble boy,
Bright as the day-star—shall transport thy soul
With new delights, and little shalt thou reck
Of the light sorrow that afflicts thee now
At parting from thy father and thy friends.

[*Sakoontalá throws herself at her foster-father's feet.*

KANWA: Blessings on thee, my child! May all my hopes of thee be realized!

ŚAKOONTALÁ [*approaching her friends*]: Come, my two loved companions, embrace me—both of you together.

PRIYAMVADÁ *and* ANASÚYÁ [*embracing her*]: Dear Śakoontalá, remember, if the King should by any chance be slow in recognizing you, you have only to show him this ring, on which his own name is engraved.

ŚAKOONTALÁ: The bare thought of it puts me in a tremor.

PRIYAMVADÁ *and* ANASÚYÁ: There is no real cause for fear, dearest. Excessive affection is too apt to suspect evil where none exists.

ŚÁRNGARAVA: Come, lady, we must hasten on. The sun is rising in the heavens.

ŚAKOONTALÁ [*looking towards the hermitage*]: Dear father, when shall I ever see this hallowed grove again?

KANWA: I will tell thee; listen—
When thou hast passed a long and blissful life
As King Dushyanta's queen, and jointly shared
With all the earth his ever-watchful care;
And hast beheld thine own heroic son,
Matchless in arms, united to a spouse
In happy wedlock; when his aged sire,
Thy faithful husband, hath to him resigned
The helm of state; then, weary of the world,
Together with Dushyanta thou shalt seek
The calm seclusion of thy former home:—
There amid holy scenes to be at peace,
Till thy pure spirit gain its last release.

GAUTAMÍ: Come, my child, the favorable time for our journey

is fast passing. Let thy father return. Venerable Sire, be thou the first to move homewards, or these last words will never end.

KANWA: Daughter, detain me no longer. My religious duties must not be interrupted.

ŚAKOONTALÁ [*again embracing her foster-father*]: Beloved father, thy frame is much enfeebled by penitential exercises. Do not, oh! do not, allow thyself to sorrow too much on my account.

KANWA [*sighing*]: How, O my child, shall my bereavèd heart
Forget its bitterness, when, day by day,
Full in my sight shall grow the tender plants
Reared by thy care, or sprung from hallowed grain
Which thy loved hands have strewn around the door—
A frequent offering to our household gods?
    Go, my daughter, and may thy journey be prosperous.

[*Exit Śakoontalá with her escort.*

PRIYAMVADÁ *and* ANASÚYÁ [*gazing after Śakoontalá*]: Alas! alas! she is gone, and now the trees hide our darling from our view.

KANWA [*sighing*]: Well, Anasúyá, your sister has departed. Moderate your grief, both of you, and follow me. I go back to the hermitage.

PRIYAMVADÁ *and* ANASÚYÁ: Holy father, the sacred grove will be a desert without Śakoontalá. How can we ever return to it?

KANWA: It is natural enough that your affection should make you view it in this light. [*Walking pensively on.*] As for me, I am quite surprised at myself. Now that I have fairly dismissed her to her husband's house, my mind is easy: for indeed,
A daughter is a loan—a precious jewel
Lent to a parent till her husband claim her.
And now that to her rightful lord and master
I have delivered her, my burdened soul
Is lightened, and I seem to breathe more freely.   [*Exeunt.*

ACT FIFTH

Scene—A Room in the Palace

The King Dushyanta and the Jester Máthavya are discovered seated.

MÁTHAVYA [*listening*]: Hark! my dear friend, listen a minute, and you will hear sweet sounds proceeding from the music-room. Someone is singing a charming air. Who

can it be? Oh! I know. The queen Hansapadiká is prac-
ticing her notes, that she may greet you with a new
song.

KING: Hush! Let me listen.

A VOICE [*sings behind the scenes*]:
How often hither didst thou rove,
Sweet bee, to kiss the mango's cheek;
Oh! leave not, then, thy early love,
The lily's honeyed lip to seek.

KING: A most impassioned strain, truly!

MÁTHAVYA: Do you understand the meaning of the words?

KING [*smiling*]: She means to reprove me, because I once
paid her great attention, and have lately deserted her
for the queen Vasumatí. Go, my dear fellow, and tell
Hansapadiká from me that I take her delicate reproof
as it is intended.

MÁTHAVYA: Very well. [*Rising from his seat.*] But stay—I
don't much relish being sent to bear the brunt of her
jealousy. The chances are that she will have me seized
by the hair of the head and beaten to a jelly. I would as
soon expose myself, after a vow of celibacy, to the
seductions of a lovely nymph, as encounter the fury of
a jealous woman.

KING: Go, go; you can disarm her wrath by a civil speech;
but give her my message.

MÁTHAVYA: What must be must be, I suppose.   [*Exit.*

KING [*aside*]: Strange! that song has filled me with a most
peculiar sensation. A melancholy feeling has come over
me, and I seem to yearn after some long-forgotten object
of affection. Singular, indeed! but,
Not seldom in our happy hours of ease,
When thought is still, the sight of some fair form,
Or mournful fall of music breathing low,
Will stir strange fancies, thrilling all the soul
With a mysterious sadness, and a sense
Of vague yet earnest longing. Can it be
That the dim memory of events long past,
Or friendships formed in other states of being,
Flits like a passing shadow o'er the spirit?
                    [*Remains pensive and sad.*

Enter the Chamberlain.

CHAMBERLAIN: Alas! to what an advanced period of life have
I attained!
Even this wand betrays the lapse of years;
In youthful days 'twas but a useless badge
And symbol of my office; now it serves
As a support to prop my tottering steps.

Ah me! I feel very unwilling to announce to the King
that a deputation of young hermits from the sage Kanwa
has arrived, and craves an immediate audience. Certainly, his majesty ought not to neglect a matter of
sacred duty, yet I hardly like to trouble him when he
has just risen from the judgment-seat. Well, well; a
monarch's business is to sustain the world, and he must
not expect much repose; because—

Onward, forever onward, in his car
The unwearied Sun pursues his daily course,
Nor tarries to unyoke his glittering steeds.
And ever moving speeds the rushing Wind
Through boundless space, filling the universe
With his life-giving breezes. Day and night,
The King of Serpents on his thousand heads
Upholds the incumbent earth; and even so,
Unceasing toil is aye the lot of kings,
Who, in return, draw nurture from their subjects.

I will therefore deliver my message. [*Walking on and looking about.*] Ah! here comes the King:—

His subjects are his children; through the day,
Like a fond father, to supply their wants,
Incessantly he labors; wearied now,
The monarch seeks seclusion and repose—
E'en as the prince of elephants defies
The sun's fierce heat, and leads the fainting herd
To verdant pastures, ere his wayworn limbs
He yields to rest beneath the cooling shade.

[*Approaching.*] Victory to the King! So please your
majesty, some hermits who live in a forest near the
Snowy Mountains have arrived here, bringing certain
women with them. They have a message to deliver from
the sage Kanwa, and desire an audience. I await your
Majesty's commands.

KING [*respectfully*]: A message from the sage Kanwa, did
you say?

CHAMBERLAIN: Even so, my liege.

KING: Tell my domestic priest, Somaráta, to receive the her-
its with due honor, according to the prescribed form.
He may then himself introduce them into my presence.
I will await them in a place suitable for the reception
of such holy guests.

CHAMBERLAIN: Your Majesty's commands shall be obeyed.

[*Exit.*

KING [*rising and addressing the Warder*]: Vetravatí, lead the
way to the chamber of the consecrated fire.

WARDER: This way, Sire.

KING [*walking on, with the air of one oppressed by the cares of government*]: People are generally contented and happy when they have gained their desires; but kings have no sooner attained the object of their aspirations than all their troubles begin.

'Tis a fond thought that to attain the end
And object of ambition is to rest;
Success doth only mitigate the fever
Of anxious expectation; soon the fear
Of losing what we have, the constant care
Of guarding it doth weary. Ceaseless toil
Must be the lot of him who with his hands
Supports the canopy that shields his subjects.

TWO HERALDS [*behind the scenes*]: May the King be victorious!

FIRST HERALD: Honor to him who labors day by day
For the world's weal, forgetful of his own.
Like some tall tree that with its stately head
Endures the solar beam, while underneath
It yields refreshing shelter to the weary.

SECOND HERALD: Let but the monarch wield his threatening rod
And e'en the guilty tremble; at his voice
The rebel spirit cowers; his grateful subjects
Acknowledge him their guardian; rich and poor
Hail him a faithful friend, a loving kinsman.

KING: Weary as I was before, this complimentary address has refreshed me. [*Walks on.*]

WARDER: Here is the terrace of the hallowed fire-chamber, and yonder stands the cow that yields the milk for the oblations. The sacred enclosure has been recently purified, and looks clean and beautiful. Ascend, Sire.

KING [*leans on the shoulders of his attendants, and ascends*]: Vetravatí, what can possibly be the message that the venerable Kanwa has sent me by these hermits?—
Perchance their sacred rites have been disturbed
By demons, or some evil has befallen
The innocent herds, their favorites, that graze
Within the precincts of the hermitage;
Or haply, through my sins, some withering blight
Has nipped the creeping plants that spread their arms
Around the hallowed grove. Such troubled thoughts
Crowd through my mind, and fill me with misgiving.

WARDER: If you ask my opinion, Sire, I think the hermits merely wish to take an opportunity of testifying their loyalty, and are therefore come to offer homage to your Majesty.

*Enter the Hermits, leading Śakoontalá, attended by Gautamí;
and, in advance of them, the Chamberlain and the domestic
Priest.*

CHAMBERLAIN: This way, reverend sirs, this way.
ŚÁRNGARAVA: O Śáradwata,
  'Tis true the monarch lacks no royal grace,
  Nor ever swerves from justice; true, his people,
  Yea such as in life's humblest walks are found,
  Refrain from evil courses; still to me,
  A lonely hermit reared in solitude,
  This throng appears bewildering, and methinks
  I look upon a burning house, whose inmates
  Are running to and fro in wild dismay.
ŚÁRADWATA: It is natural that the first sight of the King's
  capital should affect you in this manner; my own sensa-
  tions are very similar.
  As one just bathed beholds the man polluted;
  As one late purified, the yet impure:—
  As one awake looks on the yet unwakened;
  Or as the freeman gazes on the thrall,
  So I regard this crowd of pleasure-seekers.
ŚAKOONTALÁ [*feeling a quivering sensation in her right eye-
  lid, and suspecting a bad omen*]: Alas! what means this
  throbbing of my right eye-lid?
GAUTAMÍ: Heaven avert the evil omen, my child! May the
  guardian deities of thy husband's family convert it into
  a sign of good fortune!   [*Walks on.*
PRIEST [*pointing to the King*]: Most reverend sirs, there stands
  the protector of the four classess of the people; the
  guardian of the four orders of the priesthood. He has
  just left the judgment-seat, and is waiting for you. Behold him!
ŚÁRNGARAVA: Great Bráhman, we are happy in thinking that
  the King's power is exerted for the protection of all
  classes of his subjects. We have not come as petitioners
  —we have the fullest confidence in the generosity of
  his nature.
  The loftiest trees bend humbly to the ground
  Beneath the teeming burden of their fruit;
  High in the vernal sky the pregnant clouds
  Suspend their stately course, and hanging low,
  Scatter their sparkling treasures o'er the earth:—
  And such is true benevolence; the good
  Are never rendered arrogant by riches.
WARDER: So please your Majesty, I judge from the placid
  countenance of the hermits that they have no alarming
  message to deliver.

KING [*looking at Sakoontalá*]: But the lady there—
Who can she be, whose form of matchless grace
Is half concealed beneath her flowing veil?
Among the sombre hermits she appears
Like a fresh bud 'mid sear and yellow leaves.

WARDER: So please your Majesty, my curiosity is also roused,
but no conjecture occurs to my mind. This at least is
certain, that she deserves to be looked at more closely.

KING: True; but it is not right to gaze at another man's wife.

SAKOONTALÁ [*placing her hand on her bosom. Aside*]: O my
heart, why this throbbing? Remember thy lord's affection,
and take courage.

PRIEST [*advancing*]: These holy men have been received with
all due honor. One of them has now a message to deliver
from his spiritual superior. Will your Majesty deign to
hear it?

KING: I am all attention.

HERMITS [*extending their hands*]: Victory to the King!

KING: Accept my respectful greeting.

HERMITS: May the desires of your soul be accomplished!

KING: I trust no one is molesting you in the prosecution of
your religious rites.

HERMITS: Who dares disturb our penitential rites
When thou art our protector? Can the night
Prevail to cast her shadows o'er the earth
While the sun's beams irradiate the sky?

KING: Such, indeed, is the very meaning of my title—"Defender of the Just." I trust the venerable Kanwa is in
good health. The world is interested in his well-being.

HERMITS: Holy men have health and prosperity in their own
power. He bade us greet your Majesty, and, after kind
inquiries, deliver this message.

KING: Let me hear his commands.

SÁRNGARAVA: He bade us say that he feels happy in giving his
sanction to the marriage which your Majesty contracted
with this lady, his daughter, privately and by mutual
agreement. Because

By us thou art esteemed the most illustrious
Of noble husbands; and Sakoontalá
Virtue herself in human form revealed.
Great Brahmá hath in equal yoke united
A bride unto a husband worthy of her:—
Henceforth let none make blasphemous complaint
That he is pleased with ill-assorted unions.

Since, therefore, she expects soon to be the mother of
thy child, receive her into thy palace, that she may
perform, in conjunction with thee, the ceremonies prescribed by religion on such an occasion.

GAUTAMÍ: So please your Majesty, I would add a few words:
but why should I intrude my sentiments when an opportunity of speaking my mind has never been allowed
me?

She took no counsel with her kindred; thou
Didst not confer with thine, but all alone
Didst solemnize thy nuptials with thy wife.
Together, then, hold converse; let us leave you.

ŚAKOONTALÁ [*aside*]: Ah! how I tremble for my lord's reply.

KING: What strange proposal is this?

ŚAKOONTALÁ [*aside*]: His words are fire to me.

ŚÁRNGARAVA: What do I hear? Dost thou, then, hesitate? Monarch, thou art well acquainted with the ways of the
world, and knowest that

A wife, however virtuous and discreet,
If she live separate from her wedded lord,
Though under shelter of her parent's roof,
Is mark for vile suspicion. Let her dwell
Beside her husband, though he hold her not
In his affection. So her kinsmen will it.

KING: Do you really mean to assert that I married this lady?

ŚAKOONTALÁ [*despondingly. Aside*]: O my heart, thy worst mis-
givings are confirmed.

ŚÁRNGARAVA: Is it becoming in a monarch to depart from
the rules of justice, because he repents of his engage-
ments?

KING: I cannot answer a question which is based on a mere
fabrication.

ŚÁRNGARAVA: Such inconstancy is fortunately not common,
excepting in men intoxicated by power.

KING: Is that remark aimed at me?

GAUTAMÍ: Be not ashamed, my daughter. Let me remove thy
veil for a little space. Thy husband will then recognize
thee.   [*Removes her veil.*

KING [*gazing at Śakoontalá. Aside*]: What charms are here
revealed before mine eyes!

Truly no blemish mars the symmetry
Of that fair form; yet can I ne'er believe
She is my wedded wife; and like a bee
That circles round the flower whose nectared cup
Teems with the dew of morning, I must pause
Ere eagerly I taste the proffered sweetness.
                        [*Remains wrapped in thought.*

WARDER: How admirably does our royal master's behavior
prove his regard for justice! Who else would hesitate for
a moment when good fortune offered for his acceptance
a form of such rare beauty?

ŚÁRNGARAVA: Great King, why art thou silent?

KING: Holy men, I have revolved the matter in my mind; but the more I think of it, the less able am I to recollect that I ever contracted an alliance with this lady. What answer, then, can I possibly give you when I do not believe myself to be her husband, and I plainly see that she is soon to become a mother?

ŚAKOONTALÁ [*aside*]: Woe! woe! Is our very marriage to be called in question by my own husband? Ah me! is this to be the end of all my bright visions of wedded happiness?

ŚÁRNGARAVA: Beware!
Beware how thou insult the holy Sage!
Remember how he generously allowed
Thy secret union with his foster-child;
And how, when thou didst rob him of his treasure,
He sought to furnish thee excuse, when rather
He should have cursed thee for a ravisher.

ŚÁRADWATA: Śárngarava, speak to him no more. Śakoontalá, our part is performed; we have said all we had to say, and the King has replied in the manner thou hast heard. It is now thy turn to give him convincing evidence of thy marriage.

ŚAKOONTALÁ [*aside*]: Since his feeling towards me has undergone a complete revolution, what will it avail to revive old recollections? One thing is clear—I shall soon have to mourn my own widowhood. [*Aloud.*] My revered husband—— [*Stops short.*] But no—I dare not address thee by this title, since thou hast refused to acknowledge our union. Noble descendant of Puru! It is not worthy of thee to betray an innocent-minded girl, and disown her in such terms, after having so lately and so solemnly plighted thy vows to her in the hermitage.

KING [*stopping his ears*]: I will hear no more. Be such a crime far from my thoughts!
What evil spirit can possess thee, lady,
That thou dost seek to sully my good name
By base aspersions? like a swollen torrent,
That, leaping from its narrow bed, o'erthrows
The tree upon its bank, and strives to blend
Its turbid waters with the crystal stream?

ŚAKOONTALÁ: If, then, thou really believest me to be the wife of another, and thy present conduct proceeds from some cloud that obscures thy recollection, I will easily convince thee by this token.

KING: An excellent idea!

ŚAKOONTALÁ [*feeling for the ring*]: Alas! alas! woe is me! There is no ring on my finger!
[*Looks with anguish at Gautamí.*

GAUTAMÍ: The ring must have slipped off when thou wast in the act of offering homage to the holy water of Sachí's sacred pool, near Śakrávatára.

KING [*smiling*]: People may well talk of the readiness of woman's invention! Here is an instance of it.

ŚAKOONTALÁ: Say, rather, of the omnipotence of fate. I will mention another circumstance, which may yet convince thee.

KING: By all means let me hear it at once.

ŚAKOONTALÁ: One day, while we were seated in a jasmine bower, thou didst pour into the hollow of thine hand some water, sprinkled by a recent shower in the cup of a lotus blossom——

KING: I am listening; proceed.

ŚAKOONTALÁ: At that instant, my adopted child, the little fawn, with soft, long eyes, came running towards us. Upon which, before tasting the water thyself, thou didst kindly offer some to the little creature, saying fondly—"Drink first, gentle fawn." But she could not be induced to drink from the hand of a stranger; though immediately afterwards, when I took the water in my own hand, she drank with perfect confidence. Then, with a smile, thou didst say—"Every creature confides naturally in its own kind. You are both inhabitants of the same forest, and have learnt to trust each other."

KING: Voluptuaries may allow themselves to be seduced from the path of duty by falsehoods such as these, expressed in honeyed words.

GAUTAMÍ: Speak not thus, illustrious Prince. This lady was brought up in a hermitage, and has never learnt deceit.

KING: Holy matron,
E'en in untutored brutes, the female sex
Is marked by inborn subtlety—much more
In beings gifted with intelligence.
The wily Köil, ere towards the sky
She wings her sportive flight, commits her eggs
To other nests, and artfully consigns
The rearing of her little ones to strangers.

ŚAKOONTALÁ [*angrily*]: Dishonorable man, thou judgest of others by thine own evil heart. Thou, at least, art unrivalled in perfidy, and standest alone—a base deceiver in the garb of virtue and religion—like a deep pit whose yawning mouth is concealed by smiling flowers.

KING [*aside*]: Her anger, at any rate, appears genuine, and makes me almost doubt whether I am in the right. For, indeed,
When I had vainly searched my memory,
And so with stern severity denied

The fabled story of our secret loves,
Her brows, that met before in graceful curves,
Like the arched weapon of the god of love,
Seemed by her frown dissevered; while the fire
Of sudden anger kindled in her eyes.

[*Aloud.*] My good lady, Dushyanta's character is well-
known to all. I comprehend not your meaning.

ŚAKOONTALÁ: Well do I deserve to be thought a harlot for
having, in the innocence of my heart, and out of the
confidence I reposed in a Prince of Puru's race, intrusted
my honor to a man whose mouth distils honey, while
his heart is full of poison.

[*Covers her face with her mantle, and bursts into tears.*

ŚÁRNGARAVA: Thus is it that burning remorse must ever
follow rash actions which might have been avoided, and
for which one has only one's self to blame.

Not hastily should marriage be contracted,
And specially in secret. Many a time,
In hearts that know not each the other's fancies,
Fond love is changed into most bitter hate.

KING: How now! Do you give credence to this woman rather
than to me, that you heap such accusations on me?

ŚÁRNGARAVA [*sarcastically*]: That would be too absurd, certainly. You have heard the proverb—

Hold in contempt the innocent words of those
Who from their infancy have known no guile:—
But trust the treacherous counsels of the man
Who makes a very science of deceit.

KING: Most veracious Bráhman, grant that you are in the
right, what end would be gained by betraying this lady?

ŚÁRNGARAVA: Ruin.

KING: No one will believe that a Prince of Puru's race would
seek to ruin others or himself.

ŚÁRADWATA: This altercation is idle, Śárngarava. We have executed the commission of our preceptor; come, let us
return.   [*To the King.*

Sakoontalá is certainly thy bride;
Receive her or reject her, she is thine.
Do with her, King, according to thy pleasure—
The husband o'er the wife is absolute.

Go on before us, Gautamí.   [*They move away.*

ŚAKOONTALÁ: What! is it not enough to have been betrayed by
this perfidious man? Must you also forsake me, regardless of my tears and lamentations?

[*Attempts to follow them.*

GAUTAMÍ [*stopping*]: My son Śárngarava, see, Sakoontalá is
following us, and with tears implores us not to leave

her. Alas! poor child, what will she do here with a cruel husband who casts her from him?

ŚÁRNGARAVA [*turning angrily towards her*]: Wilful woman, dost thou seek to be independent of thy lord?

> [*Śakoontalá trembles with fear.*

ŚÁRNGARAVA: Sakoontalá!

If thou art really what the King proclaims thee,
How can thy father e'er receive thee back
Into his house and home? but, if thy conscience
Be witness to thy purity of soul,
E'en should thy husband to a handmaid's lot
Condemn thee, thou may'st cheerfully endure it,
When ranked among the number of his household.

Thy duty, therefore, is to stay. As for us, we must return immediately.

KING: Deceive not the lady, my good hermit, by any such expectations.

The moon expands the lotus of the night,
The rising sun awakes the lily; each
Is with his own contented. Even so
The virtuous man is master of his passions,
And from another's wife averts his gaze.

ŚÁRNGARAVA: Since thy union with another woman has rendered thee oblivious of thy marriage with Śakoontalá, whence this fear of losing thy character for constancy and virtue?

KING [*to the Priest*]: You must counsel me, revered sir, as to my course of action. Which of the two evils involves the greater or less sin?

Whether by some dark veil my mind be clouded,
Or this designing woman speak untruly,
I know not. Tell me, must I rather be
The base disowner of my wedded wife,
Or the defiling and defiled adulterer?

PRIEST [*after deliberation*]: You must take an intermediate course.

KING: What course, revered sir? Tell me at once.

PRIEST: I will provide an asylum for the lady in my own house until the birth of her child; and my reason, if you ask me, is this. Soothsayers have predicted that your first-born will have universal dominion. Now, if the hermit's daughter bring forth a son with the discus or mark of empire in the lines of his hand, you must admit her immediately into your royal apartments with great rejoicings; if not, then determine to send her back as soon as possible to her father.

KING: I bow to the decision of my spiritual adviser.

PRIEST: Daughter, follow me.

ŚAKOONTALÁ: O divine earth, open and receive me into thy bosom!

[*Exit Śakoontalá weeping, with the Priest and the Hermits. The King remains absorbed in thinking of her, though the curse still clouds his recollection.*

A VOICE [*behind the scenes*]: A miracle! a miracle!

KING [*listening*]: What has happened now?

PRIEST [*entering with an air of astonishment*]: Great Prince, a stupendous prodigy has just occurred!

KING: What is it?

PRIEST: May it please your Majesty, so soon as Kanwa's pupils had departed,

Śakoontalá, her eyes all bathed in tears,

With outstretched arms bewailed her cruel fate——

KING: Well, well, what happened then?

PRIEST: When suddenly a shining apparition,

In female shape, descended from the skies,

Near the nymphs' pool, and bore her up to heaven.

[*All remain motionless with astonishment.*

KING: My good priest, from the very first I declined having anything to do with this matter. It is now all over, and we can never, by our conjectures, unravel the mystery; let it rest; go, seek repose.

PRIEST [*looking at the King*]: Be it so. Victory to the King!
[*Exit.*

KING: Vetravatí, I am tired out; lead the way to the bed-chamber.

WARDER: This way, Sire.   [*They move away.*

KING: Do what I will, I cannot call to mind

That I did e'er espouse the sage's daughter—

Therefore I have disowned her; yet 'tis strange

How painfully my agitated heart

Bears witness to the truth of her assertion,

And makes me credit her against my judgment.   [*Exeunt.*

PRELUDE TO ACT SIXTH

Scene—A Street

Enter the King's brother-in-law as Superintendent of the city police; and with him two Constables, dragging a poor fisher-man, who has his hands tied behind his back.

BOTH THE CONSTABLES [*striking the prisoner*]: Take that for a rascally thief that you are; and now tell us, sirrah, where you found this ring—aye, the King's own signet-ring. See, here is the royal name engraved on the setting of the jewel.

FISHERMAN [*with a gesture of alarm*]: Mercy! kind sirs, mercy! I did not steal it; indeed I did not.

FIRST CONSTABLE: Oh! then I suppose the King took you for some fine Bráhman, and made you a present of it?

FISHERMAN: Only hear me. I am but a poor fisherman, living at Śakrávatára——

SECOND CONSTABLE: Scoundrel, who ever asked you, pray, for a history of your birth and parentage?

SUPERINTENDENT [*to one of the Constables*]: Súchaka, let the fellow tell his own story from the beginning. Don't interrupt him.

BOTH CONSTABLES: As you please, master. Go on, then, sirrah, and say what you've got to say.

FISHERMAN: You see in me a poor man, who supports his family by catching fish with nets, hooks, and the like.

SUPERINTENDENT [*laughing*]: A most refined occupation, certainly!

FISHERMAN: Blame me not for it, master.
The father's occupation, though despised
By others, casts no shame upon the son,
And he should not forsake it. Is the priest
Who kills the animal for sacrifice
Therefore deemed cruel? Sure a lowborn man
May, though a fisherman, be tender-hearted.

SUPERINTENDENT: Well, well; go on with your story.

FISHERMAN: One day I was cutting open a large carp I had just hooked, when the sparkle of a jewel caught my eye, and what should I find in the fish's maw but that ring! Soon afterwards, when I was offering it for sale, I was seized by your honors. Now you know everything. Whether you kill me, or whether you let me go, this is the true account of how the ring came into my possession.

SUPERINTENDENT [*to one of the Constables*]: Well, Jánuka, the rascal emits such a fishy odor that I have no doubt of his being a fisherman; but we must inquire a little more closely into this queer story about the finding of the ring. Come, we'll take him before the King's household.

BOTH CONSTABLES: Very good, master. Get on with you, you cut-purse. [*All move on.*

SUPERINTENDENT: Now attend, Súchaka; keep you guard here at the gate; and hark ye, sirrahs, take good care your prisoner does not escape, while I go in and lay the whole story of the discovery of this ring before the King in person. I will soon return and let you know his commands.

CONSTABLE: Go in, master, by all means; and may you find favor in the King's sight! [*Exit Superintendent.*

FIRST CONSTABLE [*after an interval*]: I say, Jánuka, the Super-intendent is a long time away.

SECOND CONSTABLE: Aye, aye; kings are not to be got at so easily. Folks must bide the proper opportunity.

FIRST CONSTABLE: Jánuka, my fingers itch to strike the first blow at this royal victim here. We must kill him with all the honors, you know. I long to begin binding the flowers round his head.

> [*Pretends to strike a blow at the fisherman.*

FISHERMAN: Your honor surely will not put an innocent man to a cruel death.

SECOND CONSTABLE [*looking*]: There's our Superintendent at last, I declare. See, he is coming towards us with a paper in his hand. We shall soon know the King's command; so prepare, my fine fellow, either to become food for the vultures, or to make acquaintance with some hungry cur.

SUPERINTENDENT [*entering*]: Ho, there, Súchaka! set the fish-erman at liberty, I tell you. His story about the ring is all correct.

SÚCHAKA: Oh! very good, sir; as you please.

SECOND CONSTABLE: The fellow had one foot in hell, and now here he is in the land of the living. [*Releases him.*

FISHERMAN [*bowing to the Superintendent*]: Now, master, what think you of my way of getting a livelihood?

SUPERINTENDENT: Here, my good man, the King desired me to present you with this purse. It contains a sum of money equal to the full value of the ring.

> [*Gives him the money.*

FISHERMAN [*taking it and bowing*]: His Majesty does me too great honor.

SÚCHAKA: You may well say so. He might as well have taken you from the gallows to seat you on his state elephant.

JÁNUKA: Master, the King must value the ring very highly, or he would never have sent such a sum of money to this ragamuffin.

SUPERINTENDENT: I don't think he prizes it as a costly jewel so much as a memorial of some person he tenderly loves. The moment it was shown to him he became much agitated, though in general he conceals his feelings.

SÚCHAKA: Then you must have done a great service——

JÁNUKA: Yes, to this husband of a fish-wife.

> [*Looks enviously at the fisherman.*

FISHERMAN: Here's half the money for you, my masters. It will serve to purchase the flowers you spoke of, if not to buy me your good-will.

JÁNUKA: Well, now, that's just as it should be.

SUPERINTENDENT: My good fisherman, you are an excellent

fellow, and I begin to feel quite a regard for you. Let us
seal our first friendship over a glass of good liquor.
Come along to the next wine-shop and we'll drink your
health.

ALL: By all means.   [*Exeunt.*

ACT SIXTH

Scene—The Garden of the Palace

The nymph Sánumatí is seen descending in a celestial car.

SÁNUMATÍ: Behold me just arrived from attending in my
proper turn at the nymphs' pool, where I have left the
other nymphs to perform their ablutions, whilst I seek
to ascertain, with my own eyes, how it fares with King
Dushyanta. My connection with the nymph Menaká
has made her daughter Śakoontalá dearer to me than
my own flesh and blood; and Menaká it was who
charged me with this errand on her daughter's behalf.
[*Looking round in all directions.*] How is it that I see no
preparations in the King's household for celebrating the
great vernal festival? I could easily discover the reason
by my divine faculty of meditation; but respect must be
shown to the wishes of my friend. How then shall I
arrive at the truth? I know what I will do. I will become
invisible, and place myself near those two maidens who
are tending the plants in the garden.

[*Descends and takes her station.*

*Enter a Maiden, who stops in front of a mango-tree and gazes
at the blossom. Another Maiden is seen behind her.*

FIRST MAIDEN: Hail to thee, lovely harbinger of spring!
The varied radiance of thy opening flowers
Is welcome to my sight. I bid thee hail,
Sweet mango, soul of this enchanting season.

SECOND MAIDEN: Parabaitiká, what are you saying there to
yourself?

FIRST MAIDEN: Dear Madhukariká, am I not named after the
Köil? [9] and does not the Köil sing for joy at the first
appearance of the mango-blossom?

[9] The Köil is the Indian cuckoo. It is sometimes called Parabhrita
(nourished by another) because the female is known to leave her eggs
in the nest of the crow to be hatched. The bird is a great favorite with
the Indian poets, as the nightingale with Europeans.

SECOND MAIDEN: [*approaching hastily, with transport*]: What! is spring really come?

FIRST MAIDEN: Yes, indeed, Madhukariká, and with it the season of joy, love, and song.

SECOND MAIDEN: Let me lean upon you, dear, while I stand on tip-toe and pluck a blossom of the mango, that I may present it as an offering to the god of love.

FIRST MAIDEN: Provided you let me have half the reward which the god will bestow in return.

SECOND MAIDEN: To be sure you shall, and that without asking. Are we not one in heart and soul, though divided in body? [*Leans on her friend and plucks a mango-blossom.*] Ah! here is a bud just bursting into flower. It diffuses a delicious perfume, though not yet quite expanded. [*Joining her hands reverentially.*

God of the bow, who with spring's choicest flowers
Dost point thy five unerring shafts; to thee
I dedicate this blossom; let it serve
To barb thy truest arrow; be its mark
Some youthful heart that pines to be beloved.

[*Throws down a mango-blossom.*

CHAMBERLAIN [*entering in a hurried manner, angrily*]: Hold there, thoughtless woman. What are you about, breaking off those mango-blossoms, when the King has forbidden the celebration of the spring festival?

BOTH MAIDENS [*alarmed*]: Pardon us, kind sir, we have heard nothing of it.

CHAMBERLAIN: You have heard nothing of it? Why, all the vernal plants and shrubs, and the very birds that lodge in their branches, show more respect to the King's order than you do.

Yon mango-blossoms, though long since expanded,
Gather no down upon their tender crests;
The flower still lingers in the amaranth,
Imprisoned in its bud; the tuneful Köil,
Though winter's chilly dews be overpast,
Suspends the liquid volume of his song
Scarce uttered in his throat; e'en Love, dismayed,
Restores the half-drawn arrow to his quiver.

BOTH MAIDENS: The mighty power of King Dushyanta is not to be disputed.

FIRST MAIDEN: It is but a few days since Mitrávasu, the King's brother-in-law, sent us to wait upon his Majesty; and, during the whole of our sojourn here, we have been intrusted with the charge of the royal pleasure-grounds. We are therefore strangers in this place, and heard nothing of the order until you informed us of it.

CHAMBERLAIN: Well then, now you know it, take care you don't continue your preparations.

BOTH MAIDENS: But tell us, kind sir, why has the King prohibited the usual festivities? We are curious to hear, if we may.

SÁNUMATÍ [*aside*]: Men are naturally fond of festive entertainments. There must be some good reason for the prohibition.

CHAMBERLAIN: The whole affair is now public; why should I not speak of it! Has not the gossip about the King's rejection of Śakoontalá reached your ears yet?

BOTH MAIDENS: Oh yes, we heard the story from the King's brother-in-law, as far, at least, as the discovery of the ring.

CHAMBERLAIN: Then there is little more to tell you. As soon as the King's memory was restored by the sight of his own ring, he exclaimed, "Yes, it is all true. I remember now my secret marriage with Śakoontalá. When I repudiated her, I had lost my recollection." Ever since that moment, he has yielded himself a prey to the bitterest remorse.

He loathes his former pleasures; he rejects
The daily homage of his ministers.
On his lone couch he tosses to and fro,
Courting repose in vain. Whene'er he meets
The ladies of his palace, and would fain
Address them with politeness, he confounds
Their names; or, calling them "Śakoontalá,"
Is straightway silent and abashed with shame.

SÁNUMATÍ [*aside*]: To me this account is delightful.

CHAMBERLAIN: In short, the King is so completely out of his mind that the festival has been prohibited.

BOTH MAIDENS: Perfectly right.

A VOICE [*behind the scenes*]: The King! the King! This way, Sire, this way.

CHAMBERLAIN [*listening*]: Oh! here comes his majesty in this direction. Pass on, maidens; attend to your duties.

BOTH MAIDENS: We will, sir.   [*Exeunt.*

Enter King Dushyanta, dressed in deep mourning, attended by his Jester, Máthavya, and preceded by Vetravatí.

CHAMBERLAIN [*gazing at the King*]: Well, noble forms are certainly pleasing, under all varieties of outward circumstances. The King's person is as charming as ever, notwithstanding his sorrow of mind.

Though but a single golden bracelet spans
His wasted arm; though costly ornaments

Have given place to penitential weeds;
Though oft-repeated sighs have blanched his lips,
And robbed them of their bloom; though sleepless care
And carking thought have dimmed his beaming eye;
Yet does his form, by its inherent lustre,
Dazzle the gaze; and, like a priceless gem
Committed to some cunning polisher,
Grow more effulgent by the loss of substance.

SÁNUMATÍ [*aside. Looking at the King*]: Now that I have seen
    him, I can well understand why Sakoontalá should pine
    after such a man, in spite of his disdainful rejection of
    her.

KING [*walking slowly up and down, in deep thought*]:
When fatal lethargy o'erwhelmed my soul,
My loved one strove to rouse me, but in vain:—
And now when I would fain in slumber deep
Forget myself, full soon remorse doth wake me.

SÁNUMATÍ [*aside*]: My poor Sakoontalá's sufferings are very
    similar.

MÁTHAVYA [*aside*]: He is taken with another attack of this
    odious Sakoontalá fever. How shall we ever cure him?

CHAMBERLAIN [*approaching*]: Victory to the King! Great
    Prince, the royal pleasure-grounds have been put in order.
    Your Majesty can resort to them for exercise and amuse-
    ment whenever you think proper.

KING: Vetravatí, tell the worthy Pisuna, my prime minister,
    from me, that I am so exhausted by want of sleep that
    I cannot sit on the judgment-seat to-day. If any case of
    importance be brought before the tribunal he must give
    it his best attention, and inform me of the circumstances
    by letter.

VETRAVATÍ: Your Majesty's commands shall be obeyed.

                                                        [*Exit.*

KING [*to the Chamberlain*]: And you, Vátáyana, may go
    about your own affairs.

CHAMBERLAIN: I will, Sire.   [*Exit.*

MÁTHAVYA: Now that you have rid yourself of these trouble-
    some fellows, you can enjoy the delightful coolness of
    your pleasure-grounds without interruption.

KING: Ah! my dear friend, there is an old adage—"When
    affliction has a mind to enter, she will find a crevice
    somewhere"—and it is verified in me.
Scarce is my soul delivered from the cloud
That darkened its remembrance of the past,
When lo! the heart-born deity of love
With yonder blossom of the mango barbs
His keenest shaft, and aims it at my breast.

MÁTHAVYA: Well, then, wait a moment; I will soon demolish Master Káma's arrow with a cut of my cane.

[*Raises his stick and strikes off the mango-blossom.*

KING [*smiling*]: That will do. I see very well the god of Love is not a match for a Bráhman. And now, my dear friend, where shall I sit down, that I may enchant my sight by gazing on the twining plants, which seem to remind me of the graceful shape of my beloved?

MÁTHAVYA: Do you not remember? you told Chaturiká you should pass the heat of the day in the jasmine bower; and commanded her to bring the likeness of your queen Sakoontalá, sketched with your own hand.

KING: True. The sight of her picture will refresh my soul. Lead the way to the arbor.

MÁTHAVYA: This way, Sire.

[*Both move on, followed by Sánumatí.*

MÁTHAVYA: Here we are at the jasmine bower. Look, it has a marble seat, and seems to bid us welcome with its offerings of delicious flowers. You have only to enter and sit down. [*Both enter and seat themselves.*

SÁNUMATÍ [*aside*]: I will lean against these young jasmines. I can easily, from behind them, glance at my friend's picture, and will then hasten to inform her of her husband's ardent affection.

[*Stands leaning against the creepers.*

KING: Oh! my dear friend, how vividly all the circumstances of my union with Sakoontalá present themselves to my recollection at this moment! But tell me now how it was that, between the time of my leaving her in the hermitage and my subsequent rejection of her, you never breathed her name to me! True, you were not by my side when I disowned her; but I had confided to you the story of my love and you were acquainted with every particular. Did it pass out of your mind as it did out of mine?

MÁTHAVYA: No, no; trust me for that. But, if you remember, when you had finished telling me about it, you added that I was not to take the story in earnest, for that you were not really in love with a country girl, but were only jesting; and I was dull and thick-headed enough to believe you. But so fate decreed, and there is no help for it.

SÁNUMATÍ [*aside*]: Exactly.

KING [*after deep thought*]: My dear friend, suggest some relief for my misery.

MÁTHAVYA: Come, come, cheer up; why do you give way? Such weakness is unworthy of you. Great men never surrender themselves to uncontrolled grief. Do not mountains remain unshaken even in a gale of wind?

KING: How can I be otherwise than inconsolable, when I call to mind the agonized demeanor of the dear one on the occasion of my disowning her?

When cruelly I spurned her from my presence,
She fain had left me; but the young recluse,
Stern as the Sage, and with authority
As from his saintly master, in a voice
That brooked not contradiction, bade her stay.
Then through her pleading eyes, bedimmed with tears,
She cast on me one long reproachful look,
Which like a poisoned shaft torments me still.

SÁNUMATÍ [*aside*]: Alas! such is the force of self-reproach following a rash action. But his anguish only rejoices me.

MÁTHAVYA: An idea has just struck me. I should not wonder if some celestial being had carried her off to heaven.

KING: Very likely. Who else would have dared to lay a finger on a wife, the idol of her husband? It is said that Menaká, the nymph of heaven, gave her irth. The suspicion has certainly crossed my mind that some of her celestial companions may have taken her to their own abode.

SÁNUMATÍ [*aside*]: His present recollection of every circumstance of her history does not surprise me so much as his former forgetfulness.

MÁTHAVYA: If that's the case, you will be certain to meet her before long.

KING: Why?

MÁTHAVYA: No father and mother can endure to see a daughter suffering the pain of separation from her husband.

KING: Oh! my dear Máthavya,

Was it a dream? or did some magic dire,
Dulling my senses with a strange delusion,
O'ercome my spirit? or did destiny,
Jealous of my good actions, mar their fruit,
And rob me of their guerdon? It is past,
Whate'er the spell that bound me. Once again
Am I awake, but only to behold
The precipice o'er which my hopes have fallen.

MÁTHAVYA: Do not despair in this manner. Is not this very ring a proof that what has been lost may be unexpectedly found?

KING [*gazing at the ring*]: Ah! this ring, too, has fallen from a station which it will not easily regain, and deserves all my sympathy.

O gem, deserved the punishment we suffer,
And equal is the merit of our works,
When such our common doom. Thou didst enjoy
The thrilling contact of those slender fingers,
Bright as the dawn; and now how changed thy lot!

SÁNUMATÍ [*aside*]: Had it found its way to the hand of any other person, then indeed its fate would have been deplorable.

MÁTHAVYA: Pray, how did the ring ever come upon her hand at all?

SÁNUMATÍ: I myself am curious to know.

KING: You shall hear. When I was leaving my beloved Śakoontalá that I might return to my own capital, she said to me, with tears in her eyes, "How long will it be ere my lord send for me to his palace and make me his queen?"

MÁTHAVYA: Well, what was your reply?

KING: Then I placed the ring on her finger, and thus addressed her—

Repeat each day one letter of the name
Engraven on this gem; ere thou hast reckoned
The tale of syllables, my minister
Shall come to lead thee to thy husband's palace.

But, hard-hearted man that I was, I forgot to fulfil my promise, owing to the infatuation that took possession of me.

SÁNUMATÍ [*aside*]: A pleasant arrangement! Fate, however, ordained that the appointment should not be kept.

MÁTHAVYA: But how did the ring contrive to pass into the stomach of that carp which the fisherman caught and was cutting up?

KING: It must have slipped from my Śakoontalá's hand, and fallen into the stream of the Ganges, while she was offering homage to the water of Śachí's holy pool.

MÁTHAVYA: Very likely.

SÁNUMATÍ [*aside*]: Hence it happened, I suppose, that the King, always fearful of committing the least injustice, came to doubt his marriage with my poor Śakoontalá. But why should affection so strong as his stand in need of any token of recognition?

KING: Let me now address a few words of reproof to this ring.

MÁTHAVYA [*aside*]: He is going stark mad, I verily believe.

KING: Hear me, thou dull and undiscerning bauble!

For so it argues thee, that thou couldst leave
The slender fingers of her hand, to sink
Beneath the waters. Yet what marvel is it

That thou shouldst lack discernment? let me rather
Heap curses on myself, who, though endowed
With reason, yet rejected her I loved.

MÁTHAVYA [*aside*]: And so, I suppose, I must stand here to
be devoured by hunger, whilst he goes on in this sentimental strain.

KING: O forsaken one, unjustly banished from my presence,
take pity on thy slave, whose heart is consumed by the
fire of remorse, and return to my sight.

Enter Chaturiká hurriedly, with a picture in her hand.

CHATURIKÁ: Here is the Queen's portrait. [*Shows the picture.*

MÁTHAVYA: Excellent, my dear friend, excellent! The imitation of nature is perfect, and the attitude of the figures
is really charming. They stand out in such bold relief
that the eye is quite deceived.

SÁNUMATÍ [*aside*]: A most artistic performance! I admire the
King's skill, and could almost believe that Śakoontalá
herself was before me.

KING: I own 'tis not amiss, though it portrays
But feebly her angelic loveliness.
Aught less than perfect is depicted falsely,
And fancy must supply the imperfection.

SÁNUMATÍ [*aside*]: A very just remark from a modest man,
whose affection is exaggerated by the keenness of his
remorse.

MÁTHAVYA: Tell me—I see three female figures drawn on
the canvas, and all of them beautiful; which of the
three is her Majesty, Śakoontalá?

SÁNUMATÍ [*aside*]: If he cannot distinguish her from the
others, the simpleton might as well have no eyes in his
head.

KING: Which should you imagine to be intended for her?

MÁTHAVYA: She who is leaning, apparently a little tired,
against the stem of that mango-tree, the tender leaves
of which glitter with the water she has poured upon
them. Her arms are gracefully extended; her face is
somewhat flushed with the heat; and a few flowers have
escaped from her hair, which has become unfastened,
and hangs in loose tresses about her neck. That must
be the queen Śakoontalá, and the others, I presume, are
her two attendants.

KING: I congratulate you on your discernment. Behold the
proof of my passion;
My finger, burning with the glow of love,
Has left its impress on the painted tablet;
While here and there, alas! a scalding tear

Has fallen on the cheek and dimmed its brightness.
Chaturiká, the garden in the background of the picture
is only half-painted. Go, fetch the brush that I may
finish it.

CHATURIKÁ: Worthy Máthavya, have the kindness to hold
the picture until I return.

KING: Nay, I will hold it myself.

> [*Takes the picture. Exit Chaturiká.*

KING: My loved one came but lately to my presence
And offered me herself, but in my folly
I spurned the gift, and now I fondly cling
To her mere image; even as a madman
Would pass the waters of the gushing stream,
And thirst for airy vapors of the desert.

MÁTHAVYA [*aside*]: He has been fool enough to forego the
reality for the semblance, the substance for the shadow.
[*Aloud.*] Tell us, pray, what else remains to be painted.

SÁNUMATÍ [*aside*]: He longs, no doubt, to delineate some
favorite spot where my dear Sakoontalá delighted to
ramble.

KING: You shall hear——
I wish to see the Málini portrayed,
Its tranquil course by banks of sand impeded—
Upon the brink a pair of swans: beyond,
The hills adjacent to Himálaya,
Studded with deer; and, near the spreading shade
Of some large tree, where 'mid the branches hang
The hermits' vests of bark, a tender doe,
Rubbing its downy forehead on the horn
Of a black antelope, should be depicted.

MÁTHAVYA [*aside*]: Pooh! if I were he, I would fill up the
vacant spaces with a lot of grizzly-bearded old hermits.

KING: My dear Máthavya, there is still a part of Sakoontalá's
dress which I purposed to draw, but find I have omitted.

MÁTHAVYA: What is that?

SÁNUMATÍ [*aside*]: Something suitable, I suppose, to the
simple attire of a young and beautiful girl dwelling in
a forest.

KING: A sweet Sirísha blossom should be twined
Behind her ear, its perfumed crest depending
Towards her cheek; and, resting on her bosom,
A lotus-fibre necklace, soft and bright
As an autumnal moon-beam, should be traced.

MÁTHAVYA: Pray, why does the Queen cover her lips with
the tips of her fingers, bright as the blossom of a lily,
as if she were afraid of something? [*Looking more
closely.*] Oh! I see; a vagabond bee, intent on thieving

the honey of flowers, has mistaken her mouth for a rose-bud, and is trying to settle upon it.

KING: A bee! drive off the impudent insect, will you?

MÁTHAVYA: That's your business. Your royal prerogative gives you power over all offenders.

KING: Very true. Listen to me, thou favorite guest of flowering plants; why give thyself the trouble of hovering here?

See where thy partner sits on yonder flower,
And waits for thee ere she will sip its dew.

SÁNUMATÍ [*aside*]: A most polite way of warning him off!

MÁTHAVYA: You'll find the obstinate creature is not to be sent about his business so easily as you think.

KING: Dost thou presume to disobey? Now hear me—
An thou but touch the lips of my beloved,
Sweet as the opening blossom, whence I quaffed
In happier days love's nectar, I will place thee
Within the hollow of yon lotus cup,
And there imprison thee for thy presumption.

MÁTHAVYA: He must be bold indeed not to show any fear when you threaten him with such an awful punishment. [*Smiling, aside.*] He is stark mad, that's clear; and I believe, by keeping him company, I am beginning to talk almost as wildly. [*Aloud.*] Look, it is only a painted bee.

KING: Painted? impossible!

SÁNUMATÍ [*aside*]: Even I did not perceive it; how much less should he?

KING: Oh! my dear friend, why were you so ill-natured as to tell me the truth?

While, all entranced, I gazed upon her picture,
My loved one seemed to live before my eyes,
Till every fibre of my being thrilled
With rapturous emotion. Oh! 'twas cruel
To dissipate the day-dream, and transform
The blissful vision to a lifeless image. [*Sheds tears.*

SÁNUMATÍ [*aside*]: Separated lovers are very difficult to please; but he seems more difficult than usual.

KING: Alas! my dear Máthavya, why am I doomed to be the victim of perpetual disappointment?

Vain is the hope of meeting her in dreams,
For slumber night by night forsakes my couch:
And now that I would fain assuage my grief
By gazing on her portrait here before me,
Tears of despairing love obscure my sight.

SÁNUMATÍ [*aside*]: You have made ample amends for the wrong you did Śakoontalá in disowning her.

CHATURIKÁ [*entering*]: Victory to the King! I was coming along with the box of colors in my hand——

KING: What now?

CHATURIKÁ: When I met the Queen Vasumatí, attended by Taraliká. She insisted on taking it from me, and declared she would herself deliver it into your Majesty's hands.

MÁTHAVYA: By what luck did you contrive to escape her?

CHATURIKÁ: While her maid was disengaging her mantle, which had caught in the branch of a shrub, I ran away.

KING: Here, my good friend, take the picture and conceal it. My attentions to the Queen have made her presumptuous. She will be here in a minute.

MÁTHAVYA: Conceal the picture! conceal myself, you mean. [*Getting up and taking the picture.*] The Queen has a bitter draught in store for you, which you will have to swallow as Śiva did the poison at the Deluge. When you are well quit of her, you may send and call me from the Palace of Clouds,[10] where I shall take refuge.
[*Exit, running.*

SÁNUMATÍ [*aside*]: Although the King's affections are transferred to another object, yet he respects his previous attachments. I fear his love must be somewhat fickle.

VETRAVATÍ [*entering with a despatch in her hand*]: Victory to the King!

KING: Vetravatí, did you observe the Queen Vasumatí coming in this direction?

VETRAVATÍ: I did; but when she saw that I had a despatch in my hand for your Majesty, she turned back.

KING: The Queen has too much regard for propriety to interrupt me when I am engaged with state-affairs.

VETRAVATÍ: So please your Majesty, your Prime Minister begs respectfully to inform you that he has devoted much time to the settlement of financial calculations, and only one case of importance has been submitted by the citizens for his consideration. He has made a written report of the facts, and requests your Majesty to cast your eyes over it.

KING: Hand me the paper. [*Vetravatí delivers it.*

KING [*reading*]: What have we here? "A merchant named Dhanamitra, trading by sea, was lost in a late shipwreck. Though a wealthy trader, he was childless; and the whole of his immense property becomes by law forfeited to the King." So writes the minister. Alas! alas! for his childlessness. But surely, if he was wealthy, he must have had many wives. Let an inquiry be made

---

10 Palace of King Dushyanta, so-called because it was as lofty as the clouds.

whether any one of them is expecting to give birth to a child.

VETRAVATÍ: They say that his wife, the daughter of the foreman of a guild belonging to Ayodhyá, has just completed the ceremonies usual upon such expectations.

KING: The unborn child has a title to his father's property. Such is my decree. Go, bid my minister proclaim it so.

VETRAVATÍ: I will, my liege.   [*Going.*

KING: Stay a moment.

VETRAVATÍ: I am at your Majesty's service.

KING: Let there be no question whether he may or may not have left offspring;

Rather be it proclaimed that whosoe'er
Of King Dushyanta's subjects be bereaved
Of any loved relation, an it be not
That his estates are forfeited for crimes,
Dushyanta will himself to them supply
That kinsman's place in tenderest affection.

VETRAVATÍ: It shall be so proclaimed.
                    [*Exit Vetravatí, and reënter after an interval.*

VETRAVATÍ: Your Majesty's proclamation was received with acclamations of joy, like grateful rain at the right season.

KING [*drawing a deep sigh*]: So then, the property of rich men, who have no lineal descendants, passes over to a stranger at their decease. And such, alas! must be the fate of the fortunes of the race of Puru at my death; even as when fertile soil is sown with seed at the wrong season.

VETRAVATÍ: Heaven forbid!

KING: Fool that I was to reject such happiness when it offered itself for my acceptance!

SÁNUMATÍ [*aside*]: He may well blame his own folly when he calls to mind his treatment of my beloved Śakoontalá.

KING: Ah! woe is me! when I forsook my wife—
My lawful wife—concealed within her breast
There lay my second self, a child unborn,
Hope of my race, e'en as the choicest fruit
Lies hidden in the bosom of the earth.

SÁNUMATÍ [*aside*]: There is no fear of your race being cut off for want of a son.

CHATURIKÁ [*aside to Vetravatí*]: The affair of the merchant's death has quite upset our royal master, and caused him sad distress. Had you not better fetch the worthy Máthavya from the Palace of Clouds to comfort him?

VETRAVATÍ: A very good idea.   [*Exit.*

KING: Alas! the shades of my forefathers are even now beginning to be alarmed, lest at my death they may be deprived of their funeral libations.

No son remains in King Dushyanta's place
To offer sacred homage to the dead
Of Puru's noble line: my ancestors
Must drink these glistening tears, the last libation
A childless man can ever hope to make them.

[*Falls down in an agony of grief.*

CHATURIKÁ [*looking at him in consternation*]: Great King, compose yourself.

SÁNUMATÍ [*aside*]: Alas! alas! though a bright light is shining near him, he is involved in the blackest darkness, by reason of the veil that obscures his sight. I will now reveal all, and put an end to his misery. But no; I heard the mother of the great Indra, when she was consoling Sakoontalá, say, that the gods will soon bring about a joyful union between husband and wife, being eager for the sacrifice which will be celebrated in their honor on the occasion. I must not anticipate the happy moment, but will return at once to my dear friend and cheer her with an account of what I have seen and heard.

[*Rises aloft and disappears.*

A VOICE [*behind the scenes*]: Help! help! to the rescue!

KING [*recovering himself. Listening*]: Ha! I heard a cry of distress, and in Máthavya's voice. What ho there!

VETRAVATÍ [*entering*]: Your friend is in danger; save him, great King.

KING: Who dares insult the worthy Máthavya?

VETRAVATÍ: Some evil demon, invisible to human eyes, has seized him, and carried him to one of the turrets of the Palace of Clouds.

KING [*rising*]: Impossible! Have evil spirits power over my subjects, even in my private apartments? Well, well—
Daily I seem less able to avert
Misfortune from myself, and o'er my actions
Less competent to exercise control;
How can I then direct my subjects' ways,
Or shelter them from tyranny and wrong?

A VOICE [*behind the scenes*]: Halloo there! my dear friend; help! help!

KING [*advancing with rapid strides*]: Fear nothing——

THE SAME VOICE [*behind the scenes*]: Fear nothing, indeed! How can I help fearing when some monster is twisting back my neck, and is about to snap it as he would a sugar-cane?

KING [*looking around*]: What ho there! my bow.

SLAVE [*entering with a bow*]: Behold your bow, Sire, and your armguard.

[*The King snatches up the bow and arrows.*

ANOTHER VOICE [*behind the scenes*]: Here, thirsting for thy life-blood, will I slay thee,

As a fierce tiger rends his struggling prey.

Call now thy friend Dushyanta to thy aid;

His bow is mighty to defend the weak;

Yet all its vaunted power shall be as nought.

KING [*with fury*]: What! dares he defy me to my face? Hold there, monster! Prepare to die, for your time is come. [*Stringing his bow.*] Vetravatí, lead the way to the terrace.

VETRAVATÍ: This way, Sire.   [*They advance in haste.*

KING [*looking on every side*]: How's this? there is nothing to be seen.

A VOICE [*behind the scenes*]: Help! Save me! I can see you, though you cannot see me. I am like a mouse in the claws of a cat; my life is not worth a moment's purchase.

KING: Avaunt, monster! You may pride yourself on the magic that renders you invisible, but my arrow shall find you out. Thus do I fix a shaft

That shall discern between an impious demon

And a good Bráhman; bearing death to thee,

To him deliverance—even as the swan

Distinguishes the milk from worthless water.   [*Takes aim.*

Enter Mátali, holding Máthavya, whom he releases.

MÁTALI: Turn thou thy deadly arrows on the demons;

Such is the will of Indra; let thy bow

Be drawn against the enemies of the gods;

But on thy friends cast only looks of favor.

KING [*putting back his arrow*]: What, Mátali! Welcome, most noble charioteer of the mighty Indra.

MÁTHAVYA: So, here is a monster who thought as little about slaughtering me as if I had been a bullock for sacrifice, and you must e'en greet him with a welcome.

MÁTALI [*smiling*]: Great Prince, hear on what errand Indra sent me into your presence.

KING: I am all attention.

MÁTALI: There is a race of giants, the descendants of Kála-nemi, whom the gods find difficult to subdue.

KING: So I have already heard from Nárada.

MÁTALI: Heaven's mighty lord, who deigns to call thee "friend,"

Appoints thee to the post of highest honor,

As leader of his armies; and commits

The subjugation of this giant brood

To thy resistless arms, e'en as the sun

Leaves the pale moon to dissipate the darkness.

Let your Majesty, therefore, ascend at once the celestial car of Indra; and, grasping your arms, advance to victory.

KING: The mighty Indra honors me too highly by such a mark of distinction. But tell me, what made you act thus towards my poor friend Máthavya?

MÁTALI: I will tell you. Perceiving that your Majesty's spirit was completely broken by some distress of mind under which you were laboring, I determined to rouse your energies by moving you to anger. Because

To light a flame, we need but stir the embers;
The cobra, when incensed, extends his head
And springs upon his foe; the bravest men
Display their courage only when provoked.

KING [*aside to Máthavya*]: My dear Máthavya, the commands of the great Indra must not be left unfulfilled. Go you and acquaint my minister, Piśuna, with what has happened, and say to him from me,

Dushyanta to thy care confides his realm—
Protect with all the vigor of thy mind
The interests of my people; while my bow
Is braced against the enemies of heaven.

MÁTHAVYA: I obey. [*Exit.*

MÁTALI: Ascend, illustrious Prince.

[*The King ascends the car. Exeunt.*

ACT SEVENTH

Scene—The Sky

Enter King Dushyanta and Mátali in the car of Indra, moving in the air.

KING: My good Mátali, it appears to me incredible that I can merit such a mark of distinction for having simply fulfilled the behests of the great Indra.

MÁTALI [*smiling*]: Great Prince, it seems to me that neither of you is satisfied with himself—

You underrate the service you have rendered,
And think too highly of the god's reward:
He deems it scarce sufficient recompense
For your heroic deeds on his behalf.

KING: Nay, Mátali, say not so. My most ambitious expectations were more than realized by the honor conferred on me at the moment when I took my leave. For,

Tinged with celestial sandal, from the breast
Of the great Indra, where before it hung,
A garland of the ever-blooming tree
Of Nandana was cast about my neck

By his own hand: while, in the very presence
Of the assembled gods, I was enthroned
Beside their mighty lord, who smiled to see
His son Jayanta envious of the honor.

MÁTALI: There is no mark of distinction which your Majesty
does not deserve at the hands of the immortals. See,
Heaven's hosts acknowledge thee their second saviour;
For now thy bow's unerring shafts (as erst
The lion-man's terrific claws) have purged
The empyreal sphere from taint of demons foul.

KING: The praise of my victory must be ascribed to the
majesty of Indra.
When mighty gods make men their delegates
In martial enterprise, to them belongs
The palm of victory; and not to mortals.
Could the pale Dawn dispel the shades of night,
Did not the god of day, whose diadem
Is jewelled with a thousand beams of light,
Place him in front of his effulgent car?

MÁTALI: A very just comparison. [*Driving on.*] Great King,
behold! the glory of thy fame has reached even to the
vault of heaven.
Hark! yonder inmates of the starry sphere
Sing anthems worthy of thy martial deeds,
While with celestial colors they depict
The story of thy victories on scrolls
Formed of the leaves of heaven's immortal trees.

KING: My good Mátali, yesterday, when I ascended the sky,
I was so eager to do battle with the demons, that the
road by which we were travelling towards Indra's heaven
escaped my observation. Tell me, in which path of the
seven winds are we now moving?

MÁTALI: We journey in the path of Parivaha;
The wind that bears along the triple Ganges,
And causes Ursa's seven stars to roll
In their appointed orbits, scattering
Their several rays with equal distribution.
'Tis the same path that once was sanctified
By the divine impression of the foot
Of Vishnu, when, to conquer haughty Bali,
He spanned the heavens in his second stride.

KING: This is the reason, I suppose, that a sensation of calm
repose pervades all my senses. [*Looking down at the
wheels.*] Ah! Mátali, we are descending towards the
earth's atmosphere.

MÁTALI: What makes you think so?

KING: The car itself instructs me; we are moving
O'er pregnant clouds, surcharged with rain; below us

I see the moisture-loving Chátakas
In sportive flight dart through the spokes; the steeds
Of Indra glisten with the lightning's flash;
And a thick mist bedews the circling wheels.

MÁTALI: You are right; in a little while the chariot will touch
the ground, and you will be in your own dominions.

KING [*looking down*]: How wonderful is the appearance of
the earth as we rapidly descend!

Stupendous prospect! yonder lofty hills
Do suddenly uprear their towering heads
Amid the plain, while from beneath their crests
The ground receding sinks; the trees, whose stems
Seemed lately hid within their leafy tresses,
Rise into elevation, and display
Their branching shoulders; yonder streams, whose waters,
Like silver threads, but now were scarcely seen,
Grow into mighty rivers; lo! the earth
Seems upward hurled by some gigantic power.

MÁTALI: Well described! [*Looking with awe.*] Grand, indeed,
and lovely is the spectacle presented by the earth.

KING: Tell me, Mátali, what is that range of mountains which,
like a bank of clouds illumined by the setting sun, pours
down a stream of gold? On one side its base dips into
the eastern ocean, and on the other side into the western.

MÁTALI: Great Prince, it is called "Golden-peak," [11] and is
the abode of the attendants of the god of Wealth. In
this spot the highest forms of penance are wrought out.

There Kaśyapa, the great progenitor
Of demons and of gods, himself the offspring
Of the divine Maríchi, Brahmá's son,
With Aditi, his wife, in calm seclusion,
Does holy penance for the good of mortals.

KING: Then I must not neglect so good an opportunity of
obtaining his blessing. I should much like to visit this
venerable personage and offer him my homage.

MÁTALI: By all means! An excellent idea.

[*Guides the car to the earth.*

KING [*in a tone of wonder*]: How's this?

Our chariot wheels move noiselessly. Around
No clouds of dust arise; no shock betokened
Our contact with the earth; we seem to glide
Above the ground, so lightly do we touch it.

MÁTALI: Such is the difference between the car of Indra and
that of your Majesty.

KING: In which direction, Mátali, is Kaśyapa's sacred retreat?

---

[11] A sacred range of mountains lying along the Himálaya chain immediately adjacent to Kailása, the paradise of Kuvera, the god of
wealth.

MÁTALI [*pointing*]: Where stands yon anchorite, towards the
orb
Of the meridian sun, immovable
As a tree's stem, his body half-concealed
By a huge ant-hill. Round about his breast
No sacred cord is twined, but in its stead
A hideous serpent's skin. In place of necklace,
The tendrils of a withered creeper chafe
His wasted neck. His matted hair depends
In thick entanglement about his shoulders,
And birds construct their nests within its folds.

KING: I salute thee, thou man of austere devotion.

MÁTALI [*holding in the reins of the car*]: Great Prince, we
are now in the sacred grove of the holy Kaśyapa—the
grove that boasts as its ornament one of the five trees
of Indra's heaven, reared by Aditi.

KING: This sacred retreat is more delightful than heaven itself.
I could almost fancy myself bathing in a pool of nectar.

MÁTALI [*stopping the chariot*]: Descend, mighty Prince.

KING [*descending*]: And what will you do, Mátali?

MÁTALI: The chariot will remain where I have stopped it.
We may both descend. [*Doing so.*] This way, great King.
[*Walking on.*] You see around you the celebrated region
where the holiest sages devote themselves to penitential
rites.

KING: I am filled with awe and wonder as I gaze.
In such a place as this do saints of earth
Long to complete their acts of penance; here,
Beneath the shade of everlasting trees,
Transplanted from the groves of Paradise,
May they inhale the balmy air, and need
No other nourishment; here may they bathe
In fountains sparkling with the golden dust
Of lilies, here, on jewelled slabs of marble,
In meditation rapt, may they recline;
Here, in the presence of celestial nymphs,
E'en passion's voice is powerless to move them.

MÁTALI: So true is it that the aspirations of the good and great
are ever soaring upwards. [*Turning round and speaking
off the stage.*] Tell me, Vriddha-śakalya, how is the
divine son of Maríchi now engaged? What sayest thou?
that he is conversing with Aditi and some of the wives
of the great sages, and that they are questioning him
respecting the duties of a faithful wife?

KING [*listening*]: Then we must await the holy father's leisure.

MÁTALI [*looking at the King*]: If your Majesty will rest under
the shade, at the foot of this Aśoka-tree, I will seek an

opportunity of announcing your arrival to Indra's reputed father.

KING: As you think proper.   [*Remains under the tree.*

MÁTALI: Great King, I go.   [*Exit.*

KING [*feeling his arm throb*]: Wherefore this causeless throbbing, O mine arm?

All hope has fled forever; mock me not
With presages of good, when happiness
Is lost, and nought but misery remains.

A VOICE [*behind the scenes*]: Be not so naughty. Do you begin already to show a refractory spirit?

KING [*listening*]: This is no place for petulance. Who can it be whose behavior calls for such a rebuke? [*Looking in the direction of the sound and smiling.*] A child, is it? closely attended by two holy women. His disposition seems anything but childlike. See,

He braves the fury of yon lioness
Suckling its savage offspring, and compels
The angry whelp to leave the half-sucked dug,
Tearing its tender mane in boisterous sport.

Enter a child, attended by two women of the hermitage, in the manner described.

CHILD: Open your mouth, my young lion, I want to count your teeth.

FIRST ATTENDANT: You naughty child, why do you tease the animals? Know you not that we cherish them in this hermitage as if they were our own children? In good sooth, you have a high spirit of your own, and are beginning already to do justice to the name Sarvadamana (All-taming), given you by the hermits.

KING: Strange! My heart inclines towards the boy with almost as much affection as if he were my own child. What can be the reason? I suppose my own childlessness makes me yearn towards the sons of others.

SECOND ATTENDANT: This lioness will certainly attack you if you do not release her whelp.

CHILD [*laughing*]: Oh! indeed! let her come. Much I fear her, to be sure.   [*Pouts his under-lip in defiance.*

KING: The germ of mighty courage lies concealed
Within this noble infant, like a spark
Beneath the fuel, waiting but a breath
To fan the flame and raise a conflagration.

FIRST ATTENDANT: Let the young lion go, like a dear child, and I will give you something else to play with.

CHILD: Where is it? Give it me first. [*Stretches out his hand.*

KING [*looking at his hand*]: How's this? His hand exhibits

one of those mystic marks which are the sure prognostic
of universal empire. See!

His fingers stretched in eager expectation
To grasp the wished-for toy, and knit together
By a close-woven web, in shape resemble
A lotus-blossom, whose expanding petals
The early dawn has only half unfolded.

SECOND ATTENDANT: We shall never pacify him by mere
words, dear Suvratá. Be kind enough to go to my cottage, and you will find there a plaything belonging to
Márkándeya, one of the hermit's children. It is a peacock made of China-ware, painted in many colors. Bring
it here for the child.

FIRST ATTENDANT: Very well. [*Exit.*

CHILD: No, no; I shall go on playing with the young lion.
              [*Looks at the female attendant and laughs.*

KING: I feel an unaccountable affection for this wayward
child.

How blessed the virtuous parents whose attire
Is soiled with dust, by raising from the ground
The child that asks a refuge in their arms!
And happy are they while with lisping prattle,
In accents sweetly inarticulate,
He charms their ears; and with his artless smiles
Gladdens their hearts, revealing to their gaze
His tiny teeth, just budding into view.

ATTENDANT: I see how it is. He pays me no manner of attention. [*Looking off the stage.*] I wonder whether any of
the hermits are about here. [*Seeing the King.*] Kind Sir,
could you come hither a moment and help me to release
the young lion from the clutch of this child, who is
teasing him in boyish play?

KING [*approaching and smiling*]: Listen to me, thou child of
a mighty saint.

Dost thou dare show a wayward spirit here?
Here, in this hallowed region? Take thou heed
Lest, as the serpent's young defiles the sandal,
Thou bring dishonor on the holy sage,
Thy tender-hearted parent, who delights
To shield from harm the tenants of the wood.

ATTENDANT: Gentle Sir, I thank you; but he is not the saint's
son.

KING: His behavior and whole bearing would have led me to
doubt it, had not the place of his abode encouraged the
idea.

[*Follows the child, and takes him by the hand, according to
      the request of the attendant. Speaking aside.*

I marvel that the touch of this strange child

Should thrill me with delight; if so it be,
How must the fond caresses of a son
Transport the father's soul who gave him being!

ATTENDANT [*looking at them both*]: Wonderful! Prodigious!

KING: What excites your surprise, my good woman?

ATTENDANT: I am astonished at the striking resemblance between the child and yourself; and, what is still more extraordinary, he seems to have taken to you kindly and submissively, though you are a stranger to him.

KING [*fondling the child*]: If he be not the son of the great sage, of what family does he come, may I ask?

ATTENDANT: Of the race of Puru.

KING [*aside*]: What! are we, then, descended from the same ancestry? This, no doubt, accounts for the resemblance she traces between the child and me. Certainly it has always been an established usage among the princes of Puru's race,

To dedicate the morning of their days
To the world's weal, in palaces and halls,
'Mid luxury and regal pomp abiding;
Then, in the wane of life, to seek release
From kingly cares, and make the hallowed shade
Of sacred trees their last asylum, where
As hermits they may practice self-abasement,
And bind themselves by rigid vows of penance.

[*Aloud.*] But how could mortals by their own power gain admission to this sacred region?

ATTENDANT: Your remark is just; but your wonder will cease when I tell you that his mother is the offspring of a celestial nymph, and gave him birth in the hallowed grove of Kaśyapa.

KING [*aside*]: Strange that my hopes should be again excited! [*Aloud.*] But what, let me ask, was the name of the prince whom she deigned to honor with her hand?

ATTENDANT: How could I think of polluting my lips by the mention of a wretch who had the cruelty to desert his lawful wife?

KING [*aside*]: Ha! the description suits me exactly. Would I could bring myself to inquire the name of the child's mother! [*Reflecting.*] But it is against propriety to make too minute inquiries about the wife of another man.

FIRST ATTENDANT [*entering with the china peacock in her hand*]: Sarva-damana, Sarva-damana, see, see, what a beautiful Śakoonta (bird).

CHILD [*looking round*]: My mother! Where? Let me go to her.

BOTH ATTENDANTS: He mistook the word Śakoonta for

Śakoontalá. The boy dotes upon his mother, and she is ever uppermost in his thoughts.

SECOND ATTENDANT: Nay, my dear child, I said, Look at the beauty of this Śakoonta.

KING [*aside*]: What! is his mother's name Śakoontalá? But the name is not uncommon among women. Alas! I fear the mere similarity of a name, like the deceitful vapor of the desert, has once more raised my hopes only to dash them to the ground.

CHILD [*takes the toy*]: Dear nurse, what a beautiful peacock!

FIRST ATTENDANT [*looking at the child. In great distress*]: Alas! alas! I do not see the amulet on his wrist.

KING: Don't distress yourself. Here it is. It fell off while he was struggling with the young lion. [*Stoops to pick it up.*

BOTH ATTENDANTS: Hold! hold! Touch it not, for your life. How marvellous! He has actually taken it up without the slightest hesitation.

[*Both raise their hands to their breasts and look at each other in astonishment.*

KING: Why did you try to prevent my touching it?

FIRST ATTENDANT: Listen, great Monarch. This amulet, known as "The Invincible," was given to the boy by the divine son of Maríchi, soon after his birth, when the natal ceremony was performed. Its peculiar virtue is, that when it falls on the ground, no one excepting the father or mother of the child can touch it unhurt.

KING: And suppose another person touches it?

FIRST ATTENDANT: Then it instantly becomes a serpent, and bites him.

KING: Have you ever witnessed the transformation with your own eyes?

BOTH ATTENDANTS: Over and over again.

KING [*with rapture. Aside*]: Joy! joy! Are then my dearest hopes to be fulfilled? [*Embraces the child.*

SECOND ATTENDANT: Come, my dear Suvratá, we must inform Śakoontalá immediately of this wonderful event, though we have to interrupt her in the performance of her religious vows. [*Exeunt.*

CHILD [*to the King*]: Do not hold me. I want to go to my mother.

KING: We will go to her together, and give her joy, my son.

CHILD: Dushyanta is my father, not you.

KING [*smiling*]: His contradiction convinces me only the more.

Enter Śakoontalá, in widow's apparel, with her long hair twisted into a single braid.

ŚAKOONTALÁ [*aside*]: I have just heard that Sarva-damana's amulet has retained its form, though a stranger raised it

from the ground. I can hardly believe in my good fortune.
Yet why should not Sánumatí's prediction be verified?

KING [*gazing at Sakoontalá*]: Alas! can this indeed be my
Sakoontalá?
Clad in the weeds of widowhood, her face
Emaciate with fasting, her long hair
Twined in a single braid, her whole demeanor
Expressive of her purity of soul:
With patient constancy she thus prolongs
The vow to which my cruelty condemned her.

ŚAKOONTALÁ [*gazing at the King, who is pale with remorse*]:
Surely this is not like my husband; yet who can it be
that dares pollute by the pressure of his hand my child,
whose amulet should protect him from a stranger's
touch?

CHILD [*going to his mother*]: Mother, who is this man that has
been kissing me and calling me his son?

KING: My best beloved, I have indeed treated thee most cruelly,
but am now once more thy fond and affectionate lover.
Refuse not to acknowledge me as thy husband.

ŚAKOONTALÁ [*aside*]: Be of good cheer, my heart. The anger
of Destiny is at last appeased. Heaven regards thee with
compassion. But is he in very truth my husband?

KING: Behold me, best and loveliest of women,
Delivered from the cloud of fatal darkness
That erst oppressed my memory. Again
Behold us brought together by the grace
Of the great lord of Heaven. So the moon
Shines forth from dim eclipse, to blend his rays
With the soft lustre of his Rohiní.

ŚAKOONTALÁ: May my husband be victorious——[*She stops
short, her voice choked with tears.*

KING: O fair one, though the utterance of thy prayer
Be lost amid the torrent of thy tears,
Yet does the sight of thy fair countenance,
And of thy pallid lips, all unadorned
And colorless in sorrow for my absence,
Make me already more than conqueror.

CHILD: Mother, who is this man?

ŚAKOONTALÁ: My child, ask the deity that presides over thy
destiny.

KING [*falling at Sakoontalá's feet*]: Fairest of women, banish
from thy mind
The memory of my cruelty; reproach
The fell delusion that o'erpowered my soul,
And blame not me, thy husband; 'tis the curse
Of him in whom the power of darkness reigns,
That he mistakes the gifts of those he loves

For deadly evils. Even though a friend
Should wreathe a garland on a blind man's brow,
Will he not cast it from him as a serpent?

ŚAKOONTALÁ: Rise, my own husband, rise. Thou wast not to blame. My own evil deeds, committed in a former state of being, brought down this judgment upon me. How else could my husband, who was ever of a compassionate disposition, have acted so unfeelingly? [*The King rises.*] But tell me, my husband, how did the remembrance of thine unfortunate wife return to thy mind?

KING: As soon as my heart's anguish is removed, and its wounds are healed, I will tell thee all.

Oh! let me, fair one, chase away the drop
That still bedews the fringes of thine eye;
And let me thus efface the memory
Of every tear that stained thy velvet cheek,
Unnoticed and unheeded by thy lord,
When in his madness he rejected thee. [*Wipes away the tear.*

ŚAKOONTALÁ [*seeing the signet-ring on his finger*]: Ah! my dear husband, is that the Lost Ring?

KING: Yes; the moment I recovered it, my memory was restored.

ŚAKOONTALÁ: The ring was to blame in allowing itself to be lost at the very time when I was anxious to convince my noble husband of the reality of my marriage.

KING: Receive it back, as the beautiful twining plant receives again its blossom in token of its reunion with the spring.

ŚAKOONTALÁ: Nay; I can never more place confidence in it. Let my husband retain it.

Enter Mátali.

MÁTALI: I congratulate your Majesty. Happy are you in your reunion with your wife: happy are you in beholding the face of your son.

KING: Yes, indeed. My heart's dearest wish has borne sweet fruit. But tell me, Mátali, is this joyful event known to the great Indra?

MÁTALI [*smiling*]: What is unknown to the gods? But come with me, noble Prince, the divine Kaśyapa graciously permits thee to be presented to him.

KING: Śakoontalá, take our child and lead the way. We will together go into the presence of the holy Sage.

ŚAKOONTALÁ: I shrink from entering the august presence of the great Saint, even with my husband at my side.

KING: Nay; on such a joyous occasion it is highly proper. Come, come; I entreat thee. [*All advance.*

Kaśyapa is discovered seated on a throne with his wife Aditi.

KAŚYAPA [*gazing at Dushyanta. To his wife*]: O Aditi,
This is the mighty hero, King Dushyanta,
Protector of the earth; who, at the head
Of the celestial armies of thy son,
Does battle with the enemies of heaven.
Thanks to his bow, the thunderbolt of Indra
Rests from its work, no more the minister
Of death and desolation to the world,
But a mere symbol of divinity.

ADITI: He bears in his noble form all the marks of dignity.

MÁTALI [*to Dushyanta*]: Sire, the venerable progenitors of the
celestials are gazing at your Majesty with as much affection as if you were their son. You may advance towards
them.

KING: Are these, O Mátali, the holy pair,
Offspring of Daksha and divine Maríchi,
Children of Brahmá's sons, by sages deemed
Sole fountain of celestial light, diffused
Through twelve effulgent orbs? Are these the pair
From whom the ruler of the triple world,
Sovereign of gods and lord of sacrifice,
Sprang into being? That immortal pair
Whom Vishnu, greater than the self-existent,
Chose for his parents, when, to save mankind,
He took upon himself the shape of mortals?

MÁTALI: Even so.

KING [*prostrating himself*]: Most august of beings, Dushyanta,
content to have fulfilled the commands of your son
Indra, offers you his adoration.

KAŚYAPA: My son, long may'st thou live, and happily may'st
thou reign over the earth!

ADITI: My son, may'st thou ever be invincible in the field of
battle!

ŚAKOONTALÁ: I also prostrate myself before you, most adorable beings, and my child with me.

KAŚYAPA: My daughter,
Thy lord resembles Indra, and thy child
Is noble as Jayanta, Indra's son;
I have no worthier blessing left for thee,
May'st thou be faithful as the god's own wife!

ADITI: My daughter, may'st thou be always the object of thy
husband's fondest love; and may thy son live long to be
the joy of both his parents! Be seated.

[*All sit down in the presence of Kaśyapa.*

KAŚYAPA [*regarding each of them by turns*]: Hail to the beautiful Śakoontalá!
Hail to her noble son! and hail to thee,

Illustrious Prince! Rare triple combination
Of virtue, wealth, and energy united!

KING: Most venerable Kaśyapa, by your favor all my desires
were accomplished even before I was admitted to your
presence. Never was mortal so honored that his boon
should be granted ere it was solicited. Because,

Bloom before fruit, the clouds before the rain—
Cause first and then effect, in endless sequence,
Is the unchanging law of constant nature:
But, ere the blessing issued from thy lips,
The wishes of my heart were all fulfilled.

MÁTALI: It is thus that the great progenitors of the world confer favors.

KING: Most reverend Sage, this thy handmaid was married to
me by the Gandharva ceremony, and after a time was
conducted to my palace by her relations. Meanwhile a
fatal delusion seized me; I lost my memory and rejected
her, thus committing a grievous offense against the venerable Kanwa, who is of thy divine race. Afterwards the
sight of this ring restored my faculties, and brought back
to my mind all the circumstances of my union with his
daughter. But my conduct still seems to me incompre-
hensible;

As foolish as the fancies of a man
Who, when he sees an elephant, denies
That 'tis an elephant, yet afterwards,
When its huge bulk moves onward, hesitates,
Yet will not be convinced till it has passed
Forever from his sight, and left behind
No vestige of its presence save its footsteps.

KAŚYAPA: My son, cease to think thyself in fault. Even the
delusion that possessed thy mind was not brought about
by any act of thine. Listen to me.

KING: I am attentive.

KAŚYAPA: Know that when the nymph Menaká, the mother of
Śakoontalá, became aware of her daughter's anguish in
consequence of the loss of the ring at the nymphs' pool,
and of thy subsequent rejection of her, she brought her
and confided her to the care of Aditi. And I no sooner
saw her than I ascertained by my divine power of
meditation, that thy repudiation of thy poor faithful wife
had been caused entirely by the curse of Durvásas—
not by thine own fault—and that the spell would termi-
nate on the discovery of the ring.

KING [*drawing a deep breath*]: Oh! what a weight is taken off
my mind, now that my character is cleared of reproach.

ŚAKOONTALÁ [*aside*]: Joy! joy! My revered husband did not,
then, reject me without good reason, though I have no

recollection of the curse pronounced upon me. But, in all probability, I unconsciously brought it upon myself, when I was so distracted on being separated from my husband soon after our marriage. For I now remember that my two friends advised me not to fail to show the ring in case he should have forgotten me.

KAŚYAPA: At last, my daughter, thou art happy, and hast gained thy heart's desire. Indulge, then, no feeling of resentment against thy partner. See, now,

Though he repulsed thee, 'twas the sage's curse
That clouded his remembrance; 'twas the curse
That made thy tender husband harsh towards thee.
Soon as the spell was broken, and his soul
Delivered from its darkness, in a moment
Thou didst gain thine empire o'er his heart.
So on the tarnished surface of a mirror
No image is reflected, till the dust
That dimmed its wonted lustre is removed.

KING: Holy father, see here the hope of my royal race.

[*Takes his child by the hand.*

KAŚYAPA: Know that he, too, will become the monarch of the whole earth. Observe,

Soon, a resistless hero, shall he cross
The trackless ocean, borne above the waves
In an aerial car; and shall subdue
The earth's seven sea-girt isles.[12] Now has he gained,
As the brave tamer of the forest-beasts,
The title Sarva-damana; but then
Mankind shall hail him as King Bharata,
And call him the supporter of the world.

KING: We cannot but entertain the highest hopes of a child for whom your highness performed the natal rites.

ADITI: My revered husband, should not the intelligence be conveyed to Kanwa, that his daughter's wishes are fulfilled, and her happiness complete? He is Śakoontalá's foster-father. Menaká, who is one of my attendants, is her mother, and dearly does she love her daughter.

ŚAKOONTALÁ [*aside*]: The venerable matron has given utterance to the very wish that was in my mind.

KAŚYAPA: His penances have gained for him the faculty of omniscience, and the whole scene is already present to his mind's eye.

KING: Then most assuredly he cannot be very angry with me.

KAŚYAPA: Nevertheless it becomes us to send him intelligence of this happy event, and hear his reply. What, ho there!

PUPIL [*entering*]: Holy father, what are your commands?

---

12 According to the mythical geography of the Hindoos the earth consisted of seven islands surrounded by seven seas.

KAŚYAPA: My good Gálava, delay not an instant, but hasten through the air and convey to the venerable Kanwa, from me, the happy news that the fatal spell has ceased, that Dushyanta's memory is restored, that his daughter Śakoontalá has a son, and that she is once more tenderly acknowledged by her husband.

PUPIL: Your highness's commands shall be obeyed. [*Exit.*

KAŚYAPA: And now, my dear son, take thy consort and thy child, re-ascend the car of Indra, and return to thy imperial capital.

KING: Most holy father, I obey.

KAŚYAPA: And accept this blessing—

  For countless ages may the god of gods,
  Lord of the atmosphere, by copious showers
  Secure abundant harvest to thy subjects;
  And thou by frequent offerings preserve
  The Thunderer's friendship! Thus, by interchange
  Of kindly actions, may you both confer
  Unnumbered benefits on earth and heaven!

KING: Holy father, I will strive, as far as I am able, to attain this happiness.

KAŚYAPA: What other favor can I bestow on thee, my son?

KING: What other can I desire? If, however, you permit me to form another wish, I would humbly beg that the saying of the sage Bharata be fulfilled:—

  May kings reign only for their subjects' weal!
  May the divine Saraswati, the source
  Of speech, and goddess of dramatic art,
  Be ever honored by the great and wise!
  And may the purple self-existent god,
  Whose vital Energy pervades all space,
  From future transmigrations save my soul! [*Exeunt omnes.*

Atsumori, a Nō Drama, by Seami Motokiyo

[A.D. 1363-1444]

TRANSLATED BY ARTHUR WALEY [1889-   ]

ᕼᐁᕽᓀᑯᔉᔌ

The fascination which the Japanese Nō drama has had for such outstanding 20th century poets as William Butler Yeats and Ezra Pound is no doubt attributable to its highly stylized and self-conscious form. If to the untutored reader or observer the Nō seems primitive, he must remember that primitivism is often the hallmark of sophistication.

The Nō grew out of popular Shinto dances and mimes in the 12th through the 14th centuries, but under Buddhist influence it acquired an almost hieratic character as religious ceremonial. In the hands of a famous father-son team, Kwanami and Seami Motokiyo, it achieved some artistic freedom. Its aristocratic patronage, however, encouraged the development of an abstruse, even esoteric dramatic language weighed down with obscure literary and mythological allusions. For a time even forbidden to the populace, the Nō soon became a fit vehicle for expressing the emotions of only the most refined of the Samurai class. Harassed by the moral problems involved in killing and being killed, the warrior found esthetic pleasure and religious solace in the delicate melancholy of the Nō. Its decline until recent times was accompanied by a growing interest in the Kabuki theater, which produced a more popular and more realistic drama.

The Nō is characterized by a very slight text which is eked out by elaborate conventions of acting, chanting, and dancing. As in Greek tragedy, which it somewhat resembles, masks and a chorus are used. The role of the latter is to lend emphasis to passages of the text and on occasion to speak the lines of a leading character if he is engaged in dancing. Often a character speaks of himself in the third person, with an effect of startling detachment. The text is highly lyrical and stresses, not the action, but the after-effects of the action upon the leading characters—or their ghosts.

Atsumori is one of several Nō based on the 12th century wars between the Taira and Minamoto clans. The Taira had been attacked in their place of naval retreat at Suma Bay, and Atsumori, nephew of their chief, had been killed by Kumagai, who found beside the dead body a bamboo flute.

PERSONS

THE PRIEST RENSEI (formerly the warrior Kumagai).
A YOUNG REAPER, who turns out to be the ghost of Atsumori.
HIS COMPANION.
CHORUS.

PRIEST : Life is a lying dream, he only wakes
Who casts the world aside.

I am Kumagai no Naozane, a man of the country of Musashi. I have left my home and call myself the priest Rensei; this I have done because of my grief at the death of Atsumori, who fell in battle by my hand. Hence it comes that I am dressed in priestly guise.

And now I am going down to Ichi-no-Tani to pray for the salvation of Atsumori's soul.

[*He walks slowly across the stage, singing a song descriptive of his journey.*]

I have come so fast that here I am already at Ichi-no-Tani, in the country of Tsu.

Truly the past returns to my mind as though it were a thing of to-day.

But listen! I hear the sound of a flute coming from a knoll of rising ground. I will wait here till the flute-player passes, and ask him to tell me the story of this place.

REAPERS [*together*] : To the music of the reaper's flute
No song is sung
But the sighing of wind in the fields.

YOUNG REAPER : They that were reaping,
Reaping on that hill,
Walk now through the fields
Homeward, for it is dusk.

REAPERS [*together*] : Short is the way that leads
From the sea of Suma back to my home.
This little journey, up to the hill
And down to the shore again, and up to the hill,—
This is my life, and the sum of hateful tasks.
If one should ask me
I too would answer
That on the shores of Suma
I live in sadness.
Yet if any guessed my name,
Then might I too have friends.
But now from my deep misery
Even those that were dearest
Are grown estranged. Here must I dwell abandoned
To one thought's anguish:
That I must dwell here.

PRIEST : Hey, you reapers! I have a question to ask you.

YOUNG REAPER : Is it to us you are speaking? What do you
wish to know?

PRIEST : It was a pleasant sound, and all the pleasanter because one does not look for such music from men of
your condition.

YOUNG REAPER : Unlooked for from men of our condition,
you say! Have you not read?
"Do not envy what is above you
Nor despise what is below you"?
Moreover the songs of woodmen and the flute-playing of
herdsmen,
Flute-playing even of reapers and songs of wood-fellers
Through poets' verses are known to all the world.
Wonder not to hear among us
The sound of a bamboo-flute.

PRIEST : You are right. Indeed it is as you have told me.
Songs of woodmen and flute-playing of herdsmen . . .

REAPER : Flute-playing of reapers . . .

PRIEST : Songs of wood-fellers . . .

REAPER : Guide us on our passage through this sad world.

PRIEST : Song . . .

REAPER : And dance . . .

PRIEST : And the flute . . .

REAPER : And music of many instruments . . .

CHORUS : These are the pastimes that each chooses to his
taste.

   Of floating bamboo-wood

   Many are the famous flutes that have been made;

   Little-Branch and Cicada-Cage,

   And as for the reaper's flute,

   Its name is Green-leaf;

   On the shore of Sumiyoshi

   The Corean flute they play.

   And here on the shore of Suma

   On Stick of the Salt-kilns

   The fishers blow their tune.

PRIEST : How strange it is! The other reapers have all gone
home, but you alone stay loitering here. How is that?

REAPER : How is it, you ask? I am seeking for a prayer in
the voice of the evening waves. Perhaps *you* will pray
the Ten Prayers for me?

PRIEST : I can easily pray the Ten Prayers for you, if you
will tell me who you are.

REAPER : To tell you the truth—I am one of the family of
Lord Atsumori.

PRIEST : One of Atsumori's family? How glad I am!

   Then the priest joined his hands [*he kneels down*] and
prayed:—

NAMU AMIDABU

   Praise to Amida Buddha!

   "If I attain to Buddhahood,

   In the whole world and its ten spheres

   Of all that dwell here none shall call on my name

   And be rejected or cast aside."

CHORUS: "Oh, reject me not!

   One cry suffices for salvation,

   Yet day and night

   Your prayers will rise for me.

   Happy am I, for though you know not my name,

   Yet for my soul's deliverance

   At dawn and dusk henceforward I know that you will pray."

   So he spoke. Then vanished and was seen no more.

[Here follows the Interlude between the two Acts, in which a recitation concerning Atsumori's death takes place. These interludes are subject to variation and are not considered part of the literary text of the play.]

PRIEST: Since this is so, I will perform all night the rites of prayer for the dead, and calling upon Amida's name will pray again for the salvation of Atsumori.

> *[The ghost of Atsumori appears, dressed as a young warrior.]*

ATSUMORI: Would you know who I am
That like the watchmen at Suma Pass
Have wakened at the cry of sea-birds roaming
Upon Awaji shore?
Listen, Rensei. I am Atsumori.

PRIEST: How strange! All this while I have never stopped beating my gong and performing the rites of the Law. I cannot for a moment have dozed, yet I thought that Atsumori was standing before me. Surely it was a dream.

ATSUMORI: Why need it be a dream? It is to clear the karma of my waking life that I am come here in visible form before you.

PRIEST: Is it not written that one prayer will wipe away ten thousand sins? Ceaselessly I have performed the ritual of the Holy Name that clears all sin away. After such prayers, what evil can be left? Though you should be sunk in sin as deep . . .

ATSUMORI: As the sea by a rocky shore,
Yet should I be salved by prayer.

PRIEST: And that my prayers should save you . . .

ATSUMORI: This too must spring
From kindness of a former life.

PRIEST: Once enemies . . .

ATSUMORI: But now . . .

PRIEST: In truth may we be named . . .

ATSUMORI: Friends in Buddha's Law.

CHORUS: There is a saying, "Put away from you a wicked friend; summon to your side a virtuous enemy." For you it was said, and you have proven it true.
And now come tell with us the tale of your confession, while the night is still dark.

CHORUS: He bids the flowers of Spring
Mount the tree-top that men may raise their eyes
And walk on upward paths;
He bids the moon in autumn waves be drowned
In token that he visits laggard men
And leads them out from valleys of despair.

ATSUMORI: Now the clan of Taira, building wall to wall,

Spread over the earth like the leafy branches of a great
  tree:
CHORUS: Yet their prosperity lasted but for a day;
  It was like the flower of the convolvulus.
  There was none to tell them
  That glory flashes like sparks from flint-stone,
  And after,—darkness.
  Oh wretched, the life of men!
ATSUMORI: When they were on high they afflicted the humble;
  When they were rich they were reckless in pride.
  And so for twenty years and more
  They ruled this land.
  But truly a generation passes like the space of a dream.
  The leaves of the autumn of Juyei
  Were tossed by the four winds;
  Scattered, scattered (like leaves too) floated their ships.
  And they, asleep on the heaving sea, not even in dreams
  Went back to home.
  Caged birds longing for the clouds,—
  Wild geese were they rather, whose ranks are broken
  As they fly to southward on their doubtful journey.
  So days and months went by; Spring came again
  And for a little while
  Here dwelt they on the shore of Suma
  At the first valley.
  From the mountain behind us the winds blew down
  Till the fields grew wintry again.
  Our ships lay by the shore, where night and day
  The sea-gulls cried and salt waves washed on our sleeves.
  We slept with fishers in their huts
  On pillows of sand.
  We knew none but the people of Suma.
  And when among the pine-trees
  The evening smoke was rising,
  Brushwood, as they call it,
  Brushwood we gathered
  And spread for carpet.
  Sorrowful we lived
  On the wild shore of Suma,
  Till the clan Taira and all its princes
  Were but villagers of Suma.
ATSUMORI: But on the night of the sixth day of the second
  month
  My father Tsunemori gathered us together.
  "Tomorrow," he said, "we shall fight our last fight.
  Tonight is all that is left us."
  We sang songs together, and danced.

PRIEST: Yes, I remember; we in our siege-camp
    Heard the sound of music
    Echoing from your tents that night;
    There was the music of a flute . . .
ATSUMORI: The bamboo-flute! I wore it when I died.
PRIEST: We heard the singing . . .
ATSUMORI: Songs and ballads . . .
PRIEST: Many voices
ATSUMORI: Singing to one measure.

[*Atsumori dances*]

    First comes the Royal Boat.
CHORUS: The whole clan has put its boats to sea.
    He will not be left behind;
    He runs to the shore.
    But the Royal Boat and the soldiers' boats
    Have sailed far away.
ATSUMORI: What can he do?
    He spurs his horse into the waves.
    He is full of perplexity.
    And then
CHORUS: He looks behind him and sees
    That Kumagai pursues him;
    He cannot escape.
    Then Atsumori turns his horse
    Knee-deep in the lashing waves,
    And draws his sword.
    Twice, three times he strikes; then, still saddled,
    In close fight they twine; roll headlong together
    Among the surf of the shore.
    So Atsumori fell and was slain, but now the Wheel of Fate
    Has turned and brought him back.

[*Atsumori rises from the ground and advances toward the
Priest with uplifted sword.*]

    "There is my enemy," he cries, and would strike,
    But the other is grown gentle
    And calling on Buddha's name
    Has obtained salvation for his foe;
    So that they shall be re-born together
    On one lotus-seat.
    "No, Rensei is not my enemy.
    Pray for me again, oh pray for me again."

3 SONG

I Of Man and Nature

FROM The Chinese Poets

TRANSLATED BY ROBERT PAYNE {1911-   } AND OTHERS

The poet-scholar has at all times occupied a place of respect in the culture of China, which has probably produced more poetry than any other nation in the history of the world. It is interesting that the book which Confucius himself held in highest regard was *The Book of Songs,* and that even the later great flourishing of the poetic art in Han, T'ang and Sung times tended to be looked upon as a kind of decline from an earlier golden age.

If any generalization can be made about this long history of poetic production over three millennia of time, it is perhaps that the ideal of perfect form combined with simple substance has always prevailed. Of the form little can be appreciated by those of us who must read Chinese poetry only in translation. The poems are of various genres and employ rhyme, meter, parallelism of word and line, classical and mythological allusions, and something not known in English verse—tone. The English reader can hardly be unaware, on the other hand, of the engaging simplicity of the themes of Chinese verse, which has a genius for transmuting the most prosaic matter into poetry.

The Book of Songs was recommended by Confucius for its ethical teachings, but the English reader is more likely to find in it the music which Confucius also considered essential for the well-ordered soul. These are not folk songs proper, having gone through a considerable process of refinement; but they have some of the lyric charm of old ballads as well as their dramatic quality. Their subjects are simply man and nature, but the symbolic treatment of the inner human problem in terms of outward nature stamps them as the products of antiquity. It also, curiously enough, makes them distinctly modern. It is significant that Ezra Pound should have found the sources of his poetic inspiration in the Greek Anthology, Provençal verse and Chinese poetry.

If the subjects of Chinese poetry are familiar, it should be realized that peculiarities in the society of the Chinese lend a difference to the treatment of these subjects. Love is seldom romantic. More often it is platonic—the expression of a deep friendship between man and man. Yet it will often be expressed as the love of man for wife and concubine. The numerous poems of separation, which tinge with melancholy so much of Chinese verse, are the inevitable consequence of the bureaucratic system of life which, in its desire to avoid nepotism, sent a public servant long distances from his home. The poet, who would gladly be a recluse, was often forced by economic necessity to become a bureaucrat. Hence the tyranny of the civil examinations and the longing for that period of retirement from duties when the youthtime activities of poetry might be resumed.

There is a collection of the poetry of the T'ang Dynasty (A.D. 618–906) published in 1717 which contains about 49,000 poems in 900 books filling 30 volumes. If one may regard the *Songs* as belonging to the classical age, then the T'ang period is truly the Renaissance of Chinese poetry. It is natural, therefore, that the largest representation of Chinese poetry in this anthology should come from the T'ang writers. The later Sungs (A.D. 960–1279) contributed some notable poets but they were perhaps more imitative of the past than were the T'angs. Of the latter, the best known in the West is Li Po, the most admired in China is Tu Fu, and the only rival to either is Po Chu-i. To these three have been added in this volume the names of Wang Wei, who is outstanding both as poet and painter and whose verses are accordingly the most imagistic, and the Sung poet-painter Su Tung-p'o, known to English readers as the hero of Lin Yutang's *The Gay Genius.*

The translations were made by Robert Payne in collaboration with various Chinese scholars.

From *THE BOOK OF SONGS (Pre-Confucian)*

My Lord Is Full of Delight

My lord is full of delight.
In his left hand he holds a flute,
With his right he summons me to play with him.
Oh, what sweet joy!

My lord is full of blessing.
In his left hand he holds dancing plumes,
With his right he summons me to dance with him.
Oh, what sweet joy!

Ripe Plums

Ripe plums are dropping,
Now there are only seven,
May a fine lover come for me
Now while there is yet time.

Ripe plums are dropping,
Now there are only three.
May a fine lover come for me
While there is still time.

Ripe plums are dropping,
I lay them in a shallow basket.
May a fine lover come for me.
Tell me his name.

The Moon Is Rising

The white moon in rising,
O lady so lovely and bright.
Why am I enchanted?
Why am I consumed with grief?

The white moon in rising
Is like the splendor of my lady.
Why am I caught in these chains?
Why am I consumed with grief?

The moon rising in splendor
Is the light of my love.
Why am I forsaken?
Why am I consumed with grief?

Beyond the East Gate

Beyond the east gate
Are girls shining like clouds.
Though they are shining like clouds,
There is none on whom my heart dwells.
Plain cloth and gray kerchief,
This were joy enough for me!

Beyond the gate tower
Are girls lovely as rush wool.
Though they are lovely as rush wool,
There is none on whom my heart dwells.
Plain cloth and madder kerchief,
Such is my joy!

The Cloth Cap

O why should the sight of your cloth cap
Fill me with such longing?
My heart is aflame with grief.

O why does the sight of your cloth coat
Spear my heart with grief.
Enough! I have fallen in love.

O why does the sight of your cloth leggings
Tangle my heart in knots?
Enough! Let us be joined together!

The Blind Musicians

The blind musicians, the blind musicians[1]
In the courtyard of Chou.
They have set up their pillars and crossbars,
With upright plumes and hooks for the drums and bells—
The small and larger drums are hanging there,
The tambourines, the stone-chimes, the batons and tiger-
    clappers.
When all have been struck the music begins.
Then the pipes and the flutes sound shrilly.
Sweet is the music,
August as the song of birds.
The ancestors listen:
They are our guests.
For ever and ever they gaze on our victories.

The Turbulent Waters

Amid the turbulent waters
The white rocks stand clean.
With a white coat and a red lappet
I followed you to Yueh.
Now that I have seen my lord,
Shall I not rejoice?

Amid the turbulent waters
The white rocks are washed clean.
With a white coat and a red lappet
I followed you to Kao.
Now that I have seen my lord,
Why should I be sad?

[1] Musicians in China are traditionally blind.

Amid the turbulent waters
The white rocks are dashed clean.
I have heard that you are wedded:
I dare not talk to you.

WANG WEI [699–759]

Morning

The peachblossom is redded because rain fell overnight,
The willows are greener in the morning mist:
The fallen petals are not yet swept away by servants.
Birds sing. The guest on the hill is asleep.

The Cold Mountain

The cold mountain turns dark green.
The autumn stream flows murmuring on.
Leaning on my staff beneath the wicket gate,
In the rushing wind I hear the cry of the aged cicada.

After Long Rain

The long rain falls on the empty forest. Smoke rises
Over the cooking-pots where they are preparing to feast
    the neighbours:
With immense wings the heron flows on the ricefields.
In the deep shade the yellow heron is singing.

Verses

You who come from the old village—
Tell me what is happening there?
When you left, were the chill plum-blossoms
Flowering beneath the white window?

A Song for Wei City

The morning rain of Wei city wets the white dust,
The inns are green, the willows are in spring,
May I advise you to empty one more cup,
For west of the Yuan-kuan hills you will find no friend.

Thinking of My Brother in Shantung on the Ninth Day of the Ninth Moon

To be a stranger in a strange land:
Whenever one feasts, one thinks of one's brother twice as
    much as before.
There where my brother far away is ascending,
The dogwood is flowering, and a man is missed.

Departure

I have just seen you go down the mountain:
I close the wicker gate in the setting sun.
The grass will be green again in the coming spring,
But will the wanderer ever return?

Walking at Leisure

Walking at leisure we watch laurel flowers falling:
In the silence of this night the spring mountain is empty.
The moon rises, the birds are startled
As they sing occasionally near the spring fountain.

In the Hills [2]

White pebbles jut from the river-stream,
Stray leaves red in the cold autumn:
No rain is falling on the mountain path,
But my clothes are damp in the fine green air.

LI PO [701?–762]

Conversation in the Mountains

If you were to ask me why I dwell among green mountains,
I shall laugh silently; my soul is serene.
The peach-blossom follows the moving water,
There is another heaven and earth beyond the world of men.

The Girl of Yueh

She is gathering lotos-seed in the river of Yueh.
While singing, she sees a stranger and turns around;
Then she smiles and hides among the lotos-leaves,
Pretending to be overcome by shyness.

[2] Su Tung-p'o regarded this poem as the best example to demonstrate
Wang Wei's genius in painting in words instead of in colors.

Verses

Clean is the autumn wind,
Splendid the autumn moon.
The blown leaves are heaped and scattered,
The ice-cold raven starts from its roost.
Dreaming of you—when shall I see you again?
On this night sorrow fills my heart.

The Moon over the Mountain Pass

The bright moon soars over the Mountain of Heaven,
Gliding over an ocean of clouds.
A shrill wind screaming ten thousand *li* away,
And a sound of whistling from Yu-men pass.
The imperial army marches down White Mound Road.
The Tartars search the bays of the Blue Sea.
The warriors look back to their distant homes:
Never yet has one been seen to return.
Tonight, on the high towers she is waiting.
There is only sorrow and unending grieving.

Fighting on the South Frontier

Last year we fought by the springs of Sankan river,
This year we fight on the Tsung-ho roads,
We have dipped our weapons in the waves of Chiao-chi lake,
We have pastured our horses in the snows of the T'ien
    mountains,
We have gone into battle ten thousand *li* away.
Our three armies are utterly exhausted.

The Huns think of slaughter as a kind of ploughing,
From of old they have seen only white bones in the yellow
    sands.
Where the Ch'in Emperors built walls against the Hun
    barbarians,
The sons of Han burn beacon fires.
The beacons burn without ceasing.
There is no end to war!

On the field of battle men grapple each other and die,
The horses of the fallen utter lament to heaven,
Ravens and kites peck men's guts,
And flying away, hang them on the boughs of dead trees.
So men are smeared on the desert grass,
And the generals return empty-handed.
Know that weapons of war are utterly evil—
The virtuous man uses them only when he must.

In the Mountains on a Summer Day

Lazily I stir a white feather fan,
Lying naked within the green wood.
I hang my hat on a crag,
And bare my head to the wind of the pines.

To Tan Ch'iu

My friend is dwelling in the eastern mountain,
Delighting in the beauty of valleys and hills.
In the green spring he lies in deserted forests,
And he is fast asleep when the sun rises.
The wind of the pines ripples his skirts and sleeves.
How I envy you, far from all striving,
Pillowed high in a mist of blue clouds!

The Girls of Yueh

The jade faces of the girls on Yueh Stream,
Their dusky brows, their red skirts,
Each wearing a pair of golden spiked sandals—
O, their feet are white like frost.

Boating Song

A boat of sandalwood and oars of magnolia:
At both ends sit "flutes of jade and pipes of gold." [3]
Pretty singing girls, countless flagons of sweet wine.
O let me follow the waves, wherever they take me.
I am like the fairy who rode away on a yellow crane.
Aimlessly I wander, following the white gulls.
The songs of Chu-ping [4] still shine like the sun and moon:
Of the palaces and towers of the Ch'u kings no trace is left
    on the mountains.
With a single stroke of my pen I shake the five mountains.
The poem finished, I laugh—my delight is vaster than the
    oceans.
If riches and fame could last for ever,
The Han River would flow north-westward to its source.

[3] I.e. the musicians are sitting at the prow and stern.
[4] Chu-ping is another name of Chu Yuan, who served in the state of Ch'u.

For the Dancer of the King of Wu,
When She Is Half-Drunk

The wind waves the lotoses in the scented palace by the
    water:
In the Ku-su Tower, the King of Wu is carousing.[5]
Hsi-shih, flushed with wine, dances coy and unresisting.
By the east window, laughing, she leans on a couch of white
    jade.

Saying Farewell to a Friend

The green mountain lies beyond the north wall of the city,
Where the white water winds in the east—
Here we part.
The solitary sail will attempt a flight of a thousand *li,*
The flowing clouds are the dreams of a wandering son,
The setting sun, the affection of an old friend.
So you go, waving your hands—
Only the bark of the deer.

The Summit Temple

Here it is night: I stay at the Summit Temple.
Here I can touch the stars with my hand.
I dare not speak aloud in the silence
For fear of disturbing the dwellers of Heaven.

Drinking Alone under Moonlight

Holding a jug of wine among the flowers,
And drinking alone, not a soul keeping me company,
I raise my cup and invite the moon to drink with me,
And together with my shadow we are three.
But the moon does not know the joy of drinking,
And my shadow only follows me about.
Nevertheless I shall have them as my companions,
For one should enjoy life at such a time.
The moon loiters as I sing my songs,
My shadow looks confused as I dance.
I drink with them when I am awake
And part with them when I am drunk.
Henceforward may we always be feasting,
And may we meet in the Cloudy River of Heaven.[6]

---

[5] Hsi-shih, the most beautiful of all Chinese consorts, was discovered
washing her clothes by the side of a stream by K'u-chien, the King of
Yueh, who presented her to the King of Wu.
[6] I.e. The Milky Way.

Awakening from Drunkenness on a Spring Day

Our life in the world is only a great dream.
Why should I toil my life away?
Let me be drunk all day,
Let me lie at the foot of the house-gate.
When I wake up, I blink at the garden trees:
A lonely bird is singing amid the flowers.
I demand of the bird what season it is:
He answers: "The spring wind makes the mango-bird sing."
Moved by his song, I sigh my heart away
And once more pour myself wine.
So I sing wildly till the bright moon shines.
The song over, all my senses are numb.

Drinking Alone in Moonlight

If Heaven had no love for wine,
There would be no Wine Star in Heaven;
If earth had no love for wine,
There would be no city called Wine Springs.
Since Heaven and Earth love wine,
I can love wine without shaming Heaven.

They say that clear wine is a saint,
Thick wine follows the way of the sage.
I have drunk deep of saint and sage:
What need then to study the spirits and fairies?
With three cups I penetrate the Great Tao.
Take a whole jugful—I and the world are one.
Such things as I have dreamed in wine
Shall never be told to the sober.

On Climbing the Phoenix Tower at Chinling [7]

Once in the Phoenix Tower the phoenix made her nest,
Now the phoenix has gone, the tower empty, only the river
    flowing on.
There were flowers in the garden of Wu, but the paths are
    now hidden in deep grass.
Here the great lords of Chin are buried in grave-mounds.
Half of these three mountains stretched into the blue sky.
The river's two streams wander round the White Heron Island.
Floating clouds for ever are shading the rays of the sun.
And I am grief-stricken because I cannot see Chang-an.

[7] Chinling is the modern Nanking, once the capital of Wu, Chin and
many other states and dynasties.

To Tu Fu

On the Mountain of Boiled Rice I met Tu Fu,
Wearing a bamboo hat in the hot midday;
Pray, how is it that you have grown so thin?
It is because you suffer from poetry?

A Song of War

Before the Peak of Returning Joy the sand was like snow,
Outside the surrendered city the moon was like frost.
I do not know who blew the horns at night,
But all night long the boys looked towards their homes.

TU FU [713–770]

Prelude

This fugitive between the Earth and Sky,
From the North-east storm-tossed to the South-west,
Time has left stranded in Three Valleys where
Exotic costumes mixed with ours suggest
Alliance with Huns whose loyalty suspect
Adds cause for mourning by the enforced guest.
Most desolate was Yu Hsin's life who sang
Towards its end of northern valleys best.

Night in the Villa by the River

Twilight comes down the mountain to
The villa next the dyke. By caves
On high the light clouds pitch their tents.
The moon turns over in the waves.
In silence left by flight of cranes
The wolves at feast howl while the fears
Of wartime prevent sleep from men
Powerless to adjust the spheres.

The Empty Purse

The bitter pinecone may be eaten,
The mist on high give nourishment.
The whole world takes to go-and-getting;
My way alone is difficult:

My oven is cold as the well at morning,
And the bed wants warmth from coverlets;
My purse ashamed to be found empty
Still keeps on hand a single coin.

Song of the Vermeil Phoenix

See you not Heng Mountain towering over Hunan hills,
From its summit the vermeil phoenix murmuring lean
Over to gaze, forever seeking his comrades?
His wings are folded, his mouth is closed, but his mind is
    working
With pity for all the birds that are caught in nets,
From which even the tiny oriole hardly can escape:
He would dispense to them ants and fruit of bamboo,
Provoking hawk and vulture to scream their threats.

Quatrain

Before you praise Spring's advent note
What capers the mad wind may cut:
To cast the flowers to the waves
And overturn the fishing boat.

The Return

Cliffs of scarlet cloud gleam in the west;
The sun's feet are sinking beneath the earth.
By the rustic gate sparrows are twittering.
The stranger returns to his home from a thousand *li*.
My wife is astonished that I still exist.
No longer bewildered, she wipes away her tears.
I was drifting sand in the wind of the world's anger.
It is just fate that has brought me back alive.
The fence gate is filled with neighbours' faces,
Sighing and shedding a few tears.
In the deep night we light a new candle
And see each other face to face as in a dream.

On Climbing the Heights on the Ninth Day
of the Ninth Moon

The wind keen, the sky high, the gibbons wailing,
Blue islands, white sand and sea-birds flying,
And everywhere the leaves falling,
Then the immeasurable great river in torrent.

Ten thousand *li* from home, in such an autumn,
Wasted by sickness and years, alone, climbing the heights:
Sorrows and griefs and sufferings have given me new grey
hairs.
Utterly cast down, I have just drunk a glass of wine.

Spring

Mountains and rivers lie in the opening sun.
Spring winds freshen the flowers and herbs.
Swallows are flying to fill their nests with mud.
Doves spread themselves drowsily in hot sand.

The blue river reflects the white birds
On the green mountains red flowers are burning.
Silently I watch the procession of Spring.
Then I will return to my beloved home.

Summer Night

Cool perfume of bamboo pervades my room,
Wild moonlight fills the whole courtyard:
Drop by drop falls the crystal dew.
One by one the moving stars appear.
The fleeting glow-worms sparkle in dark corners,
The waterfowl on the river bank call to one another;
Everything in the world follows the path of war—
I sit on my bed, meditating through the long night.

Chengtu

Now faintly the falling sun
Shines on my traveller's robes.
As I move onward, so does the scenery change:
Suddenly I feel as though under another sky.
I meet fresh people.
I do not know when I shall see my native home.
The Great River flows east,
As endlessly as are a wanderer's days.
Beautiful buildings fill the whole city;
The woods are dark in this late winter.
Noisily stands the famous city,
Full of the sound of flutes and reeds.
Marvellous, but I am still a stranger here.
Therefore I turn and look at the far mountains,
In the evening all birds return to their homes.

When shall I return to the centre of China?
The moon is not very high;
All the stars are shining as in a contest.
O, from the ancient days always there have been travellers.
So why should I grieve?

To Li Po on a Spring Day

Po, the unrivalled poet,
Who soars alone into the kingdom of imagination,
Yours is the delicacy of Yin,
Yours also Pao's rare freshness.
North of Wei River spring comes through the trees.
Meanwhile you wander beneath the sunset clouds of Chiang-
tung.
When shall we buy a cask of wine once more
And argue minutely on versification?

To Li Po

When the cold wind visits you from the corners of the
earth—
How are you, my beloved, what are you dreaming on?
When will the wild geese fly with your letter here?
The autumn rivers and lakes deepen and bring you my
thoughts.
The god of poetry hates those whom fortune smiles upon,
The devil bursts into laughter when real men stand close to
him.
The world is a desert! If only we could throw poems into the
Milo River
And speak with the great soul who was sacrificed to loyalty
and poetry.[8]

Thinking of My Brothers on a Moonlit Night

No one walks when the guardian drum sounds,
The cry of the wild geese marks autumn on the frontier:
Now at night the dewdrops twinkle with a starry whiteness,
Yet how much brighter shines the moon on my home!
My brothers are separated and wanderers in the land,
And there is nowhere where I can ask whether they have
survived or are dead:
A letter takes so long upon the way:
O, but I know there is much more than war in this country.

8 Chu Yuan [a notable poet of the 4th century B.C. who drowned himself in the Milo River.—Ed.]

PO CHU-I [772-846]

Sitting at Night

Against the lamp I sit by the south window,
Listening to the sleet and the wind in the dark:
Desolation deepens the night among the villages.
Through the snow I hear the lost wild goose calling . . .

Seeing Hsia Chan off by River

Because you are old and departing I have wetted my hand-
kerchief,
You who are homeless at seventy, belonging to the wilderness.
Anxiously I watch the wind rising as the boat sails away,
A white-headed man amid white-headed waves.

Lonely Night in Early Autumn

Thin leaves wave on the *wu-t'ung* tree beside the well:
Through the pounding of the washerwomen, autumn begins
to sing.
Under the eaves, I find a place and sleep alone,
And waking, I see the bed half-filled with the moon.

Song of the Pines

I like sitting alone when the moon is shining,
And there are two pines standing before the verandah;
A breeze comes from the south-west,
Creeping into the branches and leaves.
Under the brilliant moon at midnight
It whistles a cool, distant music,
Like rustling rains in empty mountains
And the serene harp-strings in the fall.
On first hearing them, the heat of summer is washed away:
And this suffocating boredom comes to an end.
So I keep awake the whole night,
Both the heart and the body becoming clear.
Along the south street coaches and horses are stirring,
In the west city sounds of playing and singing.
Who knows that under the roof-trees of this place
The ears are full, but not with noise.

The Harp

I lay my harp on the curved table,
Sitting there idly, filled only with emotions.
Why should I trouble to play?
A breeze will come and sweep the strings.

On an Ancient Tomb East of the Village

Among the ancient tombs both high and low,
There is a path for cattle and sheep.
Standing alone on the highest of them,
How carefree is my heart!
Turning to look at the village,
I see nothing but weeds in deserted fields—
The villagers are not fond of flowers,
And have planted only chestnuts and dates.
Ever since I came to live here,
I have never been delighted with the scenery:
The flowers are few, the orioles are scarce,
And when spring comes it can hardly be seen.

Visiting the Hermit Cheng

I hear you have gone to live among the village mounds
By the lonely gate where the bamboo groves abound.
I have come now only to beg you:
Lend me your south garden that I may look at the hills.

Buying Flowers

In the capital Spring comes late:
The noisy chariots and horses are passing.
They say, "It is the time of the peonies."
So they come together to buy flowers.
Prices, high and low, may change,
But also it depends on how much you buy.
Hundreds shine bright red,
There is a bouquet white as crystal,
Sheltered by curtains overhead
And constructed on a bamboo framework,
Watered and set in mud.
These are the old colors, but changed:
Every house buys them according to custom,
And nobody thinks wrong of it.

241

Only an old man from the farm
Coming by chance to the flower-market
Lowers his head, deeply sighs—
A sigh which no one understands.
Over a single posy of deep-colored flowers
Ten common families might sing!

Looking in the Lake

I look at my shadow over and over in the lake;
I see no white face, only the white hair,
I have lost my youth, and shall never find it again.
Useless to stir the lake-water!

A Flower

It seems a flower, but not a flower,
It seems a mist but not a mist.
It comes at midnight,
It goes away in the morning.
Its coming is like a spring dream that does not last long,
And its going is like the morning cloud: you will find it
     nowhere.

To the Distant One

I try to forget, but it is in vain.
I try to go, but I have no way.
There are no wings on my axles,
My head is covered with white hairs.
I sit and watch the leaves falling,
Or go up to the top of the tower.
Shades hover in boundless twilight:
A vast sadness comes to my eyes.

SU TUNG-P'O [1036–1101]

On the Tower of Gathering Remoteness

The endless blue mountains disperse,
Nor can they assemble together;
The waves roll, the clouds continually run-
     ning
Huddle into the screen beside the window.

Therefore pour out your eyes,
Define the limits of your vision:
Having this, you will not be poorer
Than a man who rules a dukedom.

Seeking Spring Beyond the City

The wild birds on the roof are bitterly complaining to man,
Suddenly ripples appear in the ice-pool in front of the balustrade:
I am becoming old, and increasingly more tired
Of getting drunk in the company of those with red skirts.
Rising from my sick-bed, in vain I am surprised
That all my hair has freshly turned white.
Lying on this couch, I hear the drum and horn of His Highness:
Therefore I bid my boys prepare my hat and dress.
Passing through the winding verandah and coming out in the arbor,
And leaving behind me this terribly pressing cold—
I find, ah what a boundless spring in the savage plain!

Spring Scene

The flowers have lost their withered red,
Small are the green apricots.
When the swallows come and fly,
The cottages are ringed round by blue
    streams.
Blown by the wind, the catkins are made
    small,
O where can I not find fragrant grass
In this boundless earth!

There is a swing within the walls,
And beyond there is a path:
Someone is walking outside,
And inside a lovely girl is laughing.
Gradually the sound of laughter is no
    more!
And the lover is vexed by the cold!

Sitting at Night with My Nephew
Who Has Just Come from Afar

My mind is worn out, my features grown sharp and
    gaunt:
You would hardly recognize me but for my old accent.

Where is our home?—I am thinking about it all night.
In my declining age I know why you have come.

Afraid of strangers, I would sit in idiot silence.
Then, enquiring about old friends, I cry in surprise
That since half of them are dead, only half survive.

The dream vanishes. The rain no longer falls.
I am awake now from my drunken stupor.
I look with a smile at a hungry mouse
Climbing up the stand of my oil-lamp.

Verses

I am old, sick and lonely.
I make my home on East Slope.
White, sparse and unkempt
My beard mingles with the wind.
Often my little boy is delightfully
        astonished
To find roses on my cheeks.
How should he know, I smile,
That they are the redness of wine.

Listening to the River

Drinking on East Slope at night,
I am tipsy and sober.
It must be the third watch,
When I reach home.
My boy snores like thunder:
No one answers my knock.
Leaning on my staff,
I listen to the river.

Always do I regret
That my being is not mine.
When shall I not remember
To hurry about after nothing?
In deep night the wind slumbers.
The white silk lies flat.
Soon the little boat will float away,
The rest of its life spent in rivers
        and seas.

FROM The Japanese Poets

ᴵᴺᴼᴵᴼᴶᴹᴵ

The poetry of Japan, like so much of its painting, is work in miniature. There never were many long poems in the language, and the tendency has been for the forms to be further shortened in the course of the more than thousand years that the art of the word has been practiced. The *Manyoshu*, the oldest anthology of Japanese poetry, which was compiled in A.D. 760 mainly out of poems written during the preceding century, contains over 4,000 *tanka* or short poems and only 324 *naga-uta* or long poems. The latter, which rarely ran over 150 lines, practically disappeared after the 8th century. The *tanka* is a five-line poem, of which the first and third lines have five syllables each and the others seven, making a total of thirty-one syllables per poem. During the 16th–18th centuries, out of this already short poem were evolved the *haiku*, seventeen syllable poems of three lines.

Japanese poetry has no rhyme, but it has other devices, some of which defy transplantation into the English language. We are familiar with punning, especially in Elizabethan verse, but aside from an occasionally successful pun by John Donne or another of the so-called metaphysical poets, we do not tolerate the trick in serious English poetry. The Japanese, on the other hand, regard word-play as a grave matter. Their pivot words, which turn in two directions, often carry a large part of the burden of a poem. Similarly, pillow words, which are stock epithets such as we find in Homer (e.g. "rosy-fingered dawn"), are employed to give added depth to the poetic content by association. What may seem to be innocuous little verses consequently often have a very sharp edge of wit. Moreover, an emotional dimension is added by the symbolical meaning that attaches to geographic or historic sites—such as, notably, Fujiyama—or to natural objects. Plum blossoms will mean love; cherry blossoms beauty; and the cuckoo and the nightingale play different roles from those which our culture has assigned to them.

Although Japanese poetry is extremely suggestive, it never loses its clarity and definiteness or its utter simplicity of form. Limited in range though it is, it achieves a kind of perfection in miniature which one is tempted to believe is the essence of poetry. Rhetoric and philosophy, which play so large a part in English poetry, are kept at arm's length by the Japanese poet, who prefers the image and its implication to the statement and its commentary. The devotee of contemporary English poetry is as likely to be pleased by this as the traditionalist is to be estranged. It should in any case not be supposed that this estheticism inspiring the poetic art of Japan has cut poetry off from the main currents of its cultural life. How intimately poetry is bound up with Japanese life and literature is amply demonstrated in the chapter from the novel *The Tale of Genji* in this anthology.

ᴵᴺᴼᴵᴼᴶᴹᴵ

From the *MANYŌ SHŪ* [compiled A.D. 760]

TRANSLATED BY ARTHUR WALEY [1889-   ]

The Priest Hakutsū [c. 704]

O pine-tree standing
At the [side of] the stone house,
When I look at you,
It is like seeing face to face
The men of old time.

Ōtomo No Tabito [665–731]

To sit silent
And look wise
Is not to be compared with
Drinking saké
And making a riotous shouting.

The Lady of Sakanoye [8th century]

It is other people who have separated
You and me.
Come, my lord!
Do not dream of listening
To the between-words of people!
My heart, thinking
"How beautiful [he is]"
Is like a swift river
[Which] though one dams it and dams it,
Will still break through.

Yakamochi

[These] meetings in dreams,
How sad they are!
When, waking up startled
One gropes about,—
And there is no contact to the hand.

Akahito

The men of valour
Have gone to the honourable hunt:
The ladies
Are trailing their red petticoats
Over the clean sea-beach.

The plum-blossom
Which I thought I would show
To my Brother
Does not seem to be one [at all];
It was [only] that snow had fallen!

Hitomaro

May the men who are born
From my time onwards
Never, never meet
With a path of love-making
Such as mine has been!

Anonymous

Loosed from Winter's prison
When Spring comes forth,
In the morning
The white dew falls:

In the evening
The mists trail:
And in the valley of Hatsu-se
Beneath the twigs of the trees
The nightingale sings.

O sea-gulls that are crying
On Sao river
How is it that,
Loving the river-beach,
You go further up the river?

From the *KOKIN SHŪ* [compiled A.D. 905–922]

Translated by Arthur Waley [1889–   ]

Ki No Akimine [9th century]

The beloved person must I think
Have entered
The summer mountain:
For the cuckoo is singing
With a louder note.

The Lady Eguchi [c. 890]

If only Life-and-Death
Were a thing
Subject to our wills,
What would be the bitterness of parting?

Hitomaro [?]

My thoughts are with a boat
Which travels island-hid
In the morning-mist
Of the shore of Akashi,—
Dim, Dim!

Anonymous

They say there is
A still pool even in the middle of
The rushing whirlpool,—
Why is there none in the whirlpool of my love?

If it were possible
To give away my life in exchange
For [your] love,
How easy a thing Death would be!

Like the ice which melts
When spring begins
Not leaving a trace behind,
May your heart melt towards me!

Can this world
From of old
[Always] have been so sad,
Or did it become so for the sake
Of me alone?

Ono No Yoshiki [died 902]

My love
Is like the grasses
Hidden in the deep mountain:
Though its abundance increases,
There is none that knows.

HAIKU

Translated by Harold G. Henderson [1889–   ]

Matsuo Basho [1644–1694]

Many, many things
   they bring to mind—
      cherry-blossoms.

On a withered branch
   A crow has settled—
      autumn nightfall.

Around existence twine
   (Oh, bridge that hangs across the gorge!)
      ropes of twisted vine.

Cool it is, and still:
   just the tip of a crescent moon
      over Black-wing Hill.

The summer grasses grow.
   Of mighty warriors' splendid dreams
      the afterglow.

Old pond:
   frog-jump-in
      water-sound.

How rough a sea—
   and, stretching over Sado Isle,
      the Galaxy—

A village where they ring
  no bells!—Oh, what *do* they do
    at dusk in spring?

Some of them with staves,
  and white-haired—a whole family
    visiting the graves!

Fall of night
  over the sea—the wild-duck voices
    shadowy and white.

No rice?—In that hour
  we put into the gourd
    a maiden-flower.

A lightning-gleam:
  into darkness travels
    a night-heron's scream.

Taniguchi Buson [1715–1783]

Spring rain! And as yet
  the little froglets' bellies
    haven't got wet!

No poem you send
  in answer—O, young lady!
    Spring is at its end!

Blossoms on the pear;
  and a woman in the moonlight
    reads a letter there. . . .

Raftsmen on their floats;
  their straw capes—see them!—in the storm
    cherry-blossom coats!

The scattering bloom
  turns into torn waste-paper,
    and a bamboo broom—

What piercing cold I feel!
  My dead wife's comb, in our bedroom,
    under my heel. . . .

That axe that I hear
  off in the woods, far away—
    and this wood-pecker, near.

II Of Man and God

FROM The *Meditations* of Ma'arri

{A.D. 973-1057}

TRANSLATED BY REYNOLD A. NICHOLSON {1868-1945}

The Arab poet al-Ma'arri deserves to be better known by readers who think well of Omar Khayyam. If he is less popular among his compatriots than the earlier Mutanabbi, it may be for the same reason that Khayyam was not formerly much favored by the Persians: because he was a free-thinking Moslem. Ma'arri's was an eminently rational mind that roamed over many subjects with a philosophical, though not systematic, comprehensiveness. Like Omar, he was a man of extensive culture, whose verses, in Reynold A. Nicholson's classification, touch upon Life and Death, Human Society, Philosophy, and Religion.

He differs from Omar, however, in the one radical respect that he is also a poet of asceticism. Omar often escapes from the vexations of life by turning to the pleasures of the senses; Ma'arri prefers the way of the hermit. This aspect of his personality may be explained in terms of his private life. He early became blind, and although he managed to acquire a prodigious education despite this disability, it apparently left him embittered with life. His later disillusioning experiences in the great city of Baghdad, whither he went as a young man in search of his fortune, were sufficient to complete the job. The last half or more of his life was devoted to study, teaching, and writing.

The work called by Nicholson the *Meditations* is that by which Ma'arri is best known in the West. It contains the pithy, trenchant, though often cautiously disguised comments upon life of an enlightened Moslem who placed reason and conscience above authority and tradition.

In the following translations, freedom has been taken with the rhymes and meters, and excerpts are often rendered as complete poems, but the translations are on the whole regarded as faithful to both the thought and the expression of the originals.

From the *MEDITATIONS* of Ma'arri

I

In the casket of the Hours
Events deep-hid
Wait on their guardian Powers
To raise the lid.

And the Maker infinite,
Whose poem is Time,
He need not weave in it
A forced stale rhyme.

The Nights pass so,
Voices dumb,
Without sense quick or slow
Of what shall come.

*   *   *

By Allah's will preserving
From misflight,
The barbs of Time unswerving
On us alight.

A loan is all he gives
And takes again;
With his gift happy lives
The folly of men.

II

Nor birth I chose nor old age nor to live:
What the Past grudged me shall the Present give?
Here must I stay, by Doom's both hands constrained,
Nor go until my going is ordained.
You who would guide me out of dark illusion,
You lie—your story does but make confusion.
For can you alter that you brand with shame,
Or is it not unalterably the same?

III

Commandments there be which some minds reckon
    lightly,
Yet no man knoweth whom shall befall perdition.
The Book of Mohammed, ay, and the Book of Moses,
The Gospel of Mary's son and the Psalms of David,
Their bans no nation heeded, their wisdom perished
In vain—and like to perish are all the people.

Two homes hath a man to dwell in, and Life resembles
A bridge that is travelled over in ceaseless passage.
Behold an abode deserted, a tomb frequented!
Nor houses nor tombs at last shall remain in being.

I V

Age after age entirely dark hath run
Nor any dawn led up a rising sun.
Things change and pass, the world unshaken stands
With all its western, all its eastern lands.

The Pen flowed and the fiat was fulfilled,
The ink dried on the parchment as Fate willed.
Chosroes could his satraps round him save,
Or Caesar his patricians—from the grave?

V

'Tis sorrow enough for man that after he roamed at will,
The Days beckon him and say, "Begone, enter now a
        grave!"
How many a time our feet have trodden beneath the dust
A brow of the arrogant, a skull of the debonair!

V I

I welcome Death in his onset and the return thereof,
That he may cover me with his garment's redundancy.
This world is such an abode that if those present here
Have their wits entire, they will never weep for the
        absent ones.
Calamities exceeding count hath it brought to light;
Beneath its arm and embosomed close how many more!
It cleaves us all with its swords asunder and smites us
        down
With its spears and finds us out, right home, with its
        sure-winged shafts.
Its prize-winners, who won the power and the wealth
        of it,
Are but little distant in plight from those who lost its
        prize.

*   *   *

And a strange thing 'tis, how lovingly doth every man
Desire the Mother of stench [9] the while he rails at her.

V I I

If Time aids thee to victory, he will aid
Thy foe anon to take a full revenge.

[9] Mother of stench—life or this world. [Ed.]

The Days' meridian heats bear off as spoil
That which was shed from the moist dawns gone by.

VIII

Thou campest, O son of Adam, the while thou marchest,
And sleep'st in thy fold, and thou on a night-long
journey.
Whoso in this world abides hath hope of profit,
Howbeit a living man is for aye a loser.
The blind folk everywhere, eastward and westward,
Have numbered amongst their riches the staves they
lean on.

IX

When I would string the pearls of my desire,
Alas, Life's too short thread denies them room.
Vast folios cannot yet contain entire
Man's hope; his life is a compendium.

X

O'er many a race the sun's bright net was spread
And loosed their pearls nor left them even a thread.
This dire World delights us, though all sup,
All whom she mothers, from one mortal cup.
A choice of ills: which rather of the twain
Wilt thou?—to perish or to live in pain?

XI

For his own sordid ends
The pulpit he ascends,
And though he disbelieves in resurrection,
Makes all his hearers quail
Whilst he unfolds a tale
Of Last Day scenes that stun the recollection.

XII

Thy thought kindled a fire that showed beside thee
A path whilst thou wert seeking light to guide thee.
Stargazers, charmers, soothsayers are cheats,
All of that sort a cunning greed dissemble:
Howbeit the aged beggar's hand may tremble,
It none the less lies open for receipts.

XIII

Wealth hushes Truth and swells loud Error's voice,
To do it homage all the sects rejoice.

The Moslem got his tax-money no more,
And left his mosque to find a church next door.

X I V

Who'll rescue me from living in a town
Where I am spoken of with praise unfit?
Rich, pious, learned: such is my renown,
But many a barrier stands 'twixt me and it.

*   *   *

I owned to ignorance, yet wise was thought
By some—and is not ours a wondrous case?
For verily we all are good-for-naught:
I am not noble nor are they not base.

My body in Life's strait grip scarce bears the strain—
How shall I move Decay to clasp it round?
O the large gifts of Death! Ease after pain
He brings to us, and silence after sound.

X V

Kneel in the day-time to thy Lord and bow,
And when thou canst bear vigil, vigil bear.
Is fine wheat dear, 'tis nobleness in thee
To give thy generous horse an equal share;
And set before thyself a relish of
Bright oil and raisins, scanty but sweet fare.
A clay jug for thy drink assign: thou'lt wish
Nor silver cup nor golden vessel there.
In summer what will hide thy nakedness
Content thee; coarse homespun thy winter wear.
I ban the judge's office, or that thou
Be seen to preach in mosque or lead the prayer;
And shun viceroyalty and to bear a whip,
As 'twere the sword a paladin doth bare.
Those things in nearest kin and truest friends
I loathe, spend as thou wilt thy soul or spare.
Shame have I found in some men's patronage:
Commit thyself to His eternal care;
And let thy wife be decked with fear of Him
Outshining pearls and emeralds ordered fair—
All praiseth Him: list how the raven's croak
And cricket's chirp His holiness declare—
And lodge thine honour where most glory is:
Not in the vale dwells he that seeks the highland air.

XVI

Humanity, in whom the best
Of this world's features are expressed—
The chiefs set over them to reign
Are but as moons that wax and wane.

If ye unto your sons would prove
By act how dearly them ye love,
Then every voice of wisdom joins
To bid you leave them in your loins.

XVII

Two fates still hold us fast,
A future and a past;
Two vessels' vast embrace
Surrounds us—Time and Space.

Whene'er we ask what end
Our Maker did intend,
Some answering voice is heard
That utters no plain word.

XVIII

If criminals are fated,
'Tis wrong to punish crime.
When God the ores created,
He knew that on a time
They should become the sources
Whence sword-blades dripping blood
Flash o'er the manes of horses
Iron-curbed, iron-shod.

XIX

The body, which gives thee during life a form,
Is but thy vase: be not deceived, my soul!
Cheap is the bowl thou storest honey in,
But precious for the contents of the bowl.

XX

We laugh, but inept is our laughter,
We should weep, and weep sore,
Who are shattered like glass and thereafter
Remoulded no more.

The *Rubaiyat* of Omar Khayyam

{DIED A.D. 1122?}

TRANSLATED BY EDWARD FITZGERALD {1809-1883}

It is doubtful whether any original English poem of real merit has had as wide a circulation as Edward Fitzgerald's translation of some quatrains by the Persian poet-scientist Omar Khayyam. In its less than one-hundred-year history it has achieved a greater fame for Khayyam than his original verses were able to do in over eight hundred years.

This has, of course, tended to confuse product with by-product. The *Rubaiyat* vogue of the late 19th and early 20th centuries was largely the work of Fitzgerald fans, who appreciated the skill with which an English author had made an old Persian poet express their *fin de siècle* mood. Thus were begot the Omar Khayyam Clubs of England and America. Thus, too, the thousand and one editions—fine, illustrated, limited, large, small, good, bad and worse—of the several Fitzgerald versions. One of these, illustrated by the American artist Elihu Vedder, weighed fifteen pounds; another, 1/4 by 3/16 inches in dimensions, is the smallest published book in the world. Still another, elaborately bound and jewelled—valued at £1000—went down with the Titanic in 1912. As an afterglow of this Omar cult, the 1920's in America found in the Old Reprobate a worthy challenger of the Volstead prohibition act and a staunch defender of the deterministic philosophy being preached by Clarence Darrow and Theodore Dreiser.

Meanwhile, the fad of the translation had given impetus to the scholarly study of the poet who inspired it. Countless versions of the quatrains appeared in almost every language of the world, including Esperanto. Some of these were translations of Fitzgerald's English version; some direct from the Persian. New manuscript discoveries, especially in very recent years, have enabled scholars to come closer to the true Omar. His world reputation might now be said to be on a par with that of his most famous English translator, and he is read widely even in his native land.

The English reader would form a better idea of the poetry of Omar if he scrambled the quatrains translated by Fitzgerald. For whether in the first edition (reproduced here) or in the more commonly reprinted fourth, Fitzgerald took the liberty of arranging the quatrains in an order that would depict a full day's cycle, from dawn to moon-rise. This plan is foreign to the original, in which the quatrains are arranged alphabetically by the last letter of the rhyming word. That is to say, each quatrain of Omar's is an individual poem and not merely a stanza, as it is in Fitzgerald. On

257

the other hand, the common notion that this is not a faithful translation is unfounded in fact. It may not always be accurate, and it certainly did not attempt to be literal; but faithful it is in the same sense that the King James version of the Bible is. And like that other great translation into the English language, it demonstrates—in the words of an Omarian—that "the human cry has no nationality."

ﺍﻥﺟﻌﺟﺍﻝ

RUBAIYAT

I

Awake! for Morning in the Bowl of Night
Has flung the Stone that puts the Stars to Flight:
   And Lo! the Hunter of the East has caught
The Sultán's Turret in a Noose of Light.

II

Dreaming when Dawn's Left Hand was in the Sky
I heard a Voice within the Tavern cry,
   "Awake, my Little ones, and fill the Cup
"Before Life's Liquor in its Cup be dry."

III

And, as the Cock crew, those who stood before
The Tavern shouted—"Open then the Door!
   "You know how little while we have to stay,
"And, once departed, may return no more."

IV

Now the New Year reviving old Desires,
The thoughtful Soul to Solitude retires,
   Where the WHITE HAND OF MOSES on the Bough
Puts out, and Jesus from the Ground suspires.[10]

V

Irám indeed is gone with all its Rose,
And Jamshýd's Sev'n-ring'd Cup[11] where no one knows;
   But still the Vine her ancient Ruby yields,
And still a Garden by the Water blows.

[10] The Hebraic and Christian "prophets" viewed, in these metaphors, as life-giving and healing. [Ed.]
[11] Jamshýd, a legendary Persian king of magic power. [Ed.]

VI

And David's Lips are lock't; but in divine
High piping Péhlevi,[12] with "Wine! Wine! Wine!
  "Red Wine!"—the Nightingale cries to the Rose
That yellow Cheek of hers to incarnadine.

VII

Come, fill the Cup, and in the Fire of Spring
The Winter Garment of Repentance fling:
  The Bird of Time has but a little way
To fly—and Lo! the Bird is on the Wing.

VIII

And look—a thousand Blossoms with the Day
Woke—and a thousand scatter'd into Clay:
  And this first Summer Month that brings the Rose
Shall take Jamshýd and Kaikobád away.

IX

But come with old Khayyám, and leave the Lot
Of Kaikobád and Kaikhosrú forgot! [13]
  Let Rustum lay about him as he will,
Or Hátim Tai [14] cry Supper—heed them not.

X

With me along some Strip of Herbage strown
That just divides the desert from the sown,
  Where name of Slave and Sultán scarce is known,
And pity Sultán Máhmúd on his Throne.

XI

Here with a Loaf of Bread beneath the Bough,
A Flask of Wine, a Book of Verse—and Thou
  Beside me singing in the Wilderness—
And Wilderness is Paradise enow.

XII

"How sweet is mortal Sovranty!"—think some:
Others—"How blest the Paradise to come!"
  Ah, take the Cash in hand and waive the Rest;
Oh, the brave Music of a *distant* Drum!

---

12 Péhlevi—the language of pre-Islamic Persia. [Ed.]
13 Kaikobád and Kaikhosrú—semi-legendary Persian monarchs symbolizing great power. [Ed.]
14 Hátim Tai—Arab chieftain traditionally famous for his hospitality. [Ed.]

XIII

Look to the Rose that blows about us—"Lo,
"Laughing," she says, "into the World I blow:
  "At once the silken Tassel of my Purse
"Tear, and its Treasure on the Garden throw."

XIV

The Worldly Hope men set their Hearts upon
Turns Ashes—or it prospers; and anon,
  Like Snow upon the Desert's dusty Face
Lighting a little Hour or two—is gone.

XV

And those who husbanded the Golden Grain,
And those who flung it to the Winds like Rain,
  Alike to no such aureate Earth are turn'd
As, buried once, Men want dug up again.

XVI

Think, in this batter'd Caravanserai [15]
Whose Doorways are alternate Night and Day,
  How Sultán after Sultán with his Pomp
Abode his Hour or two, and went his way.

XVII

They say the Lion and the Lizard keep
The Courts where Jamshýd gloried and drank deep:
  And Bahrám, that great Hunter—the Wild Ass
Stamps o'er his Head, and he lies fast asleep.

XVIII

I sometimes think that never blows so red
The Rose as where some buried Cæsar bled;
  That every Hyacinth the Garden wears
Dropt in its Lap from some once lovely Head.

XIX

And this delightful Herb whose tender Green
Fledges the River's Lip on which we lean—
  Ah, lean upon it lightly! for who knows
From what once lovely Lip it springs unseen!

XX

Ah, my Belovéd, fill the Cup that clears
TO-DAY of past Regrets and future Fears—
  To-morrow?—Why, To-morrow I may be
Myself with Yesterday's Sev'n Thousand Years.

---

15 Caravanserai—the world viewed as a roadside inn. [Ed.]

XXI

Lo! some we loved, the loveliest and best
That Time and Fate of all their Vintage prest,
    Have drunk their Cup a Round or two before,
And one by one crept silently to Rest.

XXII

And we, that now make merry in the Room
They left, and Summer dresses in new Bloom,
    Ourselves must we beneath the Couch of Earth
Descend, ourselves to make a Couch—for whom?

XXIII

Ah, make the most of what we yet may spend,
Before we too into the Dust descend;
    Dust into Dust, and under Dust, to lie,
Sans Wine, sans Song, sans Singer, and—sans End!

XXIV

Alike for those who for TO-DAY prepare,
And those that after a TO-MORROW stare,
    A Muezzín [16] from the Tower of Darkness cries
"Fools! your Reward is neither Here nor There!"

XXV

Why, all the Saints and Sages who discuss'd
Of the Two Worlds so learnedly, are thrust
    Like foolish Prophets forth; their Words to Scorn
Are scatter'd, and their Mouths are stopt with Dust.

XXVI

Oh, come with old Khayyám, and leave the Wise
To talk; one thing is certain, that Life flies;
    One thing is certain, and the Rest is Lies;
The Flower that once has blown for ever dies.

XXVII

Myself when young did eagerly frequent
Doctor and Saint, and heard great Argument
    About it and about: but evermore
Came out by the same Door as in I went.

XXVIII

With them the Seed of Wisdom did I sow,
And with my own hand labour'd it to grow:
    And this was all the Harvest that I reap'd—
"I came like Water, and like Wind I go."

16 Muezzín summons the faithful to prayer. [Ed.]

XXIX

Into this Universe, and *why* not knowing,
Nor *whence*, like Water willy-nilly flowing:
  And out of it, as Wind along the Waste,
I know not *whither*, willy-nilly blowing.

XXX

What, without asking, hither hurried *whence?*
And, without asking, *whither* hurried hence!
  Another and another Cup to drown
The Memory of this Impertinence!

XXXI

Up from Earth's Centre through the Seventh Gate
I rose, and on the Throne of Saturn sate,
  And many Knots unravel'd by the Road;
But not the Knot of Human Death and Fate.

XXXII

There was a Door to which I found no Key:
There was a Veil past which I could not see:
  Some little Talk awhile of ME and THEE
There seemed—and then no more of THEE and ME.

XXXIII

Then to the rolling Heav'n itself I cried,
Asking, "What Lamp had Destiny to guide
  "Her little Children stumbling in the Dark?"
And—"A blind Understanding!" Heav'n replied.

XXXIV

Then to this earthen Bowl did I adjourn
My Lip the secret Well of Life to learn:
  And Lip to Lip it murmur'd—"While you live
"Drink!—for once dead you never shall return."

XXXV

I think the Vessel, that with fugitive
Articulation answer'd, once did live,
  And merry-make; and the cold Lip I kiss'd
How many Kisses might it take—and give!

XXXVI

For in the Market-place, one Dusk of Day,
I watch'd the Potter thumping his wet Clay:
  And with its all obliterated Tongue
It murmur'd—"Gently, Brother, gently, pray!"

XXXVII

Ah, fill the Cup:—what boots it to repeat
How Time is slipping underneath our Feet:
    Unborn TO-MORROW, and dead YESTERDAY,
Why fret about them if TO-DAY be sweet!

XXXVIII

One Moment in Annihilation's Waste,
One Moment, of the Well of Life to taste—
    The Stars are setting and the Caravan
Starts for the Dawn of Nothing—Oh, make haste!

XXXIX

How long, how long, in infinite Pursuit
Of This and That endeavour and dispute?
    Better be merry with the fruitful Grape
Than sadden after none, or bitter, Fruit.

XL

You know, my Friends, how long since in my House
For a new Marriage I did make Carouse:
    Divorced old barren Reason from my Bed,
And took the Daughter of the Vine to Spouse.

XLI

For "Is" and "Is-NOT" though *with* Rule and Line,
And "UP-AND-DOWN" *without*, I could define,
    I yet in all I only cared to know,
Was never deep in anything but—Wine.

XLII

And lately, by the Tavern Door agape,
Came stealing through the Dusk an Angel Shape
    Bearing a Vessel on his Shoulder; and
He bid me taste of it; and 'twas—the Grape!

XLIII

The Grape that can with Logic absolute
The Two-and-Seventy jarring Sects confute:
    The subtle Alchemist that in a Trice
Life's leaden Metal into Gold transmute.

XLIV

The mighty Mahmúd,[17] the victorious Lord,
That all the misbelieving and black Horde
    Of Fears and Sorrows that infest the Soul
Scatters and slays with his enchanted Sword.

[17] Mahmúd, Persian conqueror (970–1130). [Ed.]

XLV

But leave the Wise to wrangle, and with me
The Quarrel of the Universe let be:
    And, in some corner of the Hubbub coucht,
Make Game of that which makes as much of Thee.

XLVI

For in and out, above, about, below,
'Tis nothing but a Magic Shadow-show,
    Play'd in a Box whose Candle is the Sun,
Round which we Phantom Figures come and go.

XLVII

And if the Wine you drink, the Lip you press,
End in the Nothing all Things end in—Yes—
    Then fancy while Thou art, Thou art but what
Thou shalt be—Nothing—Thou shalt not be less.

XLVIII

While the Rose blows along the River Brink,
With old Khayyám the Ruby Vintage drink:
    And when the Angel with his darker Draught
Draws up to Thee—take that, and do not shrink.

XLIX

'Tis all a Chequer-board of Nights and Days
Where Destiny with Men for Pieces plays:
    Hither and thither moves, and mates, and slays,
And one by one back in the Closet lays.

L

The Ball no Question makes of Ayes and Noes,[18]
But Right or Left, as strikes the Player goes;
    And He that toss'd Thee down into the Field,
He knows about it all—HE knows—HE knows!

LI

The Moving Finger writes; and, having writ,
Moves on: nor all thy Piety nor Wit
    Shall lure it back to cancel half a Line,
Nor all thy Tears wash out a Word of it.

LII

And that inverted Bowl we call The Sky,
Whereunder crawling coop't we live and die,

18 Ball—in the game of polo. [Ed.]

Lift not thy hands to *It* for help—for It
Rolls impotently on as Thou or I.

L I I I

With Earth's first Clay They did the Last Man's knead,
And then of the Last Harvest sow'd the Seed:
    Yea, the first Morning of Creation wrote
What the Last Dawn of Reckoning shall read.

L I V

I tell Thee this—When, starting from the Goal,
Over the shoulders of the flaming Foal [19]
    Of Heav'n Parwín and Mushtara they flung,
In my predestin'd Plot of Dust and Soul

L V

The Vine had struck a Fibre; which about
If clings my Being—let the Súfi flout;
    Of my Base Metal may be filed a Key,
That shall unlock the Door he howls without.

L V I

And this I know: whether the one True Light,
Kindle to Love, or Wrath consume me quite,
    One Glimpse of It within the Tavern caught
Better than in the Temple lost outright.

L V I I

Oh, Thou, who didst with Pitfall and with Gin
Beset the Road I was to wander in,
    Thou wilt not with Predestination round
Enmesh me, and impute my Fall to Sin?

L V I I I

Oh, Thou, who Man of baser Earth didst make,
And who with Eden didst devise the Snake;
    For all the Sin wherewith the Face of Man
Is blacken'd, Man's Forgiveness give—and take!

L I X

Listen again. One Evening at the Close
Of Ramazán,[20] ere the better Moon arose,
    In that old Potter's Shop I stood alone
With the clay Population round in Rows.

[19] Foal—allusions to heavenly constellations. [Ed.]
[20] Ramazán—Mohammedan month of fasting. [Ed.]

L X

And, strange to tell, among that Earthen Lot
Some could articulate, while others not:
 And suddenly one more impatient cried—
"Who *is* the Potter, pray, and who the Pot?"

L X I

Then said another—"Surely not in vain
"My Substance from the common Earth was ta'en,
 "That He who subtly wrought me into Shape
"Should stamp me back to common Earth again."

L X I I

Another said—"Why, ne'er a peevish Boy
"Would break the Bowl from which he drank in Joy;
 "Shall He that *made* the Vessel in pure Love
"And Fansy, in an after Rage destroy!"

L X I I I

None answer'd this; but after Silence spake
A Vessel of a more ungainly Make:
 "They sneer at me for leaning all awry;
"What! did the Hand then of the Potter shake?"

L X I V

Said one—"Folks of a surly Tapster tell,
"And daub his Visage with the Smoke of Hell;
 "They talk of some strict Testing of us—Pish!
"He's a Good Fellow, and 'twill all be well."

L X V

Then said another with a long-drawn Sigh,
"My Clay with long oblivion is gone dry:
 "But, fill me with the old familiar Juice,
"Methinks I might recover by-and-bye!"

L X V I

So while the Vessels one by one were speaking,
One spied the little Crescent all were seeking:
 And then they jogg'd each other, "Brother! Brother!
"Hark to the Porter's Shoulder-knot a-creaking!"

L X V I I

Ah, with the Grape my fading Life provide,
And wash my Body whence the Life has died,
 And in the Windingsheet of Vine-leaf wrapt,
So bury me by some sweet Garden-side.

LXVIII

That ev'n my buried Ashes such a Snare
Of Perfume shall fling up into the Air,
    As not a True Believer passing by
But shall be overtaken unaware.

LXIX

Indeed the Idols I have loved so long
Have done my Credit in Men's Eye much wrong:
    Have drown'd my Honour in a shallow Cup,
And sold my Reputation for a Song.

LXX

Indeed, indeed, Repentance oft before
I swore—but was I sober when I swore?
    And then and then came Spring, and Rose-in-hand
My thread-bare Penitence apieces tore.

LXXI

And much as Wine has play'd the Infidel,
And robb'd me of my Robe of Honour—well,
    I often wonder what the Vintners buy
One half so precious as the Goods they sell.

LXXII

Alas, that Spring should vanish with the Rose!
That Youth's sweet-scented Manuscript should close!
    The Nightingale that in the Branches sang,
Ah, whence, and whither flown again, who knows!

LXXIII

Ah Love! could thou and I with Fate conspire
To grasp this sorry Scheme of Things entire,
    Would not we shatter it to bits—and then
Re-mould it nearer to the Heart's Desire!

LXXIV

Ah, Moon of my Delight who know'st no wane,
The Moon of Heav'n is rising once again:
    How oft hereafter rising shall she look
Through this same Garden after me—in vain!

LXXV

And when Thyself with shining Foot shall pass
Among the Guests Star-scatter'd on the Grass,
    And in thy joyous Errand reach the Spot
Where I made one—turn down an empty Glass!

III Of Sacred and Profane Love

FROM **The** *Moallakat*

Ode by Imr-ul-Kais

[A.D. 520-565]

TRANSLATED BY LADY ANNE [1837-1917] AND
WILFRED S. BLUNT [1840-1922]

≈≈≈≈≈

This *Kasidah* or ode is believed to have been composed when its
author was twenty-five years old. He lived only another twenty
years, killed by poisoning in a manner that will not surprise the
reader of this poem. Kais, himself the scion of a royal Arabian
family, had been invited to the imperial court at Byzantium,
where his amorous disposition had involved him in an affair with
the Emperor's daughter. Expelled from court, he is said to have
been pursued by hired assassins who offered him a robe of honor
impregnated with the poison that brought about his end.

His earlier career was marked by several marriages, much feud-
ing against and in behalf of his tribe, and undoubtedly more
than a fair share of the "stupendously hedonistic" living which
the translators find in this ode. An amusing anecdote tells of
his vow to marry only the woman who could answer his riddle:
"What are two and four and eight?" When one damsel finally
divined that the answer was not fourteen and replied: "The two
breasts of a woman, the four milking teats of a she-camel, and
the eight dugs of a she-wolf," she qualified as his first wife and
proceeded to bear him several sons and a daughter.

The *Kasidah* form had apparently been well developed by the
Arabs when Kais took it up, but his ode is the earliest of the
great seven which constitute the *Moallakat*, the most famous collection of pre-Islamic poems that we have. The *Kasidah* follows
a well-established pattern. The poet approaches a forsaken camp-
ing ground, calls upon his traveling companions to halt while he
nostalgically recollects departed dwellers and frustrated loves,
laments the hardships of life, praises his camel or steed, describes
a storm or hunt or barbecue, and concludes with a panegyric to

the prince or governor. Tennyson's poem "Locksley Hall" is believed to have been written in imitation of these odes.

As they were primarily an oral form of literature, they show to best advantage if recited in bardic fashion. The present translation attempts to copy the rolling Arab meters but it does not retain the rhyme of the original. The accent marks indicate the syllable to be stressed.

ﻢﻌﻤﺳ

ODE

Weep, ah weep love's losing, love's with its dwelling place
    set where the hills divide Dakhúli and Háumali.

Túdiha and Mikrat! There the hearth-stones of her stand
    where the South and North winds cross-weave the sand-
    furrows.

See the white-doe droppings strewn by the wind on them,
    black on her floor forsaken, fine-grain of peppercorns.

Here it was I watched her, lading her load-camels, stood by
    these thorn-trees weeping tears as of colocynth.[21]

Here my twin-friends waited, called to me camel-borne: Man!
    not of grief thou diest. Take thy pain patiently.

Not though tears assuage thee, deem it beseemeth thee thus
    for mute stones to wail thee, all thy foes witnesses.

What though fortune flout thee! Thus Om Howéyrith did,
    thus did thy Om Rebábi, fooled thee in Másali.

O, where these two tented, sweet was the breath of them,
    sweet as of musk their fragrance, sweet as garánfoli.[22]

Mourned I for them long days, wept for the love of them,
    tears on my bosom raining, tears on my swordhandle.

Yet, was I un-vanquished. Had I not happiness, I at their
    hands in Dáret, Dáret of Júljuli?

O that day of all days! Slew I my milch-camel, feasted the
    maidens gayly,—well did they load for me!

Piled they high the meat-strings. All day they pelted me,
    pelted themselves with fatness, fringes of camel-meat.

Climbed I to her howdah, sat with Onéyzata, while at my
    raid she chided: Man! Must I walk afoot?

Swayed the howdah wildly, she and I close in it: there! my
    beast's back is galled now. Slave of Grief, down with
    thee.

Answered I: Nay, sweetheart, loosen the rein of him. Think
    not to stay my kisses. Here will I harvest them.

[21] Colocynth—a wild melon, so bitter-tasting as to cause tears. [Ed.]
[22] Garánfoli—an herb eaten by camels. [Ed.]

Grieve not for thy camel. Grudge not my croup-riding. Give
    me—and thee—to taste things sweeter than clove-apples,
Kisses on thy white teeth, teeth, nay the pure petals, even
    and clean and close-set, wreathing a camomile.
Wooed have I thy equals, maidens and wedded ones. Her, the
    nursling's mother, did I not win to her?
What though he wailed loudly, babe of the amulets, turned
    she not half towards him, half of her clasped to me?
Woe is me, the hard heart! How did she mock at me, high
    on the sand-hill sitting, vowing to leave and go!
Fátima, nay my own love, though thou wouldst break with
    me, still be thou kind awhile now, leave me not utterly.
Clean art thou mistaken. Love is my malady. Ask me the
    thing thou choosest. Straight will I execute.
If so be thou findest ought in thy lover wrong, cast from thy
    back my garments, moult thee my finery.
Woe is me, the hard heart! When did tears trouble thee save
    for my soul's worse wounding, stricken and near to die?

Fair too was that other, she the veil-hidden one, howdahed
    how close, how guarded! Yet did she welcome me.
Passed I twixt her tent-ropes,—what though her near-of-kin
    lay in the dark to slay me, blood-shedders all of them.
Came I at the mid-night, hour when the Pleiades showed as
    the links of seed-pearls binding the sky's girdle.
Stealing in, I stood there. She had cast off from her every
    robe but one robe, all but her night-garment.
Tenderly she scolded: What is this stratagem? Speak, on thine
    oath, thou mad one. Stark is thy lunacy.
Passed we out together, while she drew after us on our twin
    track to hide it, wise, her embroideries,
Fled beyond the camp-lines. There in security dark in the
    sand we lay down far from the prying eyes.
By her plaits I wooed her, drew her face near to me, won
    to her waist how frail-lined, hers of the ankle-rings.
Fair-faced she—no redness—noble of countenance, smooth
    as of glass her bosom, bare with its necklaces.
Thus are pearls yet virgin, seen through the dark water, clear
    in the sea-depths gleaming, pure, inaccessible.
Coyly she withdraws her, shows us a cheek, a lip, she a
    gazelle of Wújra,—yearling the fawn with her.
Roe-like her throat slender, white as an áriel's,[23] sleek to thy
    lips uplifted,—pearls are its ornament.
On her shoulders fallen thick lie the locks of her, dark as
    the dark date-clusters hung from the palm-branches.

---

23 Áriel—an antelope. [Ed.]

See the side-plaits pendent, high on the brows of her, tressed
    in a knot, the caught ones fast with the fallen ones.

Slim her waist,—a well-cord scarce has its slenderness. Smooth
    are her legs as reed-stems stripped at a waterhead.

The morn through she sleepeth, muck-stream in indolence,
    hardly at noon hath risen, girded her day dresses.

Soft her touch,—her fingers fluted as water-worms, sleek as
    the snakes of Thóbya, tooth-sticks of Ishali.[24]

Lighteneth she night's darkness, ay, as an evening lamp hung
    for a sign of guidance lone on a hermitage.

Who but shall desire her, seeing her standing thus, half in
    her childhood's short frock, half in her woman's robe!

Strip thee of youth's fooling, thou in thy manhood's prime.
    Yet to her love be faithful,—hold it a robe to thee.

Many tongues have spoken, warned me of craft in love. Yet
    have they failed an answer,—all were thine enemies.

Dim the drear night broodeth,—veil upon veil let down, dark
    as a mad sea raging, tempting the heart of me.

Spake I to Night stoutly, while he, a slow camel, dragged
    with his hind-feet halting,—gone the forehand of him.

Night! I cried, thou snail Night, when wilt thou turn to day?
    When? Though in sooth day's dawning worse were than
    thou to me.

Sluggard Night, what stays thee? Chained hang the stars of
    thee fast to the rocks with hempen ropes set un-moveable.

Water-skins of some folk—ay, with the thong of them laid
    on my nága's wither—borne have I joyfully,

Crossed how lone the rain-ways, bare as an ass-belly; near
    me the wolf, starved gamester, howled to his progeny.

Cried I: Wolf, thou wailest. Surely these lives of ours, thine
    and my own, go empty, robbed of prosperity.

All we won we leave here. Whoso shall follow us, seed in our
    corn-track casting, reap shall he barrenness.

Rode I forth at day-dawn—birds in their nests asleep—stout
    on my steed, the sleek-coat, him the game-vanquisher.

Lo, he chargeth, turneth,—gone is he—all in one, like to a
    rock stream-trundled, hurled from its eminence.

Red-bay he,—his loin-cloth chafing the ribs of him. Shifts as
    a rain-stream smoothing stones in a river-bed.

Hard is he,—he snorteth loud in the pride of him, fierce as
    a full pot boiling, bubbling beneath the lid.

---

[24] Ishali—made of the isha tree. [Ed.]

Straineth he how stoutly, while, as spent fishes swim, tied
    to his track the fleet ones plow his steps wearily.

See, in scorn he casteth youth from the back of him, leaveth
    the horseman cloakless, naked the hard-ride.

As a sling-stone hand-whirled, so is the might of him, loosed
    from the string that held it, hurled from the spliced
    ribbon.

Lean his flanks, gazelle-like, legs as the ostrich's; he like a
    strong wolf trotteth; lithe as a fox-cub he.

Stout his frame; behind him, look, you shall note of him full-
    filled the hind-leg gap, tail with no twist in it.

Polished, hard his quarters, smooth as the pounding-stone
    used for a bridegroom's spices, grind-slab of colocynth.

As the henna juice lies dyed on a beard grown hoar, so on
    his neck the blood-stains mark the game down-ridden.

Rushed we on the roe-herd. Sudden, as maids at play circling
    in skirts low-training, forth leaped the does of it.

Flashing fled they, jewels, shells set alternately on a young
    gallant's neck-string, his the high pedigreed.

Yet he gained their leaders, far while behind him lay bunched
    in a knot the hindmost, ere they fled scatter-wise.

'Twixt the cow and bull herds held, he in wrath his road;
    made he of both his booty,—sweatless the neck of him.

All that day we roasted, seethed the sweet meat of them, row
    upon row in cauldrons, firelighters all of us.

Nathless home at night-fall, he in the fore-front still. Where
    is the eye shall bind him? How shall it follow him?

The night through he watcheth, scorneth him down to lay,
    close, while I sleep, still saddled, bridled by side of me.

Friend, thou seest the lightning. Mark where it wavereth,
    gleameth like fingers twisted, clasped in the cloud-rivers.

Like a lamp new-lighted, so is the flash of it, trimmed by a
    hermit nightly pouring oil-sésame.

Stood I long a watcher, twin-friends how dear with me, till
    in Othéyb it faded, ended in Dáriji.

By its path we judged it: rain over Káttan is; far in Sitár it
    falleth, streameth in Yáthoboli.

Gathered gross the flood-head dammed in Kutéyfati. Woe to
    the trees, the branched ones! Woe the kanáhboli! [25]

El Kanáan hath known it, quailed from the lash of it. Down
    from their lairs it driveth hot-foot the ibexes.

Known it too hath Téyma; standeth no palm of her there,
    nor no house low-founded,—none but her rock-buildings.

[25] Kanáhboli—a tree. [Ed.]

Stricken stood Thabíra [26] whelmed by the rush of it, like an
   old chief robe-folded, bowed in his striped mantle.
Nay, but he Mujéymir, [26] tall-peaked at dawn of day, showed
   like a spinster's distaff tossed on the flood-water.
Cloud-wrecked lay the valley piled with the load of it, high
   as in sacks the Yemámi heapeth his corn-measures.
Seemed it then the song-birds, wine-drunk at sun-rising, loud
   through the valley shouted, maddened with spiceries,
While the wild beast corpses, grouped like great bulbs up-
   torn, cumbered the hollow places, drowned in the night-
   trouble.

Gita Govinda (abridged) by Jayadeva

[12TH CENTURY A.D.]

TRANSLATED BY GEORGE KEYT [1901-   ]

The Sanskrit scholar A. B. Keith calls the *Gita Govinda* a master-
piece which "surpasses in its completeness of effect any other
Indian poem," and he compares it to the works of Aeschylus,
Sophocles, and Euripides. For its 19th century English translator,
Sir Edwin Arnold, it was an "Indian Song of Songs." In the
allegorical interpretation to which it has been subjected it does
indeed resemble that Biblical book. Such an interpretation, however, is not much favored today. A religious poem it certainly
is, for it treats of the loves of Krishna, the favorite reincarnation
of a favorite deity, Vishnu. But the richly sensuous accounts of
love's dalliance with which the poem is almost overladen do not
require to be explained away as figurative pictures of a spiritual
love. Such dualism of sense and spirit, the present translator
insists, is foreign to the spirit of Indian religion. The poet Jayadeva never lets us forget that Krishna—whether as lover or warrior—is deserving of the devotee's worship because he is an
avatar of Vishnu.

This poem frankly celebrates Krishna as lover. He is seen in
his natural habitat, however, and as a cowherd. His paramour,
from whom he is temporarily estranged, is the cowherdess Rádhá.
At the climax of this pastoral drama he is ecstatically reunited
with her, but only after a full account of the poignancy of love's
reconciliation. The slight narrative is told in terms chiefly of songs
and recitatives, which describe outward scenes and inner feelings.
The only other character is a maid attendant upon Rádhá, who
acts as confidante and go-between in the subtle and delicate love-

26 Thabíra . . . Mujéymir—mountains. [Ed.]

play of Rádhá and Krishna. From time to time the poet Jayadeva intrudes to comment upon his story or characters, or to applaud his own achievement as author. These comments are so charmingly interwoven into the fabric of the poem that they become an integral part of the whole.

Mr. Keyt's translation seeks to retain as much as possible of the music and the dictional felicity of the original. It boldly holds on to the refrains, which, at first monotonous, soon reveal their important role in the ritualistic character of the Sanskrit poem. The reader of Elizabethan epithalamia or marriage poems will recognize in them a familiar effect. The slow, languorous movement of the characters in the attractions and repulsions of love constitutes an exquisite sort of verbal dance.

Approximately half of the poem is here reproduced. Some sense of the continuity of the whole piece has been provided by the editor in the brief paraphrases of the omitted portions, in brackets.

GITA GOVINDA

* * *

I

[*Rádhá's confidante has been telling her of the difficulties of parting. She now turns to an account of Krishna's wanton sporting with the other maidens.*]

Sandal and garment of yellow and lotus garlands upon his
    body of blue,
In his dance the jewels of his ears in movement dangling over
    his smiling cheeks.
Hari [27] here disports himself with charming women given to
    love!

The wife of a certain herdsman sings as Hari sounds a tune
    of love
Embracing him the while with all the force of her full and
    swelling breasts.
Hari here disports himself with charming women given to
    love!

Another artless woman looks with ardour on Krishna's lotus
    face

27 Hari—lord; here Krishna. [Ed.]

Where passion arose through restless motion of playful eyes
with sidelong glances.
Hari here disports himself with charming women given to
love!

Another comes with beautiful hips, making as if to whisper
a word,
And drawing close to his ear the adorable Krishna she kisses
upon the cheek.
Hari here disports himself with charming women given to
love!

Another on the bank of the Jamna, when Krishna goes to a
bamboo thicket,
Pulls at his garment to draw him back, so eager is she for
amorous play.
Hari here disports himself with charming women given to
love!

Hari praises another woman, lost with him in the dance of
love,
The dance where the sweet low flute is heard in the clamour
of bangles on hands that clap.
Hari here disports himself with charming women given to
love!

He embraces one woman, he kisses another, and fondles
another beautiful one,
He looks at another one lovely with smiles, and starts in
pursuit of another woman.
Hari here disports himself with charming women given to
love!

May all prosperity spread from this, Shri Jayadeva's famed
and delightful
Song of wonderful Keshava's secret play in the forest of
Vrindávana!
Hari here disports himself with charming women given to
love!

* * *

With his limbs, tender and dark like rows of clumps of blue
lotus flowers,
By herd-girls surrounded, who embrace at pleasure, any part
of his body,
Friend, in spring beautiful Hari plays like Love's own self
Conducting the love sport, with love for all, bringing delight
into being.

The wind from the Malayan range seeks Shiva's mountain,
  to plunge in its coolness,
As if tortured by heat from the coils of the serpents dwelling
  there in its caves [28]
And the voices, low-toned and loud, of the kókilas "kuhuh,
  kuhur"
Delightedly crying at sight of the buds on smooth mango-
  summits.

May the smiling captivating Hari protect you, whom Rádhá,
  blinded by love,
Violently kissed as she made as if singing a song of welcome
  saying,
"Your face is nectar, excellent," ardently clasping his bosom
In the presence of the fair-browed herd-girls dazed in the
  sport of love!

II

[*Rádhá, having expressed her desire for Krishna, now begs
her confidante to make him enjoy her.*]

O make him enjoy me, my friend, that haughty destroyer of
  Keshi, that Krishna so fickle,
Me who in darkness, unseen, to a thicket for house, departed
  with him,
Dwelling concealed in a secret place with him, only to lose
  him thereafter
And wander in anxious quest all over for him who laughs out
  his love.

O make him enjoy me, my friend, that haughty destroyer of
  Keshi, that Krishna so fickle,
I who am shy like a girl on her way to the first of her trysts
  of love,
He who is charming with flattering words, I who am tender
In speech and smiling, he on whose hip the garment lies
  loosely worn.

O make him enjoy me, my friend, that haughty destroyer of
  Keshi, that Krishna so fickle,
Me whose couch was of tender shoots beneath me, my bosom
  itself
For long which served as a bed for him, for Krishna the lips
  of whose mouth
Resembled a drink in kissing me, clasped while we were in
  each other's embrace.

[28] By reason of the Sandal Trees, among the roots of which Snakes live.

O make him enjoy me, my friend, that haughty destroyer of
    Keshi, that Krishna so fickle,
Me who sweated and moistened all over my body with love's
    exertion,
That Krishna whose cheeks were lovely with down all stand-
    ing on end as he thrilled,
Whose half-closed eyes were languid, and restless who was in
    his brimming desire.

O make him enjoy me, my friend, that haughty destroyer of
    Keshi, that Krishna so fickle,
Me whose masses of curls were like loose-slipping flowers,
    whose amorous words
Were vague as of doves and kókila birds, that Krishna whose
    bosom is marked
With scratches, surpassing all in his love that the science of
    love could teach.

O make him enjoy me, my friend, that haughty destroyer of
    Keshi, that Krishna so fickle,
To whose act of desire accomplished the anklets upon my
    feet bejewelled
Vibrated sounding, who gave his kisses seizing the hair of the
    head,
And to whom in his passionate love my girdle sounded in
    eloquence sweet.

O make him enjoy me, my friend, that haughty destroyer of
    Keshi, that Krishna so fickle,
Whose lotus eyes had closed a little, and who had drowsily
    grown—
Having tasted in bodily pleasure with me the shattering thrill
    in the end,
With me whose vine-like body collapsed, unable to bear any
    more.

O make him enjoy me, my friend, that haughty destroyer of
    Keshi, that Krishna so fickle,
And may he playfully make more pleasure, sung here by
    Shri Jayadeva
Describing his many and endless amours with amorous gópí
    women.

* * *

In the forest I see—I am thrilled—Govinda surrounded by
    herd-girls, his love-flute fallen;
At the girls with their arched eyebrows glancing, Govinda
    moist with sweat on his cheeks,

At seeing me an embarrassed nectar of a smile on his sweet
     face.

In the distance, my friend, the sight of the clustering buds of
     ashoka creepers distresses,
And the wind from over the gardens and lakes, and the
     opening of buds on the mango tops
Alive with the humming of bees; so pleasant, no pleasure to
     me.

May Krishna in this his unusual aspect, gazing a long while
     into the mind,
Cleanse you of that sin which is seen in the pleasure of
     infatuated hearts
And in the meaning smiles and loosening dishevelled hair,
     in the gleam of the surging of herd-girls,
In their wanton raising of arms above their arm-pits to display
     their breasts.

III

Kamsa's enemy, abandoning the herd-girls, placed Rádhá in
     his heart,
Rádhá as a chain through relation to the robe of the world,
     Shri Krishna.
Krishna repentant, his heart scarred by shafts of the love god,
     went about looking for Rádhá,
Searching all over, full of dejection, he went to a bower on
     the banks of the Jamna.

Rádhá so deeply wronged, troubled to see me surrounded by
     women,
She went, and I, in the fear of my guilt, made no attempt to
     stop her.
Alas, alas, she is gone in anger, her love destroyed!

Parted so long, now what will she do if I see her? What will
     she say?
What of wealth any more? What use of the herd-girls? Why
     continue to live?
Alas, alas, she is gone in anger, her love destroyed!

I think of that face of hers, wrathful, eyebrows crooked,
     knitted in anger,
A crimson lotus clouded beneath the bees which keep hover-
     ing over it!
Alas, alas, she is gone in anger, her love destroyed!

She who has come to my heart, I sport her always with
　　warmth and fervour.
Why follow her here in the forest now? Why mourn in vain
　　and lament?
Alas, alas, she is gone in anger, her love destroyed!

O my slender one, I imagine your heart is dejected through
　　anger of me—
I cannot console you kneeling in homage, I know not where
　　to find you!
Alas, alas, she is gone in anger, her love destroyed!

As if inconstant, coming and going, so you appear before me.
The ardent embrace you used to give me, O why not give it
　　again?
Alas, alas, she is gone in anger, her love destroyed!

If you pardon me now I shall never repeat this neglect of
　　you ever—
O beautiful, give me your pleasure again, I burn with desire!
Alas, alas, she is gone in anger, her love destroyed!

This of Hari alone is a song by the famed Jayadeva,
Who arose, as out of the ocean the moon, from the village of
　　Kindubilva,
Alas, alas, she is gone in anger, her love destroyed!

* * *

Not the king of serpents this lotus necklace upon my bosom,
Not the gleam of poison upon my neck this chain of blue
　　lotus,
Not ash this unguent of sandal dust upon me;
Mistake me not for Shiva,[29] O love god, assail not me!

O love god, you who won conquering all through play,
O not in your bow place your arrow, this mango sprout, not
　　in your hand!
What valour destroying the weakened?

My mind—through the pain of those other arrows of Love,
　　the looks of the deer-eyed Rádhá—
I assure you smarts me still!

[29] Allusion to Kama's assault on the ascetic God in order to inflame him
with love for Parvati [his spouse—Ed.].

On Rádhá, embodying his victory, Love, who conquers all
    things
Placed his bow, her sprout-like eyebrows; his arrows, her
    fluttering glances;
His bow-string, the tips of the curves of her ears;—the
    weapons of Love.

So your arrow of eye-play placed on your bow of an eyebrow
    wounds me;
Death's work is done too, my slender one, by your curly
    black tresses;
Your lip, like a bimba fruit, but infatuates further;
And your bosom, so chaste, how it ravages playing with my
    life!

These are with her the pleasures of being intimate:
The charms vibrant and moist of her eyes and the scent of
    her lotus mouth,
The ambiguous sweet nectar-dripping of her words and the
    sweetness of her bimba lips;
On these the mind dwelling attached, even so is increased the
    pain of being parted.

May welfare befall you from waves of sidelong glances
The love god's looks in Rádhá's moon of a face
Artlessly sweet, and of nectar, disclosed by the signs of the
    women who send their devotion
To the shining place of his flute, of him with his swaying
    head, whose earrings keep dangling across his neck!

I V

[*The confidante tells Krishna of Rádhá's pining for love of
him and upbraids him.*]

V

"I stay here; you go to Rádhá; conciliate her with my words,
    and bring her!"
So himself did Madhu's enemy say to the friend; and she
    came to Rádhá and said:

When breezes blow from the Malayan mountain, longing
    grows and increases;
When clusters of flowers open in bloom, torn are the hearts
    that are parted.
He droops, separated from you, O friend, the wearer of
    garlands!
When he appears to be dead, at the time, even then, when
    the cold moon is burning,
He wails in dejection beneath the falling of shafts from the
    god of desire.

He droops, separated from you, O friend, the wearer of
garlands!

When he hears the noise of swarms of bees, he covers his
ears from their humming;
Pain he feels, night after night, of a heart in love that is
parted.
He droops, separated from you, O friend, the wearer of
garlands!

He dwells beneath the roof of the forest, discards his lovely
garland;
He tosses in bed, on the floor of the forest, repeating your
name in murmurs.
He droops, separated from you, O friend, the wearer of
garlands!

Give his place in your heart to Hari, when the poet Jayadeva
has spoken,
Your heart full of passion because of this poem which sings
of love's separation.
He droops, separated from you, O friend, the wearer of
garlands!

* * *

Again in the grove of the love-god, Mádhava dwells on the
past events of his amours—
His amours with you—and ceaselessly mutters, repeating the
talks between you;
And yearns for that nectar again, the embrace of your breasts
like pitchers.

He has gone into the trysting place, full of all desired bliss,
O you of lovely hips, delay no more!
O go forth now and seek him out, him the master of your
heart, him endowed with passion's lovely form.
He dwells, the garland wearer, in the forest by the Jamna, in
the gentle breezes there,
The swelling breasts of gópí [30] girls who crushes ever with
his restless hands.

Softly on his flute he plays, calling to the meeting place,
naming it with notes and saying where;
And the pollen by the breezes borne, the breezes which have
been on you, that pollen in his sight has high esteem.
He dwells, the garland wearer, in the forest by the Jamna, in
the gentle breezes there,
The swelling breasts of gópí girls who crushes ever with his
restless hands.

[30] Gópí girls—milkmaids. [Ed.]

On fallen feathers of the birds, on leaves about the forest
    floor, he lies excited making there his bed,
And he gazes out upon the path, looks about with trembling
    eyes, anxious, looking out for your approach.
He dwells, the garland wearer, in the forest by the Jamna, in
    the gentle breezes there,
The swelling breasts of gópí girls who crushes ever with his
    restless hands.

Depart, my friend, now to that grove, impenetrable in this
    dark, and put upon yourself your cloak of black;
Discard the anklets on your feet, betraying—noisy timid
    foes—which dance with clatter in the sport of love!
He dwells, the garland wearer, in the forest by the Jamna, in
    the gentle breezes there,
The swelling breasts of gópí girls who crushes ever with his
    restless hands.

O you with your complexion fair, Hari's breast will make you
    shine, that cloud with necklace as of fluttering cranes,
And there where merit-fruit is eaten, lightning you will seem
    in radiance, Krishna then in love-play lying beneath you!
He dwells, the garland wearer, in the forest by the Jamna, in
    the gentle breezes there,
The swelling breasts of gópí girls who crushes ever with his
    restless hands.

There on that bed of tender leaves, O lotus-eyed, embrace his
    hips, his naked hips from whence the girdle drops,
Those hips from whence the garment falls, those loins which
    are a treasure heap, the fountain and the source of all
    delight!
He dwells, the garland wearer, in the forest by the Jamna, in
    the gentle breezes there,
The swelling breasts of gópí girls who crushes ever with his
    restless hands.

O act according to my words, and satisfy with no delay the
    longing in the love of Hari now!
Or otherwise now, like the ceasing of this night close on its
    end, that haughty one's desire will cease for you.
He dwells, the garland wearer, in the forest by the Jamna, in
    the gentle breezes there,
The swelling breasts of gópí girls who crushes ever with his
    restless hands.

O worship Hari, to be welcomed in resembling merit, and
    who shows so much of mercy to
His devotee, the poet Shri Jayadeva, who now makes this
    utterance of a very lovely song!

He dwells, the garland wearer, in the forest by the Jamna, in
the gentle breezes there,
The swelling breasts of gópí girls who crushes ever with his
restless hands.

* * *

Among couples drunken with lust and gone with adulterous
intent, attained to confusion, indulging in talk,
What shameless delights are there not in the darkness, after
embracing and scratching and rousing desire and kissing,
After excitement, and starting the actions fulfilling desire!

O lovely face, the adorable one after seeing how you cast
your trembling and fearful glances along the darkened
road,
Pausing at every tree, tardily walking, arriving in secret, your
limbs in motion like waves of Love,
May he then realise his desire!

On the sweet and lotus-like face of Rádhá, he who resembles
a bee,
Devaki's son, as a blue gem fit for the crests of the lords of
the triple world,
He who is death to the lords of the earth,
And among the herd-girls whenever he wishes a source of
pleasure-disturbance,
And to Kamsa the star of destruction; may he protect you!

VI–VII

[*Rádhá bemoans Krishna's absence, envying the girl with
whom he now lies.*]

Dressed for the occasion in the customary garb of love,
Her hair all dishevelled and the flowers there all disarranged—
A certain girl, excelling in her charms unrivalled, dallies with
the enemy of Madhu.

Transformed into another being, it seems, by the embrace of
Hari,
All quivering the necklaces upon her breast curved like a
jar—
A certain girl, excelling in her charms unrivalled, dallies with
the enemy of Madhu.

Her face, a moon, is fondled by the fluttering petals in her
hair,
The exciting moisture of his lips induces languor in her
limbs—
A certain girl, excelling in her charms unrivalled, dallies with
the enemy of Madhu.

Her earrings bruise her cheeks while dancing with the motion
  of her head,
Her girdle by the tremor of her moving hips is made to
  tinkle—
A certain girl, excelling in her charms unrivalled, dallies with
  the enemy of Madhu.

She laughs because she gets embarrassed when she looks
  upon her lover,
In many ways she utters senseless sounds, through fever of
  her love—
A certain girl, excelling in her charms unrivalled, dallies with
  the enemy of Madhu.

Very great her wide and wave-like tremor of upstanding hairs,
Very large her passion blossoms with the closing of her
  eyes—
A certain girl, excelling in her charms unrivalled, dallies with
  the enemy of Madhu.

Beautiful her body with the drops of sweat through love's
  exertion,
She who is unswerving in love's conflict, fallen on his
  breast—
A certain girl, excelling in her charms unrivalled, dallies with
  the enemy of Madhu.

May the sport of Hari's amours in the song of Shri Jayadeva
Bring completely to an end the sins of this the age of
  Kali [31]—
A certain girl, excelling in her charms unrivalled, dallies with
  the enemy of Madhu.

* * *

Like the lotus face of Mura's foe this moon in radiance,
Pale through a separation that surpasses usual pain,
And, in alliance with the god of love,
Spreads all throughout my heart the anguish of desire.

A brow-mark on a lovely woman's lovely face he makes with
  musk, as if it were the deer-mark on the moon,
And passion there begins to rise within that face whose lips
  are thrilled beneath the kisses over them that smother.
In a forest on an island in the Jamna he sports, Mura's
  enemy, defeating me today.

He decorates with crimson flowers her curly tresses, curls
  which are upon her lively face a mass of clouds,

[31] Kali—female consort of Shiva, god of destruction. [Ed.]

Flowers with crimson flashings lovely in the forest of her
   tresses, haunt of that wild creature love's desire.
In a forest on an island in the Jamna he sports, Mura's
   enemy, defeating me today.

Around the spacious heaven of her firm set breasts besmeared
   with musk, adorned with hare-shaped marks made with
   his nails,
He winds about and fastens there upon her neck the necklaces, of pure and precious pearls the necklaces.
In a forest on an island in the Jamna he sports, Mura's
   enemy, defeating me today.

Diamond bracelets that resemble bees in clusters he puts
   upon her hands so snowy and so tender and so cool,
Her hands with tender lotus palms surpassing in their smooth-
   ness the tenderness of stalks of lotuses.
In a forest on an island in the Jamna he sports, Mura's
   enemy, defeating me today.

A girdle set with jewels, like a festal wreath, he binds around
   her large and lovely hips, her ample loins,
From whence her thighs, clothed modestly, are always as the
   home of Love and where upon his golden throne Love
   sits.
In a forest on an island in the Jamna he sports, Mura's
   enemy, defeating me today.

Upon her lotus stalks of feet he smears lac, as if they are
   being covered by an outer garment there,
Her feet adorned with toe-nails as of gems, and to the heart
   of him attached with love whose home is Kamalá.
In a forest on an island in the Jamna he sports, Mura's
   enemy, defeating me today.

While with some girl of lovely eyes Hala's that wicked brother
   sports, tell me, O my friend, wherefore must I
Keep dwelling here so uselessly, here beneath this branch,
   and without taste for all the pleasures of desire?
In a forest on an island in the Jamna he sports, Mura's
   enemy, defeating me today.

Acquired in this Kali age may no sin abide in him, that prince
   of poets who is Jayadeva,
Whose place to Madhu's slayer is devotion, and who glows
   with taste, praising all the qualities of Hari!
In a forest on an island in the Jamna he sports, Mura's
   enemy, defeating me today.

* * *

O my friend, if that heartless rogue has failed to come,
Why, O my messenger, should you be anxious!
If he sports, the much beloved, as he pleases, how may the
  fault be yours?
Know that this heart of mine,
Drawn into union, drawn by his virtue to him my lover,
Will go of itself to him, breaking through the pain of my
  longing!

* * *

VIII

Then having somehow passed the night, and withered by the
  arrows of love,
She reproachfully said to her lover at dawn, though he bowed
  in her presence imploring with soothing words:

By breaking so much rest at night, his eyes today look very
  reddened, and resemble passion in their colour,
His eyes the abode of drowsiness, and showing his addiction
  to desire that so readily awakens.
Alas! Alas! Go Mádhava! Go, Keshava! Desist from uttering
  these deceitful words!
Follow her, you lotus-eyed, she who can dispel your trouble,
  go to her!

Your mouth, O Krishna, darkened, enhances—making beautiful—the crimson beauty of your lovely body,
Enhances with a darkness, a blackness that arises from the
  kissing of eyes coloured with black unguent.
Alas! Alas! Go, Mádhava! Go, Keshava! Desist from uttering
  these deceitful words!
Follow her, you lotus-eyed, she who can dispel your trouble,
  go to her!

Like a letter that declares the victory of love, and done in
  silver and in gold and set with gems,
So your body now assumes the look—with scars of love-war
  marked upon it, scratches made there by her fingernail.
Alas! Alas! Go, Mádhava! Go, Keshava! Desist from uttering
  these deceitful words!
Follow her, you lotus-eyed, she who can dispel your trouble,
  go to her!

As if upon the tree of love, its foliage, the patches there, the
  coverings of the tender leaves and sprouts,
So on this haughty breast of yours the patches here, the
  markings from the red of lac made by her lotus foot.

Alas! Alas! Go, Mádhava! Go, Keshava! Desist from uttering
    these deceitful words!
Follow her, you lotus-eyed, she who can dispel your trouble,
    go to her!

Made by her tooth the bruise, an imprint, on your lip I see,
    makes pain for me, gives anguish to my mind;
And your body—does it not proclaim that you are no more
    mine, that you have parted now from me, that you have
    changed?
Alas! Alas! Go, Mádhava! Go, Keshava! Desist from uttering
    these deceitful words!
Follow her, you lotus-eyed, she who can dispel your trouble,
    go to her!

I who follow you devoted—how can you deceive me, so
    tortured by love's fever as I am?
O Krishna, like the look of you, your body which appears so
    black, that heart of yours a blackness shall assume!
Alas! Alas! Go, Mádhava! Go, Keshava! Desist from uttering
    these deceitful words!
Follow her, you lotus-eyed, she who can dispel your trouble,
    go to her!

In your wanderings through the forest the way you ravish
    women, O what is there so wonderful in that?
The Putaniká yakshi proclaims to all your feat of youth—in
    your pitiless destruction of the women!
Alas! Alas! Go, Mádhava! Go, Keshava! Desist from uttering
    these deceitful words!
Follow her, you lotus-eyed, she who can dispel your trouble,
    go to her!

Let those who understand give ear to this—the lamentation,
    the wail of women destitute in love,
The grief of being neglected, sung by Shri Jayadeva, in
    heaven even rare and sweet as nectar.
Alas! Alas! Go, Mádhava! Go, Keshava! Desist from uttering
    these deceitful words!
Follow her, you lotus-eyed, she who can dispel your trouble,
    go to her!

* * *

The sight of your flow of a love of a bosom aglow with
    patches of lac from the foot of your sweetheart
Causes my shame to take the place of my sorrow born of
    my great love being destroyed.

May blessings be bestowed by the sound of the flute of
    Kamsa's foe,

The sound of the flute removing the difficult grief of the gods
  by the dánavas humbled,
The sound of the flute, the great invitation to the deer-eyed
  women, stirring, delighting, and making them bold,
The sound bringing down from the crests of the dwellers of
  heaven, swaying with pleasure, the mandára flowers!

IX

[*Rádhá's confidante urges her to put aside pride and go to
  Krishna.*]

X

Then in the day's decline when Rádhá—softened in anger,
  weak in restraint against her ceaseless sighs—
Was awaiting the message her friend would bring, Hari with
  faltering steps of joy, shyly went to that beautiful one
  and said:

If you speak but a little the moon-like gleam of your teeth
  will destroy the darkness frightful, so very terrible,
  come over me;
Your moon of a face which glitters upon my eye, the moon-
  bird's eye, now makes me long for the sweet of your
  lips.
O loved one, O beautiful, give up that baseless pride against
  me!
My heart is burnt by the fire of longing; give me that drink
  so sweet of your lotus face!

O you with beautiful teeth, if you are in anger against me,
  strike me then with your fingernails, sharp and like
  arrows,
Bind me, entwining, with the cords of your arms, and bite
  me then with your teeth, and feel happy punishing!
O loved one, O beautiful, give up that baseless pride against
  me!
My heart is burnt by the fire of longing; give me that drink
  so sweet of your lotus face!

You are my life, and you are my ornament, you are the
  jewel, the gem, in the depth of the ocean of all my being,
So be gracious to me, and thus continue to be, and my heart
  shall always endeavour to be most worthy of you!
O loved one, O beautiful, give up that baseless pride against
  me!
My heart is burnt by the fire of longing; give me that drink
  so sweet of your lotus face!

O slender one, in your anger today even your eye, a blue
    lotus, assumes now the look of a crimson lotus;
But if through the power of the flower-arrowed one, the love
    god, you make the blue Krishna crimson that action is
    only right!
O loved one, O beautiful, give up that baseless pride against
    me!
My heart is burnt by the fire of longing; give me that drink
    so sweet of your lotus face!

Let the radiant cluster of gems that glitter upon your jar-
    shaped breast make bright the region of your heart!
Let your girdle upon the swelling curve of your hips so firm
    make a tinkling sound, proclaiming Love's command!
O loved one, O beautiful, give up that baseless pride against
    me!
My heart is burnt by the fire of longing; give me that drink
    so sweet of your lotus face!

O you with your gentle voice, but speak! With lac I shall
    redden the soles of your feet and make them glisten
    with oil,
Your pair of feet surpassing hibiscus flowers, delighting my
    heart, your feet unrivalled in amorous play.
O loved one, O beautiful, give up that baseless pride against
    me!
My heart is burnt by the fire of longing; give me that drink
    so sweet of your lotus face!

As an ornament place upon my head your proud and stalk-
    like feet, as a cure for the venom of desire!
O let your feet remove the change now made by the pitiless
    fire of love, which burns and which destroys!
O loved one, O beautiful, give up that baseless pride against
    me!
My heart is burnt by the fire of longing; give me that drink
    so sweet of your lotus face!

All this song with these words of Mura's foe, adorned with
    the beautiful speech of the poet Jayadeva,
Tender and skilful and full of delight, prevails, having won
    over Rádhá, and flattering haughty women.
O loved one, O beautiful, give up that baseless pride against
    me!
My heart is burnt by the fire of longing; give me that drink
    so sweet of your lotus face!

* * *

Abandon your fears, O anxious one, but for the love god—
    that bodiless one—none is so blest as to enter my heart,
    tenanted ever by you with your hips and breasts so firm.
When you embrace me, my sweetheart, inflict upon me then,
    as a penalty, all the things that result in the bondage of
    that embrace!

Pressing upon me your breasts so hard, entwining me with
    your vine-like arms, biting me with your merciless teeth,
    inflict upon me, foolish one, the suitable penalty!
Then through the blows of Love—that base one, the five-
    arrowed—my life will depart from me, you rogue, and
    you shall be happy!

A cure unfailing, O moon-face one, is the nectar of your lips,
A cure for destroying the fear in the hearts of the young men
    who see in their infatuation your eyebrow-curve as a
    deadly serpent.

To no purpose, O slender one, you pain me with silence!
Make music, O you of sweet notes, and dispel my heat with
    your glances!
O you of the beautiful face, but give up aversion to me, to
    me your lover, sweet one, so tenderly waiting on you;
    elude not me!

Your lips are one with the colour of bandhuka blossoms, and
    the tender skin of your cheek, you rogue, gleams pale
    like the madhuka flower;
The beautiful blue of the lotus is shown in your eyes; your
    nose resembles the sesamum flower;
And altogether, O loved one, with you, O you with your
    teeth of jasmine, the god whose weapons are flowers
    conquers the world with the hosts of your face!

With your languorous eyes, your glistening mouth like the
    moon, your gait the delight of the people, your thighs
    excelling the trunk of the plantain;
With your skilful amorous play, with the sweet and beautiful
    streaks of your eyebrows;
How wonderful, slender one, though on earth, the way you
    bear in your person the nymphs of heaven! [32]

May that Hari bestow more happiness, that Hari who met the
    Kuvalayapída demon in the battle and saw in the jar-

[32] An elaborate pun here, untranslatable, giving the names of the
nymphs.

shaped hands of the demon the likeness of Rádhá's
breasts, and sweated and closed his eyes a moment;
So that Kamsa, deluded, began to cry, "Subdued! He is conquered! He is overcome!"

X I

At nightfall, which robs one of sight, when Keshava, suitably
clothed, after soothing the deer-eyed one, and gone to
the thicket,
A certain young woman said to Rádhá—who was cheerful
now and had put on her jewels and looked like the sun:

Who made a song of coaxing words, bowing at your feet in
homage,
And gone now to the lovely clump of bamboos, to the bed of
passion,
O foolish woman, follow him who looks with favour now,
O Rádhá, Madhu's slayer!

O you who bear the weight of heavy thighs and heavy breasts,
come hither
With tardy tread that shames the goose and with your jewelled
anklets tinkling,
O foolish woman, follow him who looks with favour now,
O Rádhá, Madhu's slayer!

Listen to his lovely noise, infatuating, end your yearning
Where the flocks of cuckoos praise the reign of him whose
bow is flowers!
O foolish woman, follow him who looks with favour now,
O Rádhá, Madhu's slayer!

O you with thighs like elephant trunks, these creepers with
their hands aflutter,
Their tendrils waving in the wind, appear to ask you to the
meeting!
O foolish woman, follow him who looks with favour now,
O Rádhá, Madhu's slayer!

Consult your jar-shaped breast on which are spotless streams
of necklaces,
Which quivers undulating on the waves, the surging force of
passion!
O foolish woman, follow him who looks with favour now,
O Rádhá, Madhu's slayer!

Your friends are all aware, you rogue, that you are ready for
     love's conflict,
Go, your belt aloud with bells, shameless, amorous, to the
     meeting!
O foolish woman, follow him who looks with favour now,
     O Rádhá, Madhu's slayer!

O you with arrows of Love for nails, leaning on your friend,
     seductive
Go to Hari, his ways are known, and know him by his
     bracelets' tinkling!
O foolish woman, follow him who looks with favour now,
     O Rádhá, Madhu's slayer!

May this song of Jayadeva dwell upon the necks of people
Given to Hari, necks the beauty of their necklaces surpassing.
O foolish woman, follow him who looks with favour now,
     O Rádhá, Madhu's slayer!

* * *

She will see me, her speech that of love, herself in the bliss
     of a close embrace, intimate, limb to limb, sporting in
     dalliance, O friend, having come!
Full of this thought the lover he sees her, imagining, in the
     grove in a mass of deep darkness,
And he trembles, thrilled, feels glad, perspires, and attempts
     to step forward, and swoons.

Beautiful, a robe of black, the darkness which has caused
     them to smear on their eyelids black unguent.
And wreaths of clusters of tapiccha blossoms over their ears
     and garlands of dark coloured lotuses over their heads
     and streaks of musk across their bosoms, O friend,
The darkness embracing the limbs of those beautiful rogues,
     the herd-girls, excited, in haste to go to the tryst.

Dark like tender tamála leaves the darkness shaped with an
     outline everywhere by the flashing clusters of jewels of
     the women gone to the tryst,
The women whose bodies are yellow with saffron,
The darkness the touchstone, the test of the gold of his love.

Then in the entrance to his hut in the thicket, lit by the
     central gems of his gold belt's pendant and the gems of
     his garland and on his anklets and earrings,

She pointed out Hari to Rádhá her friend, Rádhá so shy, and said:

* * *

He is tired, having borne you so long in his heart, he is burned by Love, and desires to drink of your lips contracted with nectar;
So adorn his lap for a moment here in this place that was given in fear to your slave, your slave who was bought with a little part of the wealth of a frown,
Your slave who has worshipped your lotus foot.

Her eyes to Govinda turning desirous, anxious and with delight
She entered the abode of Love, her beautiful anklets tinkling.

She looked on Hari who desired only her, on him who for long wanted dalliance,
Whose face with his pleasure was overwhelmed, and who was possessed with Desire,
Hari on whose body the waves of many changes appeared at the sight of her face
Like the ocean in dance with its waves ascending when seeing the face of the moon.

She looked on Hari who desired only her, on him who for long wanted dalliance,
Whose face with his pleasure was overwhelmed, and who was possessed with Desire,
After embracing her long and ardently, Hari with his necklace of pearls,
Hari like the Jamna in a mighty flood with its necklace of specks of foam.

She looked on Hari who desired only her, on him who for long wanted dalliance,
Whose face with his pleasure was overwhelmed, and who was possessed with Desire,
On Hari whose body was dark and tender, clothed in a garment of yellow,
Like a lotus blue-coloured whose centre is circled around by a mass of pollen.

She looked on Hari who desired only her, on him who for long wanted dalliance,

Whose face with his pleasure was overwhelmed, and who was
　　possessed with Desire,
Who engendered passion with his face made lovely through
　　tremblings of glancing eyes,
Like a pond in autumn with a pair of wagtails at play in a
　　full blown lotus.

She looked on Hari who desired only her, on him who for
　　long wanted dalliance,
Whose face with his pleasure was overwhelmed, and who was
　　possessed with Desire,
Who was adorned with earrings like suns come to clasp his
　　lotus of a face,
And who for her lips—with a sweet smile gleaming, lovely,
　　like sprouts—felt a longing.

She looked on Hari who desired only her, on him who for
　　long wanted dalliance,
Whose face with his pleasure was overwhelmed, and who was
　　possessed with Desire,
Whose hair had beautiful flowers, like a cloud with moon-
　　beams studded within,
And whose brow had the sandal spot unblemished, like the
　　disc of the moon in the dark.

She looked on Hari who desired only her, on him who for
　　long wanted dalliance,
Whose face with his pleasure was overwhelmed, and who was
　　possessed with Desire,
Whose body was thrilling all over, restless, because of his
　　skill in love,
Whose body was lovely because of the ornaments, flashings
　　of many gems.

She looked on Hari who desired only her, on him who for
　　long wanted dalliance,
Whose face with his pleasure was overwhelmed, and who was
　　possessed with Desire,
O people, place Hari for ever in your hearts, Hari the source
　　of all merit,
By whom, in the wealth of Jayadeva's poem, all beauty of
　　art has been doubled!

* * *

Like the gushing of the shower of sweat in the effort of her
　　travel to come to his hearing,

Rádhá's eyes let fall a shower of tears when she met her beloved,
Tears of delight which went to the ends of her eyes and fell
on her flawless necklace.

When she went near the couch and her friends left the
bower, scratching their faces to hide their smiles,
And she looked on the mouth of her loved one, lovely with
longing, under the power of love,
The modest shame of that deer-eyed one departed.

May Nanda's son be happy to show you infinite joy,
Nanda's son laying gentle hands on Rádhá, and placing her
in his arms, and suddenly stirred and embracing her
close,
And looking round over his back, craning his neck, and
fearing, "May her firm high breast not pierce and break
through my body!"

The rod-like punishing arm of Mura's slayer prevails,
That arm which drips with the blood of the demon, playfully
killed,
Kuvalayapída, elephant-like, that arm upon which the goddess of victory scattered the mandára flowers,
That arm self-marked, as it were, with lac, the blood, the
sign of the joy of fighting the demon.

XII

When the group of her friends had departed, Hari looked on
his sweetheart Rádhá, she who was amorous, her eyes
on the couch of flowers, a smile of desire on her lip,
Rádhá released of her heavy load of shame, and he said:

O you woman with desire, place upon this patch of flower-
strewn floor your lotus foot, upon this bed of sprouts,
And let your foot through beauty win, contending with the
bed's appearance, this bed of sprouts which is so fair
to see!
To me who am Naráyana,[33] O be attached, now always yours!
O follow me, my little Rádhá!

You came here journeying from afar, enduring much, so
with my lotus flowers of hands I shall adore your feet;
Use me always on the bed, me, valiant in being attached, as
if I were an anklet for your use!

[33] Vishnu.

To me who am Naráyana, O be attached, now always yours!
  O follow me, my little Rádhá!

Make pleasant conversation now and make complacent speech
  like drops of nectar falling from your face, the moon;
As if it were the garment on your bosom which conceals
  your breasts, I shall remove the pain of being parted!
To me who am Naráyana, O be attached, now always yours!
  O follow me, my little Rádhá!

To extinguish now my fire of passion lay your breast upon
  my bosom, place your jar-shaped breast against my
  breast,
Which seemed so hard for me to have, your lovely breast,
  elusive, and impatient for the pleasures of embrace!
To me who am Naráyana, O be attached, now always yours!
  O follow me, my little Rádhá!

O lovely woman, give me now the nectar of your lips, infuse
  new life into this slave of yours, so dead,
This slave whose heart is placed in you, whose body burned
  in separation, this slave denied the pleasures of your
  love!
To me who am Naráyana, O be attached, now always yours!
  O follow me, my little Rádhá!

O moon-face woman, make the bells upon your jewelled
  girdle tinkle, mimicking the noises of your throat,
And now at last destroy that pain of those from loved ones
  severed—the agony of listening to the cuckoos!
To me who am Naráyana, O be attached, now always yours!
  O follow me, my little Rádhá!

Your eyes now looked upon by me extinguish that me which
  was embodiment of very shame itself,
Me made unhappy by your anger undeserved, me made to
  feel so uselessly the agony of longing!
To me who am Naráyana, O be attached, now always yours!
  O follow me, my little Rádhá!

Among all tasteful people may this song of Jayadeva create
  a state of passionate delight,
This poem which in every verse proclaims the satisfaction in
  the pleasure of the love of Madhu's slayer.
To me who am Naráyana, O be attached, now always yours!
  O follow me, my little Rádhá!

* * *

Their love play grown great was very delightful, the love
play where thrills were a hindrance to firm embraces,
Where their helpless closing of eyes was a hindrance to longing looks at each other, and their secret talk to their
drinking of each the other's nectar of lips, and where
the skill of their love was hindered by boundless delight!

She performed as never before throughout the course of the
conflict of love, to win, lying over his beautiful body, to
triumph over her lover;
And so through taking the active part her thighs grew lifeless,
and languid her vine-like arms, and her heart beat
fast, and her eyes grew heavy and closed;
For how many women prevail in the male performance!

In the morning most wondrous, the heart of her lord was
smitten with arrows of Love, arrows which went through
his eyes,
Arrows which were her nail-scratched bosom, her reddened
sleep-denied eyes, her crimson lips from a bath of kisses,
her hair disarranged with the flowers awry, and her
girdle all loose and slipping.
With hair knot loosened and stray locks waving, her cheeks
perspiring, her glitter of bimba lips impaired,
And the necklace of pearls not appearing fair because of
her jar-shaped breasts being denuded,
And her belt, her glittering girdle, dimmed in beauty,
And all of a sudden placing her hands on her naked breasts,
and over her naked loins, to hide them, and looking
embarrassed;
Even so, with her tender loveliness ravaged, she continued
to please!

The happy one drank of the face where the lips were washed
with the juice of his mouth,
His mouth half open uttering amorous noises, vague and
delirious, the rows of teeth in the breath of an indrawn
sigh delightedly chattering.
Drank of the face of that deer-eyed woman whose body lay
helpless, released of excessive delight, the thrilling delight of embraces, making the breasts both flaccid and
firm.

Then Rádhá—free of love's obstacles, Rádhá whose lover lay
prone in her power, exhausted through pleasure of
love—
Said with a wish for adornment:

She said to the joy of her heart, the delight of the Yadus,
O delight of the Yadus, depict here and make a design, a
    pattern, with musk on my breast,
My breast the twin of the festal pitcher of love, depict with
    your hand which is cool!

She said to the joy of her heart, the delight of the Yadus,
O loved one, renew the kohl on my eyelids, shaming a cluster
    of bees, being blacker,
The kohl you have smudged with your kisses, the black on
    my eyelids releasing the arrows of Love!

She said to the joy of her heart, the delight of the Yadus,
O you apparelled so lovely, wear on the lobes of your ears
    earrings which shame
Your dancing deer-eyes on the lobes of your ears which bear
    the noose of the play of Desire!

She said to the joy of her heart, the delight of the Yadus,
Adorn the curl on my brow which puts the lotus to shame,
    my spotless brow,
The curl which brings about laughter, which makes on my
    beautiful forehead a cluster of bees!

She said to the joy of her heart, the delight of the Yadus,
O lotus face, make a beautiful spot on my forehead, a spot
    with the paste of the sandal,
Like a digit of the hare-marked moon, make on the moon of
    my brow, which is sweating no more!

She said to the joy of her heart, the delight of the Yadus,
O giver of pride, on my tresses, untidy now on account of
    desire, place flowers,
My curls, excelling the feathers of peacocks, in which the
    whisk is the banner of Love!

She said to the joy of her heart, the delight of the Yadus,
O you with a beautiful heart, place on my hips the girdle,
    the clothes, and the jewels—
Cover my beautiful loins, luscious and firm, the cavern of
    Love to be feared!

She said to the joy of her heart, the delight of the Yadus,
Full of compassion, O place your heart in the words of the
    song of Shri Jayadeva

Ridding with nectar this sinful age of its fever recalling the
feet of Hari!

* * *

Make a pattern upon my breasts and a picture on my cheeks
and fasten over my loins a girdle,
Bind my masses of hair with a beautiful garland and place
many bracelets upon my hands and jewelled anklets
upon my feet!
And so he who wore the yellow garment did as she told him.

* * *

Whatever is of the condition of love's discernment shown
with beauty in poetic form, and all skill in the art of
heaven's musicians, and all of reflection on Vishnu,
All such you may joyfully see, wise people, in this the song
of the Lord of Herds, made by the poet devoted to him,
the wise Jayadeva.

May the art of poetry seen in this poem be in the mouths of
those who are dear to Paráshara and the others,
This poem of Shri Jayadeva the son of Rámádevi and Shri
Bhojadeva.
Jayadeva's words of insight wherever known, like love's own
glorious flavour,
There, O drink, not pleasant is the thought of you any more;
and hardly sweet you become, O sugar; and who, O
wine, would want to look on you?
O nectar, you are no more immortal; and like water you
taste, O milk; and you have to lament, O mango; and
cease to compare, O beautiful lip.

May pure and unclouded joy and prosperity come from the
movements of hands of the Best of Men, amorous hands
delighting in breasts resembling the prayága fruit,
Hands in performance of many forms of amorous play with
Rádhá beside the Jamna
On the bank where coquettish tresses were waving, at the
tryst where his black hair mixed with her necklace of
pearls, where the dark Jamna meets the Ganges' white
stream at Prayága.

FROM The *Dīvāni Shamsi Tabrīz* of Rumi

{A.D. 1207-1273}

TRANSLATED BY REYNOLD A. NICHOLSON {1868-1945}

ᕀᗢᑤᑕᕗᐁ

The *Mathnawi* embodies the deepest philosophical insights and ethical teachings of Rumi, but his *Divan* (collection of odes) contains the purest distillation of his gift for lyrical poetry. It is in the *Divan* that one finds the ecstatic spiritual devotee whom his English translator has called "the greatest mystical poet of any age." Rumi (so named from his residence in the European or Roman portion of the Turkish domains) was the founder of the colourful order of the whirling dervishes, who seek, through the exhilaration of mystic dance and song, to place themselves at the perfect center of the divine order of things. Some of the heady music of their votive dance can be heard in these inspired songs, and it has been marvelously preserved in a number of Reynold A. Nicholson's translations, the first four of which are quite literal, the last five somewhat free.

The poems that make up the *Divan* were apparently composed under the influence of an inspired if uncouth fanatic known as the Sun of Tabrīz (whence the name of this collection). This is a curious instance of the attribution of authorship to the true begetter, as it were. Nicholson has called Shams the Socrates to Rumi's Plato. Whatever may have been the relationship of the two men, the poetry of Rumi obviously required at least the inspiration provided by the absence of Shams. This platonic love is regarded by the Sufi poets as generating an intuition of the divine, and the similarity to neoplatonic thought is very striking. Use is made—as it is in all mystic love poetry—of the language of the senses, but this expression only provides "shadow pictures of the soul's passionate longing to be reunited with God," in Nicholson's felicitous phrase. For comparison, the English reader may turn to the seventeenth century metaphysical poets Herbert, Vaughan, and Crashaw.

The form in which the poems are cast is the familiar *ghazal* or ode used in most Moslem love poetry, whether sacred or profane.

ᕀᗢᑤᑕᕗᐁ

From the *DĪVĀNI SHAMSI TABRĪZ*

I

The man of God is drunken without wine,
The man of God is full without meat.
The man of God is distraught and bewildered,
The man of God has no food or sleep.

300

The man of God is a king 'neath darvish–cloak,
The man of God is a treasure in a ruin.
The man of God is not of air and earth,
The man of God is not of fire and water.
The man of God is a boundless sea,
The man of God rains pearls without a cloud.
The man of God hath hundred moons and skies,
The man of God hath hundred suns.
The man of God is made wise by the Truth,
The man of God is not learned from book.
The man of God is beyond infidelity and religion,
To the man of God right and wrong are alike.
The man of God has ridden away from Not-being,
The man of God is gloriously attended.
The man of God is concealed, Shamsi Dīn;
The man of God do thou seek and find!

II

A beauty that all night long teaches love-tricks to Venus and
    the moon,
Whose two eyes by their witchery seal up the two eyes of
    heaven.
Look to your hearts! I, whate'er betide, O Moslems,
Am so mingled with him that no heart is mingled with me.
I was born of his love at the first, I gave him my heart at
    the last;
When the fruit springs from the bough, on that bough it
    hangs.
The tip of his curl is saying, "Ho! betake thee to rope-
    dancing."
The cheek of his candle is saying, "Where is a moth that it
    may burn?"
For the sake of dancing on that rope, O heart, make haste,
    become a hoop;
Cast thyself on the flame, when his candle is lit.
Thou wilt never more endure without the flame, when thou
    hast known the rapture of burning;
If the water of life should come to thee, it would not stir
    thee from the flame.

III

Thee I choose, of all the world, alone;
Wilt thou suffer me to sit in grief?
My heart is as a pen in thy hand,
Thou art the cause if I am glad or melancholy.

Save what thou willest, what will have I?
Save what thou showest, what do I see?
Thou mak'st grow out of me now a thorn and now a rose;
Now I smell roses and now pull thorns.
If thou keep'st me that, that I am;
If thou would'st have me this, I am this.
In the vessel where thou givest colour to the soul
Who am I, what is my love and hate?
Thou wert first, and last thou shalt be;
Make my last better than my first.
When thou art hidden, I am of the infidels;
When thou art manifest, I am of the faithful.
I have nothing except thou hast bestowed it;
What dost thou seek from my bosom and sleeve?

I V

Happy the moment when we are seated in the palace, thou
    and I,
With two forms and with two figures but with one soul,
    thou and I.
The colours of the grove and the voice of the birds will be-
    stow immortality
At the time when we come into the garden, thou and I.
The stars of heaven will come to gaze upon us;
We shall show them the moon itself, thou and I.
Thou and I, individuals no more, shall be mingled in ecstasy,
Joyful, and secure from foolish babble, thou and I.
All the bright-plumed birds of heaven will devour their hearts
    with envy
In the place where we shall laugh in such a fashion, thou
    and I.
This is the greatest wonder, that thou and I, sitting here in
    the same nook,
Are at this moment both in 'Irāq and Khorāsān, thou and I.

V

He comes, a moon whose like the sky ne'er saw, awake or
    dreaming,
Crowned with eternal flame no flood can lay.
Lo, from the flagon of thy love, O Lord, my soul is swim-
    ming,
And ruined all my body's house of clay!

When first the Giver of the grape my lonely heart befriended,
Wine fired my bosom and my veins filled up,

But when his image all mine eye possessed, a voice descended:
"Well done, O sovereign Wine and peerless Cup!"

Love's mighty arm from roof to base each dark abode is
    hewing
Where chinks reluctant catch a golden ray.
My heart, when Love's sea of a sudden burst into its viewing,
Leaped headlong in, with "Find me now who may!"

    As, the sun moving, clouds behind him run,
    All hearts attend thee, O Tabrīz's Sun!

    V I

    Poor copies out of heaven's original,
    Pale earthly pictures mouldering to decay,
    What care altho' your beauties break and fall,
    When that which gave them life endures for aye?

    O never vex thine heart with idle woes:
    All high discourse enchanting the rapt ear,
    All gilded landscapes and brave glistering shows
    Fade—perish, but it is not as we fear.

    While far away the living fountains ply,
    Each petty brook goes brimful to the main.
    Since brook nor fountain can forever die,
    Thy fears how foolish, thy lament how vain!

    What is this fountain, wouldst thou rightly know?
    The Soul whence issue all created things.
    Doubtless the rivers shall not cease to flow,
    Till silenced are the everlasting springs.

    Farewell to sorrow, and with quiet mind
    Drink long and deep: let others fondly deem
    The channel empty they perchance may find,
    Or fathom that unfathomable stream.

    The moment thou to this low world wast given,
    A ladder stood whereby thou mightst aspire;
    And first thy steps, which upward still have striven,
    From mineral mounted to the plant: then higher.

    To animal existence: next, the Man,
    With knowledge, reason, faith. O wondrous goal!

This body, which a crumb of dust began—
How fairly fashioned the consummate whole!

Yet stay not here thy journey: thou shalt grow
An angel bright and home far off in heaven.
Plod on, plunge last in the great Sea, that so
Thy little drop make oceans seven times seven.

"The Son of God!" Nay, leave that word unsaid,
Say, "God is One, the pure, the single Truth."
What tho' thy frame be withered, old, and dead,
If the soul save her fresh immortal youth?

VII

Lo, for I to myself am unknown, now in God's name what
    must I do?
I adore not the Cross nor the Crescent, I am not a Giaour [34]
    nor a Jew.
East nor West, land nor sea is my home, I have kin nor with
    angel nor gnome,
I am wrought not of fire nor of foam, I am shaped not of
    dust nor of dew.
I was born not in China afar, not in Saqsīn and not in
    Bulghār [35];
Not in India, where five rivers are, nor 'Irāq nor Korāsān I
    grew.
Not in this world nor that world I dwell, not in Paradise,
    neither in Hell;
Not from Eden and Rizwān [36] I fell, not from Adam my
    lineage I drew.
In a place beyond uttermost Place, in a tract without shadow
    of trace,
Soul and body transcending, I live in the soul of my Loved
    One anew!

VIII

Up, O ye lovers, and away! 'Tis time to leave the world for
    aye.
Hark, loud and clear from heaven the drum of parting calls
    —let none delay!

[34] Giaour—an infidel. [Ed.]
[35] Saqsīn—a city in the Caucasus; Bulghār—a town on the Volga. [Ed.]
[36] Rizwān—the angel who holds the keys to Paradise. [Ed.]

The cameleer hath risen amain, made ready all the camel-
    train,
And quittance now desires to gain: why sleep ye, travellers,
    I pray?
Behind us and before there swells the din of parting and of
    bells;
To shoreless Space each moment sails a disembodied spirit
    away.
From yonder starry lights and through those curtain-awnings
    darkly blue
Mysterious figures float in view, all strange and secret things
    display.
From this orb, wheeling round its pole, a wondrous slumber
    o'er thee stole:
O weary life that weighest nought, O sleep that on my soul
    dost weigh!
O heart, toward thy heart's love wend, and O friend, fly
    toward the Friend,
Be wakeful, watchman, to the end: drowse seemingly no
    watchman may.

IX

Why wilt thou dwell in mouldy cell, a captive, O my heart?
Speed, speed the flight! a nursling bright of yonder world
    thou art.
He bids thee rest upon his breast, he flings the veil away:
Thy home wherefore make evermore this mansion of decay?
O contemplate thy true estate, enlarge thyself, and rove
From this dark world, thy prison, whirled to that celestial
    grove.
O honoured guest in Love's high feast, O bird of the angel-
    sphere,
'Tis cause to weep, if thou wilt keep thy habitation here.
A voice at morn to thee is borne—God whispers to the soul—
"If on the way the dust thou lay, thou soon wilt gain the
    goal."
That road be thine toward the Shrine! and lo, in bush and
    briar,
The many slain by love and pain in flower of young desire,
Who on the track fell wounded back and saw not, ere the
    end,
A ray of bliss, a touch, a kiss, a token of the Friend!

FROM The *Divan* of Hafiz

{A.D. 1320-1391}

TRANSLATED BY GERTRUDE LOWTHIAN BELL {1868-1926}

١٤٩٣٤١

Hafiz has probably had more English translators than his better known compatriot, Omar Khayyam. His fame was entering upon its second century in England when the *Rubaiyat* of Omar Khayyam began to acquire its coterie of readers. In the late 18th century he had inspired the father of British Orientalism, Sir William Jones; and through the latter's translations, he had reached Byron, Moore and other Romantic poets. A German version of the *Divan* had begotten Goethe's *West–Eastern Divan* in imitation, and the continent had come to know "the sweet singer of Shiraz." Poetasters in both hemispheres adopted the name of Hafiz as a nom de plume in order to reach readers whom their verses could not otherwise command. Even that connoisseur of miscellaneous wit and wisdom, Sherlock Holmes, embellished a classical solution by coupling the authority of Hafiz with that of Horace.

John Payne, who temporarily set aside a translation of the complete *Divan* on which he was engaged in order to do a complete *Rubaiyat* of Omar, regarded Hafiz as one of the three greatest poets of the world, the other two being Dante and Shakespeare. Such an evaluation might sound more excessive if Ralph Waldo Emerson had not similarly coupled Hafiz with Shakespeare as types of the pure poet. To all, Hafiz has been "the Prince of Persian poets," and no decade has passed without a fresh attempt to transfuse his lyricism into English verse. Although he has yet to find a Fitzgerald, there is fairly general agreement that Gertrude Lowthian Bell has come nearest to plucking the heart of his mystery.

The continued appeal of Hafiz to contemporary readers undoubtedly lies in a certain pleasing ambiguity at the very base of his poetry. Hafiz wrote in the tradition of Sufism, but he was not a true Sufi as Rumi certainly was. If there is anything divine in the love which he celebrates, that divinity must be found in the very *human* nature of it. His *Divan* is a symbolical rather than an allegorical expression of man's fate, cast as that is somewhere between the two worlds. Wine, love, and roses do not stand for some religious equivalent as in the Sufi lexicon; rather, in these very objects of nature, spirituality is to be found. The mysticism of Hafiz, then, if mystic he is, more closely resembles Shelley's than it does St. Theresa's. His poems project at once the sweetness of the joys of this world and its inadequacies. The *Weltschmerz*, the sense of the tears in things, the heavy weight of all this unintelligible world, are all there; but they are carried lightly, without metaphysical baggage, as though the song were sufficient comment on the human lot.

For the most part, the *Divan* consists of *ghazals* or odes. In form these are poems of varying length, made up of a number of couplets that play a sort of variations on a theme. This makes for a thin continuity, judged by our standards of unity and coherence. "Wonderful is the inconsecutiveness of the Persian poets," said Emerson, who had a little of the quality himself. In part Miss Bell has made the reader's task easier by expanding couplet into stanza; the reader can further help himself by looking for an organic rather than a logical unity in the odes.

From the *DIVAN* of Hafiz

I

Wind from the east, oh Lapwing of the day,
I send thee to my Lady, though the way
Is far to Saba, where I bid thee fly;
Lest in the dust thy tameless wings should lie,
Broken with grief, I send thee to thy nest,
　　Fidelity.

Or far or near there is no halting-place
Upon Love's road—absent, I see thy face,
And in thine ear my wind-blown greetings sound,
North winds and east waft them where they are bound,
Each morn and eve convoys of greeting fair
　　I send to thee.

Unto mine eyes a stranger, thou that art
A comrade ever-present to my heart,
What whispered prayers and what full meed of praise
　　I send to thee.

Lest Sorrow's army waste thy heart's domain,
I send my life to bring thee peace again,
Dear life thy ransom! From thy singers learn
How one that longs for thee may weep and burn;
Sonnets and broken words, sweet notes and songs
　　I send to thee.

Give me the cup! a voice rings in mine ears
Crying: "Bear patiently the bitter years!
For all thine ills, I send thee heavenly grace.
God the Creator mirrored in thy face
Thine eyes shall see, God's image in the glass
　　I send to thee.

"Hafiz, thy praise alone my comrades sing;
Hasten to us, thou that art sorrowing!
A robe of honor and a harnessed steed
  I send to thee."

II

A flower-tinted cheek, the flowery close
Of the fair earth, these are enough for me—
Enough that in the meadow wanes and grows
The shadow of a graceful cypress tree.
I am no lover of hypocrisy;
Of all the treasures that the earth can boast,
A brimming cup of wine I prize the most—
  This is enough for me!

To them that here renowned for virtue live,
A heavenly palace is the meet reward;
To me, the drunkard and the beggar, give
The temple of the grape with red wine stored!
Beside a river seat thee on the sward;
It floweth past—so flows thy life away,
So sweetly, swiftly, fleets our little day—
  Swift, but enough for me!

Look upon all the gold in the world's mart,
On all the tears the world hath shed in vain;
Shall they not satisfy thy craving heart?
I have enough of loss, enough of gain;
I have my Love, what more can I obtain?
Mine is the joy of her companionship
Whose healing lip is laid upon my lip—
  This is enough for me!

I pray thee send not forth my naked soul
From its poor house to seek for Paradise;
Though heaven and earth before me God unroll,
Back to my village still my spirit flies,
And, Hafiz, at the door of Kismet lies
No just complaint—a mind like water clear,
A song that swells and dies upon the ear,
  These are enough for thee!

III

The rose has flushed red, the bud has burst,
And drunk with joy is the nightingale—
Hail, Sufis! lovers of wine, all hail!
For wine is proclaimed to a world athirst.
Like a rock your repentance seemed to you;

Behold the marvel! of what avail
Was your rock, for a goblet has cleft it in two!

Bring wine for the king and the slave at the gate!
Alike for all is the banquet spread,
And drunk and sober are warmed and fed.
When the feast is done and the night grows late,
And the second door of the tavern gapes wide,
The low and the mighty must bow the head
'Neath the archway of Life, to meet what . . . outside?

Except thy road through affliction pass,
None may reach the halting-station of mirth;
God's treaty: Am I not Lord of the earth?
Man sealed with a sigh: Ah yes, alas!
Nor with Is nor Is Not let thy mind contend;
Rest assured all perfection of mortal birth
In the great Is Not at the last shall end.

For Assaf's [37] pomp, and the steeds of the wind,
And the speech of birds, down the wind have fled,
And he that was lord of them all is dead;
Of his mastery nothing remains behind.
Shoot not thy feathered arrow astray!
A bowshot's length through the air it has sped,
And then . . . dropped down in the dusty way.

But to thee, O Hafiz, to thee, O Tongue
That speaks through the mouth of the slender reed,
What thanks to thee when thy verses speed
From lip to lip, and the song thou hast sung?

I V

What is wrought in the forge of the living and life—
All things are naught! Ho! fill me the bowl,
For naught is the gear of the world and the strife!
One passion has quickened the heart and the soul,
The Beloved's presence alone they have sought—
Love at least exists; yet if Love were not,
Heart and soul would sink to the common lot—
    All things are naught!

Like an empty cup is the fate of each,
That each must fill from Life's mighty flood;
Naught thy toil, though to Paradise gate thou reach,
If Another has filled up thy cup with blood;
Neither shade from the sweet-fruited trees could be
      bought
By thy praying—oh Cypress of Truth, dost not see

[37] Assaf—the minister of Solomon, who had magical powers. [Ed.]

That Sidreh and Tuba [38] were naught, and to thee
  All then were naught!

The span of thy life is as five little days,
Brief hours and swift in this halting-place;
Rest softly, ah rest! while the Shadow delays,
For Time's self is naught and the dial's face.
On the lip of oblivion we linger, and short
Is the way from the Lip to the Mouth, where we pass—
While the moment is thine, fill, oh Saki, the glass
  Ere all is naught!

Consider the rose that breaks into flower,
Neither repines though she fade and die—
The powers of the world endure for an hour,
But naught shall remain of their majesty.
Be not too sure of your crown, you who thought
That virtue was easy and recompense yours;
From the monastery to the wine tavern doors
  The way is naught!

What though I, too, have tasted the salt of my tears,
Though I, too, have burnt in the fires of grief,
Shall I cry aloud to unheeding ears?
Mourn and be silent! naught brings relief.
Thou, Hafiz, art praised for the songs thou hast wrought,
But bearing a stained or an honored name,
The lovers of wine shall make light of thy fame—
  All things are naught!

V

I cease not from desire till my desire
Is satisfied; or let my mouth attain
My love's red mouth, or let my soul expire,
Sighed from those lips that sought her lips in vain.
Others may find another love as fair;
Upon her threshold I have laid my head:
The dust shall cover me, still lying there,
When from my body life and love have fled.

My soul is on my lips ready to fly,
But grief beats in my heart and will not cease,
Because not once, not once before I die,
Will her sweet lips give all my longing peace.
My breath is narrowed down to one long sigh
For a red mouth that burns my thoughts like fire;
When will that mouth draw near and make reply
To one whose life is straitened with desire?

[38] Sidreh and Tuba—trees of Paradise. [Ed.]

When I am dead, open my grave and see
The cloud of smoke that rises round thy feet:
In my dead heart the fire still burns for thee;
Yea, the smoke rises from my winding-sheet!
Ah come, Beloved! for the meadows wait
Thy coming, and the thorn bears flowers instead
Of thorns, the cypress fruit, and desolate
Bare winter from before thy steps has fled.

Hoping within some garden ground to find
A red rose soft and sweet as thy soft cheek
Through every meadow blows the western wind,
Through every garden he is fain to seek.
Reveal thy face! that the whole world may be
Bewildered by thy radiant loveliness;
The cry of man and woman comes to thee,
Open thy lips and comfort their distress!

Each curling lock of thy luxuriant hair
Breaks into barbed hooks to catch my heart,
My broken heart is wounded everywhere
With countless wounds from which the red drops start.
Yet when sad lovers meet and tell their sighs,
Not without praise shall Hafiz' name be said,
Not without tears, in those pale companies
Where joy has been forgot and hope has fled.

VI

Where is my ruined life, and where the fame
  Of noble deeds?
Look on my long-drawn road, and whence it came,
  And where it leads!

Can drunkenness be linked to piety
  And good repute?
Where is the preacher's holy monody,
  Where is the lute?

From monkish cell and lying garb released,
  Oh heart of mine,
Where is the Tavern fane, the Tavern priest,
  Where is the wine?

Past days of meeting, let the memory
  Of you be sweet!
Where are those glances fled, and where for
  Reproaches meet?

His friend's bright face warms not the enemy
  When love is done—

Where is the extinguished lamp that made night day,
    Where is the sun?

Balm to mine eyes the dust, my head I bow
    Upon thy stair.
Where shall I go, where from thy presence? thou
    Art everywhere.

Look not upon the dimple of her chin,
    Danger lurks there!
Where wilt thou hide, oh trembling heart, fleeing in
    Such mad haste—where?

To steadfastness and patience, friend, ask not
    If Hafiz keep—
Patience and steadfastness I have forgot,
    And where is sleep?

VII

Mirth, Spring, to linger in a garden fair,
What more has earth to give? All ye that wait,
Where is the Cup-bearer, the flagon where?
When pleasant hours slip from the hand of Fate,
Reckon each hour as a certain gain;
Who seeks to know the end of mortal care
Shall question his experience in vain.

Thy fettered life hangs on a single thread—
Some comfort for thy present ills devise,
But those that time may bring thou shalt not dread.
Waters of Life and Irem's [39] Paradise—
What meaning do our dreams and pomp convey,
Save that beside a mighty stream, wide-fed,
We sit and sing of wine and go our way!

The modest and the merry shall be seen
To boast their kinship with a single voice;
There are no differences to choose between,
Thou art but flattering thy soul with choice!
Who knows the Curtain's secret? . . . Heaven is mute
And yet with Him who holds the Curtain, e'en
With Him, oh Braggart, thou would'st raise dispute!

Although His thrall shall miss the road and err,
'Tis but to teach him wisdom through distress,
Else Pardon and Compassionate Mercy were
But empty syllables and meaningless.
The Zealot thirsts for draughts of Kausar's [40] wine,

39 Irem—a fabulous garden. [Ed.]
40 Kausar—a fountain in Paradise. [Ed.]

And Hafiz doth an earthly cup prefer—
But what, between the two, is God's design?

VIII

From Canaan Joseph shall return, whose face
A little time was hidden: weep no more—
Oh, weep no more! in sorrow's dwelling-place
The roses yet shall spring from the bare floor!
And heart bowed down beneath a secret pain—
Oh stricken heart! joy shall return again,
Peace to the love-tossed brain—oh, weep no more!

Oh, weep no more! for once again Life's Spring
Shall throne her in the meadows green, and o'er
Her head the minstrel of the night shall fling
A canopy of rose leaves, score on score.
The secret of the world thou shalt not learn,
And yet behind the veil Love's fire may burn—
Weep'st thou? let hope return and weep no more!

Today may pass, tomorrow pass, before
The turning wheel give me my heart's desire;
Heaven's self shall change, and turn not evermore
The universal wheel of Fate in ire.
Oh Pilgrim nearing Mecca's holy fane,
The thorny maghilan [41] wounds thee in vain,
The desert blooms again—oh, weep no more!

What though the river of mortality
Round the unstable house of Life doth roar,
Weep not, oh heart, Noah shall pilot thee,
And guide thine ark to the desiréd shore!
The goal lies far, and perilous is thy road,
Yet every path leads to that same abode
Where thou shalt drop thy load—oh, weep no more!

Mine enemies have persecuted me,
My love has turned and fled from out my door—
God counts our tears and knows our misery;
Ah, weep not! He has heard thy weeping sore.
And chained in poverty and plunged in night,
Oh Hafiz, take thy Koran and recite
Litanies infinite, and weep no more!

---

[41] Maghilan—a thorny shrub which grows in the deserts of Arabia near Mecca. When the Pilgrims see it they know that they have almost reached their goal, and forget the hardships of the journey and the barrenness of the wastes through which their road lies.

4 *SCRIPTURE*

I Confucian

FROM The *Analects* of Confucius

{551-479 B.C.}

TRANSLATED BY JAMES LEGGE {1815-1897}

୧୬୭ୖ୬ଽଡ଼୭ୖ

A fair portion of the whole history of China might be told in terms of the Confucian classics, of which the *Analects* are a part. At present these books are in disrepute among the Chinese, Nationalist and Communist alike, because of their association with autocracy in general and with the Manchu Dynasty (overthrown in 1911) in particular. Since the 12th century, when the Sung scholars canonized them, the Classics have served as a body of orthodox dogma. A thousand years earlier, they had been given official recognition by the Han emperors, who rescued them from the destruction to which they had been doomed by a pre-Han emperor desirous of ruling without benefit of the traditions which they embodied. This was still several centuries after the time of Master Kung Fu Tze himself, who was credited with the collecting and editing of some of the books and the authorship of others. The *Analects* are perhaps the most authentic records of his teachings, being statements of his own or of his disciples. Thus they enable us to get back to the teacher behind the apotheosized saint.

Confucius thought of himself as a transmitter and not an originator of ideas. His doctrines presumably came down from a still older period of history and were derived from the rule and conduct of legendary or half-legendary sovereigns regarded as Divine Sages. From them it was that the Tao or Way was learned, the correct principles of governing both self and state. Confucius believed that this art of living according to the old rituals had been forgotten in his time; he conceived it as his duty to recall people to it. Fundamentally a rationalistic doctrine of moderation in all things, it little concerned itself with supernatural sanctions.

314

It can therefore more properly be called a philosophy than a religion.

Of humble origins and fairly low position, Confucius sought—on the whole vainly—to find a governor who would put his principles into practice. His disciples provided him with audience and later developed and disseminated his ideas. Of the twenty books of the *Analects,* those here reproduced (III-IX) are regarded as least touched by the hands of commentators and emendators. Thus they may be taken as the very seeds of that doctrine of Confucianism which for 2500 years governed the destinies of the Chinese people.

ᛁᚾᛞᚲᛞᚲᛘᛁ

BOOK III

I. Confucius said of the head of the Ke family, who had eight rows of pantomimes in his area, "If he can bear to do this, what may he not bear to do?" [1]

II. The three families used the Yung ode, while the vessels were being removed, at the conclusion of the sacrifice. The Master said, " 'Assisting are the princes;—the emperor looks profound and grave:'—what application can these words have in the hall of the three families?"

III. The Master said, "If a man be without the virtues proper to humanity, what has he to do with the rites of propriety? If a man be without the virtues proper to humanity, what has he to do with music?"

IV. 1. Lin Fang asked what was the first thing to be attended to in ceremonies.

2. The Master said, "A great question indeed!

3. "In festive ceremonies, it is better to be sparing than extravagant. In the ceremonies of mourning, it is better that there be deep sorrow than a minute attention to observances."

V. The Master said, "The rude tribes of the east and north have their princes, and are not like the States of our great land which are without them."

VI. The chief of the Ke family was about to sacrifice to the T'ae mountain. The Master said to Yenyew, "Can you not

[1] Sections I–VI deal with the impropriety of family heads' usurping the duties of the Duke in conducting rites. The eight rows of dancers in I symbolize the ostentation of the usurpers. The quotation from a sacrificial ode in II points up their disregard for tradition. [Ed.]

save him from this?" He answered, "I cannot." Confucius said, "Alas! will you say that the T'ae mountain is not so discerning as Lin Fang?"

vii. The Master said, "The student of virtue has no contentions. If it be said he cannot avoid them shall this be in archery? But he bows complaisantly to his competitors; thus he ascends the hall, descends, and exacts the forfeit of drinking. In his contention, he is still the Keun-tsze [2]."

viii. 1. Tsze-hea asked, saying, "What is the meaning of the passage—'The pretty dimples of her artful smile! The well defined black and white of her eye! The plain ground for the colours'?"

2. The Master said, "The business of laying on the colours follows the preparation of the plain ground."

3. "Ceremonies then are a subsequent thing." The Master said, "It is Shang [3] who can bring out my meaning! Now I can begin to talk about the odes with him."

ix. The Master said, "I am able to describe the ceremonies of the Hea dynasty, but Ke cannot sufficiently attest my words. I am able to describe the ceremonies of the Yin dynasty but Sung cannot sufficiently attest my words. They cannot do so because of the insufficiency of their records and wise men. If those were sufficient, I could adduce them in support of my words."

x. The Master said, "At the great sacrifice, after the pouring out of the libation, I have no wish to look on."

xi. Some one asked the meaning of the great sacrifice. The Master said, "I do not know. He who knew its meaning would find it as easy to govern the empire as to look on this";—pointing to his palm.

xii. 1. He sacrificed to the dead, as if they were present. He sacrificed to the spirits, as if the spirits were present.

2. The Master said, "I consider my not being present at the sacrifice, as if I did not sacrifice."

xiii. 1. Wang-sun Kea asked, saying, "What is the meaning of the saying, 'It is better to pay court to the furnace than to the south-west corner'?"

2. The Master said, "Not so. He who offends against Heaven has none to whom he can pray."

---

[2] Keun-tsze—gentleman. [Ed.]
[3] Shang—Tsze-hea. [Ed.]

xiv. The Master said, "Chow [4] had the advantage of viewing the two past dynasties. How complete and elegant are its regulations! I follow Chow."

xv. The Master, when he entered the grand temple, asked about everything. Some one said, "Who will say that the son of the man of Tsow [5] knows the rules of propriety? He has entered the grand temple and asks about everything." The Master heard the remark and said, "This is a rule of propriety."

xvi. The Master said, "In archery it is not going through the leather which is the principal thing;—because people's strength is not equal. This was the old way." [6]

xvii. 1. Tsze-kung wished to do away with the offering of a sheep connected with the inauguration of the first day of each month.

2. The Master said, "Tsze, you love the sheep; I love the ceremony."

xviii. The Master said, "The full observance of the rules of propriety in serving one's prince is accounted by people to be flattery."

xix. The duke Ting asked how a prince should employ his ministers, and how ministers should serve their prince. Confucius replied, "A prince should employ his ministers according to the rules of propriety; ministers should serve their prince with faithfulness."

xx. The Master said, "The Kwan Ts'eu is expressive of enjoyment without being licentious, and of grief without being hurtfully excessive."

xxi. 1. The duke Gae asked Tsae Go about the altars of the spirits of the land. Tsae Go replied, "The Hea sovereign used the pine tree; the man of the Yin used the cypress; and the man of the Chow used the chestnut tree, meaning thereby to cause the people to be in awe."

2. When the Master heard it, he said, "Things that are done, it is needless to speak about; things that have had their course, it is needless to remonstrate about; things that are past, it is needless to blame."

---

4 Chow—a dynasty that could look back to the Hea and Yin dynasties. [Ed.]
5 Tsow—supposedly Confucius's family home. [Ed.]
6 That is, the ancients were not violent but persuasive. [Ed.]

XXII. 1. The Master said, "Small indeed was the capacity of Kwan Chung!"

2. Some one said, "Was Kwan Chung parsimonious?" "Kwan," was the reply, "had the San Kwei, and his officers performed no double duties; how can he be considered parsimonious?"

3. "Then, did Kwan Chung know the rules of propriety?" The Master said, "The princes of states have a screen intercepting the view at their gates. Kwan had likewise a screen at his gate. The princes of states, on any friendly meeting between two of them, had a stand on which to place their inverted cups. Kwan had also such a stand. If Kwan knew the rules of propriety, who does not know them?"

XXIII. The Master instructing the Grand music-master of Loo, said, "How to play music may be known. At the commencement of the piece, all the parts should sound together. As it proceeds, they should be in harmony, severally distinct and flowing without break, and thus on to the conclusion."

XXIV. The border-warden at E requested to be introduced to the Master, saying, "When men of superior virtue have come to this, I have never been denied the privilege of seeing them." The followers of the sage introduced him, and when he came out from the interview, he said, "My friends, why are you distressed by your master's loss of office? The empire has long been without the principles of truth and right; Heaven is going to use your master as a bell with its wooden tongue."

XXV. The Master said of the Shaou that it was perfectly beautiful and also perfectly good. He said of the Woo that it was perfectly beautiful but not perfectly good.[7]

XXVI. The Master said, "High station filled without indulgent generosity; ceremonies performed without reverence; mourning conducted without sorrow;—wherewith should I contemplate such ways?"

BOOK IV

I. The Master said, "It is virtuous manners which constitute the excellence of a neighbourhood. If a man, in selecting a

[7] Shaou . . . Woo—the succession dance and the war dance (Arthur Waley). [Ed.]

residence, do not fix on one where such prevail, how can he be wise?"

II. The Master said, "Those who are without virtue cannot abide long either in a condition of poverty and hardship, or in a condition of enjoyment. The virtuous rest in virtue; the wise desire virtue."

III. The Master said, "It is only the truly virtuous man who can love, or who can hate, others."

IV. The Master said, "If the will be set on virtue, there will be no practice of wickedness."

V. 1. The Master said, "Riches and honours are what men desire. If it cannot be obtained in the proper way, they should not be held. Poverty and meanness are what men dislike. If it cannot be obtained in the proper way, they should not be avoided.

2. "If a superior man abandon virtue, how can he fulfil the requirements of that name?"

3. "The superior man does not, even for the space of a single meal, act contrary to virtue. In moments of haste, he cleaves to it. In seasons of danger, he cleaves to it."

VI. 1. The Master said, "I have not seen a person who loved virtue, or one who hated what was not virtuous. He who loved would esteem nothing above it. He who hated what is not virtuous, would practice virtue in such a way that he would not allow anything that is not virtuous to approach his person.

2. "Is any one able for one day to apply his strength to virtue? I have not seen the case in which his strength would be insufficient.

3. "Should there possibly be any such case, I have not seen it."

VII. The Master said, "The faults of men are characteristic of the class to which they belong. By observing a man's faults, it may be known that he is virtuous."

VIII. The Master said, "If a man in the morning hear the right way, he may die in the evening without regret."

IX. The Master said, "A scholar, whose mind is set on truth, and who is ashamed of bad clothes and bad food, is not fit to be discoursed with."

x. The Master said, "The superior man, in the world, does not set his mind either for any thing, or against any thing; what is right he will follow."

xi. The Master said, "The superior man thinks of virtue; the small man thinks of comfort. The superior man thinks of the sanctions of law; the small man thinks of favours which he may receive."

xii. The Master said, "He who acts with a constant view to his own advantage will be much murmured against."

xiii. The Master said, "Is a prince able to govern his kingdom with the complaisance proper to the rules of propriety, what difficulty will he have? If he cannot govern it with that complaisance, what has he to do with the rules of propriety?"

xiv. The Master said, "A man should say, I am not concerned that I have no place, I am concerned how I may fit myself for one. I am not concerned that I am not known, I seek to be worthy to be known."

xv. 1. The Master said, "Sin, my doctrine is that of an all-pervading unity." The disciple Tsang replied, "Yes."

2. The Master went out, and the other disciples asked, saying, "What do his words mean?" Tsang said, "The doctrine of our master is to be true to the principles of our nature and the benevolent exercise of them to others,—this and nothing more."

xvi. The Master said, "The mind of the superior man is conversant with righteousness; the mind of the mean man is conversant with gain."

xvii. The Master said, "When we see men of worth, we should think of equalling them; when we see men of a contrary character, we should turn inwards and examine ourselves."

xviii. The Master said, "In serving his parents, a son may remonstrate with them, but gently; when he sees that they do not incline to follow his advice, he shows an increased degree of reverence, but does not abandon his purpose; and should they punish him, he does not allow himself to murmur."

XIX. The Master said, "While his parents are alive, the son may not go abroad to a distance. If he does go abroad, he must have a fixed place to which he goes."

XX. The Master said, "If the son for three years does not alter from the way of his father, he may be called filial."

XXI. The Master said, "The years of parents may by no means not be kept in the memory, as an occasion at once for joy and for fear."

XXII. The Master said, "The reason why the ancients did not readily give utterance to their words, was that they feared lest their actions should not come up to them."

XXIII. The Master said, "The cautious seldom err."

XXIV. The Master said, "The superior man wishes to be slow in his words and earnest in his conduct."

XXV. The Master said, "Virtue is not left to stand alone. He who practices it will have neighbours."

XXVI. Tsze-yew said, "In serving a prince, frequent remonstrances lead to disgrace. Between friends, frequent reproofs make the friendship distant."

BOOK V

I. 1. The Master said of Kung-yay Ch'ang that he might be wived; although he was put in bonds, he had not been guilty of any crime. Accordingly, he gave him his own daughter to wife.

2. Of Nan Yung he said that if the country were well governed, he would not be out of office, and if it were ill governed, he would escape punishment and disgrace. He gave him the daughter of his own elder brother to wife.

II. The Master said, of Tsze-tseen, "Of superior virtue indeed is such a man! If there were not virtuous men in Loo, how could this man have acquired this character?"

III. Tsze-kung asked, "What do you say of me, Tsze?" The Master said, "You are an utensil." "What utensil?" "A gemmed sacrificial utensil."

IV. 1. Some one said, "Yung is truly virtuous, but he is not ready with his tongue."

2. The Master said, "What is the good of being ready with the tongue? They who meet men with smartnesses of speech, for the most part procure themselves hatred. I know not whether he be truly virtuous, but why should he show readiness of the tongue?"

V. The Master was wishing Tseih-teaou K'ae to enter on official employment. He replied, "I am not yet able to rest in the assurance of This." The Master was pleased.

VI. The Master said, "My doctrines make no way. I will get upon a raft, and float about on the sea. He that will accompany me will be Yew, I dare to say." Tsze-loo hearing this was glad, upon which the Master said, "Yew is fonder of daring than I am. He does not exercise his judgment upon matters."

VII. 1. Mang Woo asked about Tsze-loo, whether he was perfectly virtuous. The Master said, "I do not know."

2. He asked again, when the Master replied, "In a kingdom of a thousand chariots, Yew might be employed to manage the military levies, but I do not know whether he be perfectly virtuous."

3. "And what do you say of K'ew?" The Master replied, "In a city of a thousand families, or a house of a hundred chariots, K'ew might be employed as governor, but I do not know whether he is perfectly virtuous."

4. "What do you say of Ch'ih?" The Master replied, "With his sash girt and standing in a court, Ch'ih might be employed to converse with the visitors and guests, but I do not know whether he is perfectly virtuous."

VIII. 1. The Master said to Tsze-kung, "Which do you consider superior, yourself or Hwuy?"

2. Tsze-kung replied, "How dare I compare myself with Hwuy? Hwuy hears one point and knows all about a subject; I hear one point and know a second."

3. The Master said, "You are not equal to him. I grant you, you are not equal to him."

IX. 1. Tsae Yu being asleep during the day time, the Master said, "Rotten wood cannot be carved; a wall of dirty earth will not receive the trowel. This Yu!—what is the use of my reproving him?"

2. The Master said, "At first, my way with men was

to hear their words, and give them credit for their conduct. Now my way is to hear their words, and look at their conduct. It is from Yu that I have learned to make this change."

x. The Master said, "I have not seen a firm and unbending man." Some one replied, "There is Shin Ch'ang." "Ch'ang," said the Master, "is under the influence of his passions; how can he be pronounced firm and unbending?"

xi. Tsze-kung said, "What I do not wish men to do to me, I also wish not to do to men." The Master said, "Tsze, you have not attained to that."

xii. Tsze-kung said, "The Master's personal displays of his principles, and ordinary descriptions of them may be heard. His discourses about man's nature, and the way of Heaven, cannot be heard."

xiii. When Tsze-loo heard anything, if he had not yet carried it into practice, he was only afraid lest he should hear something else.

xiv. Tsze-kung asked saying, "On what ground did Kung-wan get that title of Wan?" The Master said, "He was of an active nature and yet fond of learning, and he was not ashamed to ask and learn of his inferiors!—On these grounds he has been styled Wan." [8]

xv. The Master said of Tsze-ch'an that he had four of the characteristics of a superior man:—in his conduct of himself, he was humble; in serving his superiors, he was respectful; in nourishing the people, he was kind; in ordering the people, he was just.

xvi. The Master said, "Gan P'ing knew well how to maintain friendly intercourse. The acquaintance might be long, but he showed the same respect as at first."

xvii. The Master said, "Tsang Wan kept a large tortoise in a house, on the capitals of the pillars of which he had hills made, with representations of duckweed on the small pillars above the beams supporting the rafters. Of what sort was his wisdom?"

xviii. 1. Tsze-chang asked, saying, "The minister Tsze-wan thrice took office, and manifested no joy in his countenance.

[8] Wan—a man of learning. [Ed.]

Thrice he retired from office, and manifested no displeasure. He made it a point to inform the new minister of the way in which he had conducted the government;—what do you say of him?" The Master replied, "He was loyal." "Was he perfectly virtuous?" "I do not know. How can he be pronounced perfectly virtuous?"

2. Tsze-chang proceeded, "When the officer Ts'uy killed the prince of Ts'e, Ch'in Wan, though he was the owner of forty horses, abandoned them and left the country. Coming to another state, he said, 'They are here like our great officer, Ts'uy,' and left it. He came to a second state, and with the same observation left it also;—what do you say of him?" The Master replied, "He was pure." "Was he perfectly virtuous?" "I do not know. How can he be pronounced perfectly virtuous?"

xix. Ke Wan thought thrice, and then acted. When the Master was informed of it, he said, "Twice may do."

xx. The Master said, "When good order prevailed in his country, Ning Woo acted the part of a wise man. When his country was in disorder, he acted the part of a stupid man. Others may equal his wisdom, but they cannot equal his stupidity."

xxi. When the Master was in Ch'in, he said, "Let me return! Let me return! The little children of my school are ambitious and too hasty. They are accomplished and complete so far, but they do not know how to restrict and shape themselves."

xxii. The Master said, "Pih-e and Shuh-ts'e did not keep the former wickednesses of men in mind, and hence the resentments directed towards them were few."

xxiii. The Master said, "Who says of Wei-shang Kaou that he is upright? One begged some vinegar of him, and he begged it of a neighbour and gave it him."

xxiv. The Master said, "Fine words, an insinuating appearance, and excessive respect;—Tso-k'ew Ming was ashamed of them. I also am ashamed of them. To conceal resentment against a person, and appear friendly with him;—Tso-k'ew Ming was ashamed of such conduct. I also am ashamed of it."

xxv. 1. Yen Yuen and Ke Loo being by his side, the Master said to them, "Come, let each of you tell his wishes."

2. Tsze-loo said, "I should like, having chariots and horses, and light fur dresses, to share them with my friends, and though they should spoil them, I would not be displeased."

3. Yen Yuen said, "I should like not to boast of my excellence, nor to make a display of my meritorious deeds."

4. Tsze-loo then said, "I should like, sir, to hear your wishes." The Master said, "They are, in regard to the aged, to give them rest; in regard to friends, to show them sincerity; in regard to the young, to treat them tenderly."

XXVI. The Master said, "It is all over! I have not yet seen one who could perceive his faults, and inwardly accuse himself."

XXVII. The Master said, "In a hamlet of ten families, there may be found one honourable and sincere as I am, but not so fond of learning."

BOOK VI

I. 1. The Master said, "There is Yung!—He might occupy the place of a prince."

2. Chung-kung asked about Tsze-sang Pih-tsze. The Master said, "He may pass. He does not mind small matters."

3. Chung-kung said, "If a man cherish in himself a reverential feeling of the necessity of attention to business, though he may be easy in small matters, in his government of the people, that may be allowed. But if he cherish in himself that easy feeling, and also carry it out in his practice, is not such an easy mode of procedure excessive?"

4. The Master said, "Yung's words are right."

II. The duke Gae asked which of the disciples loved to learn. Confucius replied to him, "There was Yen Hwuy; he loved to learn. He did not transfer his anger; he did not repeat a fault. Unfortunately, his appointed time was short and he died; and now there is not such another. I have not yet heard of any one who loves to learn as he did."

III. 1. Tsze-hwa being employed on a mission to Ts'e, the disciple Yen requested grain for his [9] mother. The Master said, "Give her a foo." Yen requested more. "Give her an yu," said the Master. Yen gave her five ping.

2. The Master said, "When Ch'ih [9] was proceeding to

[9] His . . . Ch'ih—Both references are to Tsze-hwa, who was improvident of his mother and prodigal toward himself. [Ed.]

Ts'e, he had fat horses to his carriage, and wore light furs. I have heard that a superior man helps the distressed, but does not add to the wealth of the rich."

3. Yuen Sze being made governor of his town by the Master, he gave him nine hundred measures of grain, but Sze declined them.

4. The Master said, "Do not decline them. May you not give them away in the neighborhoods, hamlets, towns, and villages?"

IV.   The Master, speaking of Chung-kung, said, "If the calf of a brindled cow be red and horned, although man may not wish to use it, would the spirits of the mountains and rivers put it aside?"

V.   The Master said, "Such was Hwuy that for three months there would be nothing in his mind contrary to perfect virtue. The others may attain to this on some days or in some months, but nothing more."

VI.   Ke K'ang asked, "Is Chung-yew fit to be employed as an officer of government?" The Master said, "Yew is a man of decision; what difficulty would he find in being an officer of government?" K'ang asked, "Is Tsze fit to be employed as an officer of government?" and was answered, "Tsze is a man of intelligence; what difficulty would he find in being an officer of government?" And to the same question about K'ew the Master gave the same reply, saying, "K'ew is a man of various ability."

VII.   The chief of the Ke family sent to ask Min Tsze-k'een to be governor of Pe. Min Tsze-k'een said, "Decline the offer for me politely. If any one come again to me with a second invitation, I shall be obliged to go and live on the banks of the Wan."

VIII.   Pih-new being sick, the Master went to ask for him. He took of his hand through the window, and said, "It is killing him. It is the appointment of Heaven, alas! That such a man should have such a sickness! That such a man should have such a sickness!"

IX.   The Master said, "Admirable indeed was the virtue of Hwuy! With a single bamboo dish of rice, a single gourd dish of drink, and living in his mean narrow lane, while others could not have endured the distress, he did not allow his joy to be affected by it. Admirable indeed was the virtue of Hwuy!"

x. Yen K'ew said, "It is not that I do not delight in your doctrines, but my strength is insufficient." The Master said, "Those whose strength is insufficient give over in the middle of the way, but now you limit yourself."

xi. The Master said to Tsze-hea, "Do you be a scholar after the style of the superior man, and not after that of the mean man."

xii. Tsze-yew being governor of Woo-shing, the Master said to him, "Have you got good men there?" He answered, "There is Tan-t'ae Mee-ming, who never in walking takes a short cut, and never comes to my office, excepting on public business."

xiii. The Master said, "Mang Che-fan does not boast of his merit. Being in the rear on an occasion of flight, when they were about to enter the gate, he whipt up his horse saying, 'It is not that I dare to be last. My horse would not advance.' "

xiv. The Master said, "Without the specious speech of the litanist T'o, and the beauty of the prince Chaou of Sung, it is difficult to escape in the present age."

xv. The Master said, "Who can go out but by the door? How is it that men will not walk according to these ways?"

xvi. The Master said, "Where the solid qualities are in excess of accomplishments, we have rusticity; where the accomplishments are in excess of the solid qualities, we have the manners of a clerk. When the accomplishments and solid qualities are equally blended, we then have the man of complete virtue."

xvii. The Master said, "Man is born for uprightness. If a man lose his uprightness, and yet live, his escape from death is the effect of mere good fortune."

xviii. The Master said, "They who know the truth are not equal to those who love it, and they who love it are not equal to those who find pleasure in it."

xix. The Master said, "To those whose talents are above mediocrity, the highest subjects may be announced. To those who are below mediocrity, the highest subjects may not be announced."

xx. Fan Ch'e asked what constituted wisdom. The Master said, "To give one's-self earnestly to the duties due to men, and, while respecting spiritual beings, to keep aloof from them, may be called wisdom." He asked about perfect virtue. The Master said, "The man of virtue makes the difficulty to be overcome his first business, and success only a subsequent consideration;—this may be called perfect virtue."

xxi. The Master said, "The wise find pleasure in water; the virtuous find pleasure in hills. The wise are active; the virtuous are tranquil. The wise are joyful, the virtuous are long-lived."

xxii. The Master said, "Tse, by one change, would come to the state of Loo. Loo, by one change, would come to a state where true principles predominated."

xxiii. The Master said, "A cornered vessel without corners. —A strange-cornered vessel! A strange-cornered vessel!" [10]

xxiv. Tsae Go asked, saying, "A benevolent man though it be told him,—'There is a man in the well,' will go in after him I suppose." Confucius said, "Why should he do so? A superior man may be made to go to the well, but he cannot be made to go down into it. He may be imposed upon, but he cannot be befooled."

xxv. The Master said, "The superior man, extensively studying all learning, and keeping himself under the restraint of the rules of propriety, may thus likewise not overstep what is right."

xxvi. The Master having visited Nan-tsze,[11] Tsze-loo was displeased, on which the Master swore, saying, "Wherein I have done improperly, may Heaven reject me! may Heaven reject me!"

xxvii. The Master said, "Perfect is the virtue which is according to the Constant Mean! Rare for a long time has been its practice among the people."

xxviii. 1. Tsze-kung said, "Suppose the case of a man extensively conferring benefits on the people, and able to assist

[10] A metaphorical allusion to an anomalous political situation in China. [Ed.]
[11] Nan-tsze—"The wicked concubine of Duke Ling of Wei." (Arthur Waley). [Ed.]

all, what would you say of him? Might he be called perfectly virtuous?" The Master said, "Why speak only of virtue in connection with him! Must he not have the qualities of a sage? Even Yaou and Shun [12] were still solicitous about this.

2. "Now the man of perfect virtue, wishing to be established himself, seeks also to establish others; wishing to be enlarged himself, he seeks also to enlarge others.

3. "To be able to judge of others by what is nigh in ourselves;—this may be called the art of virtue."

BOOK VII

I. The Master said, "A transmitter and not a maker, believing in and loving the ancients, I venture to compare myself with our old P'ang."

II. The Master said, "The silent treasuring up of knowledge; learning without satiety; and instructing others without being wearied:—what one of these things belongs to me?"

III. The Master said, "The leaving virtue without proper cultivation; the not thoroughly discussing what is learned; not being able to move towards righteousness of which a knowledge is gained; and not being able to change what is not good:—these are the things which occasion me solicitude."

IV. When the Master was unoccupied with business, his manner was easy, and he looked pleased.

V. The Master said, "Extreme is my decay. For a long time, I have not dreamed as I was wont to do, that I saw the duke of Chow."

VI. 1. The Master said, "Let the will be set on the path of duty.

2. "Let every attainment in what is good be firmly grasped.

3. "Let perfect virtue be accorded with.

4. "Let relaxation and enjoyment be found in the polite arts."

VII. The Master said, "From the man bringing his bundle of dried flesh for my teaching upwards, I have never refused instruction to any one."

12 Yaou and Shun—mythological sages who ruled wisely according to the Way. [Ed.]

VIII. The Master said, "I do not open up the truth to one who is not eager to get knowledge, nor help out any one who is not anxious to explain himself. When I have presented one corner of a subject to any one, and he cannot from it learn the other three, I do not repeat my lesson."

IX. 1. When the Master was eating by the side of a mourner, he never ate to the full.

2. He did not sing on the same day in which he had been weeping.

X. 1. The Master said to Yen Yuen, "When called to office to undertake its duties; when not so called, to lie retired;—it is only I and you who have attained to this."

2. Tsze-loo said, "If you had the conduct of the armies of a great state, whom would you have to act with you?"

3. The Master said, "I would not have him to act with me, who will unarmed attack a tiger, or cross a river without a boat, dying without regret. My associate must be the man who proceeds to action full of solicitude, who is fond of adjusting his plans, and then carries them into execution."

XI. The Master said, "If the search for riches is sure to be successful, though I should become a groom with whip in hand to get them, I will do so. As the search may not be successful, I will follow after that which I love."

XII. The things in reference to which the Master exercised the greatest caution were—fasting, war, and sickness.

XIII. When the Master was in Ts'e, he heard the Shaou, and for three months did not know the taste of flesh. "I did not think," he said, "that music could have been made so excellent as this."

XIV. 1. Yen Yew said, "Is our Master for the prince of Wei?" Tsze-kung said, "Oh! I will ask him."

2. He went in accordingly, and said, "What sort of men were Pih-e and Shuh-ts'e?" "They were ancient worthies," said the Master. "Did they have any repinings because of their course?" The Master again replied, "They sought to act virtuously, and they did so; and what was there for them to repine about?" On this, Tsze-kung went out and said, "Our Master is not for him."

XV. The Master said, "With coarse rice to eat, with water to drink, and my bended arm for a pillow;—I have still joy in the midst of these things. Riches and honours acquired by unrighteousness are to me as a floating cloud."

XVI.   The Master said, "If some years were added to my life, I would give fifty to the study of the Yih, and then I might come to be without great faults."

XVII.   The Master's frequent themes of discourse were—the Odes, the History, and the maintenance of the Rules of propriety. On all these he frequently discoursed.

XVIII.   1. The duke of She asked Tsze-loo about Confucius, and Tsze-loo did not answer him.

2. The Master said, "Why did you not say to him,—He is simply a man, who in his eager pursuit of knowledge forgets his food, who in the joy of its attainment forgets his sorrows, and who does not perceive that old age is coming on?"

XIX.   The Master said, "I am not one who was born in the possession of knowledge; I am one who is fond of antiquity, and earnest in seeking it there."

XX.   The subjects on which the Master did not talk, were—extraordinary things, feats of strength, disorder, and spiritual beings.

XXI.   The Master said, "When I walk along with two others, they may serve me as my teachers. I will select their good qualities and follow them, their bad qualities and avoid them."

XXII.   The Master said, "Heaven produced the virtue that is in me. Hwan T'uy—what can he do to me?"

XXIII.   The Master said, "Do you think, my disciples, that I have any concealments? I conceal nothing from you. There is nothing which I do that is not shown to you, my disciples; —that is my way."

XXIV.   There were four things which the Master taught,—letters, ethics, devotion of soul, and truthfulness.

XXV.   1. The Master said, "A sage it is not mine to see; could I see a man of real talent and virtue, that would satisfy me."

2. The Master said, "A good man it is not mine to see; could I see a man possessed of constancy, that would satisfy me.

3. "Having not and yet affecting to have, empty and yet affecting to be full, straightened and yet affecting to be at ease:—it is difficult with such characteristics to have constancy."

XXVI. The Master angled,—but did not use a net. He shot, —but not at birds perching.

XXVII. The Master said, "There may be those who act without knowing why. I do not do so. Hearing much and selecting what is good and following it, seeing much and keeping it in memory; this is the second style of knowledge."

XXVIII. 1. It was difficult to talk with people of Hoo-heang, and a lad of that place having had an interview with the Master, the disciples doubted.

2. The Master said, "I admit people's approach to me without committing myself as to what they may do when they have retired. Why must one be so severe? If a man purify himself to wait upon me, I receive him so purified, without guaranteeing his past conduct."

XXIX. The Master said, "Is virtue a thing remote? I wish to be virtuous, and lo! virtue is at hand."

XXX. 1. The minister of crime of Ch'in asked whether the duke Ch'aou knew propriety, and Confucius said, "He knew propriety."

2. Confucius having retired, the minister bowed to Woo-ma K'e to come forward, and said, "I have heard that the superior man is not a partizan. May the superior man be a partizan also? The prince married a daughter of the house of Woo, of the same surname with himself, and called her,— 'The elder lady Tsze of Woo.' If the prince knew propriety, who does not know it?"

3. Woo-ma K'e reported these remarks, and the Master said, "I am fortunate! If I have any errors, people are sure to know them."

XXXI. When the Master was in company with a person who was singing, if he sang well, he would make him repeat the song, while he accompanied it with his own voice.

XXXII. The Master said, "In letters I am perhaps equal to other men, but the character of the superior man, carrying out in his conduct what he professes, is what I have not yet attained to."

XXXIII. The Master said, "The sage and the man of perfect virtue;—how dare I rank myself with them? It may simply be said of me, that I strive to become such without satiety, and teach others without weariness." Kung-se Hwa said, "This is just what we, the disciples, cannot imitate you in."

XXXIV. The Master being very sick, Tsze-loo asked leave to pray for him. He said, "May such a thing be done?" Tsze-loo replied, "It may. In the Prayers it is said, 'Prayer has been made to the spirits of the upper and lower worlds.'" The Master said, "My praying has been for a long time."

XXXV. The Master said, "Extravagance leads to insubordination, and parsimony to meanness. It is better to be mean than to be insubordinate."

XXXVI. The Master said, "The superior man is satisfied and composed; the mean man is always full of distress."

XXXVII. The Master was mild, and yet dignified; majestic, and yet not fierce; respectful, and yet easy.

BOOK VIII

I. The Master said, "T'ae-pih may be said to have reached the highest point of virtuous action. Thrice he declined the empire, and the people in ignorance of his motives could not express their approbation of his conduct."

II. 1. The Master said, "Respectfulness, without the rules of propriety, becomes laborious bustle; carefulness, without the rules of propriety, becomes timidity; boldness, without the rules of propriety, becomes insubordination; straightforwardness, without the rules of propriety, becomes rudeness.

2. "When those who are in high stations perform well all their duties to their relations, the people are aroused to virtue. When old friends are not neglected by them, the people are preserved from meanness."

III. The philosopher Tsang [13] being sick, he called to him the disciples of his school, and said, "Uncover my feet, uncover my hands. It is said in the Book of Poetry, 'We should be apprehensive and cautious, as if on the brink of a deep gulf, as if treading on thin ice,' and so have I been. Now and hereafter, I know my escape from all injury to my person, O ye, my little children."

[13] Tsang—one of the more important of Confucius' disciples. [Ed.]

IV. 1. The philosopher Tsang being sick, Mang King went to ask how he was.

2. Tsang said to him, "When a bird is about to die, its notes are mournful; when a man is about to die, his words are good.

3. "There are three principles of conduct which the man of high rank should consider specially important:—that in his deportment and manner he keep from violence and heedlessness; that in regulating his countenance he keep near to sincerity; and that in his words and tones he keep far from lowness and impropriety. As to such matters as attending to the sacrificial vessels, there are the proper officers for them."

V. The philosopher Tsang said, "Gifted with ability, and yet putting questions to those who were not so; possessed of much, and yet putting questions to those possessed of little; having, as though he had not; full, and yet counting himself as empty; offended against and yet entering into no altercation:—formerly I had a friend who pursued this style of conduct."

VI. The philosopher Tsang said, "Suppose that there is an individual who can be entrusted with the charge of a young orphan prince, and can be commissioned with authority over a state of a hundred *le*, and whom no emergency however great can drive from his principles;—is such a man a superior man? He is a superior man indeed."

VII. 1. The philosopher Tsang said, "The scholar may not be without breadth of mind and vigorous endurance. His burden is heavy and his course is long.

2. "Perfect virtue is the burden which he considers it is his to sustain;—is it not heavy? Only with death does his course stop;—is it not long?"

VIII. 1. The Master said, "It is by the Odes that the mind is aroused.

2. "It is by the Rules of propriety that the character is established.

3. "It is from Music that the finish is received."

IX. The Master said, "The people may be made to follow a path of action, but they may not be made to understand it."

X. The Master said, "The man who is fond of daring and is dissatisfied with poverty, will proceed to insubordination.

So will the man who is not virtuous, when you carry your dislike of him to an extreme."

XI. The Master said, "Though a man have abilities as admirable as those of the duke of Chow, yet if he be proud and niggardly, those other things are really not worth being looked at."

XII. The Master said, "It is not easy to find a man who has learned for three years without coming to be good."

XIII. 1. The Master said, "With sincere faith he unites the love of learning; holding firm to death, he is perfecting the excellence of his course.

2. "Such an one will not enter a tottering state, nor dwell in a disorganized one. When right principles of government prevail in the empire, he will show himself; when they are prostrated, he will keep concealed.

3. "When a country is well governed, poverty and a mean condition are things to be ashamed of. When a country is ill governed, riches and honour are things to be ashamed of."

XIV. The Master said, "He who is not in any particular office has nothing to do with plans for the administration of its duties."

XV. The Master said, "When the music-master, Che, first entered on his office, the finish with the Kwan Ts'ew was magnificent;—how it filled the ears!"

XVI. The Master said, "Ardent and yet not upright; stupid and yet not attentive; simple and yet not sincere:—such persons I do not understand."

XVII. The Master said, "Learn as if you could not reach your object, and were always fearing also lest you should lose it."

XVIII. The Master said, "How majestic was the manner in which Shun and Yu held possession of the empire, as if it were nothing to them!"

XIX. 1. The Master said, "Great indeed was Yaou as a sovereign! How majestic was he! It is only Heaven that is grand, and only Yaou corresponded to it. How vast was his virtue! The people could find no name for it.

2. "How majestic was he in the works which he accomplished? How glorious in the elegant regulations which he instituted!"

xx. 1. Shun had five ministers, and the empire was well governed.

2. King Woo said, "I have ten able ministers."

3. Confucius said, "Is not the saying that talents are difficult to find, true? Only when the dynasties of T'ang and Yu met, were they more abundant than in this of Chow, yet there was a woman among them. The able ministers were no more than nine men.

4. "King Wan possessed two of the three parts of the empire, and with those he served the dynasty of Yin. The virtue of the house of Chow may be said to have reached the highest point indeed."

xxi. The Master said, "I can find no flaw in the character of Yu. He used himself coarse food and drink, but displayed the utmost filial piety towards the spirits. His ordinary garments were poor but he displayed the utmost elegance in his sacrificial cap and apron. He lived in a low mean house, but expended all his strength on the ditches and water-channels. I can find nothing like a flaw in Yu."

BOOK IX

i. The subjects of which the Master seldom spoke were— profitableness, and also the appointments of Heaven, and perfect virtue.

ii. 1. A man of the village of Ta-heang said, "Great indeed is the philosopher K'ung! His learning is extensive, and yet he does not render his name famous by any particular thing."

2. The Master heard the observation, and said to his disciples, "What shall I practice? Shall I practice charioteering, or shall I practice archery? I will practice charioteering."

iii. 1. The Master said, "The linen cap is that prescribed by the rules of ceremony, but now a silk one is worn. It is economical, and I follow the common practice.

2. "The rules of ceremony prescribe the bowing below the hall, but now the practice is to bow only after ascending it. That is arrogant. I continue to bow below the hall, though I oppose the common practice."

IV. There were four things from which the Master was entirely free. He had no foregone conclusions, no arbitrary predeterminations, no obstinacy, and no egoism.

V. 1. The Master was put in fear in K'wang.

2. He said, "After the death of King Wan, was not the cause of truth lodged here in me?

3. "If Heaven had wished to let this cause of truth perish, then I, a future mortal, should not have got such a relation to that cause. While Heaven does not let the cause of truth perish, what can the people of K'wang do to me?"

VI. 1. A high officer asked Tsze-kung saying, "May we not say that your Master is a sage? How various is his ability!"

2. Tsze-kung said, "Certainly Heaven has endowed him unlimitedly. He is about a sage. And, moreover, his ability is various."

3. The Master heard the conversation and said, "Does the high officer know me? When I was young, my condition was low, and therefore I acquired my ability in many things, but they were mean matters. Must the superior man have such variety of ability? He does not need variety of ability."

4. Laou said, "The Master said, 'Having no official employment, I acquired many arts.'"

VII. The Master said, "Am I indeed possessed of knowledge? I am not knowing. But if a mean person who appears quite empty-like, ask anything of me, I set it forth from one end to the other, and exhaust it."

VIII. The Master said, "The Fung bird does not come; the river sends forth no map: [55]—it is all over with me."

IX. When the Master saw a person in a mourning dress, or any one with the cap and upper and lower garments of full dress, or a blind person, on observing them approaching, though they were younger than himself, he would rise up, and if he had to pass by them he would do so hastily.

X. 1. Yen Yuen, in admiration of the Master's doctrines sighed and said, "I looked up to them, and they seemed to become more high; I tried to penetrate them, and they seemed to become more firm; I looked at them before me, and suddenly they seemed to be behind.

2. "The Master, by orderly method, skilfully leads men on. He enlarged my mind with learning, and taught me the restraints of propriety.

[55] Signs of the coming of a sage. [Ed.]

3. "When I wish to give over the study of his doctrines, I cannot do so, and having exerted all my ability, there seems something to stand right up before me; but though I wish to follow and lay hold of it, I really find no way to do so."

XI. 1. The Master being very ill, Tsze-loo wished the disciples to act as ministers to him.

2. During a remission of his illness, he said, "Long has the conduct of Yew been deceitful! By pretending to have ministers when I have them not, whom should I impose upon? Should I impose upon Heaven?

3. "Moreover, than that I should die in the hands of ministers, is it not better that I should die in the hands of you, my disciples? And though I may not get a great burial, shall I die upon the road?"

XII. Tsze-kung said, "There is a beautiful gem here. Should I lay it up in a case and keep it? Or should I seek for a good price and sell it?" The Master said, "Sell it! Sell it! But I would wait till the price was offered."

XIII. 1. The Master was wishing to go and live among the nine wild tribes of the east.

2. Some one said, "They are rude. How can you do such a thing?" The Master said, "If a superior man dwelt among them what rudeness would there be?"

XIV. The Master said, "I returned from Wei to Loo, and then the music was reformed, and the pieces in the Imperial songs and Praise songs found all their proper place."

XV. The Master said, "Abroad, to serve the high ministers and officers; at home, to serve one's father and elder brother; in all duties to the dead, not to dare not to exert one's-self; and not to be overcome of wine:—what one of these things do I attain to?"

XVI. The Master standing by a stream, said, "It passes on just like this, not ceasing day or night!"

XVII. The Master said, "I have not seen one who loves virtue as he loves beauty."

XVIII. The Master said, "The prosecution of learning may be compared to what may happen in raising a mound. If there want but one basket of earth to complete the work, and I stop, the stopping is my own work. It may be compared to throwing down the earth on the level ground. Though but one basketful is thrown at a time, the advancing with it is my own going forward."

XIX. The Master said, "Never flagging when I set forth anything to him;—ah! that Hwuy."

XX. The Master said of Yen Yuen, "Alas! I saw his constant advance. I never saw him stop in his progress."

XXI. The Master said, "There are cases in which the blade springs, but the plant does not go on to flower! There are cases where it flowers, but no fruit is subsequently produced!"

XXII. The Master said, "A youth is to be regarded with respect. How do we know that his future will not be equal to our present? If he reach the age of forty or fifty, and has not made himself heard of, then indeed he will not be worth being regarded with respect."

XXIII. The Master said, "Can men refuse to assent to the words of strict admonition? But it is reforming the conduct because of them which is valuable. Can men refuse to be pleased with words of gentle advice? But it is unfolding their aim which is valuable. If a man be pleased with these words, but does not unfold their aim, and assents to those, but does not reform his conduct, I can really do nothing with him."

XXIV. The Master said, "Hold faithfulness and sincerity as first principles. Have no friends not equal to yourself. When you have faults, do not fear to abandon them."

XXV. The Master said, "The commander of the forces of a large state may be carried off, but the will of even a common man cannot be taken from him."

XXVI. 1. The Master said, "Dressed himself in a tattered robe quilted with hemp, yet standing by the side of men dressed in furs, and not ashamed;—ah! it is Yew who is equal to this.

2. " 'He dislikes none, he courts nothing;—what can he do but what is good?' "

3. Tsze-loo kept continually repeating these words of the ode, when the Master said, "Those things are by no means sufficient to constitute perfect excellence."

XXVII. The Master said, "When the year becomes cold, then we know how the pine and the cypress are the last to lose their leaves."

XXVIII.   The Master said, "The wise are free from perplexities; the virtuous from anxiety; and the bold from fear."

XXIX.   The Master said, "There are some with whom we may study in common, but we shall find them unable to go along with us to principles. Perhaps we may go on with them to principles, but we shall find them unable to get established in those along with us. Or if we may get so established along with them we shall find them unable to weigh occurring events along with us."

XXX.   1. How the flowers of the aspen-plum flutter and turn! Do I not think of you? But your house is distant.[15]

2. The Master said, "It is the want of thought about it. How is it distant?"

II *Taoist*

FROM The *Tao Teh Ching*

{4TH CENTURY B.C.}

TRANSLATED BY PAUL CARUS {1852-1919}

The Bible excepted, no Asian scripture has been more often translated into English than the *Tao Teh Ching*, the central book of Taoism. In part this is accountable by the supposed resemblance between the Taoist and Christian teachings, a fact which is eloquent of the universality of the sentiments that have inspired the great teachers of the world. The *Tao Teh Ching* is perhaps the best expression of the attitude of quietistic withdrawal from action which has appealed to every nation at some time in its history.

The book is probably a product of the 4th century before Christ and represents the mystic's reply to the arguments of other schools of Chinese philosophy. It aims particularly at the ethical-minded Confucianists who sought ultimate values in well-ordered social conduct, but also at the *real* politicians or legalists, who eschewed moral sanctions altogether. The *Tao Teh Ching* probably

---

15 Apparently lines from a song, upon which Confucius then makes his comment. [Ed.]

embodies ideas that were old even at the time it was composed. Hence the traditional attribution of the book to Master Lao Tan or Lao Tzu, a more or less legendary figure who reputedly lived in the time of Confucius! Little credence is given to this tradition by scholars, but the story of the meeting of the two sages has charmed generations of Chinese, in whom—as perhaps in all people—there is a mixture of the practicality of Confucius and the mysticism of Lao Tzu.

The title itself of this book has been variously translated. The three words denote "way," "virtue," and "book." But whether together they read "the book of the way of virtue" or "the book of the power [or virtue] of the way" is much mooted. The present version renders the favorite Chinese word Tao as reason; hence the title of Carus's translation: *The Canon of Reason and Virtue.* The notion of Tao may have signified to the Chinese not merely the path to truth, but the particularly rational way supposedly followed by the revered sages of antiquity. In the doctrine of the Taoists, Tao represents the unity that underlies all multiplicity and change; thus it is analogous to the Brahma of Indian Vedanta philosophy and to the One of Neo-Platonism. The *Tao Teh Ching* counsels a life of passive adherence to the Way, a spiritual detachment from desire, and a close conformity with nature. It takes its stand finally on a grand paradox: the less one does, the more is done. Its basic injunction might best be paraphrased by an inversion of the New Testament words: Ask not, and it shall be given you; seek not, and ye shall find; knock not, and it shall be opened unto you.

Twenty-six of the eighty-one chapters constituting the *Tao Teh Ching* are here reproduced.

4. SOURCELESS

1. Reason is empty, but its use is inexhaustible. In its profundity, verily, it resembleth the arch-father of the ten thousand things.

2. "It will blunt its own sharpness,
   Will its tangles adjust;
   It will dim its own radiance
   And be one with its dust."

3. Oh, how calm it seems to remain! I know not whose son it is. Apparently even the Lord it precedes.

7. DIMMING RADIANCE

1. Heaven endures and earth is lasting. And why can heaven and earth endure and be lasting? Because they do

not live for themselves. On that account can they endure.
2. Therefore

The holy man puts his person behind and his person comes to the front. He surrenders his person and his person is preserved. Is it not because he seeks not his own? For that reason he can accomplish his own.

8. EASY BY NATURE

1. Superior goodness resembleth water. The water's goodness benefiteth the ten thousand things, yet it quarreleth not.
2. Water dwelleth in the places which the multitudes of men shun; therefore it is near unto the eternal Reason.
3. The dwelling of goodness is in lowliness. The heart of goodness is in commotion. When giving, goodness showeth benevolence. In words, goodness keepeth faith. In government goodness standeth for order. In business goodness exhibiteth ability. The movements of goodness keep time.
4. It quarreleth not. Therefore it is not rebuked.

9. PRACTISING PLACIDITY

1. Grasp to the full, are you not likely foiled? Scheme too sharply, can you wear long? If gold and jewels fill the hall no one can protect it.
2. Rich and high but proud, brings about its own doom. To accomplish merit and acquire fame, then to withdraw, that is Heaven's Way.

11. THE FUNCTION OF THE NON-EXISTENT

1. Thirty spokes unite in one nave and on that which is non-existent [on the hole in the nave] depends the wheel's utility. Clay is moulded into a vessel and on that which is non-existent [on its hollowness] depends the vessel's utility. By cutting out doors and windows we build a house and on that which is non-existent [on the empty space within] depends the house's utility.
2. Therefore, existence renders actual but non-existence renders useful.

14. PRAISING THE MYSTERIOUS

1. We look at Reason and do not see it; its name is Colorless. We listen to Reason and do not hear it; its name is Soundless. We grope for Reason and do not grasp it; its name is Bodiless.
2. These three things cannot further be analyzed. Thus they are combined and conceived as a unity which on its surface is not clear and in its depth not obscure.
3. Forever and aye Reason remains unnamable, and again and again it returns home to non-existence.
4. This is called the form of the formless, the image of the imageless. This is called the transcendentally abstruse.
5. In front its beginning is not seen. In the rear its end is not seen.
6. By holding fast to the Reason of the ancients, the present is mastered and the origin of the past understood. This is called Reason's clue.

16. RETURNING TO THE ROOT [16]

1. By attaining the height of abstraction we gain fulness of rest.
2. All the ten thousand things arise, and I see them return. Now they bloom in bloom but each one homeward returneth to its root.
3. Returning to the root means rest. It signifies the return according to destiny. Return according to destiny means the eternal. Knowing the eternal means enlightenment. Not knowing the eternal causes passions to rise; and that is evil.
4. Knowing the eternal renders comprehensive. Comprehensiveness renders broad. Breadth renders royal. Royalty renders heavenly. Heaven renders Reason-like. Reason renders lasting. Thus the decay of the body implies no danger.

19. RETURNING TO SIMPLICITY [17]

1. Abandon your saintliness; put away your prudence; and the people will gain a hundredfold!
2. Abandon your benevolence; put away your justice; and the people will return to filial piety and paternal devotion.
3. Abandon smartness; give up greed; and thieves and robbers will no longer exist.

[16] The syllogistic reasoning of this chapter depends upon the resemblance of word characters denoting different ideas. [Ed.]
[17] How to achieve the ends of *realpolitik* by means of Taoist virtue. [Ed.]

4. These are three things for which culture is insufficient. Therefore it is said:

"Hold fast to that which will endure,
Show thyself simple, preserve thee pure,
And lessen self with desires fewer."

20. DIFFERENT FROM THE VULGAR

1. Abandon learnedness, and you have no vexation. The "yes" compared with the "yea," how little do they differ! But the good compared with the bad, how much do they differ!

2. If what the people dread cannot be made dreadless, there will be desolation, alas! and verily, there will be no end of it.

3. The multitudes of men are happy, so happy, as though celebrating a great feast. They are as though in springtime ascending a tower. I alone remain quiet, alas! like one that has not yet received an omen. I am like unto a babe that does not yet smile.

4. Forlorn am I, O so forlorn! It appears that I have no place whither I may return home.

5. The multitude of men all have plenty and I alone appear empty. Alas! I am a man whose heart is foolish.

6. Ignorant am I, O, so ignorant! Common people are bright, so bright, I alone am dull.

7. Common people are smart, so smart, I alone am confused, so confused.

8. Desolate am I, alas! like the sea. Adrift, alas! like one who has no place where to stay.

9. The multitude of men all possess usefulness. I alone am awkward and a rustic too. I alone differ from others, but I prize seeking sustenance from our mother.[18]

22. HUMILITY'S INCREASE

1. "The crooked shall be straight,
Crushed ones recuperate,
The empty find their fill.
The worn with strength shall thrill;
Who little have receive,
And who have much will grieve."

2. Therefore

[18] This entire chapter stands in marked contrast to the Confucian doctrine of social accommodation as a basic virtue. [Ed.]

The holy man embraces unity and becomes for all the
    world a model.
Not self-displaying he is enlightened;
Not self-approving he is distinguished;
Not self-asserting he acquires merit;
Not self-seeking he gaineth life.
Since he does not quarrel, therefore no one in the world
    can quarrel with him.

3. The saying of the ancients: "The crooked shall be
straight," is it in any way vainly spoken? Verily, they will
be straightened and return home.

26. THE VIRTUE OF GRAVITY

1. The heavy is of the light the root, and rest is motion's
master.

2. Therefore the holy man in his daily walk does not depart from gravity. Although he may have magnificent sights,
he calmly sits with liberated mind.

3. But how is it when the master of the ten thousand
chariots in his personal conduct is too light for the empire?
If he is too light he will lose his vassals. If he is too passionate he will lose the throne.

31. QUELLING WAR

1. Even victorious arms are unblest among tools, and people had better shun them. Therefore he who has Reason does
not rely on them.

2. The superior man when residing at home honors the
left. When using arms, he honors the right.

3. Arms are unblest among tools and not the superior man's
tools. Only when it is unavoidable he uses them. Peace and
quietude he holdeth high.

4. He conquers but rejoices not. Rejoicing at a conquest
means to enjoy the slaughter of men. He who enjoys the
slaughter of men will most assuredly not obtain his will in
the empire.

33. THE VIRTUE OF DISCRIMINATION

1. One who knows others is clever, but one who knows
himself is enlightened.

2. One who conquers others is powerful, but one who conquers himself is mighty.

3.   One who knows contentment is rich and one who pushes with vigor has will.
4.   One who loses not his place endures.
5.   One who may die but will not perish, has life everlasting.

43. *ITS UNIVERSAL APPLICATION*

1.   The world's weakest overcomes the world's hardest.
2.   Non-existence enters into the impenetrable.
3.   Thereby I comprehend of non-assertion the advantage. There are few in the world who obtain of non-assertion the advantage and of silence the lesson.

45. *GREATEST VIRTUE*

1.   "Greatest perfection imperfect will be,
     But its work ne'er waneth
     Greatest fulness is vacuity,
     Its work unexhausted remaineth."
2.   "Straightest lines resemble curves;
     Greatest skill like a tyro serves;
     Greatest eloquence stammers and swerves."
3.   Motion conquers cold. Quietude conquers heat. Purity and clearness are the world's standard.

46. *MODERATION OF DESIRE*

1.   When the world possesses Reason, race horses are reserved for hauling dung. When the world is without Reason, war horses are bred in the common.
2.   No greater sin than yielding to desire. No greater misery than discontent. No greater calamity than greed.
3.   Therefore, he who knows content's content is always content.

47. *VIEWING THE DISTANT*

1.   "Without passing out of the gate
     The world's course I prognosticate.
     Without peeping through the window
     The heavenly Reason I contemplate.
     The further one goes,
     The less one knows."

2. Therefore the holy man does not travel, and yet he has knowledge. He does not see things, and yet he defines them. He does not labor, and yet he completes.

51. *NURSING VIRTUE*

1. Reason quickens all creatures. Virtue feeds them. Reality shapes them. The forces complete them. Therefore among the ten thousand things there is none that does not esteem Reason and honor virtue.
2. Since the esteem of Reason and the honoring of virtue is by no one commanded, it is forever spontaneous.
3. Therefore it is said that Reason quickens all creatures, while virtue feeds them, raises them, nurtures them, completes them, matures them, rears them, and protects them.
4. To quicken but not to own, to make but not to claim, to raise but not to rule, this is called profound virtue.

54. *THE CULTIVATION OF INTUITION*

1. "What is well planted is not uprooted;
   What's well preserved cannot be looted!"
2. By sons and grandsons the sacrificial celebrations shall not cease.
3. Who cultivates Reason in his person, his virtue is genuine.

   Who cultivates it in his house, his virtue is overflowing.
   Who cultivates it in his township, his virtue is lasting.
   Who cultivates it in his country, his virtue is abundant.
   Who cultivates it in the world, his virtue is universal.
4. Therefore,
   By one's person one tests persons.
   By one's house one tests houses.
   By one's township one tests townships.
   By one's country one tests countries.
   By one's world one tests worlds.
5. How do I know that the world is such? Through IT.

56. *THE VIRTUE OF THE MYSTERIOUS*

1. One who knows does not talk. One who talks does not know. Therefore the sage keeps his mouth shut and his sense-gates closed.

2. "He will blunt his own sharpness,
    His own tangles adjust;
    He will dim his own radiance,
    And be one with his dust." [19]
3. This is called profound identification.
4. Thus he is inaccessible to love and also inaccessible to enmity. He is inaccessible to profit and inaccessible to loss. He is also inaccessible to favor and inaccessible to disgrace. Thus he becomes world-honored.

57. SIMPLICITY IN HABITS

1. With rectitude one governs the state; with craftiness one leads the army; with non-diplomacy one takes the empire. How do I know that it is so? Through IT.
2. The more restrictions and prohibitions are in the empire, the poorer grow the people. The more weapons the people have, the more troubled is the state. The more there is cunning and skill, the more startling events will happen. The more mandates and laws are enacted, the more there will be thieves and robbers.
3. Therefore the holy man says: I practise non-assertion, and the people of themselves reform. I love quietude, and the people of themselves become righteous. I use no diplomacy, and the people of themselves become rich. I have no desire, and the people of themselves remain simple.

61. THE VIRTUE OF HUMILITY

1. A great state, one that lowly flows, becomes the empire's union, and the empire's wife.
2. The wife always through quietude conquers her husband, and by quietude renders herself lowly.
3. Thus a great state through lowliness toward small states will conquer the small states, and small states through lowliness towards great states will conquer great states.
4. Therefore some render themselves lowly for the purpose of conquering; others are lowly and therefore conquer.
5. A great state desires no more than to unite and feed the people; a small state desires no more than to devote itself to the service of the people; but that both may obtain their wishes, the greater one must stoop.

[19] Cf. Chapter 4 above. [Ed.]

66. PUTTING ONESELF BEHIND

1. That rivers and oceans can of the hundred valleys be kings is due to their excelling in lowliness. Thus they can of the hundred valleys be the kings.
2. Therefore the holy man, when anxious to be above the people, must in his words keep underneath them. When anxious to lead the people, he must with his person keep behind them.
3. Therefore the holy man dwells above, but the people are not burdened. He is ahead, but the people suffer no harm.
4. Therefore the world rejoices in exalting him and does not tire. Because he strives not, no one in the world will strive with him.

76. BEWARE OF STRENGTH

1. Man during life is tender and delicate. When he dies he is stiff and stark.
2. The ten thousand things, the grass as well as the trees, while they live are tender and supple. When they die they are rigid and dry.
3. Thus the hard and the strong are the companions of death. The tender and the delicate are the companions of life.
   Therefore he who in arms is strong will not conquer.
4. When a tree has grown strong it is doomed.
5. The strong and the great stay below. The tender and the delicate stay above.

78. TRUST IN FAITH

1. In the world nothing is tenderer and more delicate than water. In attacking the hard and the strong nothing will surpass it. There is nothing that herein takes its place.
2. The weak conquer the strong, the tender conquer the rigid. In the world there is no one who does not know it, but no one will practise it.
3. Therefore the holy man says:
   "Him who the country's sin makes his,
   We hail as priest at the great sacrifice.
   Him who the curse bears of the country's failing,
   As king of the empire we are hailing."
4. True words seem paradoxical.

1. True words are not pleasant; pleasant words are not true.
The good are not contentious; the contentious are not good.
The wise are not learned; the learned are not wise.
2. The holy man hoards not. The more he does for others,
the more he owns himself. The more he gives to others, the
more will he himself lay up an abundance.
3. Heaven's Reason is to benefit but not to injure; the holy
man's Reason is to accomplish but not to strive.

III Hindu

FROM The *Bhagavad Gita*

{1ST CENTURY B.C.}

TRANSLATED BY SIR EDWIN ARNOLD {1832-1904}

The *Bhagavad Gita* presents the classic treatment of the problem
of moral man in immoral society. This sublime poem occurs in
the epic *Mahabharata* at a time when the wars between the two
branches of the Bharata family, the Pandavas and the Kuravas, are
drawing to a crisis. The Pandava hero Arjuna is preparing to go
into battle against his cousins. As his charioteer he has Krishna,
one of the reincarnations of the god Vishnu. At the moment of
commitment to the fight, Arjuna is overcome by doubts about the
morality of his undertaking. He does not wish to be guilty of the
death of his kin, and would almost rather be killed than kill.

Krishna undertakes to resolve his doubts in the long dialogue
between the two which constitutes the bulk of the poem, and
which is reported by the charioteer Sanjaya to an elder of the
Bharata family who is viewing the struggle.

In the eighteen books of the *Bhagavad Gita* Krishna argues
eloquently, if not always logically, for a detached commitment to
action without involvement in its good or evil consequences. The
various systems of Hindu philosophy are drawn upon, notably the
Sankhya, which counsels salvation through knowledge, and
the Yoga, which seeks it through ascetic practice. To these is
added, most prominently in the theophany of the eleventh book,
the doctrine of *bhakti* or love of God, which permits a form of
divine grace to be put out by Vishnu for those who give them-

selves up to him. Any inconsistencies of system whether in religion or philosophy are overwhelmingly absorbed in the organic unity of this "song of the lord." In the words of Rabindranath Tagore:

> Thus was rounded up the entire range of Indian spiritual and philosophical speculation and practice, and were reconciled the paths of dispassionate contemplation of the Impersonal, of ecstatic devotion to the Personal, of disinterested living in the world of the actual. Sacrifice of desire and not of the object, renunciation of the Self, not of the world, were made the keynote of this harmony of spiritual endeavors. [*Hindu Scriptures,* ed. Nicol Macnicol: London, J. M. Dent & Sons, 1938, Foreword, pp. vi-vii.]

Books VI-XI, representing the core of the poem, are here offered.

CHAPTER VI

KRISHNA:

Therefore, who doeth work rightful to do,
Not seeking gain from work, that man, O Prince!
Is Sânyasi and Yôgi [20]—both in one!
And he is neither who lights not the flame
Of sacrifice, nor setteth hand to task.

Regard as true Renouncer him that makes
Worship by work, for who renounceth not
Works not as Yôgin. So is that well said
"By works the votary doth rise to saint,
And saintship is the ceasing from all works";
Because the perfect Yôgin acts—but acts
Unmoved by passions and unbound by deeds,
Setting result aside.

　　　　　Let each man raise
The Self by Soul, not trample down his Self,
Since Soul that is Self's friend may grow Self's foe.
Soul is Self's friend when Self doth rule o'er Self
But self turns enemy if Soul's own self
Hates Self as not itself. [21]

　　　　　The sovereign soul
Of him who lives self-governed and at peace
Is centered in itself, taking alike
Pleasure and pain; heat, cold; glory and shame.

[20] Sânyasi and Yôgi—monk and ascetic. [Ed.]
[21] The Sanskrit has this play on the double meaning of *Atman.*

He is the Yôgi, he is *Yûkta*, glad
With joy of light and truth; dwelling apart
Upon a peak, with senses subjugate
Whereto the clod, the rock, the glistering gold
Show all as one. By this sign is he known
Being of equal grace to comrades, friends,
Chance-comers, strangers, lovers, enemies,
Aliens and kinsmen; loving all alike,
Evil or good.

Sequestered should he sit,
Steadfastly meditating, solitary,
His thoughts controlled, his passions laid away,
Quit of belongings. In a fair, still spot
Having his fixed abode,—not too much raised,
Nor yet too low,—let him abide, his goods
A cloth, a deerskin, and the Kusa-grass.
There, setting hard his mind upon The One,
Restraining heart and senses, silent, calm,
Let him accomplish Yôga, and achieve
Pureness of soul, holding immovable
Body and neck and head, his gaze absorbed
Upon his nose-end, rapt from all around,
Tranquil in spirit, free of fear, intent
Upon his Brahmacharya [22] vow, devout,
Musing on Me, lost in the thought of Me.
That Yôgin, so devoted, so controlled,
Comes to the peace beyond,—My peace, the peace
Of high Nirvana!

But for earthly needs
Religion is not his who too much fasts
Or too much feasts, nor his who sleeps away
An idle mind; nor his who wears to waste
His strength in vigils. Nay, Arjuna! call
That the true piety which most removes
Earth-aches and ills, where one is moderate
In eating and in resting, and in sport;
Measured in wish and act; sleeping betimes,
Waking betimes for duty.

When the man,
So living, centres on his soul the thought
Straitly restrained—untouched internally
By stress of sense—then is he *Yûkta*. See!
Steadfast a lamp burns sheltered from the wind;
Such is the likeness of the Yôgi's mind
Shut from sense-storms and burning bright to Heaven.
When mind broods placid, soothed with holy wont;

22 Brahman disciple. [Ed.]

When Self contemplates self, and in itself
Hath comfort; when it knows the nameless joy
Beyond all scope of sense, revealed to soul—
Only to soul! and, knowing, wavers not,
True to the farther Truth; when, holding this,
It deems no other treasure comparable,
But, harbored there, cannot be stirred or shook
By any gravest grief, call that state "peace,"
That happy severance Yôga, call that man
The perfect Yôgin!

                Steadfastly the will
Must toil thereto, till efforts end in ease,
And thought has passed from thinking. Shaking off
All longings bred by dreams of fame and gain,
Shutting the doorways of the senses close
With watchful ward; so, step by step, it comes
To gift of peace assured and heart assuaged,
When the mind dwells self-wrapped, and the soul broods
Cumberless. But, as often as the heart
Breaks—wild and wavering—from control, so oft
Let him re-curb it, let him rein it back
To the soul's governance! for perfect bliss
Grows only in the bosom tranquillized,
The spirit passionless, purged from offence,
Vowed to the Infinite. He who thus vows
His soul to the Supreme Soul, quitting sin,
Passes unhindered to the endless bliss
Of unity with Brahma. He so vowed,
So blended, sees the Life-Soul resident
In all things living, and all living things
In that Life-Soul contained. And whoso thus
Discerneth Me in all, and all in Me,
I never let him go; nor looseneth he
Hold upon Me; but, dwell he where he may,
Whate'er his life, in Me he dwells and lives
Because he knows and worships Me, Who dwell
In all which lives, and cleaves to Me in all.
Arjuna! if a man sees everywhere—
Taught by his own similitude—one Life,
One Essence in the Evil and the Good,
Hold him a Yôgi, yea! well-perfected!

ARJUNA:

Slayer of Madhu! yet again, this Yôg,
This Peace, derived from equanimity,
Made known by thee—I see no fixity
Therein, no rest, because the heart of men

Is unfixed, Krishna! rash, tumultuous,
Wilful and strong. It were all one, I think,
To hold the wayward wind, as tame man's heart.

KRISHNA:

Hero long-armed! beyond denial, hard
Man's heart is to restrain, and wavering;
Yet may it grow restrained by habit, Prince!
By wont of self-command. This Yôg, I say,
Cometh not lightly to th' ungoverned ones;
But he who will be master of himself
Shall win it, if he stoutly strive thereto.

ARJUNA:

And what road goeth he who, having faith,
Fails, Krishna! in the striving; falling back
From holiness, missing the perfect rule?
Is he not lost, straying from Brahma's light,
Like the vain cloud, which floats 'twixt earth and Heaven
When lightning splits it, and it vanisheth?
Fain would I hear thee answer me herein,
Since, Krishna! none save thou can clear the doubt.

KRISHNA:

He is not lost, thou Son of Prithâ! No!
Nor earth, nor heaven is forfeit, even for him,
Because no heart that holds one right desire
Treadeth the road of loss! He who should fail,
Desiring righteousness, cometh at death
Unto the Region of the Just; dwells there
Measureless years, and being born anew,
Beginneth life again in some fair home
Amid the mild and happy. It may chance
He doth descend into a Yôgin house
On Virtue's breast; but that is rare! Such birth
Is hard to be obtained on this earth, Chief!
So hath he back again what heights of heart
He did achieve, and so he strives anew
To perfectness, with better hope, dear Prince!
For by the old desire he is drawn on
Unwittingly; and only to desire
The purity of Yôga is to pass
Beyond the *Sabdabrahm*, the spoken Ved.[23]
But, being Yôgi, striving strong and long,
Purged from transgressions, perfected by births
Following on births, he plants his feet at last

[23] Ved—Veda, the basis of Hinduism. [Ed.]

Upon the farther path. Such an one ranks
Above ascetics, higher than the wise,
Beyond achievers of vast deeds! Be thou
Yôgi, Arjuna! And of such believe,
Truest and best is he who worships Me
With inmost soul, stayed on My Mystery!

CHAPTER VII

KRISHNA:

Learn now, dear Prince! how, if thy soul be set
Ever on Me—still exercising Yôg,
Still making Me thy Refuge—thou shalt come
Most surely unto perfect hold of Me.
I will declare to thee that utmost lore,
Whole and particular, which, when thou knowest,
Leaveth no more to know here in this world.

Of many thousand mortals, one, perchance,
Striveth for Truth; and of those few that strive—
Nay, and rise high—one only—here and there—
Knoweth Me, as I am, the very Truth.

Earth, water, flame, air, ether, life, and mind,
And individuality—those eight
Make up the showing of Me, Manifest.

These be my lower Nature; learn the higher,
Whereby, thou Valiant One! this Universe
Is, by its principle of life, produced;
Whereby the worlds of visible things are born
As from a *Yoni.* Know! I am that womb:
I make and I unmake this Universe:
Than me there is no other Master, Prince!
No other Maker! All these hang on me
As hangs a row of pearls upon its string.
I am the fresh taste of the water; I
The silver of the moon, the gold o' the sun,
The word of worship in the Veds, the thrill
That passeth in the ether, and the strength
Of man's shed seed. I am the good sweet smell
Of the moistened earth, I am the fire's red light,
The vital air moving in all which moves,
The holiness of hallowed souls, the root
Undying, whence hath sprung whatever is;
The wisdom of the wise, the intellect
Of the informed, the greatness of the great,
The splendor of the splendid. Kunti's Son!

These am I, free from passion and desire;
Yet am I right desire in all who yearn,
Chief of the Bhâratas! for all those moods,
Soothfast, or passionate, or ignorant,
Which Nature frames, deduce from me; but all
Are merged in me—not I in them! The world—
Deceived by those three qualities of being—
Wotteth not Me Who am outside them all,
Above them all, Eternal! Hard it is
To pierce that veil divine of various shows
Which hideth Me; yet they who worship Me
Pierce it and pass beyond.

                  I am not known
To evil-doers, nor to foolish ones,
Nor to the base and churlish; nor to those
Whose mind is cheated by the show of things,
Nor those that take the way of Asuras.[24]

Four sorts of mortals know me: he who weeps,
Arjuna! and the man who yearns to know;
And he who toils to help; and he who sits
Certain of me, enlightened.

                 Of these four,
O Prince of India! highest, nearest, best
That last is, the devout soul, wise, intent
Upon "The One." Dear, above all, am I
To him; and he is dearest unto me!
All four are good, and seek me; but mine own,
The true of heart, the faithful—stayed on me,
Taking me as their utmost blessedness,
They are not "mine," but I—even I myself!
At end of many births to Me they come!
Yet hard the wise Mahatma is to find,
That man who sayeth, "All is Vâsudey!" [25]

There be those, too, whose knowledge, turned aside
By this desire or that, gives them to serve
Some lower gods, with various rites, constrained
By that which mouldeth them. Unto all such—
Worship what shrine they will, what shapes, in faith—
'Tis I who give them faith! I am content!
The heart thus asking favor from its God,
Darkened but ardent, hath the end it craves,
The lesser blessing—but 'tis I who give!
Yet soon is withered what small fruit they reap
Those men of little minds, who worship so,
Go where they worship, passing with their gods.

24 Beings of low and devilish nature.
25 Krishna.

But Mine come unto me! Blind are the eyes
Which deem th' Unmanifested manifest,
Not comprehending Me in my true Self!
Imperishable, viewless, undeclared,
Hidden behind my magic veil of shows,
I am not seen by all; I am not known—
Unborn and changeless—to the idle world.
But I, Arjuna! know all things which were,
And all which are, and all which are to be,
Albeit not one among them knoweth Me!

By passion for the "pairs of opposites,"
By those twain snares of Like and Dislike, Prince!
All creatures live bewildered, save some few
Who, quit of sins, holy in act, informed,
Freed from the "opposites," and fixed in faith,
Cleave unto Me.

Who cleave, who seek in Me
Refuge from birth and death, those have the Truth!
Those know Me BRAHMA; know Me Soul of Souls,
The ADHYATMAN; know KARMA, my work; [26]
Know I am ADHIBHUTA, Lord of Life,
And ADHIDAIVA, Lord of all the Gods,
And ADHIYAJNA, Lord of Sacrifice;
Worship Me well, with hearts of love and faith,
And find and hold Me in the hour of death.

CHAPTER VIII

ARJUNA:

WHO is that BRAHMA? What that Soul of Souls,
The ADHYATMAN? What, Thou Best of All!
Thy work, the KARMA? Tell me what it is
Thou namest ADHIBHUTA? What again
Means ADHIDAIVA? Yea, and how it comes
Thou canst be ADHIYAJNA in thy flesh?
Slayer of Madhu! Further, make me know
How good men find thee in the hour of death?

KRISHNA:

I BRAHMA am! the One Eternal GOD,
And ADHYATMAN is My Being's name,
The Soul of Souls! What goeth forth from Me,

---

[26] Brahma—the cosmic principle; Adhyatman—what Emerson called the Oversoul; Karma—the doctrine of works, by which one's reincarnations are determined. [Ed.]

Causing all life to live, is KARMA called:
And, Manifested in divided forms,
I am the ADHIBHUTA, Lord of Lives;
And ADHIDAIVA, Lord of all the Gods,
Because I am PURUSHA, who begets.
And ADHIYAJNA, Lord of Sacrifice,
I—speaking with thee in this body here—
Am, thou embodied one! (for all the shrines
Flame unto Me!) And, at the hour of death,
He that hath meditated Me alone,
In putting off his flesh, comes forth to Me,
Enters into My Being—doubt thou not!
But, if he meditated otherwise
At hour of death, in putting off the flesh,
He goes to what he looked for, Kunti's Son!
Because the Soul is fashioned to its like.

Have Me, then, in thy heart always! and fight!
Thou too, when heart and mind are fixed on Me,
Shalt surely come to Me! All come who cleave
With never-wavering will of firmest faith,
Owning none other Gods: all come to Me,
The Uttermost, Purusha, Holiest!

Whoso hath known Me, Lord of sage and singer,
   Ancient of days; of all the Three Worlds Stay,
Boundless,—but unto every atom Bringer
   Of that which quickens it: whoso, I say,

Hath known My form, which passeth mortal knowing;
   Seen my effulgence—which no eye hath seen—
Than the sun's burning gold more brightly glowing,
   Dispersing darkness,—unto him hath been

Right life! And, in the hour when life is ending,
   With mind set fast and trustful piety,
Drawing still breath beneath calm brows unbending,
   In happy peace that faithful one doth die,—

In glad peace passeth to Purusha's heaven,
   The place which they who read the Vedas name
AKSHARAM, "Ultimate"; whereto have striven
   Saints and ascetics—their road is the same.

That way—the highest way—goes he who shuts
The gates of all his senses, locks desire
Safe in his heart, centres the vital airs
Upon his parting thought, steadfastly set;
And, murmuring OM, the sacred syllable—
Emblem of BRAHM—dies, meditating Me.

For who, none other Gods regarding, looks
Ever to Me, easily am I gained
By such a Yôgi; and, attaining Me,
They fall not—those Mahatmas—back to birth,
To life, which is the place of pain, which ends,
But take the way of utmost blessedness.

The worlds, Arjuna!—even Brahma's world—
Roll back again from Death to Life's unrest;
But they, O Kunti's Son! that reach to Me,
Taste birth no more. If ye know Brahma's Day
Which is a thousand Yugas; if ye know
The thousand Yugas making Brahma's Night,
Then know ye Day and Night as He doth know!
When that vast Dawn doth break, th' Invisible
Is brought anew into the Visible;
When that deep Night doth darken, all which is
Fades back again to Him Who sent it forth;
Yea! this vast company of living things—
Again and yet again produced—expires
At Brahma's Nightfall; and, at Brahma's Dawn,
Riseth, without its will, to life new-born.
But—higher, deeper, innermost—abides
Another Life, not like the life of sense,
Escaping sight, unchanging. This endures
When all created things have passed away:
This is that Life named the Unmanifest,
The Infinite! the All! the Uttermost.
Thither arriving none return. That Life
Is Mine, and I am there! And, Prince! by faith
Which wanders not, there is a way to come
Thither. I, the PURUSHA, I Who spread
The Universe around me—in Whom dwell
All living Things—may so be reached and seen!

. . . .

Richer than holy fruit on Vedas growing,
    Greater than gifts, better than prayer or fast,
Such wisdom is! The Yôgi, this way knowing,
    Comes to the Utmost Perfect Peace at last

CHAPTER IX

KRISHNA:

Now will I open unto thee—whose heart
Rejects not—that last lore, deepest-concealed,
That farthest secret of My Heavens and Earths,

Which but to know shall set thee free from ills,—
A Royal lore! a Kingly mystery!
Yea! for the soul such light as purgeth it
From every sin; a light of holiness
With inmost splendor shining; plain to see;
Easy to walk by, inexhaustible!

They that receive not this, failing in faith
To grasp the greater wisdom, reach not Me,
Destroyer of thy foes! They sink anew
Into the realm of Flesh, where all things change!

By Me the whole vast Universe of things
Is spread abroad;—by Me, the Unmanifest!
In Me are all existences contained;
Not I in them!

           Yet they are not contained,
Those visible things! Receive and strive to embrace
The mystery majestical! My Being—
Creating all, sustaining all—still dwells
Outside of all!

           See! as the shoreless airs
Move in the measureless space, but are not space,
[And space were space without the moving airs];
So all things are in Me, but are not I.

At closing of each Kalpa,[27] Indian Prince!
All things which be back to My Being come:
At the beginning of each Kalpa, all
Issue newborn from Me.

           By Energy
And help of Prakritî,[28] my outer Self,
Again, and yet again, I make go forth
The realms of visible things—without their will—
All of them—by the power of Prakritî.

Yet these great makings, Prince! involve Me not,
Enchain Me not! I sit apart from them,
Other, and Higher, and Free; nowise attached!

Thus doth the stuff of worlds, moulded by Me,
Bring forth all that which is, moving or still,
Living or lifeless! Thus the worlds go on!

The minds untaught mistake Me, veiled in form;—
Nought see they of My secret Presence, nought
Of My hid Nature, ruling all which lives.
Vain hopes pursuing, vain deeds doing; fed

[27] Kalpa—a cycle of time. [Ed.]
[28] Prakritî—primordial matter. [Ed.]

On vainest knowledge, senselessly they seek
An evil way, the way of brutes and fiends.
But My Mahatmas, those of noble soul
Who tread the path celestial, worship Me
With hearts unwandering,—knowing Me the Source,
Th' Eternal Source, of Life. Unendingly
They glorify Me; seek Me; keep their vows
Of reverence and love, with changeless faith
Adoring Me. Yea, and those too adore,
Who, offering sacrifice of wakened hearts,
Have sense of one pervading Spirit's stress,
One Force in every place, though manifold!
I am the Sacrifice! I am the Prayer!
I am the Funeral-Cake set for the dead!
I am the healing herb! I am the ghee,
The Mantra, and the flame, and that which burns!
I am—of all this boundless Universe—
The Father, Mother, Ancestor, and Guard!
The end of Learning! That which purifies
In lustral water! I am OM! I am
Rig-Veda, Sama-Veda, Yajur-Ved;
The Way, the Fosterer, the Lord, the Judge,
The Witness; the Abode, the Refuge-House,
The Friend, the Fountain and the Sea of Life
Which sends, and swallows up; Treasure of Worlds
And Treasure-Chamber! Seed and Seed-Sower,
Whence endless harvests spring! Sun's heat is mine;
Heaven's rain is mine to grant or to withhold;
Death am I, and Immortal Life I am,
Arjuna! SAT and ASAT, Visible Life,
And Life Invisible!

Yea! those who learn
The threefold Veds, who drink the Soma-wine,
Purge sins, pay sacrifice—from Me they earn
Passage to Swarga; where the meats divine

Of great gods feed them in high Indra's heaven.
Yet they, when that prodigious joy is o'er,
Paradise spent, and wage for merits given,
Come to the world of death and change once more.

They had their recompense! they stored their treasure,
Following the threefold Scripture and its writ;
Who seeketh such gaineth the fleeting pleasure
Of joy which comes and goes! I grant them it!

But to those blessèd ones who worship Me,
Turning not otherwise, with minds set fast,
I bring assurance of full bliss beyond.

Nay, and of hearts which follow other gods
In simple faith, their prayers arise to me,
O Kunti's Son! though they pray wrongfully:
For I am the Receiver and the Lord
Of every sacrifice, which these know not
Rightfully; so they fall to earth again!
Who follow gods go to their gods; who vow
Their souls to Pitris go to Pitris; minds
To evil Bhûts given o'er sink to the Bhûts;
And whoso loveth Me cometh to Me.
Whoso shall offer Me in faith and love
A leaf, a flower, a fruit, water poured forth,
That offering I accept, lovingly made
With pious will. Whate'er thou doest, Prince!
Eating or sacrificing, giving gifts,
Praying or fasting, let it all be done
For Me, as Mine. So shalt thou free thyself
From *Karmabandh,* the chain which holdeth men
To good and evil issue, so shalt come
Safe unto Me—when thou art quit of flesh—
By faith and abdication joined to Me!
    I am alike for all! I know not hate,
I know not favor! What is made is Mine!
But them that worship Me with love, I love;
They are in Me, and I in them!

                                        Nay, Prince!
If one of evil life turn in his thought
Straightly to Me, count him amidst the good;
He hath the highway chosen; he shall grow
Righteous ere long; he shall attain that peace
Which changes not. Thou Prince of India!
Be certain none can perish, trusting Me!
O Prithâ's Son! whoso will turn to Me,
Though they be born from the very womb of Sin,
Woman or man; sprung of the Vaisya caste
Or lowly disregarded Sudra,—all
Plant foot upon the highest path; how then
The holy Brahmans and My Royal Saints?
Ah! ye who into this ill world are come—
Fleeting and false—set your faith fast on Me!
Fix heart and thought on Me! Adore Me! Bring
Offerings to Me! Make Me prostrations! Make
Me your supremest joy! and, undivided,
Unto My rest your spirits shall be guided.

CHAPTER X

KRISHNA: [29]

HEAR farther yet thou Long-Armed Lord! these latest words
    I say—
Uttered to bring thee bliss and peace, who lovest Me alway—
Not the great company of gods nor kingly Rishis [30] know
My Nature, who have made the gods and Rishis long ago;
He only knoweth—only he is free of sin, and wise,
Who seeth Me, Lord of the Worlds, with faith-enlightened
    eyes,
Unborn, undying, unbegun. Whatever Natures be
To mortal men distributed, those natures spring from Me!
Intellect, skill, enlightenment, endurance, self-control,
Truthfulness, equability, and grief or joy of soul,
And birth and death, and fearfulness, and fearlessness, and
    shame,
And honor, and sweet harmlessness, and peace which is the
    same
Whate'er befalls, and mirth, and tears, and piety, and thrift,
And wish to give, and will to help,—all cometh of My gift!
The Seven Chief Saints, the Elders Four, the Lordly Manus
    set—
Sharing My work—to rule the worlds, these too did I beget;
And Rishis, Pitris, Manus, all, by one thought of My mind;
Thence did arise, to fill this world, the races of mankind;
Wherefrom who comprehends My Reign of mystic Majesty—
That truth of truths—is thenceforth linked in faultless faith
    to Me:
Yea! knowing Me the source of all, by Me all creatures
    wrought,
The wise in spirit cleave to Me, into My Being brought;
Hearts fixed on Me; breaths breathed to Me; praising Me,
    each to each,
So have they happiness and peace, with pious thought and
    speech;
And unto these—thus serving well, thus loving ceaselessly—
I give a mind of perfect mood, whereby they draw to Me;
And, all for love of them, within their darkened souls I dwell,
And, with bright rays of wisdom's lamp, their ignorance
    dispel.

[29] The Sanskrit poem here rises to an elevation of style and manner
which I have endeavored to mark by change of metre.
[30] Rishis—seers. [Ed.]

ARJUNA:

Yes! Thou art Parabrahm! The High Abode!
The Great Purification! Thou art God
Eternal, All-creating, Holy, First,
Without beginning! Lord of Lords and Gods!
Declared by all the Saints—by Narada,
Vyâsa, Asita, and Devalas;
And here Thyself declaring unto me!
What Thou hast said now know I to be truth,
O Kesava! that neither gods nor men
Nor demons comprehend Thy mystery
Made manifest, Divinest! Thou Thyself
Thyself alone dost know, Maker Supreme!
Master of all the living! Lord of Gods!
King of the Universe! To Thee alone
Belongs to tell the heavenly excellence
Of those perfections wherewith Thou dost fill
These worlds of Thine; Pervading, Immanent!
How shall I learn, Supremest Mystery!
To know Thee, though I muse continually?
Under what form of Thine unnumbered forms
Mayst Thou be grasped? Ah! yet again recount,
Clear and complete, Thy great appearances,
The secrets of Thy Majesty and Might,
Thou High Delight of Men! Never enough
Can mine ears drink the Amrit [81] of such words!

KRISHNA:

Hanta! So be it! Kuru Prince! I will to thee unfold
Some portions of My Majesty, whose powers are manifold!
I am the Spirit seated deep in every creature's heart;
From Me they come; by Me they live; at My word they
    depart!
Vishnu of the Adityas I am,[82] those Lords of Light;
Marîtchi of the Maruts, the Kings of Storm and Blight;
By day I gleam, the golden Sun of burning cloudless Noon;
By Night, amid the asterisms I glide, the dappled Moon!
Of Vedas I am Sâma-Ved, of gods in Indra's Heaven
Vâsava; of the faculties to living beings given
The mind which apprehends and thinks; of Rudras Sankara;
Of Yakshas and of Râkshasas, Vittesh; and Pâvaka
Of Vasus, and of mountain-peaks Meru; Vrihaspati
Know Me 'mid planetary Powers; 'mid Warriors heavenly

[81] The nectar of immortality.
[82] Despite the density of the allusions which follow, and because its
general meaning is clear, this passage has been retained. [Ed.]

Skanda; of all the water-floods the Sea which drinketh each,
And Bhrigu of the holy Saints, and OM of sacred speech;
Of prayers the prayer ye whisper; of hills Himâla's snow,
And Aswattha, the fig-tree, of all the trees that grow;
Of the Devarshis, Narada; and Chitrarath of them
That sing in Heaven, and Kapila of Munis, and the gem
Of flying steeds, Uchchaisravas, from Amrit-wave which
    burst;
Of elephants Airâvata; of males the Best and First;
Of weapons Heav'n's hot thunderbolt; of cows white
    Kâmadhuk,
From whose great milky udder-teats all hearts' desires are
    strook;
Vâsuki of the serpent-tribes, round Mandara entwined;
And thousand-fanged Ananta, on whose broad coils reclined
Leans Vishnu; and of water-things Varuna; Aryam
Of Pitris, and, of those that judge, Yama the Judge I am;
Of Daityas dread Prahlâda; of what metes days and years,
Time's self I am; of woodland-beasts—buffaloes, deers, and
    bears—
The lordly-painted tiger; of birds the vast Garûd,
The whirlwind 'mid the winds; 'mid chiefs Rama with blood
    imbrued,
Makar 'mid fishes of the sea, and Ganges 'mid the streams;
Yea! First, and Last, and Centre of all which is or seems
I am, Arjuna! Wisdom Supreme of what is wise,
Words on the uttering lips I am, and eyesight of the eyes,
And "A" of written characters, Dwandwa of knitted speech,
And Endless Life, and boundless Love, whose power sustain-
    eth each;
And bitter Death which seizes all, and joyous sudden Birth,
Which brings to light all beings that are to be on earth;
And of the viewless virtues, Fame, Fortune, Song am I,
And Memory, and Patience; and Craft, and Constancy:
Of Vedic hymns the Vrihatsâm, of metres Gayatrî,
Of months the Mârgasirsha, of all the seasons three
The flower-wreathed Spring; in dicer's-play the conquering
    Double-Eight;
The splendor of the splendid, and the greatness of the great,
Victory I am, and Action! and the goodness of the good,
And Vâsudev of Vrishni's race, and of this Pandu brood
Thyself!—Yea, my Arjuna! thyself; for thou art Mine!
Of poets Usana, of saints Vyâsa, sage divine;
The policy of conquerors, the potency of kings,
The great unbroken silence in learning's secret things;
The lore of all the learnèd, the seed of all which springs.
Living or lifeless, still or stirred, whatever beings be,

None of them is in all the worlds, but it exists by Me!
Nor tongue can tell, Arjuna! nor end of telling come
Of these My boundless glories, whereof I teach thee some;
For wheresoe'er is wondrous work, and majesty, and might,
From Me hath all proceeded. Receive thou this aright!
Yet how shouldst thou receive, O Prince! the vastness of
    this word?
I, who am all, and made it all, abide its separate Lord!

CHAPTER XI

ARJUNA:

THIS, for my soul's peace, have I heard from Thee,
The unfolding of the Mystery Supreme
Named Adhyâtman; comprehending which,
My darkness is dispelled; for now I know—
O Lotus-eyed!—whence is the birth of men,
And whence their death, and what the majesties
Of thine immortal rule. Fain would I see,
As thou Thyself declar'st it, Sovereign Lord!
The likeness of that glory of Thy Form
Wholly revealed. O Thou Divinest One!
If this can be, if I may bear the sight,
Make Thyself visible, Lord of all prayers!
Show me Thy very self, the Eternal God!

KRISHNA:

Gaze, then, thou Son of Prithâ! I manifest for thee
Those hundred thousand thousand shapes that clothe my
    Mystery;
I show thee all my semblances, infinite, rich, divine,
My changeful hues, my countless forms. See! in this face of
    mine,
Adityas, Vasus, Rudras, Aswins, and Maruts; see
Wonders unnumbered, Indian Prince! revealed to none save
    thee.
Behold! this is the Universe!—Look! what is live and dead
I gather all in one—in Me! Gaze, as thy lips have said,
On GOD ETERNAL, VERY GOD! See ME! see what thou prayest!

.   .   .   .

Thou canst not!—nor, with human eyes, Arjuna! ever
    mayest!

Therefore I give thee sense divine. Have other eyes, new
   light!
   And look! This is My glory, unveiled to mortal sight!

SANJAYA:

Then, O King! the God, so saying,
Stood, to Prithâ's Son displaying
All the splendor, wonder, dread
Of His vast Almighty-head.
Out of countless eyes beholding,
Out of countless mouths commanding,
Countless mystic forms enfolding
In one Form: supremely standing
Countless radiant glories wearing,
Countless heavenly weapons bearing,
Crowned with garlands of star-clusters,
Robed in garb of woven lustres,
Breathing from His perfect Presence
Breaths of all delicious essence
Of all sweetest odors; shedding
Blinding brilliance, overspreading—
Boundless, beautiful—all spaces
From His all-regarding faces;
So He showed! If there should rise
Suddenly within the skies
Sunburst of a thousand suns
Flooding earth with rays undeemed-of,
Then might be that Holy One's
Majesty and glory dreamed of!

   So did Pandu's Son behold
All this universe enfold
All its huge diversity
Into one great shape, and be
Visible, and viewed, and blended
In one Body—subtle, splendid,
Nameless—th' All-comprehending
God of Gods, the Never-Ending
Deity!

       But, sore amazed,
   Thrilled, o'erfilled, dazzled, and dazed,
   Arjuna knelt, and bowed his head,
   And clasped his palms, and cried, and said:

ARJUNA:

Yea! I have seen! I see!
Lord! all is wrapped in Thee!
The gods are in Thy glorious frame! the creatures
  Of earth, and heaven, and hell
  In Thy Divine form dwell,
And in Thy countenance show all the features

  Of Brahma, sitting lone
  Upon His lotus-throne;
Of saints and sages, and the serpent races
  Ananta, Vâsuki.
  Yea! mightiest Lord! I see
Thy thousand thousand arms, and breasts, and faces,

  And eyes,—on every side
  Perfect, diversified;
And nowhere end of Thee, nowhere beginning,
  Nowhere a centre! Shifts
  Wherever soul's gaze lifts
Thy central Self, all-willing, and all-winning!

  Infinite King! I see
  The anadem on Thee,
The club, the shell, the discus; see Thee burning
  In beams insufferable,
  Lighting earth, heaven, and hell
With brilliance blinding, glorious, flashing, turning

  Darkness to dazzling day,
  Look I whichever way.
Ah, Lord! I worship Thee, the Undivided,
  The Uttermost of thought,
  The Treasure-Palace wrought
To hold the wealth of the worlds; the shield provided

  To shelter Virtue's laws;
  The Fount whence Life's stream draws
All waters of all rivers of all being:
  The One Unborn, Unending:
  Unchanging and unblending!
With might and majesty, past thought, past seeing!

  Silver of moon and gold
  Of sun are glances rolled
From Thy great eyes; Thy visage beaming tender
  Over the stars and skies,
  Doth to warm life surprise
Thy Universe. The worlds are filled with wonder

Of Thy perfections! Space
Star-sprinkled, and the place
From pole to pole of the heavens, from bound to bound,
Hath Thee in every spot,
Thee, Thee!—Where Thou art not
O Holy, Marvellous Form! is nowhere found!

O Mystic, Awful One!
At sight of Thee, made known,
The Three Worlds quake; the lower gods draw nigh Thee;
They fold their palms, and bow
Body, and breast, and brow,
And, whispering worship, laud and magnify Thee!

Rishis and Siddhas cry
"Hail! Highest Majesty!"
From sage and singer breaks the hymn of glory
In holy melody,
Sounding the praise of Thee,
While countless companies take up the story,

Rudras, who rides the storms,
Th' Adityas' shining forms,
Vasus and Sâdhyas, Viswas, Ushmapas,
Maruts, and those great Twins,
The heavenly, fair, Aswins,
Gandharvas, Rakshasas, Siddhas, Asuras,—

These see Thee, and revere
In silence-stricken fear;
Yea! the Worlds,—seeing Thee with form stupendous,
With faces manifold,
With eyes which all behold,
Unnumbered eyes, vast arms, members tremendous,

Flanks, lit with sun and star,
Feet planted near and far,
Tushes of terror, mouths wrathful and tender;—
The Three wide Worlds before Thee
Adore, as I adore Thee,
Quake, as I quake, to witness so much splendor!

I mark Thee strike the skies
With front in wondrous wise
Huge, rainbow-painted, glittering; and thy mouth
Opened, and orbs which see
All things, whatever be,
In all Thy worlds, east, west, and north and south.

O Eyes of God! O Head!
My strength of soul is fled,

Gone is heart's force, rebuked is mind's desire!
   When I behold Thee so,
   With awful brows a-glow,
With burning glance, and lips lighted with fire,

   Fierce as those flames which shall
   Consume, at close of all,
Earth, Heaven! Ah me! I see no Earth and Heaven!
   Thee, Lord of Lords! I see,
   Thee only—only Thee!
Ah! let Thy mercy unto me be given!

   Thou Refuge of the World!
   Lo! to the cavern hurled
Of Thy wide-opened throat, and lips white-tushed,
   I see our noblest ones,
   Great Dhritarashtra's sons,[33]
Bhishma, Drona, and Karna, caught and crushed!

   The Kings and Chiefs drawn in,
   That gaping gorge within;
The best of all both armies torn and riven!
   Between Thy jaws they lie
   Mangled fell bloodily,
Ground into dust and death! Like streams down driven

   With helpless haste, which go
   In headlong furious flow
Straight to the gulfing maw of th' unfilled ocean,
   So to that flaming cave
   These heroes great and brave
Pour, in unending streams, with helpless motion!

   Like moths which in the night
   Flutter towards a light,
Drawn to their fiery doom, flying and dying,
   So to their death still throng,
   Blind, dazzled, borne along
Ceaselessly, all these multitudes, wild flying!

   Thou, that hast fashioned men,
   Devourest them agen,
One with another, great and small, alike!
   The creatures whom Thou mak'st,
   With flaming jaws Thou tak'st,
Lapping them up! Lord God! Thy terrors strike

   From end to end of earth,
   Filling life full, from birth
To death, with deadly, burning, lurid dread!

---

[33] The opposing faction in the wars of the Bharatas. [Ed.]

Ah, Vishnu! make me know
  Why is Thy visage so?
Who art Thou, feasting thus upon Thy dead?

Who? awful Deity!
  I bow myself to Thee,
Nâmostu Tê Devavara! Prasîd! [34]
  O Mightiest Lord! rehearse
  Why hast Thou face so fierce?
Whence did this aspect horrible proceed?

KRISHNA:

Thou seest Me as Time who kills, Time who brings all to
    doom,
The Slayer Time, Ancient of Days, come hither to consume;
Excepting thee, of all these hosts of hostile chiefs arrayed,
There shines not one shall leave alive the battlefield! Dis-
    mayed
No longer be! Arise! obtain renown! destroy thy foes!
Fight for the kingdom waiting thee when thou hast van-
    quished those.
By Me they fall—not thee! the stroke of death is dealt them
    now,
Even as they stand thus gallantly; My instrument art thou!
Strike, strong-armed Prince! at Drona! at Bhishma strike!
    deal death
To Karna, Jyadratha; stay all this warlike breath!
'Tis I who bid them perish! Thou wilt but slay the slain.
Fight! they must fall, and thou must live, victor upon this
    plain!

SANJAYA:

Hearing mighty Keshav's word,
Tremblingly that helmèd Lord
Clasped his lifted palms, and—praying
Grace of Krishna—stood there, saying,
With bowed brow and accents broken,
These words, timorously spoken:

ARJUNA:

  Worthily, Lord of Might!
  The whole world hath delight
In Thy surpassing power, obeying Thee;
  The Rakshasas, in dread
  At sight of Thee, are sped
To all four quarters; and the company

[34] "Hail to Thee, God of Gods! Be favorable!"

Of Siddhas sound Thy name.
How should they not proclaim
Thy Majesties, Divinest, Mightiest?
  Thou Brahm, than Brahma greater!
  Thou Infinite Creator!
Thou God of gods, Life's Dwelling-place and Rest!

Thou, of all souls the Soul!
The Comprehending Whole!
Of Being formed, and formless Being the Framer;
  O Utmost One! O Lord!
  Older than eld, Who stored
The worlds with wealth of life. O Treasure-claimed,

Who wottest all, and art
Wisdom Thyself! O Part
In all, and all, for all from Thee have risen!
  Numberless now I see
  The aspects are of Thee!
Vayu [35] Thou art, and He who keeps the prison

Of Narak, Yama dark,
And Agni's shining spark.
Varuna's waves are Thy waves. Moon and star-light
  Are Thine! Prajâpati
  Art Thou, and 'tis to Thee
Men kneel in worshipping the old world's far light,

The first of mortal men.
Again, Thou God! again
A thousand thousand times be magnified!
  Honor and worship be—
  Glory and praise,—to Thee
Namô, Namastê, cried on every side.

Cried here, above, below,
Uttered when Thou dost go,
Uttered when Thou dost come! *Namô!* we call.
  Namôstu! God adored!
  Namôstu! Nameless Lord!
Hail to Thee! Praise to Thee! Thou One in all.

For Thou art All! Yea, Thou!
Ah! if in anger now
Thou shouldst remember I did think Thee Friend,
  Speaking with easy speech,
  As men use each to each;
Did call Thee "Krishna," "Prince," nor comprehend

[35] The wind.

Thy hidden majesty,
  The might, the awe of Thee;
Did, in my heedlessness, or in my love,
  On journey, or in jest,
  Or when we lay at rest,
Sitting at council, straying in the grove,

  Alone, or in the throng,
  Do Thee, most Holy wrong,
Be Thy grace granted for that witless sin!
  For Thou art now I know,
  Father of all below,
Of all above, of all the worlds within,

  Guru of Gurus, more
  To reverence and adore
Than all which is adorable and high!
  How, in the wide worlds three
  Should any equal be?
Shall any other share Thy majesty?

  Therefore, with body bent
  And reverent intent,
I praise, and serve, and seek Thee, asking grace.
  As father to a son,
  As friend to friend, as one
Who loveth to his lover; turn Thy face

  In gentleness on me!
  Good is it I did see
This unknown marvel of Thy Form! But fear
  Mingles with joy! Retake,
  Dear Lord! for pity's sake
Thine earthly shape, which earthly eyes may bear!

  Be merciful, and show
  The visage that I know;
Let me regard Thee, as of yore, arrayed
  With disc and forehead-gem,
  With mace and anedem,
Thou who sustainest all things! Undismayed

  Let me once more behold
  The form I loved of old,
Thou of the thousand arms and countless eyes!
  My frightened heart is fain
  To see restored again
The Charioteer, my Krishna's kind disguise.

KRISHNA:

Yea! thou hast seen, Arjuna! because I loved thee well,
The secret countenance of Me, revealed by mystic spell,
Shining, and wonderful, and vast, majestic, manifold,
Which none save thou in all the years had favor to behold:
For not by Vedas cometh this, nor sacrifice, nor alms,
Nor works well-done, nor penance long, nor prayers nor
    chaunted psalms,
That mortal eyes should bear to view the Immortal Soul un-
    clad,
Prince of the Kurus! This was kept for thee alone! Be glad!
Let no more trouble shake thy heart because thine eyes have
    seen
My terror with My glory. As I before have been
So will I be again for thee; with lightened heart behold!
Once more I am thy Krishna, the form thou knew'st of old!

SANJAYA:

These words to Arjuna spake
Vâsudev, and straight did take
Back again the semblance dear
Of the well-loved charioteer;
Peace and joy it did restore
When the Prince beheld once more
Mighty BRAHMA's form and face
Clothed in Krishna's gentle grace.

ARJUNA:

Now that I see come back, Janardana!
This friendly human frame, my mind can think
Calm thoughts once more; my heart beats still again!

KRISHNA:

Yea! it was wonderful and terrible
To view me as thou didst, dear Prince! The gods
Dread and desire continually to view!
Yet not by Vedas, nor from sacrifice,
Nor penance, nor gift-giving, nor with prayer
Shall any so behold, as thou hast seen!
Only by fullest service, perfect faith,
And uttermost surrender am I known
And seen, and entered into, Indian Prince!
Who doeth all for Me; who findeth Me
In all; adoreth always; loveth all
Which I have made, and Me, for Love's sole end,
That man, Arjuna! unto Me doth wend.

IV 𝔅uddhist

FROM **The** *Dhammapada*

[1ST CENTURY B.C.]

TRANSLATED BY F. MAX MÜLLER [1823–1900]

ᶦᴺᴬᴵᴬ

During the 6th century B.C.—which also saw the flourishing of the Zoroastrian, Hebraic, Confucian and Taoist religions—the old Vedic religion of India experienced two internal reforms that resulted in the establishment of the Jain and Buddhist faiths. The former of these two has remained a small but significant ascetic religion of India. The latter, after exercising considerable influence in its native land for several centuries, practically disappeared as a faith distinct from Hinduism, but spread to all parts of Asia to become one of the great world religions. The high regard in which it is held by Arnold Toynbee is but one instance of the powerful appeal which Buddhism has among intellectual circles in Europe and America.

Its founder, Siddharta Gotama, was a nobly born youth of many endowments who escaped the sheltered life of his father's court to observe the travails of the world. At the age of twenty-nine, he made the great renunciation and set out to live the life of a mendicant. Six years of asceticism brought him no peace, but a long period of meditation under the famous Bo tree, climaxed by his successful resistance of Mara the Tempter, at last enabled him to attain to enlightenment or the state of the Buddha. He then announced the four great truths of Buddhism:

I. that life is sorrow
II. that the cause of sorrow is desire
III. that escape is through the destruction of desire
IV. that this destruction is to be achieved by the eight-fold path, of which the steps are: 1) right belief, 2) right resolve, 3) right speech, 4) right behavior, 5) right occupation, 6) right effort, 7) right contemplation, 8) right concentration.

These basic teachings have produced the two main branches of the Buddhist religion: the Hinayana or Lesser Vehicle, which is the primitive faith flourishing mainly in southern Asia; and the Mahayana or Greater Vehicle, which has had its followers chiefly in Tibet, China, and Japan. The literature of the latter is mainly in Sanskrit and of course subsequently in Chinese and Japanese; of the former, mainly in Pali, an old Indian dialect.

The Buddhist Canon is divided into "three baskets" or Tripitakas.

The first of these, the Vinaya, contains the rules of the order. The second, the Sutta (Sanskrit *sutra* or thread), contains the sermons or teachings of the Buddha. The third, the Abhidhamma, contains the special *dharma* or laws for the training of the mind. Of these three, the most significant from the point of view of literary scripture is the Sutta. By the 3rd century B.C., this "basket" had been subdivided into five sections called Nikayas. The very last of these five, a collection of miscellaneous pieces that could not be grouped in the other four, and called the "smallish" Nikaya, holds the *Dhammapada*.

Among the sublimest of scriptural writings in the world, the *Dhammapada* is more notable, however, as a statement of a psychology than as an ethical or metaphysical creed. It enunciates a mode of disciplining the mind, heart, will and body to overcome the fires of passion, hatred, and stupidity. Neither negatively sentimental nor excessively ascetic, it depicts a widely humanistic middle way. Unlike some mystical systems which it superficially resembles, it never loses sight of the distinction between moral good and evil. Its most striking characteristic is that the salvation which it offers does not require a supreme deity. It rather pessimistically accepts the fact of man's subjection to endless transmigrations (an idea adopted from Hinduism) unless he can free himself by the exercise of the discipline that leads to the bliss of Nirvana.

Ten of the twenty-six chapters of the *Dhammapada* are reproduced below.

ﺑﺴﻤﻠﺔ

CHAPTER XI

OLD AGE

How is there laughter, how is there joy, as this world is always burning? Do you not seek a light, ye who are surrounded by darkness?

Look at this dressed-up lump, covered with wounds, joined together, sickly, full of many schemes, but which has no strength, no hold!

This body is wasted, full of sickness, and frail; this heap of corruption breaks to pieces, life indeed ends in death.

After one has looked at those gray bones, thrown away like gourds in the autumn, what pleasure is there left in life!

After a stronghold has been made of the bones, it is covered with flesh and blood, and there dwell in it old age and death, pride and deceit.

The brilliant chariots of kings are destroyed, the body also approaches destruction, but the virtue of good people never approaches destruction—thus do the good say to the good.

A man who has learnt little, grows old like an ox; his flesh grows, but his knowledge does not grow.

Looking for the maker of this tabernacle, I have run through a course of many births, not finding him; and painful is birth again and again. But now, maker of the tabernacle, thou hast been seen; thou shalt not make up this tabernacle again. All thy rafters are broken, thy ridge-pole is sundered; the mind, approaching the Eternal (Visankhâra, Nirvâna), has attained to the extinction of all desires.

Men who have not observed proper discipline, and have not gained wealth in their youth, perish like old herons in a lake without fish.

Men who have not observed proper discipline, and have not gained wealth in their youth, lie, like broken bows, sighing after the past.

CHAPTER XII

SELF

If a man hold himself dear, let him watch himself carefully; during one at least out of the three watches a wise man should be watchful.

Let each man direct himself first to what is proper, then let him teach others; thus a wise man will not suffer.

If a man make himself as he teaches others to be, then, being himself well subdued, he may subdue others; for one's own self is difficult to subdue.

Self is the lord of self, who else could be the lord? With self well subdued, a man finds a lord such as few can find.

The evil done by one's self, self-forgotten, self-bred, crushes the foolish, as a diamond breaks even a precious stone.

He whose wickedness is very great brings himself down to that state where his enemy wishes him to be, as a creeper does with the tree which it surrounds.

Bad deeds, and deeds hurtful to ourselves, are easy to do; what is beneficial and good, that is very difficult to do.

The foolish man who scorns the rule of the venerable (Arhat), of the elect (Ariya), of the virtuous, and follows a false doctrine, he bears fruit to his own destruction, like the fruits of the Katthaka reed.

By one's self the evil is done, by one's self one suffers; by one's self evil is left undone, by one's self one is purified. The pure and the impure stand and fall by themselves, no one can purify another.

Let no one forget his own duty for the sake of another's, however great; let a man, after he has discerned his own duty, be always attentive to his duty.

CHAPTER XIII

THE WORLD

Do not follow the evil law! Do not live on in thoughtlessness! Do not follow false doctrine! Be not a friend of the world.

Rouse thyself! do not be idle! Follow the law of virtue! The virtuous rest in bliss in this world and in the next.

Follow the law of virtue; do not follow that of sin. The virtuous rest in bliss in this world and in the next.

Look upon the world as you would on a bubble, look upon it as you would on a mirage: the king of death does not see him who thus looks down upon the world.

Come, look at this world, glittering like a royal chariot; the foolish are immersed in it, but the wise do not touch it.

He who formerly was reckless and afterwards became sober brightens up this world, like the moon when freed from clouds.

He whose evil deeds are covered by good deeds, brightens up this world, like the moon when freed from clouds.

This world is dark, few only can see here; a few only go to heaven, like birds escaped from the net.

The swans go on the path of the sun, they go miraculously through the ether; the wise are led out of this world, when they have conquered Mâra and his train.

If a man has transgressed the one law, and speaks lies, and scoffs at another world, there is no evil he will not do.

The uncharitable do not go to the world of the gods; fools only do not praise liberality; a wise man rejoices in liberality, and through it becomes blessed in the other world.

Better than sovereignty over the earth, better than going to heaven, better than lordship over all worlds, is the reward of Sotâpatti, the first step in holiness.

CHAPTER XIV

THE BUDDHA—THE AWAKENED

He whose conquest cannot be conquered again, into whose conquest no one in this world enters, by what track can you lead him, the Awakened, the Omniscient, the trackless?

He whom no desire with its snares and poisons can lead astray, by what track can you lead him, the Awakened, the Omniscient, the trackless?

Even the gods envy those who are awakened and not forgetful, who are given to meditation, who are wise, and who delight in the repose of retirement from the world.

Difficult to obtain is the conception of men, difficult is the life of mortals, difficult is the hearing of the True Law, difficult is the birth of the Awakened (the attainment of Buddhahood).

Not to commit any sin, to do good, and to purify one's mind, that is the teaching of all the Awakened.

The Awakened call patience the highest penance, long-suffering the highest Nirvâna; for he is not an anchorite (Pravragita) who strikes others, he is not an ascetic (Sramana) who insults others.

Not to blame, not to strike, to live restrained under the law, to be moderate in eating, to sleep and sit alone, and to dwell on the highest thoughts—this is the teaching of the Awakened.

There is no satisfying lusts, even by a shower of gold pieces; he who knows that lusts have a short taste and cause pain, he is wise; even in heavenly pleasures he finds no satisfaction, the disciple who is fully awakened delights only in the destruction of all desires.

Men, driven by fear, go to many a refuge, to mountains and forests, to groves and sacred trees.

But that is not a safe refuge, that is not the best refuge; a man is not delivered from all pains after having gone to that refuge.

He who takes refuge with Buddha, the Law, and the Church; he who, with clear understanding, sees the four holy truths: pain, the origin of pain, the destruction of pain, and the eightfold holy way that leads to the quieting of pain;—that is the safe refuge, that is the best refuge; having gone to that refuge, a man is delivered from all pain.

A supernatural person (a Buddha) is not easily found: he is not born everywhere. Wherever such a sage is born, that race prospers.

Happy is the arising of the Awakened, happy is the teaching of the True Law, happy is peace in the church, happy is the devotion of those who are at peace.

He who pays homage to those who deserve homage, whether the awakened (Buddha) or their disciples, those who have overcome the host of evils, and crossed the flood of sorrow, he who pays homage to such as have found deliverance and know no fear, his merit can never be measured by anyone.

CHAPTER XV

HAPPINESS

We live happily indeed, not hating those who hate us! among men who hate us we dwell free from hatred!

We live happily indeed, free from ailments among the ailing! among men who are ailing let us dwell free from ailments!

We live happily indeed, free from greed among the greedy! among men who are greedy let us dwell free from greed!

We live happily indeed, though we call nothing our own! We shall be like the bright gods, feeding on happiness!

Victory breeds hatred, for the conquered is unhappy. He who has given up both victory and defeat, he, the contented, is happy.

There is no fire like passion; there is no losing throw like hatred; there is no pain like this body; there is no happiness higher than rest.

Hunger is the worst of diseases, the elements of the body the greatest evil; if one knows this truly, that is Nirvâna, the highest happiness.

Health is the greatest of gifts, contentedness the best riches; trust is the best of relationships, Nirvâna the highest happiness.

He who has tasted the sweetness of solitude and tranquillity is free from fear and free from sin, while he tastes the sweetness of drinking in the law.

The sight of the elect (Ariya) is good, to live with them is always happiness; if a man does not see fools, he will be truly happy.

He who walks in the company of fools suffers a long way; company with fools, as with an enemy, is always painful; company with the wise is pleasure, like meeting with kinsfolk.

Therefore, one ought to follow the wise, the intelligent, the learned, the much enduring, the dutiful, the elect; one ought to follow such a good and wise man, as the moon follows the path of the stars.

CHAPTER XVI

PLEASURE

He who gives himself to vanity, and does not give himself to meditation, forgetting the real aim of life and grasping at pleasure, will in time envy him who has exerted himself in meditation.

Let no man ever cling to what is pleasant, or to what is unpleasant. Not to see what is pleasant is pain, and it is pain to see what is unpleasant.

Let, therefore, no man love anything; loss of the beloved is evil. Those who love nothing, and hate nothing, have no fetters.

From pleasure comes grief, from pleasure comes fear; he who is free from pleasure knows neither grief nor fear.

From affection comes grief, from affection comes fear; he who is free from affection knows neither grief nor fear.

From lust comes grief, from lust comes fear; he who is free from love knows neither grief nor fear.

From love comes grief, from love comes fear; he who is free from love knows neither grief nor fear.

From greed comes grief, from greed comes fear; he who is free from greed knows neither grief nor fear.

He who possesses virtue and intelligence, who is just, speaks the truth, and does what is his own business, him the world will hold dear.

He in whom a desire for the Ineffable (Nirvâna) has sprung up, who in his mind is satisfied, and whose thoughts are not bewildered by love, he is called ûrdhvamsrotas (carried upwards by the stream).

Kinsmen, friends, and lovers salute a man who has been long away, and returns safe from afar.

In like manner his good works receive him who has done good, and has gone from this world to the other;—as kinsmen receive a friend on his return.

CHAPTER XX

THE WAY

The best of ways is the eightfold; the best of truths the four words; the best of virtues passionlessness; the best of men he who has eyes to see.

This is the way, there is no other that leads to the purifying of intelligence. Go on this path! This is the confusion of Mâra, the tempter.

If you go on this way, you will make an end of pain! The way preached by me, when I had understood the removal of the thorns in the flesh.

You yourself must make an effort. The Tathâgatas (Buddhas) are only preachers. The thoughtful who enter the way are freed from the bondage of Mâra.

"All created things perish," he who knows and sees this becomes passive in pain; this is the way to purity.

"All created things are grief and pain," he who knows and sees this becomes passive in pain; this is the way that leads to purity.

"All forms are unreal," he who knows and sees this becomes passive in pain; this is the way that leads to purity.

He who does not rouse himself when it is time to rise, who, though young and strong, is full of sloth, whose will and thought are weak, that lazy and idle man never finds the way to knowledge.

Watching his speech, well restrained in mind, let a man never commit any wrong with his body! Let a man but keep these three roads of action clear, and he will achieve the way which is taught by the wise.

Through zeal knowledge is gained, through lack of zeal knowledge is lost; let a man who knows this double path of gain and loss thus place himself that knowledge may grow.

Cut down the whole forest of desires, not a tree only! Danger comes out of the forest of desires. When you have cut down both the forest of desires and its undergrowth, then, Bhikshus,[36] you will be rid of the forest and of desires!

So long as the desire of man towards women, even the smallest, is not destroyed, so long is his mind in bondage, as the calf that drinks milk is to its mother.

Cut out the love of self, like an autumn lotus, with thy hand! Cherish the road of peace. Nirvâna has been shown by Sugata (Buddha).

"Here I shall dwell in the rain, here in winter and summer," thus the fool meditates, and does not think of death.

Death comes and carries off that man, honored for his children and flocks, his mind distracted, as a flood carries off a sleeping village.

Sons are no help, nor a father, nor relations; there is no help from kinsfolk for one whom death has seized.

A wise and well-behaved man who knows the meaning of this should quickly clear the way that leads to Nirvâna.

CHAPTER XXIII

THE ELEPHANT

Silently I endured abuse as the elephant in battle endures the arrow sent from the bow: for the world is ill-natured.

They lead a tamed elephant to battle, the king mounts a

36 Bhikshus—mendicants. [Ed.]

tamed elephant; the tamed is the best among men, he who silently endures abuse.

Mules are good, if tamed, and noble Sindhu horses, and elephants with large tusks; but he who tames himself is better still.

For with these animals does no man reach the untrodden country (Nirvâna), where a tamed man goes on a tamed animal—on his own well-tamed self.

The elephant called Dhanapâlaka, his temples running with pungent sap, and who is difficult to hold, does not eat a morsel when bound; the elephant longs for the elephant grove.

If a man becomes fat and a great eater, if he is sleepy and rolls himself about, that fool, like a hog fed on grains, is born again and again.

This mind of mine went formerly wandering about as it liked, as it listed, as it pleased; but I shall now hold it in thoroughly, as the rider who holds the hook holds in the furious elephant.

Be not thoughtless, watch your thoughts! Draw yourself out of the evil way, like an elephant sunk in mud.

If a man find a prudent companion who walks with him, is wise, and lives soberly, he may walk with him, overcoming all dangers, happy, but considerate.

If a man find no prudent companion who walks with him, is wise, and lives soberly, let him walk alone, like a king who has left his conquered country behind—like an elephant in the forest.

It is better to live alone: there is no companionship with a fool; let a man walk alone, let him commit no sin, with few wishes, like an elephant in the forest.

If the occasion arises, friends are pleasant; enjoyment is pleasant, whatever be the cause; a good work is pleasant in the hour of death; the giving up of all grief is pleasant.

Pleasant in the world is the state of a mother, pleasant the state of a father, pleasant the state of a Samana, pleasant the state of a Brâhmana.[37]

Pleasant is virtue lasting to old age, pleasant is a faith firmly rooted; pleasant is attainment of intelligence, pleasant is avoiding of sins.

---

[37] Samana—ascetic; Brâhmana—member of the priestly caste. [Ed.]

CHAPTER XXIV.

THIRST

The thirst of a thoughtless man grows like a creeper; he runs from life to life, like a monkey seeking fruit in the forest.

Whomsoever this fierce poisonous thirst overcomes, in this world, his sufferings increase like the abounding Bîrana grass.

But from him who overcomes this fierce thirst, difficult to be conquered in this world, sufferings fall off, like water-drops from a lotus leaf.

This salutary word I tell you, "Do ye, as many as are here assembled, dig up the root of thirst, as he who wants the sweet-scented Usîra root must dig up the Bîrana grass, that Mâra, the tempter, may not crush you again and again, as the stream crushes the reeds."

As a tree, even though it has been cut down, is firm so long as its root is safe, and grows again, thus, unless the feeders of thirst are destroyed, this pain of life will return again and again.

He whose thirty-six streams are strongly flowing in the channels of pleasure, the waves—his desires which are set on passion—will carry away that misguided man.

The channels run everywhere, the creeper of passion stands sprouting; if you see the creeper springing up, cut its root by means of knowledge.

A creature's pleasures are extravagant and luxurious; given up to pleasure and deriving happiness, men undergo again and again birth and decay.

Beset with lust, men run about like a snared hare; held in fetters and bonds, they undergo pain for a long time, again and again.

Beset with lust, men run about like a snared hare; let therefore the mendicant drive out thirst, by striving after passionlessness for himself.

He who, having got rid of the forest of lust (after having reached Nirvâna), gives himself over to forest-life (to lust), and who, when free from the forest (from lust), runs to the forest (to lust), look at that man! though free, he runs into bondage.

Wise people do not call that a strong fetter which is made of iron, wood, or hemp; passionately strong is the care for precious stones and rings, for sons and a wife.

That fetter wise people call strong which drags down, yields, but is difficult to undo; after having cut this at last, people leave the world, free from cares, and leaving the pleasures of love behind.

384

Those who are slaves to passions, run down the stream of desires, as a spider runs down the web which he has made himself; when they have cut this, at last, wise people go onwards, free from cares, leaving all pain behind.

Give up what is before, give up what is behind, give up what is between, when thou goest to the other shore of existence; if thy mind is altogether free, thou wilt not again enter into birth and decay.

If a man is tossed about by doubts, full of strong passions, and yearning only for what is delightful, his thirst will grow more and more, and he will indeed make his fetters strong.

If a man delights in quieting doubts, and, always reflecting, dwells on what is not delightful, he certainly will remove, nay, he will cut the fetter of Mâra.

He who has reached the consummation, who does not tremble, who is without thirst and without sin, he has broken all the thorns of life: this will be his last body.

He who is without thirst and without affection, who understands the words and their interpretation, who knows the order of letters (those which are before and which are after), he has received his last body, he is called the great sage, the great man.

"I have conquered all, I know all, in all conditions of life I am free from taint; I have left all, and through the destruction of thirst I am free; having learnt myself, whom should I indicate as my teacher?"

The gift of the law exceeds all gifts; the sweetness of the law exceeds all sweetness; the delight in the law exceeds all delights; the extinction of thirst overcomes all pain.

Riches destroy the foolish, if they look not for the other shore; the foolish by his thirst for riches destroys himself, as if he were destroying others.

The fields are damaged by weeds, mankind is damaged by passion: therefore a gift bestowed on the passionless brings great reward.

The fields are damaged by weeds, mankind is damaged by hatred: therefore a gift bestowed on those who do not hate brings great reward.

The fields are damaged by weeds, mankind is damaged by vanity: therefore a gift bestowed on those who are free from vanity brings great reward.

The fields are damaged by weeds, mankind is damaged by lust: therefore a gift bestowed on those who are free from lust brings great reward.

CHAPTER XXVI

THE BRÂHMANA

Stop the stream valiantly, drive away the desires, O Brâhmana! When you have understood the destruction of all that was made, you will understand that which was not made.

If the Brâhmana has reached the other shore in both laws, in restraint and contemplation, all bonds vanish from him who has obtained knowledge.

He for whom there is neither the hither nor the further shore, nor both, him, the fearless and unshackled, I call indeed a Brâhmana.

He who is thoughtful, blameless, settled, dutiful, without passions, and who has attained the highest end, him I call indeed a Brâhmana.

The sun is bright by day, the moon shines by night, the warrior is bright in his armor, the Brâhmana is bright in his meditation; but Buddha, the Awakened, is bright with splendor day and night.

Because a man is rid of evil, therefore he is called Brâhmana; because he walks quietly, therefore he is called Samana; because he has sent away his own impurities, therefore he is called Pravragita (Pabbagita, a pilgrim).

No one should attack a Brâhmana, but no Brâhmana, if attacked, should let himself fly at his aggressor! Woe to him who strikes a Brâhmana, more woe to him who flies at his aggressor!

It advantages a Brâhmana not a little if he holds his mind back from the pleasures of life; the more all wish to injure has vanished, the more all pain will cease.

Him I call indeed a Brâhmana who does not offend by body, word, or thought, and is controlled on these three points.

He from whom he may learn the law, as taught by the Well-awakened (Buddha), him let him worship assiduously, as the Brâhmana worships the sacrificial fire.

A man does not become a Brâhmana by his plaited hair, by his family, or by birth; in whom there is truth and righteousness, he is blessed, he is a Brâhmana.

What is the use of plaited hair, O fool! what of the raiment of goat-skins? Within thee there is ravening, but the outside thou makest clean.

The man who wears dirty raiments, who is emaciated and covered with veins, who meditates alone in the forest, him I call indeed a Brâhmana.

I do not call a man a Brâhmana because of his origin or of his mother. He is indeed arrogant, and he is wealthy: but the poor, who is free from all attachments, him I call indeed a Brâhmana.

Him I call indeed a Brâhmana who, after cutting all fetters, never trembles, is free from bonds and unshackled.

Him I call indeed a Brâhmana who, after cutting the strap and the thong, the rope with all that pertains to it, has destroyed all obstacles, and is awakened.

Him I call indeed a Brâhmana who, though he has committed no offence, endures reproach, stripes, and bonds: who has endurance for his force, and strength for his army.

Him I call indeed a Brâhmana who is free from anger, dutiful, virtuous, without appetites, who is subdued, and has received his last body.

Him I call indeed a Brâhmana who does not cling to sensual pleasures, like water on a lotus leaf, like a mustard seed on the point of a needle.

Him I call indeed a Brâhmana who, even here, knows the end of his own suffering, has put down his burden, and is unshackled.

Him I call indeed a Brâhmana whose knowledge is deep, who possesses wisdom, who knows the right way and the wrong, and has attained the highest end.

Him I call indeed a Brâhmana who keeps aloof both from laymen and from mendicants, who frequents no houses, and has but few desires.

Him I call indeed a Brâhmana who without hurting any creatures, whether feeble or strong, does not kill nor cause slaughter.

Him I call indeed a Brâhmana who is tolerant with the intolerant, mild with the violent, and free from greed among the greedy.

Him I call indeed a Brâhmana from whom anger and hatred, pride and hypocrisy have dropped like a mustard seed from the point of a needle.

Him I call indeed a Brâhmana who utters true speech, instructive and free from harshness, so that he offend no one.

Him I call indeed a Brâhmana who takes nothing in the world that is not given him, be it long or short, small or large, good or bad.

Him I call indeed a Brâhmana who fosters no desires for this world or for the next, has no inclinations, and is unshackled.

Him I call indeed a Brâhmana who has no interests, and when he has understood the truth, does not say How, how? and who has reached the depth of the Immortal.

Him I call indeed a Brâhmana who in this world has risen above both ties, good and evil, who is free from grief, from sin, and from impurity.

Him I call indeed a Brâhmana who is bright like the moon, pure, serene, undisturbed, and in whom all gayety is extinct.

Him I call indeed a Brâhmana who has traversed this miry road, the impassable world, difficult to pass, and its vanity, who has gone through, and reached the other shore, is thoughtful, steadfast, free from doubts, free from attachment, and content.

Him I call indeed a Brâhmana who in this world, having abandoned all desires, travels about without a home, and in whom all concupiscence is extinct.

Him I call indeed a Brâhmana who, having abandoned all longings, travels about without a home, and in whom all covetousness is extinct.

Him I call indeed a Brâhmana who, after leaving all bondage to men, has risen above all bondage to the gods, and is free from all and every bondage.

Him I call indeed a Brâhmana who has left what gives pleasure and what gives pain, who is cold, and free from all germs of renewed life: the hero who has conquered all the worlds.

Him I call indeed a Brâhmana who knows the destruction and the return of beings everywhere, who is free from bondage, welfaring (Sugata), and awakened (Buddha).

Him I call indeed a Brâhmana whose path the gods do not know, nor spirits (Gandharvas), nor men, whose passions are extinct, and who is an Arhat.[38]

Him I call indeed a Brâhmana who calls nothing his own, whether it be before, behind, or between; who is poor, and free from the love of the world.

Him I call indeed a Brâhmana, the manly, the noble, the hero, the great sage, the conqueror, the indifferent, the accomplished, the awakened.

Him I call indeed a Brâhmana who knows his former abodes, who sees heaven and hell, has reached the end of births, is perfect in knowledge, a sage, and whose perfections are all perfect.

[38] Arhat—one who has gone through the required discipline. [Ed.]

V Islamic

FROM The *Koran*

[7TH CENTURY A.D.]

TRANSLATED BY
MOHAMMED MARMADUKE PICKTHALL [1875-1936]

Iᐱᗢᓚᑍᗢᑎᕳᘔᐱ

Until about a century ago, there was little disposition in the West to regard the *Koran* as anything but the work of an impostor. When Carlyle pointed out how unlikely it was that more than 300 million people would follow the religion of an impostor, it began to appear that the book of the Prophet must be an important document in the history of religion. Its subsequent sympathetic study by scholars of the West as well as the East has indeed enhanced its status as scripture. But as a work of literature it still labors under a great disadvantage because it is inevitably brought into comparison with the scriptures of the other great Semitic religions of the world.

This is of course understandable in view of the fact that a considerable part of the *Koran* is derived from the Hebrew-Christian Bible. But in its inception the *Koran* was an original revelation which sought to replace the polytheism of the peninsular Arabs with a monotheistic faith. Mohammed's acquaintance with the People of the Book, as he referred to Christians and Jews, was, at first, slight and based on chance contacts rather than on any study of their writings. In the course of the enunciation of his creed, however, he had more and more to do with these peoples. As his knowledge of their religion grew, their influence upon his own teachings was increased, and he adapted various aspects of Jewish and Christian religion to his own purposes. Both Satan and the angels were appropriated into his theology; fasts, prayers, dietary laws, and other social legislation were borrowed in varying degrees and with modifications. And most important, many Old and New Testament narratives were assimilated into the *Koran*. This process of absorption of Judaic-Christian materials transformed many stories familiar and dear to readers of the Bible. Apart from an obvious error such as the confusion of Mary, the mother of Jesus, with Miriam, mother of Moses, there was a new light cast upon most of the Biblical characters. A case in point is the story of Joseph and his brothers. Its familiar parts were retained in the Koranic version, but of far greater interest are the additions, which are characteristically Islamic. The Bible reader must learn to look at these differences with tolerant eyes. The hero Joseph has become a sort of Adonis, and the very archetype of young manhood and beauty. This necessarily throws into higher relief the episode of Joseph and Potiphar's wife. This passionate love story has had a tremendous appeal to the imagination of Moslem poets. Thomas Mann's magnificent retelling in our own day owes much to their inspiration, which Mann rightly perceived as the creation—or rather re-creation—of one of the oldest myths of the world.

A certain roughness of continuity perhaps more than anything else militates against the ready acceptance of *Koran* stories by Bible readers. This is explainable by the composition of the various *surahs* or chapters. They are not organic units, but were pieced together from revelations made at various times and perhaps recorded by different hands. For the *Koran* was revealed to Mohammed in the quiet hours of midnight meditation by a process that might be compared to Wordsworth's emotion recollected in tranquillity. These depositions of the revelation, directly from God and through the archangel Gabriel, were recorded on palm leaves, pieces of leather, stones, and bones of animals, or kept in "the breasts of men," from the time of their first utterance by Mohammed (from about A.D. 610 to 630) until an authorized rescension of the *Koran* was ordered by Abu Bekr, the first successor or Caliph.

Although this task was undertaken by one of Mohammed's secretaries, Zaid bin Thabit, the credit for the composition of the *Koran* is given by most scholars to Mohammed himself. This unquestionably inspired though on the whole moderate man, without benefit of learning or possibly even literacy, was about forty years old when the Call came to him to found the new faith. Although he was eager to avoid the charge of being a soothsayer or *kahin*—so much so that he reviled even poets—Mohammed's utterances are couched in the rhymed prose or *saj'* used by the soothsayers. Most of the oracular verses of his Book are presumed to be the words of Allah speaking either to Mohammed or to the Arab people. Occasionally, God speaks in the third person; more often in the first person plural. In one or two instances, the speaker is apparently Gabriel.

With the exception of the opening verses, the surahs are usually arranged in a descending order of length. The earlier and longer ones belong mainly to later revelation, when Mohammed was at Medina, following the Hegira or flight in A.D. 622. The shorter, more poetic surahs contain the earlier or Meccan revelations. The following excerpts are from a notable translation of the *Koran* by an English Moslem who brings to the task an appropriate spirit of reverence as well as scholarly qualifications.

ﺑﺴﻢﺍﻟﻠﻪ

SÛRAH I

TRANSLATOR'S NOTE: I have retained the word Allah throughout, because there is no corresponding word in English. The word *Allâh* (the stress is on the last syllable) has neither feminine nor plural, and has never been applied to anything other than the unimaginable Supreme Being. I use the word "God" only where the corresponding word *ilâh* is found in the Arabic.

The words in parentheses are interpolated to explain the meaning.

THE OPENING

Revealed at Mecca

In the name of Allah, the Beneficent, the Merciful.

1. Praise be to Allah, Lord of the Worlds,
2. The Beneficent, the Merciful.
3. Owner of the Day of Judgment,
4. Thee (alone) we worship; Thee (alone) we ask for help.
5. Show us the straight path,
6. The path of those whom Thou hast favoured;
7. Not (the path) of those who earn Thine anger nor of those who go astray.

SÛRAH XII

Yûsuf takes its name from its subject which is the life-story of Joseph. It differs from all other Sûrahs in having only one subject. The differences from the Bible narrative are striking. Jacob is here a Prophet, who is not deceived by the story of his son's death, but is distressed because, through a suspension of his clairvoyance, he cannot see what has become of Joseph. The real importance of the narrative, its psychic burden, is emphasized throughout, and the manner of narration, though astonishing to Western readers, is vivid.

Tradition says that it was recited by the Prophet at Mecca to the first converts from Yathrib (Al-Madînah), *i.e.* in the second year before the Hijrah; but that, as Nöldeke points out, does not mean that it was not revealed till then, but that it had been revealed by then.

A late Meccan Sûrah.

JOSEPH

Revealed at Mecca

In the name of Allah, the Beneficent, the Merciful.

1. Alif. Lâm. Râ.[39] These are verses of the Scripture that maketh plain.
2. Lo! We have revealed it, a Lecture [40] in Arabic, that ye may understand.
3. We narrate unto thee (Muhammad) the best of narratives in that We have inspired in thee this Qur'ân, though aforetime thou wast of the heedless.
4. When Joseph said unto his father: O my father! Lo! I

[39] Unexplained Arabic letters appear before the surahs. [Ed.]
[40] Ar. *Qur'ân.*

saw in a dream eleven planets and the sun and the moon,
I saw them prostrating themselves unto me.

5. He said: O my dear son! Tell not thy brethren of thy
vision, lest they plot a plot against thee. Lo! Satan is for
man an open foe.

6. Thus thy Lord will prefer thee and will teach thee the
interpretation of events, and will perfect his grace upon thee
and upon the family of Jacob as he perfected it upon thy
forefathers, Abraham and Isaac. Lo! thy Lord is Knower,
Wise.

7. Verily in Joseph and his brethren are signs (of Allah's
Sovereignty) for the inquiring.

8. When they said: Verily Joseph and his brother are
dearer to our father than we are, many though we be. Lo!
our father is in plain aberration.

9. (One said): Kill Joseph or cast him to some (other)
land, so that your father's favor may be all for you, and
(that) ye may afterward be righteous folk.

10. One among them said: Kill not Joseph but, if ye must
be doing, fling him into the depth of the pit; some caravan
will find him.

11. They said: O our father! Why wilt thou not trust us
with Joseph, when lo! we are good friends to him?

12. Send him with us to-morrow that he may enjoy himself and play. And lo! we shall take good care of him.

13. He said: Lo! in truth it saddens me that ye should
take him with you, and I fear lest the wolf devour him
while ye are heedless of him.

14. They said: If the wolf should devour him when we
are (so strong) a band, then surely we should have already
perished.

15. Then, when they led him off, and were of one mind
that they should place him in the depth of the pit, We inspired in him: Thou wilt tell them of this deed of theirs when
they know (thee) not.

16. And they came weeping to their father in the evening.

17. Saying: O our father! We went racing one with another, and left Joseph by our things, and the wolf devoured
him, and thou believest not our sayings even when we speak
the truth.

18. And they came with false blood on his shirt. He said:
Nay, but your minds have beguiled you into something. (My
course is) comely patience. And Allah it is whose help is
to be sought in that (predicament) which ye describe.

19. And there came a caravan, and they sent their water-
drawer. He let down his pail (into the pit). He said: Good
luck! Here is a youth. And they hid him as a treasure, and
Allah was Aware of what they did.

20. And they sold him for a low price, a number of silver coins; and they attached no value to him.

21. And he of Egypt who purchased him said unto his wife: Receive him honorably. Perchance he may prove useful to us or we may adopt him as a son. Thus We established Joseph in the land that We might teach him the interpretation of events. And Allah was predominant in his career, but most of mankind know not.

22. And when he reached his prime We gave him wisdom and knowledge. Thus We reward the good.

23. And she, in whose house he was, asked of him an evil act. She bolted the doors and said: Come! He said: I seek refuge in Allah! Lo! he is my lord, who hath treated me honourably. Wrong-doers never prosper.

24. She verily desired him, and he would have desired her if it had not been that he saw the argument of his lord. Thus it was, that We might ward off from him evil and lewdness. Lo! he was of Our chosen slaves.

25. And they raced with one another to the door, and she tore his shirt from behind, and they met her lord and master at the door. She said: What shall be his reward, who wisheth evil to thy folk, save prison or a painful doom?

26. (Joseph) said: She it was who asked of me an evil act. And a witness of her own folk testified: If his shirt is torn from before, then she speaketh truth and he is of the liars.

27. And if his shirt is torn from behind, then she hath lied and he is of the truthful.

28. So when he saw his shirt torn from behind, he said: Lo! this is of the guile of you women. Lo! the guile of you is very great.

29. O Joseph! Turn away from this, and thou (O woman), ask forgiveness for thy sin. Lo! thou art of the sinful.

30. And women in the city said: The ruler's wife is asking of her slave-boy an ill deed. Indeed he has smitten her to the heart with love. We behold her in plain aberration.

31. And when she heard of their sly talk, she sent to them and prepared for them a cushioned couch (to lie on at the feast) and gave to every one of them a knife and said (to Joseph): Come out unto them! And when they saw him they exalted him and cut their hands, exclaiming: Allah Blameless! This is not a human being. This is no other than some gracious angel.

32. She said: This is he on whose account ye blamed me. I asked of him an evil act, but he proved continent, but if he do not my behest he verily shall be imprisoned, and verily shall be of those brought low.

33. He said: O my Lord! Prison is more dear than that unto which they urge me, and if Thou fend not off their

wiles from me I shall incline unto them and become of the foolish.

34. So his Lord heard his prayer and fended off their wiles from him. Lo! He is Hearer, Knower.

35. And it seemed good to them (the men-folk) after they had seen the signs (of his innocence) to imprison him for a time.

36. And two young men went to prison with him. One of them said: I dreamed that I was pressing wine. The other said: I dreamed that I was carrying upon my head bread whereof the birds were eating. Announce unto us the interpretation, for we see thee of those good (at interpretation.)

37. He said: The food which ye are given (daily) shall not come unto you but I shall tell you the interpretation ere it cometh unto you. This is of that which my Lord hath taught me. Lo! I have forsaken the religion of folk who believe not in Allah and are disbelievers in the Hereafter.

38. And I have followed the religion of my fathers, Abraham and Isaac and Jacob. It never was for us to attribute aught as partner to Allah. This is of the bounty of Allah unto us (the seed of Abraham) and unto mankind; but most men give not thanks.

39. O my two fellow-prisoners! Are divers lords better, or Allah the One, the Almighty?

40. Those whom ye worship beside Him are but names which ye have named, ye and your fathers. Allah hath revealed no sanction for them. The decision rests with Allah only, Who hath commanded you that ye worship none save Him. This is the right religion, but most men know not.

41. O my two fellow-prisoners! As for one of you, he will pour out wine for his lord to drink; and as for the other, he will be crucified so that the birds will eat from his head. Thus is the case judged concerning which ye did inquire.

42. And he said unto him of the twain who he knew would be released: Mention me in the presence of thy lord. But Satan caused him to forget to mention it to his lord, so he (Joseph) stayed in prison for some years.

43. And the king said: Lo! I saw in a dream seven fat kine which seven lean were eating, and seven green ears of corn and other (seven) dry. O notables! Expound for me my vision, if ye can interpret dreams.

44. They answered: Jumbled dreams! And we are not knowing in the interpretation of dreams.

45. And he of the two who was released, and (now) at length remembering, said: I am going to announce unto you the interpretation, therefore send me forth.

46. (And when he came to Joseph in the prison, he exclaimed): Joseph! O thou truthful one! Expound for us the seven fat kine which seven lean were eating and the seven green ears of corn and other (seven) dry, that I may return unto the people, so that they may know.

47. He said: Ye shall sow seven years as usual, but that which ye reap, leave it in the ear, all save a little which ye eat.

48. Then after that will come seven hard years which will devour all that ye have prepared for them, save a little of that which ye have stored.

49. Then, after that, will come a year when the people will have plenteous crops and when they will press (wine and oil).

50. And the king said: Bring him unto me. And when the messenger came unto him, he (Joseph) said: Return unto thy lord and ask him what was the case of the women who cut their hands. Lo! my lord knoweth their guile.

51. He (the king) (then sent for those women and) said: What happened when ye asked an evil act of Joseph? They answered: Allah Blameless! We know no evil of him. Said the wife of the ruler: Now the truth is out. I asked of him an evil act, and he is surely of the truthful.

52. (Then Joseph said: I asked for) this, that he (my lord) may know that I betrayed him not in secret, and that surely Allah guideth not the snare of the betrayers.

53. I do not exculpate myself. Lo! the (human) soul enjoineth unto evil, save that whereon my Lord hath mercy. Lo! my Lord is Forgiving, Merciful.

54. And the king said: Bring him unto me that I may attach him to my person. And when he had talked with him he said: Lo! thou art to-day in our presence established and trusted.

55. He said: Set me over the storehouses of the land. Lo! I am a skilled custodian.

56. Thus gave We power to Joseph in the land. He was the owner of it where he pleased. We reach with Our mercy whom We will. We lose not the reward of the good.

57. And the reward of the Hereafter is better, for those who believe and ward off (evil).

58. And Joseph's brethren came and presented themselves before him, and he knew them but they knew him not.

59. And when he provided them with their provision he said: Bring unto me a brother of yours from your father. See ye not that I fill up the measure and I am the best of hosts?

60. And if ye bring him not unto me, then there shall be no measure for you with me, nor shall ye draw near.

61. They said: We will try to win him from his father: that we will surely do.

62. He said unto his young men: Place their merchandise in their saddlebags, so that they may know it when they go back to their folk, and so will come again.

63. So when they went back to their father they said: O our father! The measure is denied us, so send with us our brother that we may obtain the measure, surely we will guard him well.

64. He said: Can I entrust him to you save as I entrusted his brother to you aforetime? Allah is better at guarding, and He is the Most Merciful of those who show mercy.

65. And when they opened their belongings they discovered that their merchandise had been returned to them. They said: O our father! What (more) can we ask? Here is our merchandise returned to us. We shall get provision for our folk and guard our brother, and we shall have the extra measure of a camel (load). This (that we bring now) is a light measure.

66. He said: I will not send him with you till ye give me an undertaking in the name of Allah that ye will bring him back to me, unless ye are surrounded. And when they gave him their undertaking he said: Allah is the Warden over what we say.

67. And he said: O my sons! Go not in by one gate; go in by different gates. I can naught avail you as against Allah. Lo! the decision rests with Allah only. In Him do I put my trust, and in Him let all the trusting put their trust.

68. And when they entered in the manner which their father had enjoined, it would have naught availed them as against Allah; it was but a need of Jacob's soul which he thus satisfied; [41] and lo! he was a lord of knowledge because We had taught him; but most of mankind know not.

69. And when they went in before Joseph, he took his brother unto himself, saying: Lo! I, even I, am thy brother, therefore sorrow not for what they did.

70. And when he provided them with their provision, he put the drinking-cup in his brother's saddlebag, and then a crier cried: O camel-riders! Ye are surely thieves!

71. They cried, coming toward them: What is it ye have lost?

72. They said: We have lost the king's cup, and he who bringeth it shall have a camel-load, and I (said Joseph) am answerable for it.

[41] There is a prevalent superstition in the East that the members of a large family ought not to appear all together, for fear of the ill luck that comes from envy in the hearts of others.

73. They said: By Allah, well ye know we came not to do evil in the land, and are no thieves.

74. They said: And what shall be the penalty for it, if ye prove liars?

75. They said: The penalty for it! He in whose bag (the cup) is found, he is the penalty for it. Thus we requite wrongdoers.

76. Then he (Joseph) began the search with their bags before his brother's bag, then he produced it from his brother's bag. Thus did We contrive for Joseph. He could not have taken his brother according to the king's law unless Allah willed. We raise by grades (of mercy) whom We will, and over every lord of knowledge there is one more knowing.

77. They said: If he stealeth, a brother of his stole before. But Joseph kept it secret in his soul and revealed it not unto them. He said (within himself): Ye are in worse case and Allah knoweth best (the truth of) that which ye allege.

78. They said: O ruler of the land; Lo! he hath an aged father, so take one of us instead of him. Lo! we behold thee of those who do kindness.

79. He said: Allah forbid that we should seize save him with whom we found our property; then truly we should be wrongdoers.

80. So, when they despaired of (moving) him, they conferred together apart. The eldest of them said: Know ye not how your father took an undertaking from you in Allah's name and how ye failed in the case of Joseph aforetime? Therefore I shall not go forth from the land until my father giveth leave or Allah judgeth for me. He is the Best of Judges.

81. Return unto your father and say: O our father! Lo! thy son hath stolen. We testify only to that which we know; we are not guardians of the unseen.

82. Ask the township where we were, and the caravan with which we travelled hither. Lo! we speak the truth.

83. (And when they came unto their father and had spoken thus to him) he said: Nay, but your minds have beguiled you into something. (My course is) comely patience! It may be that Allah will bring them all unto me. Lo! He, only He, is the Knower, the Wise.

84. And he turned away from them and said: Alas, my grief for Joseph! And his eyes were whitened with the sorrow that he was suppressing.

85. They said: By Allah, thou wilt never cease remembering Joseph till thy health is ruined or thou art of those who perish!

86. He said: I expose my distress and anguish only unto Allah, and I know from Allah that which ye know not.

87. Go, O my sons, and ascertain concerning Joseph and his brother, and despair not of the Spirit of Allah. Lo! none despaireth of the Spirit of Allah save disbelieving folk.

88. And when they came (again) before him (Joseph) they said: O ruler! Misfortune hath touched us and our folk, and we bring but poor merchandise, so fill for us the measure and be charitable unto us. Lo! Allah will requite the charitable.

89. He said: Know ye what ye did unto Joseph and his brother in your ignorance?

90. They said: Is it indeed thou who art Joseph? He said: I am Joseph and this is my brother. Allah hath shown us favour. Lo! he who wardeth off (evil) and endureth (findeth favour); for verily Allah loseth not the wages of the kindly.

91. They said: By Allah, verily Allah hath preferred thee above us, and we were indeed sinful.

92. He said: Have no fear this day! May Allah forgive you, and He is the Most Merciful of those who show mercy.

93. Go with this shirt of mine and lay it on my father's face, he will become (again) a seer; and come to me with all your folk.

94. When the caravan departed their father had said: Truly I am conscious of the breath of Joseph, though ye call me dotard.

95. (Those around him) said: By Allah, lo! thou art in thine old aberration.

96. Then, when the bearer of glad tidings came, he laid it on his face and he became a seer once more. He said: Said I not unto you that I know from Allah that which ye know not?

97. They said: O our father! Ask forgiveness of our sins for us, for lo! we were sinful.

98. He said: I shall ask forgiveness for you of my Lord. Lo! He is the Forgiving, the Merciful.

99. And when they came in before Joseph, he took his parents unto him, and said: Come into Egypt safe, if Allah will!

100. And he placed his parents on the daïs and they fell down before him prostrate, and he said: O my father! This is the interpretation of my dream of old. My Lord hath made it true, and He hath shown me kindness, since He took me out of the prison and hath brought you from the desert after Satan had made strife between me and my brethren. Lo! my Lord is tender unto whom He will. He is the Knower, the Wise.

101. O my Lord! Thou hast given me (something) of sovereignty and hast taught me (something) of the interpretation of events—Creator of the heavens and the earth! Thou

art my Protecting Friend in the world and the Hereafter. Make me to die submissive (unto Thee), and join me to the righteous.

102. This is of the tidings of the Unseen which We inspire in thee (Muhammad). Thou wast not present with them when they fixed their plan and they were scheming.

103. And though thou try much, most men will not believe.

104. Thou askest them no fee for it. It is naught else than a reminder unto the peoples.

105. How many a portent is there in the heavens and the earth which they pass by with face averted!

106. And most of them believe not in Allah except that they attribute partners (unto Him).

107. Deem they themselves secure from the coming on them of a pall of Allah's punishment, or the coming of the Hour suddenly while they are unaware?

108. Say: This is my Way: I call on Allah with sure knowledge, I and whosoever followeth me—Glory be to Allah!—and I am not of the idolaters.

109. We sent not before thee (any messengers) save men whom We inspired from among the folk of the townships— Have they not travelled in the land and seen the nature of the consequence for those who were before them? And verily the abode of the Hereafter, for those who ward off (evil), is best. Have ye then no sense?—

110. Till, when the messengers despaired and thought that they were denied, then came unto them Our help, and whom We would was saved. And our wrath cannot be warded from the guilty.

111. In their history verily there is a lesson for men of understanding. It is no invented story but a confirmation of the existing (Scripture) and a detailed explanation of everything, and a guidance and a mercy for folk who believe.

SÛRAH XIX

MARY

Revealed at Mecca

In the name of Ollah, the Beneficent, the Merciful.

1. Kâf. Hâ. Yâ. A'în. Sad.

2. A mention of the mercy of thy Lord unto His servant Zachariah.

3. When he cried unto his Lord a cry in secret,

4. Saying: My Lord! Lo! the bones of me wax feeble and my head is shining with grey hair, and I have never been unblest in prayer to Thee, my Lord.

5. Lo! I fear my kinsfolk after me, since my wife is barren. Oh, give me from Thy presence a successor

6. Who shall inherit of me and inherit (also) of the house of Jacob. And make him, my Lord, acceptable (unto Thee).

7. (It was said unto him): O Zachariah! Lo! We bring thee tidings of a son whose name is John; We have given the same name to none before (him).

8. He said: My Lord! How can I have a son when my wife is barren and I have reached infirm old age?

9. HE said: So (it will be). Thy Lord saith: It is easy for Me, even as I created thee before, when thou wast naught.

10. He said: My Lord! Appoint for me some token. HE said: Thy token is that thou, with no bodily defect, shalt not speak unto mankind three nights.

11. Then he came forth unto his people from the sanctuary, and signified to them: Glorify your Lord at break of day and fall of night.

12. (And it was said unto his son): O John! Hold fast the Scripture. And We gave him wisdom when a child.

13. And compassion from Our presence, and purity; and he was devout,

14. And dutiful toward his parents. And he was not arrogant, rebellious.

15. Peace on him the day he was born, and the day he dieth and the day he shall be raised alive!

16. And make mention of Mary in the Scripture, when she had withdrawn from her people to a chamber looking East,

17. And had chosen seclusion from them. Then We sent unto her Our spirit and it assumed for her the likeness of a perfect man.

18. She said: Lo! I seek refuge in the Beneficent One from thee, if thou art God-fearing.

19. He said: I am only a messenger of thy Lord, that I may bestow on thee a faultless son.

20. She said: How can I have a son when no mortal hath touched me, neither have I been unchaste?

21. He said: So (it will be). Thy Lord saith: It is easy for Me. And (it will be) that We may make of him a revelation for mankind and a mercy from Us, and it is a thing ordained.

22. And she conceived him, and she withdrew with him to a far place.

23. And the pangs of childbirth drove her unto the trunk of the palm tree. She said: Oh, would that I had died ere this and had become a thing of naught, forgotten!

24. Then (one) cried unto her from below her, saying: Grieve not! Thy Lord hath placed a rivulet beneath thee,

25. And shake the trunk of the palm tree toward thee, thou wilt cause ripe dates to fall upon thee.

26. So eat and drink and be consoled. And if thou meetest any mortal, say: Lo! I have vowed a fast unto the Beneficent, and may not speak this day to any mortal.

27. Then she brought him to her own folk, carrying him. They said: O Mary! Thou hast come with an amazing thing.

28. Oh sister of Aaron! [42] Thy father was not a wicked man nor was thy mother a harlot.

29. Then she pointed to him. They said: How can we talk to one who is in the cradle, a young boy?

30. He spake: Lo! I am the slave of Allah. He hath given me the Scripture and hath appointed me a Prophet,

31. And hath made me blessed wheresoever I may be, and hath enjoined upon me prayer and alms-giving so long as I remain alive.

32. And (hath made me) dutiful toward her who bore me, and hath not made me arrogant, unblest.

33. Peace on me the day I was born, and the day I die, and the day I shall be raised alive!

34. Such was Jesus, son of Mary: (this is) a statement of the truth concerning which they doubt.

35. It befitteth not (the Majesty of) Allah that He should take unto Himself a son. Glory be to Him! When He decreeth a thing, He saith unto it only: Be! and it is.

36. And lo! Allah is my Lord and your Lord. So serve Him. That is the right path.

37. The sects among them differ: but woe unto the disbelievers from the meeting of an awful Day.

38. See and hear them on the Day they come unto Us! Yet the evil-doers are to-day in error manifest.

39. And warn them of the Day of anguish when the case hath been decided. Now they are in a state of carelessness, and they believe not.

40. Lo! We inherit the earth and all who are thereon, and unto Us they are returned.

41. And make mention (O Muhammad) in the Scripture of Abraham. Lo! he was a saint, a Prophet.

42. When he said unto his father: O my father! Why worshippest thou that which heareth not nor seeth, nor can in aught avail thee?

43. O my father! Lo! there hath come unto me of knowledge that which came not unto thee. So follow me, and I will lead thee on a right path.

[42] Pickthall denies that the Koran anachronistically confuses Mary, mother of Jesus, with Miriam, sister of Moses. [Ed.]

44. O my father! Serve not the devil. Lo! the devil is a rebel unto the Beneficent.

45. O my father! Lo! I fear lest a punishment from the Beneficent overtake thee so that thou become a comrade of the devil.

46. He said: Rejectest thou my gods, O Abraham? If thou cease not, I shall surely stone thee. Depart from me a long while!

47. He said: Peace be unto thee! I shall ask forgiveness of my Lord for thee. Lo! He was ever gracious unto me.

48. I shall withdraw from you and that unto which ye pray beside Allah, and I shall pray unto my Lord. It may be that, in prayer unto my Lord, I shall not be unblest.

49. So, when he had withdrawn from them and that which they were worshipping beside Allah, We gave him Isaac and Jacob. Each of them We made a Prophet.

50. And We gave them of Our mercy, and assigned to them a high and true renown.

51. And make mention in the Scripture of Moses. Lo! he was chosen, and he was a messenger (of Allah), a Prophet.

52. We called him from the right slope of the Mount, and brought him nigh in communion.

53. And We bestowed upon him of Our mercy his brother Aaron, a Prophet (likewise).

54. And make mention in the Scripture of Ishmael. Lo! he was a keeper of his promise, and he was a messenger (of Allah), a Prophet.

55. He enjoined upon his people worship and almsgiving, and was acceptable in the sight of his Lord.

56. And make mention in the Scripture of Idrîs.[43] Lo! he was a saint, a Prophet;

57. And We raised him to high station.

58. These are they unto whom Allah showed favor from among the Prophets, of the seed of Adam and of those whom We carried (in the ship) with Noah, and of the seed of Abraham and Israel, and from among those whom We guided and chose. When the revelations of the Beneficent were recited unto them, they fell down, adoring and weeping.

59. Now there hath succeeded them a later generation who have ruined worship and have followed lusts. But they will meet deception.

60. Save him who shall repent and believe and do right. Such will enter the Garden, and they will not be wronged in aught—

61. Gardens of Eden, which the Beneficent hath promised to His slaves in the Unseen. Lo! His promise is ever sure of fulfilment—

[43] Identified with Enoch.

62. They hear therein no idle talk, but only Peace; and therein they have food for morn and evening.

63. Such is the Garden which We cause the devout among Our bondmen to inherit.

64. We (angels) come not down save by commandment of thy Lord. Unto Him belongeth all that is before us and all that is behind us and all that is between those two, and thy Lord was never forgetful—

65. Lord of the heavens and the earth and all that is between them! Therefor, worship thou Him and be thou steadfast in His service. Knowest thou one that can be named along with Him?

66. And man saith: When I am dead, shall I forsooth be brought forth alive?

67. Doth not man remember that We created him before, when he was naught?

68. And, by thy Lord, verily We shall assemble them and the devils, then We shall bring them, crouching, around hell.

69. Then We shall pluck out from every sect whichever of them was most stubborn in rebellion to the Beneficent.

70. And surely We are best aware of those most worthy to be burned therein.

71. There is not one of you but shall approach it. That is a fixed ordinance of thy Lord.

72. Then We shall rescue those who kept from evil, and leave the evil-doers crouching there.

73. And when Our clear revelations are recited unto them, those who disbelieve say unto those who believe: Which of the two parties (yours or ours) is better in position, and more imposing as an army?

74. How many a generation have We destroyed before them, who were more imposing in respect of gear and outward seeming!

75. Say: As for him who is in error, the Beneficent will verily prolong his span of life until, when they behold that which they were promised, whether it be punishment (in the world), or the Hour (of Doom), they will know who is worse in position and who is weaker as an army.

76. Allah increaseth in right guidance those who walk aright, and the good deeds which endure are better in thy Lord's sight for reward, and better for resort.

77. Hast thou seen him who disbelieveth in Our revelations and saith: Assuredly I shall be given wealth and children?

78. Hath he perused the Unseen, or hath he made a pact with the Beneficent?

79. Nay, but We shall record that which he saith and prolong for him a span of torment.

80. And We shall inherit from him that whereof he spake, and he will come unto Us, alone (without his wealth and children).

81. And they have chosen (other) gods beside Allah that they may be a power for them.

82. Nay, but they will deny their worship of them, and become opponents unto them.

83. Seest thou not that We have set the devils on the disbelievers to confound them with confusion?

84. So make no haste against them (O Muhammad). We do but number unto them a sum (of days).

85. On the Day when We shall gather the righteous unto the Beneficent, a goodly company.

86. And drive the guilty unto Hell, a weary herd,

87. They will have no power of intercession, save him who hath made a covenant with his Lord.

88. And they say: The Beneficent hath taken unto Himself a son.

89. Assuredly ye utter a disastrous thing,

90. Whereby almost the heavens are torn, and the earth is split assunder and the mountains fall in ruins,

91. That ye ascribe unto the Beneficent a son,

92. When it is not meet for (the Majesty of) the Beneficent that He should choose a son.

93. There is none in the heavens and the earth but cometh unto the Beneficent as a slave.

94. Verily He knoweth them and numbereth them with (right) numbering.

95. And each one of them will come unto Him on the Day of Resurrection, alone.

96. Lo! those who believe and do good works, the Beneficent will appoint for them love.

97. And We make (this Scripture) easy in thy tongue, (O Muhammad) only that thou mayst bear good tidings therewith unto those who ward off (evil), and warn therewith the froward folk.

98. And how many a generation before them have We destroyed! Canst thou (Muhammad) see a single man of them, or hear from them the slightest sound?

SÛRAH LVI

THE EVENT
Revealed at Mecca

In the name of Allah, the Beneficent, the Merciful.

1. When the event befalleth—
2. There is no denying that it will befall—

3. Abasing (some), exalting (others);

4. When the earth is shaken with a shock

5. And the hills are ground to powder

6. So that they become a scattered dust,

7. And ye will be three kinds:

8. (First) those on the right hand; what of those on the right hand?

9. And (then) those on the left hand; what of those on the left hand?

10. And the foremost in the race, the foremost in the race:

11. Those are they who will be brought nigh

12. In gardens of delight;

13. A multitude of those of old

14. And a few of those of later time,

15. On lined couches,

16. Reclining therein face to face.

17. There wait on them immortal youths

18. With bowls and ewers and a cup from a pure spring

19. Wherefrom they get no aching of the head nor any madness,

20. And fruit that they prefer

21. And flesh of fowls that they desire.

22. And (there are) fair ones with wide, lovely eyes,

23. Like unto hidden pearls,

24. Reward for what they used to do.

25. There hear they no vain speaking nor recrimination

26. (Naught) but the saying: Peace, (and again) Peace.

27. And those on the right hand; what of those on the right hand?

28. Among thornless lote-trees

29. And clustered plantains,

30. And spreading shade,

31. And water gushing,

32. And fruit in plenty

33. Neither out of reach nor yet forbidden,

34. And raised couches;

35. Lo! We have created them a (new) creation

36. And made them virgins,

37. Lovers, friends,

38. For those on the right hand;

39. A multitude of those of old

40. And a multitude of those of later time.

41. And those on the left hand: What of those on the left hand?

42. In scorching wind and scalding water

43. And shadow of black smoke,

44. Neither cool nor refreshing.

45. Lo! heretofore they were effete with luxury

46. And used to persist in the awful sin.

47. And they used to say: When we are dead and have become dust and bones, shall we then, forsooth, be raised again,

48. And also our forefathers?

49. Say (unto them, O Muhammad): Lo! those of old and those of later time

50. Will all be brought together to the tryst of an appointed day.

51. Then lo! ye, the erring, the deniers,

52. Ye verily will eat of a tree called Zaqqûm

53. And will fill your bellies therewith;

54. And thereon ye will drink of boiling water,

55. Drinking even as the camel drinketh.

56. This will be their welcome on the Day of Judgment.

57. We created you. Will ye then admit the truth?

58. Have ye seen that which ye emit?

59. Do ye create it or are We the Creator?

60. We mete out death among you, and We are not to be outrun,

61. That We may transfigure you and make you what ye know not.

62. And verily ye know the first creation. Why, then, do ye not reflect?

63. Have ye seen that which ye cultivate?

64. Is it ye who foster it, or are We the Fosterer?

65. If We willed, We verily could make it chaff, then would ye cease not to exclaim:

66. Lo! we are laden with debt!

67. Nay, but we are deprived!

68. Have ye observed the water which ye drink?

69. Is it ye who shed it from the raincloud, or are We the shedder?

70. If We willed We verily could make it bitter. Why, then, give ye not thanks?

71. Have ye observed the fire which ye strike out;

72. Was it ye who made the tree thereof to grow, or were We the grower?

73. We, even We, appointed it a memorial and a comfort for the dwellers in the wilderness.

74. Therefor (O Muhammad), praise the name of thy Lord, the Tremendous.

75. Nay, I swear by the places of the stars—

76. And lo! that verily is a tremendous oath, if ye but knew—

77. That (this) is indeed a noble Qur'ân

78. In a Book kept hidden

79. Which none toucheth save the purified,

80. A revelation from the Lord of the Worlds.

81. Is it this Statement that ye scorn,

82. And make denial thereof your livelihood?

83. Why, then, when (the soul) cometh up to the throat (of the dying)

84. And ye are at that moment looking

85. —And We are nearer unto him than ye are, but ye see not—

86. Why then, if ye are not in bondage (unto Us),

87. Do ye not force it back, if ye are truthful?

88. Thus if he is of those brought nigh,

89. Then breath of life, and plenty, and a Garden of delight.

90. And if he is of those on the right hand,

91. Then (the greeting) "Peace be unto thee" from those on the right hand.

92. But if he is of the rejecters, the erring,

93. Then the welcome will be boiling water

94. And roasting at hell fire.

95. Lo! this is certain truth.

96. Therefor (O Muhammad) praise the name of thy Lord, the Tremendous.

SÛRAH LXXXI

At-Takwîr takes its name from a word in verse 1. Verses 8 and 9 contain an allusion to the practice of the pagan Arabs of burying alive girl-children whom they deemed superfluous. An early Meccan Sûrah.

THE OVERTHROWING

Revealed at Mecca

In the name of Allah, the Beneficent, the Merciful.

1. When the sun is overthrown,

2. And when the stars fall,

3. And when the hills are moved,

4. And when the camels big with young are abandoned,

5. And when the wild beasts are herded together,

6. And when the seas rise,

7. And when souls are reunited,

8. And when the girl-child that was buried alive is asked

9. For what sin she was slain,

10. And when the pages are laid open,

11. And when the sky is torn away,
12. And when hell is lighted,
13. And when the garden is brought nigh,
14. (Then) every soul will know what it hath made ready.
15. Oh, but I call to witness the planets,
16. The stars which rise and set,
17. And the close of night,
18. And the breath of morning
19. That this is in truth the word of an honoured messenger,
20. Mighty, established in the presence of the Lord of the Throne,
21. (One) to be obeyed, and trustworthy;
22. And your comrade is not mad.
23. Surely he beheld him on the clear horizon.[44]
24. And he is not avid of the Unseen.
25. Nor is this the utterance of a devil worthy to be stoned.
26. Whither then go ye?
27. This is naught else than a reminder unto creation,
28. Unto whomsoever of you willeth to walk straight.
29. And ye will not, unless (it be) that Allah willeth, the Lord of Creation.

SÛRAH LXXXII

THE CLEAVING

Revealed at Mecca

In the name of Allah, the Beneficent, the Merciful.

1. When the heaven is cleft asunder,
2. When the planets are dispersed,
3. When the seas are poured forth,
4. And the sepulchres are overturned,
5. A soul will know what it hath sent before (it) and what left behind.
6. O man! What hath made thee careless concerning thy Lord, the Bountiful,
7. Who created thee, then fashioned, then proportioned thee?
8. Into whatsoever form He will, He casteth thee.
9. Nay, but they deny the Judgement.
10. Lo! there are above you guardians,
11. Generous and recording,

---

[44] The reference is to the Prophet's vision at Mt. Hirâ.

12. Who know (all) that ye do.

13. Lo! the righteous verily will be in delight.

14. And lo! the wicked verily will be in hell;

15. They will burn therein on the Day of Judgement,

16. And will not be absent thence.

17. Ah, what will convey unto thee what the Day of Judgement is!

18. Again, what will convey unto thee what the Day of Judgement is!

19. A day on which no soul hath power at all for any (other) soul. The (absolute) command on that day is Allah's.

SÛRAH XCVI

Al-'Alaq takes its name from a word in verse 2. Verses 1–5 are the words which the Prophet received in the vision at Hirâ, therefore the first of the Koran to be revealed.

A very early Meccan Sûrah.

THE CLOT

Revealed at Mecca

In the name of Allah, the Beneficent, the Merciful.

1. Read: In the name of thy Lord who createth,

2. Createth man from a clot.

3. Read: And thy Lord is the Most Bounteous,

4. Who teacheth by the pen,

5. Teacheth man that which he knew not.

6. Nay, but verily man is rebellious

7. That he thinketh himself independent!

8. Lo! unto thy Lord is the return.

9. Hast thou seen him who dissuadeth

10. A slave when he prayeth?

11. Hast thou seen if he (relieth) on the guidance (of Allah)

12. Or enjoineth piety?

13. Hast thou seen if he denieth (Allah's guidance) and is froward?

14. Is he then unaware that Allah seeth?

15. Nay, but if he cease not. We will seize him by the forelock—

16. The lying, sinful forelock—

17. Then let him call upon his henchmen!
18. We will call the guards of hell.
19. Nay! Obey not thou him. But prostrate thyself, and draw near (unto Allah).

SÛRAH CXII

At-Tauhîd, "The Unity," takes its name from its subject. It has been called the essence of the Koran, of which it is really the last Sûrah. Some authorities ascribe this Sûrah to the Madînah period, and think that it was revealed in answer to a question of some Jewish doctors concerning the nature of God.

It is generally held to be an early Meccan Sûrah.

THE UNITY

Revealed at Mecca

In the name of Allah, the Beneficent, the Merciful.

1. Say: He is Allah, the One!
2. Allah, the eternally Besought of all!
3. He begotteth not nor was begotten.
4. And there is none comparable unto Him.

BIBLIOGRAPHIES and CHRONOLOGIES

Bibliographies

Note

The following bibliographies are intended to be useful to the general reader, to whom this book is addressed, rather than to the specialized student; hence only readily available books in the English language are listed. A number of important sources of information are therefore omitted in each list. The interested person will surely be led to them, however, by any of several books here recommended. The Wisdom of the East Series, inexpensively published by John Murray of London, contains numerous titles of interest to the reader of Asian literature; but with one exception these titles are not itemized in the following bibliographies. Also excluded are the publications from which the selections in the present anthology have been taken. In conformity with the principles of this anthology, only first-hand translations are listed; the very few departures from this rule are properly noted. It has been thought advisable to classify translations under the translator's rather than the author's name.

GENERAL

BALLOU, ROBERT O., ed., *The Bible of the World* (selections from various scriptures), New York, Viking Press, 1939.

CEADEL, ERIC B., ed., *Literatures of the East: An Appreciation* (with bibliographies), Wisdom of the East Series, London, John Murray, 1953.

DURANT, WILL, *The Story of Civilization,* New York, Simon and Schuster, 1935, 1950.

——— a) *Our Oriental Heritage,* Chaps. XIV-XXI, XXIII-XXVI.

——— b) *The Age of Faith,* Chaps. VIII-XIV.

GROUSSET, RENÉ, *Civilizations of the East* (histories of the arts of India, China, Japan, the Near East), 4 vols., New York, Knopf, 1931–34.

JURJI, EDWARD J., ed., *The Great Religions of the Modern World,* Princeton University Press, 1946.

MOORE, CHARLES A., ed., *Philosophy—East and West,* Princeton University Press, 1944.

411

NEHRU, JAWAHARLAL, *Glimpses of World History*, New York, John Day, 1942.

TIETJENS, EUNICE, *Poetry of the Orient* (an anthology of lyrics), New York, Knopf, 1928.

VAN DOREN, MARK, ed., *An Anthology of World Poetry*, New York, A. & C. Boni, 1928.

ARABIAN LITERATURE

Reference Works

ANDRAE, TOR, *Mohammed: The Man and His Faith*, New York, Charles Scribner's Sons, 1936.

ARNOLD, THOMAS and GUILLAUME, A., eds., *The Legacy of Islam*, London, Oxford Press, 1931.

BELL, RICHARD, *Introduction to the Qur'ān*, Edinburgh University Press, 1953.

BROCKELMANN, CARL, *History of the Islamic Peoples*, London, Routledge, Kegan Paul, 1949.

FARIS, NABIH A., ed., *The Arab Heritage*, Princeton University Press, 1944.

GIBB, H. A. R., *Arabic Literature: An Introduction*, London, Oxford Press, 1926.

—— *Mohammedanism*, London, Oxford Press, 1949. Also as Mentor Book, 1955.

HITTI, P. K., *The Arabs: A Short History*, Princeton University Press, 1943.

NICHOLSON, REYNOLD A., *A Literary History of the Arabs*, Cambridge University Press, 1953.

SCHROEDER, ERIC, *Muhammad's People: A Tale by Anthology*, Portland, Maine, The Bond Wheelwright Company, 1955.

VON GRUNEBAUM, G. E., *Medieval Islam*, Chicago University Press, 1946.

WICKENS, G. M., ed., *Avicenna: Scientist and Philosopher*, London, Luzac, 1952.

Translations

ARBERRY, ARTHUR J., *The Holy Koran: An Introduction with Selections*, London, Allen and Unwin, 1953.

—— *The Koran Interpreted*, 2 vols., London, Allen and Unwin, 1955.

—— *Moorish Poetry* (an anthology), Cambridge University Press, 1953.

—— *The Ring of the Dove* (by Ibn Hazm), London, Luzac, 1953.

—— *Scheherazade: Tales from the Thousand and One Nights*, London, Allen and Unwin, 1953.

LYALL, CHARLES, *Translations of Ancient Arabian Poetry*, Columbia University Press, 1930.

NICHOLSON, REYNOLD A., *Studies in Islamic Mysticism*, Cambridge University Press, 1921.

——— *Studies in Islamic Poetry*, Cambridge University Press, 1921.

——— *Translations of Eastern Poetry and Prose*, Cambridge University Press, 1922.

PALMER, E. H., *The Koran* (Oxford World's Classics), London, Oxford Press.

PAYNE, JOHN, *The Portable Arabian Nights*, New York, Viking Press, 1952.

ROLWELL, J. M., *The Koran*, Everyman's Library, London, J. M. Dent, 1933.

WATT, W. M., *The Faith and Practice of Al-Ghazālī*, London, Allen and Unwin, 1953.

PERSIAN LITERATURE

Reference Works

ARBERRY, ARTHUR J., *Sufism*, London, Allen and Unwin, 1950.

——— ed., *The Legacy of Persia*, Oxford Press, 1953.

BROWNE, EDWARD G., *A Literary History of Persia*, 4 vols., Cambridge Press, 1928.

JACKSON, A. V. W., *Persia Past and Present*, New York, The Macmillan Co., 1906.

LEVY, REUBEN, *Persian Literature: An Introduction*, Oxford Press, 1923.

Translations

ARBERRY, ARTHUR J., *Fifty Poems of Hafiz*, Cambridge Press, 1947.

——— *Immortal Rose* (an anthology), London, Luzac, 1948.

——— *Kings and Beggars* (selections from *Gulistan*), London, Luzac, 1945.

——— *Omar Khayyam: A New Version*, London, 1952.

——— ed., *Persian Poems*, Everyman's Library, London, J. M. Dent, 1954.

——— *The Rubaiyat of Rumi*, London, Emery Walker, 1949.

DARAB, G. H., *The Treasury of Mysteries* (by Nizami), London, Probsthain, 1945.

FITZGERALD, EDWARD, *Salaman and Absal . . . together with a Bird's Eye View of Fariduddin Attar's Bird Parliament*, Boston, Page and Co., 1899.

HERON-ALLEN, EDWARD, *Edward Fitzgerald's Rubaiyat of Omar*

Khayyam with Their Original Persian Sources, London, Quar-
itch, 1899.

JACKSON, A. V. W., *Early Persian Poetry,* New York, Columbia
University Press, 1920.

LEVY, REUBEN, *A Mirror for Princes,* New York, Dutton, 1951.

———— *Stories from Sadi's Bustan and Gulistan,* London, Chapman and Hall, 1928.

MASANI, R. P., *The Conference of the Birds,* London, Oxford
Press, 1924.

NICHOLSON, REYNOLD A., *Rumi, Poet and Mystic,* London, Allen
and Unwin, 1950.

———— *Tales of Mystic Meaning,* London, Chapman and Hall,
1931.

WARNER, A. G. and E., *The Sháhnáma of Firdausi,* 9 vols., London, Truebner, 1905–1925.

WILSON, C. E., *The Half Paikar* (by Nizami), London, Probsthain,
1924.

ZIMMERN, HELEN, *Epic of Kings* (prose retelling of *Shahnamah*),
New York, The Macmillan Co., 1926.

INDIAN LITERATURE

Reference Works

ARNOLD, EDWIN, *The Light of Asia* (a poetic life of Buddha),
London, Kegan Paul, 1891.

DASGUPTA, S., ed., *A History of Classical Sanskrit Literature,*
University of Calcutta, 1947.

FRAZER, R. W., *A Literary History of India,* New York, Charles
Scribner's Sons, 1898.

GARRAT, G., ed., *The Legacy of India,* Oxford, Clarendon Press,
1937.

GOWEN, HERBERT, *A History of Indian Literature,* New York,
D. Appleton, 1931.

HIRIYANA, MYSORE, *The Essentials of Indian Philosophy,* London,
Allen and Unwin, 1949.

KEITH, A. B., *A History of Sanskrit Literature,* Oxford Press, 1928.

———— *The Sanskrit Drama,* Oxford Press, 1924.

MACDONNELL, A., *India's Past,* Oxford, Clarendon Press, 1927.

MORGAN, KENNETH, ed., *The Religion of the Hindus,* New York,
Ronald Press, 1953.

RAWLINSON, H. G., *India: A Short Cultural History,* New York,
Praeger, 1952.

SCHWEITZER, ALBERT, *Indian Thought and Its Development,* London, Hodder and Stoughton, 1936.

THOMAS, E. J., *The History of Buddhist Thought,* New York,
Knopf, 1933.

————— *The Life of Buddha as Legend and History*, New York, Knopf, 1927.

WINTERNITZ, MORIZ, *A History of Indian Literature* (trans. from the German by Mrs. S. Ketkar and Miss H. Kohn), University of Calcutta, 2 vols., 1927–33.

Translations

BABBITT, IRVING, *Dhammapada*, New York, Oxford Press, 1936.

BESANT, ANNIE, *The Bhagavad Gita*, Chicago, Theosophical Press, 1923.

BURTT, E. A., *Teachings of the Compassionate Buddha*, Mentor Book, 1955.

COLLIS, M., *Quest for Sita* (prose adaptation from *Ramayana*), New York, John Day, 1947.

DAVIDS, MRS. RHYS, *Stories of the Buddha*, New York, Frederick Stokes, 1929.

DUTT, ROMESH, *Ramayana and Mahabharata* (abridgements in verse), Everyman's Library.

EDGERTON, FRANKLIN, *The Bhagavad Gita* (translation and interpretation), 2 vols., Harvard University Press, 1944.

FRANCIS, H. T. and THOMAS, E. W., *Jataka Tales*, Cambridge University Press, 1916.

HILL, W. D. P., *The Bhagavad Gita*, London, Oxford Press, 1928.

HUME, ROBERT E., *The Thirteen Principal Upanishads*, London, Milford, 1931.

LIN YUTANG, *The Wisdom of China and India* (Part I), New York, Random House, 1942.

MACDONNELL, A., *Hymns from the Rigveda*, London, Oxford Press, 1922.

MENEN, AUBREY, *The Ramayana* (a modernized prose retelling), New York, Scribner's, 1954.

RYDER, ARTHUR W., *Bhagavad Gita*, Chicago University Press, 1929.

————— *Gold's Gloom* (from *Panchatantra*), Chicago University Press, 1925.

————— *The Little Clay Cart* (by Shudraka), Harvard University Press, 1905.

————— *The Panchatantra*, Chicago University Press, 1925.

————— *Shakuntala and Other Writings* (by Kalidasa), Everyman's Library, London, J. M. Dent.

————— *The Ten Princes* (by Dandin), Chicago University Press, 1927.

SEEGER, ELIZABETH, *The Five Brothers: The Story of the Mahabharata* (a prose adaptation), New York, John Day, 1948.

CHINESE LITERATURE

Reference Works

CREEL, H. G., *Confucius, The Man and the Myth*, New York, John Day, 1949.

FITZGERALD, C. P., *China, A Short Cultural History*, London, Cresset Press, 1942.

GILES, H. A., *A History of Chinese Literature*, New York, D. Appleton, 1923.

GOODRICH, LUTHER C., *A Short History of the Chinese People*, New York, Harper, 1943.

HIGHTOWER, J. R., *Topics in Chinese Literature*, Harvard University, 1950.

HUGHES, E. R., *Chinese Philosophy in Classical Times*, Everyman's Library, London, J. M. Dent.

HUNG, WILLIAM, *Tu Fu, China's Greatest Poet*, Harvard University Press, 1952.

LIN YUTANG, *The Gay Genius: The Life and Times of Su Tung-po*, New York, John Day, 1947.

WALEY, ARTHUR, *The Life and Times of Po Chü-i*, London, Allen and Unwin, 1949.

―――― *The Poetry and Career of Li Po*, New York, The Macmillan Co., 1950.

―――― *Three Ways of Thought in Ancient China*, London, Allen and Unwin, 1939.

ZUCKER, A. E., *The Chinese Theater*, Boston, Little Brown, 1925.

Translations

ACKER, W., *T'ao the Hermit*, New York and London, Thames and Hudson, 1952.

ACTON, HAROLD and LEE YI-HSIEH, *Four Cautionary Tales*, London, Lehman, 1947.

AYSCOUGH, FLORENCE, *Tu Fu: The Autobiography of a Chinese Poet*, Boston, Houghton Mifflin, 1929.

―――― *Travels of a Chinese Poet* (vol. II of *Tu Fu*), 1934.

―――― (with Amy Lowell), *Fir-Flower Tablets: Poems Translated from the Chinese*, Boston, Houghton Mifflin, 1921.

BLAKNEY, R. B., *The Way of Life: Lao Tzu*, Mentor Book, 1955.

BUCK, PEARL S., *All Men Are Brothers* (*Shui Hu Chuan*, 17th century novel), New York, John Day, 1933.

BYNNER, WITTER and KIANG KANG-HU, *The Jade Mountain* (an anthology of poetry), New York, Knopf, 1931.

CLARK, C. D. L., *Selections from the Works of Su Tung-po*, London, Jonathan Cape, 1931.

DOEBLIN, ALFRED, *The Living Thoughts of Confucius*, London, Cassell, 1948.

EDWARDS, EVANGELINE D., *Chinese Prose Literature of the T'ang Period*, 2 vols., London, Probsthain, 1937–38.

GILES, H. A., *The Travels of Fa-Hsien*, Cambridge University Press, 1923.

HART, HENRY, *Poems of the Hundred Names*, Stanford University Press, 1954.

———— *The West Chamber, A Medieval Drama*, Stanford University Press, 1936.

HSIUNG, S. I., *Romance of the Western Chamber*, London, Methuen, 1935.

LIN YUTANG, *The Wisdom of Confucius*, New York, Modern Library, 1943.

———— *Famous Chinese Short Stories*, John Day, 1952.

———— *The Wisdom of China and India*, Part II, New York, Random House, 1942.

———— *The Wisdom of Laotse*, New York, Random House (Modern Library), 1943.

MIALL, B. and F. KUHN, *Chin P'ing Mei* (16th century novel), 2 vols., New York, G. P. Putnam's Sons, 1947.

POUND, EZRA, *Cathay* (free translations and adaptations of verse), London, Elkin Mathews, 1915.

———— *The Classic Anthology Defined by Confucius*, Harvard University Press, 1954.

———— *The Confucian Analects*, New York, Hudson Review, 1951.

WALEY, ARTHUR, *The Adventures of Monkey* (from *Hsi Yu Chi*, 16th century novel), New York, John Day, 1944.

———— *The Analects of Confucius*, London, Allen and Unwin, 1938.

———— *The Book of Songs*, New York, Houghton Mifflin, 1937.

———— *Chinese Poems*, London, Allen and Unwin, 1948.

———— *More Translations from the Chinese*, New York, Knopf, 1919.

———— *170 Chinese Poems*, New York, Knopf, 1935.

———— *The Temple and Other Poems*, New York, Knopf, 1923.

———— *Translations from the Chinese*, New York, Knopf, 1941.

———— *The Way and Its Power* (*Tao Teh Ching*), New York, Houghton Mifflin, 1935.

WANG, C. C., *Dream of the Red Chamber* (*Hung Lou Mêng*, 18th century novel), New York, Doubleday Doran, 1929.

WARE, JAMES R., *The Best of Confucius*, Garden City, Halcyon House, 1950.

———— *The Sayings of Confucius*, Mentor Book, 1955.

JAPANESE LITERATURE

Reference Works

ASTON, W. G., *A History of Japanese Literature*, New York, D. Appleton, 1937.

BOWERS, F., *The Japanese Theater*, New York, Hermitage House, 1952.

BRYAN, J. I., *The Literature of Japan*, New York, Henry Holt, 1930.

CHAMBERLAIN, B. H., *Things Japanese*, London, Trench Truebner, 1939.

KEENE, DONALD, *Japanese Literature, An Introduction*, New York, Grove Press, 1955.

KINCAID, ZOË, *Kabuki, The Popular Stage of Japan*, New York, The Macmillan Co., 1925.

LOMBARD, F. A., *Outline History of Japanese Drama*, London, Allen and Unwin, 1928.

SADLER, A. L., *Japanese Plays*, Sydney, Angus and Robertson, 1934.

SANSOM, G. B., *Japan: A Short Cultural History*, New York, Appleton-Century, 1943.

Translations

BLYTH, R. H., *Haiku*, 4 vols., Tokyo, Hokuseido Press, 1950–52.

FRENCH, JOSEPH L., ed., *Lotus and Chrysanthemum: An Anthology of Chinese and Japanese Poetry*, New York, Boni and Liveright, 1927.

KEENE, DONALD, *Japanese Literature: An Introduction*, New York, Grove Press, 1955.

——— *The Battles of Coxinga* (drama by Chikamatsu), London, Taylor's, 1951.

Many'ōshū, One Thousand Poems, Tokyo, Nippon Gakujutsu Shinkōkai, 1940.

MIYAMORI, ASATARŌ, *The Masterpieces of Chikamatsu*, London, Kegan Paul, 1926.

——— *Masterpieces of Japanese Poetry*, 2 vols., Tokyo, 1936.

PORTER, WILLIAM N., *Tosa Diary* (by Tsurayuki), London, Henry Frowde, 1912.

POUND, EZRA and E. FENOLLOSA, *Noh or Accomplishment*, New York, Macmillan, 1916.

REISCHAUER, E. O. and J. K. YAMAGIWA, *Translations from Early Japanese Literature*, Harvard University Press, 1951.

SHIVELY, DONALD, *The Love Suicide of Amijima* (drama by Chikamatsu), Harvard University Press, 1953.

WALEY, ARTHUR, *Nō Plays of Japan*, New York, Knopf, 1922.

——— *The Pillow-Book of Sei Shōnagon*, Boston, Houghton Mifflin, 1929.

——— *The Tale of Genji*, 2 vols., Boston, Houghton Mifflin.

YASUDA, KENNETH, *A Pepper-Pod* (translations of *haiku*), New York, Knopf, 1947.

Chronologies

ARABIA

CULTURAL HISTORY	LITERATURE

I. Pre-Islamic "age of barbarism" (c. A.D. 500–622)

Period of tribal feuds, blood revenge, and idolatry, including worship of Black Stone in Kaa'ba at Mecca. Influences from Jewish and Christian thought. Arab preference for "the birth of a boy, the coming to light of a poet, and the foaling of a mare."

Absence of literacy, hence of plain prose. Tradition of oral recitation by *rawis*. *Kasidah*, a rhymed purpose poem, dominant form. Main sources of information collections of poems edited in 8th and 9th centuries, such as: *Moallakat*, *Muffadaliyat*, and *Hamasa* of Abu Tammam.

570 Birth of MOHAMMED
622 Hegira or flight of Mohammed from Mecca to Medina, first year of Islamic calendar.

Seven great poets of *Moallakat*: IMR-UL-KAIS, TARAFA, AMR IBN KHULTUM, HARITH, ANTARA, ZUHAYR, and LABID.

II. Islamic Age (A.D. 622–present)

1. THE ORTHODOX CALIPHATE (RULED FROM MEDINA, A.D. 632–661)

632 Death of Mohammed. His father-in-law, ABU BEKR, elected first Caliph or successor.

Period barren of non-religious literature, possibly because of Mohammed's aversion to poets as *kahins* or soothsayers.

633–643 Conquest of Persia and Syria.
634–644 OMAR, second Caliph.

Collection of chapters of *Koran* from written notations and from the "breasts of men."

644–656 OSMAN, third Caliph.
656–661 ALI, Mohammed's son-in-law, fourth Caliph. Assassinated in civil war.

646 Authorized rescension of *Koran*.

2. THE OMMAYAD CALIPHATE (RULED FROM DAMASCUS, A.D. 661–750)

Ascendancy of Arabian aristocracy, high in morality, low in culture. Growth of sciences of grammar, law, history and theology to elucidate the *Koran*.

Vogue of court poetry: poems of rivalry and panegyrics to kings.

d. 710 Poet AL-AKHTAL, Christian convert.

680 Massacre of Husain, son of Ali, at Kerbela forms basis of Shia heresy in Islam.

705–715 Conquest of Transoxania, parts of India, Spain.
8th cent. Rise of Mutazilite free thought.

d. 720 OMAR, love lyrist.
d. 728 FARAZDAQ and JARIR, major poets.

First evidences of Sufi mysticism.
Arabic translation of *Kalila and Dimna,* Sanskrit fables of Bidpai.

Popular verses attributed to a Majnun, hero of later Islamic romances.

3. THE ABBASID CALIPHATE (RULED FROM BAGHDAD, A.D. 750–1258)

Rule of 37 successive Caliphs who claimed divine right through Abbas, Mohammed's uncle. Prevailing Persian influence, especially of BARMECIDE family, during first century. Subsequent decline of Caliphate and rise of local temporal dynasties.

"Golden Age" of literature to 1055; "Silver Age" to 1258. Gradual tendency away from veneration of pagan poets and development of originality, but with strong Hellenistic and Persian influences.

Notable early Caliphs:
754–775 MANSUR
786–809 HAROUN-AL-RASHID
813–833 MAMUN, founder of "House of Science."

d. 766 IBN ISHAQ, author of Life of Mohammed.
d. 801 RABIA of Basra, Sufi poetess.
d. 810 ABU NUWAS, greatest Arab lyrist, celebrated in *Arabian Nights.*
d. 826 ABUL ATAHIYA, poet of simple style and religious themes.

Notable later dynasties:
874–999 Samanids of Transoxania.
926–1003 Hamdanids of Syria.
932–1055 Buwayhids of West Iran, Iraq.
909–1171 Fatimids of Egypt.
976–1186 Ghaznevids of Afghanistan.

d. 923 TABARI, historian.
d. c. 930 RHAZES, physician.
d. 950 AL-FARABI, philosopher.
937–1048 AL-BIRUNI, historian, scientist.
980–1037 IBN SINA (AVICENNA), poet, physician, philosopher.

915–965 MUTANNABI, poet of highest rank among Arabs.
988 *Fihrist,* index of Arabic books.
d. 1057 AL-MA'ARRI, freethinking poet.

1040–1095 MUTAMID, ruler-poet of Spanish Islam.

1059–1111 AL-GHAZALI, "Proof of Islam," defender of orthodoxy.

1126–1198 IBN RASHD (AVERROES), defender of philosophy against Ghazali.

1258 Sack of Baghdad by HULAGU KHAN and end of Caliphate.

d. 1064 IBN HAZM, greatest of Islamic scholars in Spain.

d. 1071 IBN ZAYDUN, greatest Islamic poet of Spain.

d. 1122 HARIRI, author of *Assemblies,* popular didactic work in rhymed prose.

d. 1235 IBN'L FARID, leading Arab mystical poet.

4. FROM THE FALL OF BAGHDAD (A.D. 1258)

Period of Mongol, Turkish, and Persian ascendancy and of Arab decline. Main centers of Arab culture in Egypt, Syria, and (until 1492) Spain.

1250–1517 Mameluke ("slave") Dynasty of Egypt, ruling with "mock" caliphs in Cairo.

d. 1282 IBN KHALLIKAN, author of famous biographical dictionary.

d. 1377 IBN BATTUTA, traveler-geographer.

1453 Ottoman Turks take Constantinople.

1492 End of Arabs in Spain.

1683 Siege of Vienna by Turks.

1798 Napoleon in Egypt.

1918 End of Ottoman Empire lays basis for modern Arab states.

Poetry in low estate, but considerable historical and biographical writing. *Romance of Antar,* popular tales about pre-Islamic hero, probably composed in time of Crusades. *Thousand and One Nights* given final form under Mamelukes.

1883–1931 KAHLIL GIBRAN, distinguished Syrian writer.

IRAN (*Persia*)

CULTURAL HISTORY

LITERATURE

I. *Old Persian* (c. 800 B.C.–A.D. 224)

7th cent. B.C. Zoroaster, prophet of ancient Iran.

550–330 Achaemenian monarchs.

331 Invasion by Alexander the Great ends period and inaugurates age of anarchy followed by rule of Parthians.

Rock inscriptions only traces of Old Persian language, but Avestan *Gathas* (religious hymns) represent a sister dialect.

II. *Middle Persian* (A.D. 224–651)

Period of Sassanian kings.
b. A.D. 215 MANES, founder of Manichean heresy.
531–578 NUSHIRVAN, THE JUST, patron of Greek and Sanskrit learning and of philosopher-refugees from court of Emperor Justinian.

Pahlavi language, a descendant of Old Persian, now official tongue of Zoroastrian church and state.

Literary documents mainly legendary history and surviving in fragments.

Zand, Pahlavi commentary on Zoroastrian *Avesta*.

III. *Modern or Islamic Persian* (A.D. 615–present)

1. ARAB HEGEMONY (A.D. 651–c. 850)

Gradual islamization of Persia following Arab conquest. Flight of many Zoroastrians (Parsees) to India in 8th century.

Arabic the language of learning. Modern Persian, the descendant of Pahlavi, now written in Arabic characters.

661–750 Rule of Ommayad caliphs (Damascus).
750–850 Rule of Abbasid caliphs (Baghdad), with aid of Persian family of the Barmecides.
786–809 HAROUN AL-RASHID, caliph.
839–923 TABARI, Persian historian who wrote in Arabic.

Arab verse forms borrowed:
  kasidah (ode)
  ghazal (love poem or short ode)

Native Persian literary forms:
  rubaiyat (quatrains)
  mathnawi (long poem in couplets)

Prose either 1) simple; 2) rhymed without meter; or 3) metrical but without rhyme.

2. PERSIAN RENAISSANCE (c. A.D. 850–1258)

874–999 Samanid dynasty of Khorasan.
d. 923 AL-RHAZI (RHAZES), physician.
937–1048 AL-BIRUNI, historian, geographer.
976–1186 Ghaznevid dynasty of Afghanistan.
998–1030 Rule of MAHMUD THE GREAT of Ghazna.

d. 940 RUDAGI, first major Persian poet; little of his work extant.
d. 975 DAKIKI, initiator of *Shahnamah*, Book of Kings.

d. 932–1020 FIRDAUSI, author of Persian epic *Shahnamah*.

1003–1061   NASR-I-KHUSRAW,

980–1037 IBN SINA (AVICENNA), philosopher, physician, and poet.

1037–1157 Seljuk Turk dominion.

d. 1092 NIZAM-UL-MULK, minister of state to early Seljuk kings and founder of Nizamiyah School, Baghdad.

1059–1111 AL-GHAZALI, "Proof of Islam," defender of Moslem orthodoxy, wrote mainly in Arabic and aided growth of Sufism, a pantheistic mysticism affecting most poetry.

1219–1227 Invasion of Persia by GENGHIS KHAN.

1255–1265 Invasion of Persia by HULAGU KHAN.

poet and propagandist of Ismaeli religious sect.

d. 1122? OMAR KHAY-YAM ⎫
11th cent. BABA TAHIR ⎬ poets of *rubaiyat.*
967–1049 ABU SAID B.AB'L-KHAYR ⎭

d. c. 1150 SANAI, first great Sufi poet.

d. 1190 ANWARI ⎫ pane-
1106–1185 KHAKANI ⎬ gyrists.

1141–1203 NIZAMI OF GANJA, romancer.

1150–1230 FARIDUDDIN ATTAR, mystic poet.

3. AFTER MONGOL CONQUEST OF BAGHDAD (A.D. 1258)

1265–1337 Rule of Mongol Il-Khans.

13th cent. Mongol conversion to Islam.

1247–1318 RASHIDAD-DIN, author of encyclopedic history.

1337–1380 Rival dynasties at Fars, Kerman, Baghdad, Tabriz, and Herat.

1357–1384 SHAH SHUJA of Muzzafari dynasty, patron of poet Hafiz.

1391–1405 Conquests of TIMUR-I-LANG (Tamerlane) in Persia, Syria, India, Egypt.

1405–1502 Fall of Timur's empire and rise of Uzbek and Turkish powers.

1499–1736 Safawi dynasty of Persia.

1794–1925 Kajar Dynasty.

1849 Babi insurrection; subse-

1207–1273 RUMI, author of *Mathnawi, Divan.*

d. 1289 IRAQI, religious poet.

?1184–1292 SADI, author of *Gulistan, Bostan.*

d. 1320 MAHMUD B. SHABISTARI, author of *Gulshan-i-Raz,* mystical treatise.

1253–1325 AMIR KHUSRAW, Indian poet of Turkish blood, wrote in Persian.

1320–1390 HAFIZ of Shiraz, lyrist.

1414–1492 JAMI, last great classical Persian poet, mystic, scholar.

Strong Persian influence upon Turkish literature. Mogul Indian courts attract Persian poets.

d. 1520 HATIFI, poet.

19th cent. Growth of religious,

quent rise of Bahai faith.
1906 Persian constitution established.
1925 Pahlavi Dynasty founded.

especially Bahai, poetry and of political satire.

Growth of popular press and translation of European literary classics.

INDIA

(Note: Dates in Indian history are often approximate or conjectural.)

CULTURAL HISTORY

LITERATURE

I. *Vedic Age* (c. 1200–500 B.C.)

1200 B.C. Indo-Aryan society of Indus River basin at first tribal, patriarchal and pastoral; later monarchic and agricultural.

Vedic literature an aspect of religious worship. Includes:
1000 B.C. I. *Samhitas:*
  1) *Rigveda*—oldest. Book of metrical hymns to gods as nature powers.
  2) *Yajurveda*—prose formulas added for sacrifices.
  3) *Samaveda*—vedas arranged for purposes of chanting.
  4) *Atharva veda*—latest. Spells and incantations.

800 Growth of Brahman (priestly) caste through control of rituals. Main deities: Indra (warrior—thunderer), Varuna (sky-god of truth, order), Mitra (god of sun and of contracts).

600 *Brahma* (originally prayer) becomes cosmic principle; *atman* (breath) its psychic counterpart in man. Doctrines of *samsara* (transmigration of souls) and of *karma* (law of action determining rebirths).

800–600 II. Later *Brahmanas*, theological ritual books explaining the *Samhitas.*
600–300 III. *Upanishads*—speculative treatises, basis of later Vedanta philosophy.

599–527 VARDHAMANA MAHAVIRA, founder of Jain religion.
563–483? SIDDHARTA GOTAMA, founder of the Buddhist religion.

500 Brahmi script in use.

II. *Epic and Buddhist Age* (c. 500 B.C.–A.D.)

Indian *Trimurti* (trinity):
  Brahma (creator)
  Vishnu (preserver)
  Shiva (destroyer)
New pessimistic spirit traceable to Buddhism and Jainism. Doctrine of *maya* (material world as illusion).
Main schools of Indian philosophy:
  Sankhya—atheistic dualism
  Yoga—asceticism
  Mimamsa—Vedic doctrine of salvation by works.
  Vedanta—Vedic doctrine of salvation by knowledge.
400 PANINI, noted grammarian.
327–325 ALEXANDER THE GREAT'S conquest of Punjab. Contacts with Greece and Persia produce influence on Buddhist art and possibly Indian literature.

274–236 ASOKA on throne. Established canons of Buddhism, which spread to Ceylon.
150 PATANJALI, grammarian.

Period of composition of two great epics by slow accretion. Development of *sloka* verse (four octosyllabic lines).
Mahabharata (in 100,000 *slokas*) an *itihasa* or legendary epic, based on 10th century B.C. battle. Contains stories of Rama and Shakuntala as well as the *Bhagavad Gita*.

Ramayana (in 24,000 *slokas*), epic poem and first sample of *kavya* or formal poetry. Attributed to VALMIKI.

Simultaneous growth of:
1) later Vedic literature *(Puranas)*
2) new Sanskrit literature
3) Buddhist literature in Pali tongue.

Buddhist *Tripitaka* ("three baskets"):
1) *sutra* (doctrine)
2) *vinaya* (monastic code)
3) *abidharma* (philosophy)

1st cent. *Dhammapada* probably composed.

III. *Classical Age* (A.D.–1000 A.D.)

300 B.C. or A.D. 300 *Arthashastra*, science and art of government.
200 B.C. to A.D. 200 The Laws of MANU, a *dharmashastra*, religious and moral treatise.

4th cent. A.D. VATSYAYANA'S *Kamasutra* (art of love) influential on Indian drama.

320–480 Revival of Brahmanism, especially under CHANDRAGUPTA II at Ayodhya and Ujjain.
Spread of Indian culture south-

Flourishing of *kavya* poetry and of Sanskrit language.

ASVAGHOSA, author of life of Buddha in *kavya* form, and first Indian dramatist of note.
2nd cent. *Panchatantra* probably composed.

4th cent. BHASA, distinguished early dramatist. *The Little Clay Cart*, famous drama attributed to SHUDRAKA.
5th cent. KALIDASA, India's greatest poet-dramatist.
7th cent. SUBANDHU and BANA,

ward, and extensive relations with Far East.

Prevalence of Vishnu, Shiva worship.

kavya writers. BHARTRIHARI and AMARU, lyrists.

8th cent. DANDIN, author of *Ten Princes.* BHAVABHUTI, popular later dramatist.

IV. *Medieval and Modern Age* (A.D. 1000–present)

10th cent. Temple of Somnath sacked by Moslem ruler, MAHMUD OF GHAZNA.

1194 Afghan capture of Benares and subsequent destruction of Bihar, center of Buddhist learning.

1206 First Moslem sultan in Delhi.

13th–14th cent. Persian arts, especially architecture, introduced.

1398–99 Invasion by TAMERLANE leading to establishment of Mogul dynasty (1525–1761).

b. 1469 NANAK, founder of Sikh religion.

16th cent. Portuguese in India.

1582 AKBAR PADISHAH establishes divine faith based on all creeds.

1632–53 SHAH JEHAN builds Taj Mahal.

18th cent. Rule by East India Company.

1858 India under British Crown.

1869–1948 MAHATMA GANDHI, spiritual leader.

1947 Indian independence.

Persian the court language of Moslem rulers: Persian influence on literature considerable.

12th cent. JAYADEVA, author of *Gita Govinda.*

1253–1325 AMIR KHUSRAW, Turkish poet of India who wrote in Persian language.

1373 Oldest manuscript of *Hitopadesa,* a late adaptation of *Panchatantra.*

b. 1532 TULSI DAS, distinguished poet of medieval India.

1861–1941 RABINDRANATH TAGORE, Bengali poet.

1873–1938 MUHAMMAD IQBAL, Urdu poet.

CHINA

CULTURAL HISTORY   LITERATURE

I. *First Millennium* (c. 1100 B.C.–207 B.C.)

1. CHOU DYNASTIES (c. 1100 B.C.–221 B.C.)

To c. 800 B.C. Legendary age.

770–500 Feudal period: inde-

551–479 CONFUCIUS, supposed editor of the Classics of his-

pendent states under Chou suzerainty. People divided into four classes. Sacrifices to "Son of Heaven." Bamboo tablet and stylus used. Ancient documents collected, embodying traditions of filial piety, respect for history, and love of music and poetry.

Philosophical speculation in schools of CONFUCIUS, LAO TZU, MO TI, and the Legalists.

tory and of song, author of *Spring and Autumn Annals* and of conversations in *Analects*.

6th cent. LAO TZU, semi-legendary Taoist thinker.

5th cent. MO TI, author of *Mo-Tzu*, book of anti-Confucian doctrine.

4th cent. *Tao Teh Ching*, chief book of Taoism. *Chuang Tzu*, mystic book of Taoism.

372–289 MENCIUS, Confucian scholar.

332–296 CHU YUAN, author of famous long poem *Li Sao* (Falling into Trouble).

2. CH'IN DYNASTIES (221 B.C.–207 B.C.)

EMPEROR SHIH HUANG ("First Emperor"), builder of Great Wall.

Roll silk and camel's hair brush used as writing materials.

Script simplified and standardized.

213 Non-scientific books dealing with past burned, and writers put to death.

II. *Second Millennium* (207 B.C.–A.D. 960)

1. HAN DYNASTIES (207 B.C.–A.D. 220)

Capital at Chang-an and Lo-yang.

Restoration of learning and discovery of *Book of History*. Fourth and sixth Han emperors also poets.

145 B.C. SSU MA CH'IEN, father of Chinese history born.

136 *Five Classics* established: *Changes, Odes, History, Annals, Rituals*.

2nd & 1st cent. B.C. Wars against Huns. Buddhism introduced; Taoism flourishing as cult of magic.

1st cent A.D. Paper invented or perfected.

d. 140 B.C. MEI SHENG, author of *fu* prose poems, father of modern verse.

32–36 B.C. LADY PAN, notable woman poet.

d. A.D. 120 HSU SHEN, author of first Chinese dictionary.

187–226 TS'AO P'EI, author of essay on literary criticism.

220–264 Empire divided into 3 kingdoms.

3rd cent. LU CHI, author of notable work of literary criticism in *fu* form.

2. CHIN AND MINOR DYNASTIES (A.D. 265–618)

Capital at Nanking. Period of civil wars; little literature. Tea and chairs in use in China.

2nd–3rd cent. "Seven scholars of Chien An."
3rd cent. "Seven Sages of Bamboo Grove."
365–427 TAO CH'IEN, major poet.

5th cent. Growth of Buddhism after journey of FA HSIEN to India. Buddhist cave temples built.
606 A.D. Master of arts degree examination instituted by EMPEROR YANG TI.

501–531 HSIAO T'UNG published collection of choice works by various authors.

3. T'ANG AND FIVE DYNASTIES (A.D. 618–960)

Period of high culture, especially in poetry. Pure Land or Lotus School of Buddhism popular; Taoism influential on poetry. Loyang and Chang-an, eastern and western capitals. Gunpowder used for fireworks.

7th cent. Lu-shih (regulated verse) and Chueh-Chu (broken-off lines) used.

Notable poets of period:
699–759 WANG WEI, famous also as painter.
701–762 LI PO, best known in the West.
713–770 TU FU, favorite poet of China.
772–846 PO CHU-I, author of *Everlasting Wrong,* famous poem about YANG KUEI FEI, mistress of MING HUANG.
791–817 LI HO, notable later T'ang poet.
836–847 12 Classics cut in stone.
932–953 9 Classics printed from wood blocks.
936–978 LI YU, last emperor of southern T'angs and poet-musician-painter.

635 Nestorian Christian mission in China.
645 75 Sanskrit books translated by HSUAN-TSANG and others.
715–756 EMPEROR MING HUANG founded Academy of Letters (725).
c. 845 Ch'an (Zen) school of Buddhism founded in China.
868 Earliest extant printed book.
907–959 Period of Five Dynasties.

III. *Third Millenium* (A.D. 960–present)

1. SUNG DYNASTY (A.D. 960–1279)

Age inferior to preceding in literary arts but greater in diffu-

Professional poets replaced by amateur writers.

sion of learning. Tang chronicles rewritten. Capitals: Kai-Feng Fu, Hang-Chow.

1069–1074 Socialist reforms by WANG AN-SHIH.
11th cent. Golden age of landscape painting.
1130–1200 CHU HSI, famous historian and commentator, author of encyclopedias, re-interpreter of Confucius.

1036–1101 SU TUNG-PO, poet, painter, essayist, statesman.
1050–1100 HUANG TING-CHIEN, poet and calligraphist.
1125–1209 LU YU, prolific author of 11,000 poems of minor merit.

Flourishing of ceramic arts. Use of movable type for printing and of gunpowder for war.

Development of *tzu*, song form using colloquial language.

2. LATER DYNASTIES (A.D. 1260–1912)

1260–1368 Yuan (Mongol) Dynasty. Capital at Peking. KUBLA KHAN, a Buddhist, appreciated Confucianism.
1223–1296 WANG YING-LING, author of primer used for 600 years.
1275–1292 MARCO POLO's travels.
1368–1644 Ming Dynasty. Historical, medical, encyclopedic books compiled. Courtezans prominent as writers. Growth of arts of pottery. Tobacco introduced.
16th cent. Trade with Europeans.
1644–1912 Ching (Manchu) Dynasty, which adopted Confucianism, then allowed it to petrify.
1662–1722 SHENG TSU, patron of learning.

1850–1864 Tai Ping (Christian) revolt quelled.

1912 Chinese Republic founded by SUN YAT SEN.

Growth of drama in colloquial language and decline of the language of learning.

13th cent. *Romance of the Western Chamber*, famous play by WANG SHIH-FU.

1311–1375 LIU CHI, poet and prose writer.
Collections of short stories in colloquial language.

Notable novels:
16th cent. *Records of Journey to West. Chin Ping Mei.*
17th cent. *Romance of the Three Kingdoms. All Men Are Brothers,* famous novel of 12th century brigands.

18th cent. *Dream of the Red Chamber* given form as novel by TSAO CHAN and KAO NGOH.

20th cent. Literary Revolution led by HU SHIH.

JAPAN

CULTURAL HISTORY	LITERATURE

I. The Ancient Age (to A.D. 1185)

1. THE ARCHAIC PERIOD (TO A.D. 646)

1st cent. B.C. JIMMU, first Japanese emperor, mythically placed in 660 B.C. Clan society with animistic-polytheistic Shinto religion and prominent nature myths.

c. A.D. 405 Chinese script brought to Japan by WANI.

4th cent. A.D. Conquest of part of Korea brings in Chinese influences.

Confucianism gradually adopted but accommodated to Shintoism.

538 Advent of Buddhism.

604 PRINCE SHOTOKU's constitution establishing Buddhism, Confucian bureaucracy, Chinese sciences.

Probably some poetry of this period included in chronicles and anthologies of Nara period.

630 Embassy to T'ang China.

2. NARA PERIOD (A.D. 646–794)

Name of period from capital at Nara.

Golden age of court poetry. Lyric verse on nature, love, death in form of *tanka* (short) and *naga-uta* (long poem).

Foreign influences:
Chinese on politics
Buddhist on art, religion
Korean on education.

712 *Kojiki* (Records of Ancient Matters) containing 111 poems in Chinese characters representing Japanese words.

7th cent. Golden Hall built (burned about 1948).

720 *Nihongi*, early history in Chinese, containing 132 poems.

752 Great bronze Buddha statue erected.

725–94 *Tempyo* or golden age of Buddhist Japanese art.

760 *Manyoshu*, greatest of early anthologies, containing more than 4,000 poems by HITOMARO, AKAHITO and others.

3. HEIAN PERIOD (A.D. 794–1185)

Name from capital presently Kyoto. Period of peace and prosperity, of esthetic refinement and artificial manners.

9th cent. *Kana* or script derived from Chinese characters for writing Japanese phonetically.

805 Founding of new Buddhist sects:
Tendai (source of later sects)
Shingon (esoteric Buddhism)
838 Decline of Chinese influence begins.
942–1017 GENSHIN, monk who preached worship of Amida Buddha according to *Jodo* (Pure Land) sect.
1100 Dual Shinto, which regarded Shinto gods as Boddhisatvas (Buddhas to be).

866–1160 Dominance of Fujiwara clan of hereditary regents.
1160–1185 Dominance of Taira clan.

LADY KOMACHI ⎰ outstanding
NARIHARA ⎱ authors

905–922 *Kokin-shu,* anthology of ancient and modern poetry, edited by author of *Tosa Diary,* TSURAYUKI.
c. 900 *Ise Monogotari* and *Taketori Monogotari,* early prose fiction.
?967–1025 SEI SHONAGON, authoress of *Pillow-Book,* court lady's sketches.
?978–1031 MURASAKI SHIKIBU, authoress of *Tale of Genji,* greatest work of fiction in Japanese.

II. *The Medieval Age* (1185–1603)

1. KAMAKURA PERIOD (1185–1336)

Kyoto still center, but new administration from Kamakura by *shoguns* (generalissimos) who dictated to emperors. Land feudalized and *bushido* (way of the horse and the bow) adopted by *samurai* or warrior class and supported by rising Zen Buddhism.

1274–1281 Mongol invasions repelled. Growth of arts of picture scroll, ceramics, and tea-drinking; and final flourishing of architecture.

Distinct written and spoken tongues.

Literature not abreast of other arts, but some notable prose.

1153–1216 KAMO NO CHOMEI, author of *Hojoki,* account of hermit life.

1213–1250 *Heike Monogotari,* historical war tales of Taira clan.
1283–1350 YOSHIDA KENKO, author of *Grasses of Idleness,* notable prose work.

2. MUROMACHI PERIOD (1336–1603)

Name from Kyoto street where the Ashikaga *shoguns* resided. Period of strife, feudal unrest, drift of warriors to cities, and rise of commerce backed by Buddhist monasteries. Educa-

Period considered a dark age, but much historical study promoted.

13th cent. Growth of organized poetry contests and artificial

tion (in hands of Zen priests) and arts flourish under demand for culture by samurai.

writing of *renga* (linked verse).

14th cent. Development of Nō drama.

1329 "Literature of Five Monasteries," academy imitative of Chinese.

d. 1408 YOSHIMITSU, *shogun* patron of arts.

1420–1506 SESSHU, famous painter.

15th cent. Golden and Silver Pavilions built. High points of arts of tea ceremony, screen painting, pottery.

16th cent. European religious and trade missions.

1333–84 KWANAMI	chief creators of Nō
1364–1443 SEAMI, his son	

16th cent. Movable type introduced. *Aesop's Fables* translated.

III. *Modern Age* (1603–present)

Capital at Edo (Tokyo). Strong feudal rule by Tokugawas to 1868. Exclusion policy against Europeans. Suppression of Christianity, decline of Buddhism, rise of 12th century Chinese Confucianism.

Considerable learned writing about Confucian classics. Growth of *kabuki*, popular theater, and *joruri*, puppet stage.

1688–1704 *Genroku*, period of *chonin* (townspeople) ascendency despite restrictive measures. High bourgeois culture. Arts of "floating world," "gay quarter."

1642–1693 SAIKAKU, popular novelist.

1644–1694 BASHO, most famous poet of *haiku*, short poems of 17 syllables.

1653–1725 CHIKAMATSU MONZAEMON, leading dramatist of Japan.

1700 Case of 47 *ronin*, martyred samurai.

Growth of classical studies; commentaries on Nara and Heian writings.

1798 *Kojikiden*, commentaries, revived Shinto.

1754–1806 UTAMARO	distinguished wood-block artists.
1760–1849 HOKUSAI	
1797–1858 HIROSHIGE	

1867 Meiji Restoration puts end to Shogunate.

1904–1905 Russo-Japanese War.

1945 Allied occupation of Japan.

1763–1828 ISSA, reviver of *haiku* poems.

1767–1848 BAKIN, last great novelist.

European influences in literature manifest in translations and imitations, especially of fiction.